Thus Came The Dawn

SHAMSHER SINGH NARULA

Published by: Opender Bansal, www.7peaksent.com 7peaksent@gmail.com

First Edition, 2015

—

Published in United States of America.

ISBN 10: 0692412662
ISBN-13: 978-0692412664 (Opender Bansal)

A novel about the last phase Of British rule in India and early years of Independence.

CONTENTS

THUS CAME THE DAWN

ACKNOWLEDGMENTS

I wish to express my great gratitude to SARDAR SHAMSHER SINGH NARULA for being so gracious and providing me an opportunity to publish this work of his as an Independent Publisher by granting me full Copyright to Publish Anywhere in the World except India. There is no way I can pay him back for his guidance, generosity, and love over the years since I began my Journalism Career back in India. I endeavour to express my gratitude through this and other efforts to follow.

I sincerely thank VARTOOTI BANSAL, for her steady support and encouragement for me to publish this historical fiction. ANSHUVIJAY RODE for countless hours spent in designing the cover, formatting, proof reading the book. Finally, Iwish to express my gratitude to my late brother IQBAL SINGH BANSAL, my late parents, my friends, family members, and others over the years who pushed me to do some in this field.

- Opender Singh Bansal

CHAPTER ONE

Earsplitting silence of a city under curfew, now and then made more resounding, by the sound of gunshots. Footfall of the British soldiers parading the deserted streets added alarm to the dreadful quiet. It was again the time of death in the city of Amritsar. The serene blue of a rain washed sky was a useless waste of loveliness. All of a sudden flocks of crows 'whirled against 'the blue sky .A solitary bird was twittering in the distance.

Held captive' by a British sergeant 'and four riflemen, Hira Singh stood with his head held high outside his haveli, a square-shaped palatial house with high walls excepting the vaulted front entrance porch. His face exhibited more composure than it normally did. Its grace was enhanced by radiant eyes, saintly black beard and spotless white turban.

The British Mercantile Bank in the nearby Hall Bazaar was plundered four days ago and set on fire burning alive its British manager and his wife. Some of the plundered wares were dumped in the well in the middle of the square courtyard of Hira Singh's haveli, The ground floor of the building was open to all without. any restriction. The arched roof of the entrance porch had no gate or doorman, Two vertical beams collared by a curved engraved marquee stood on an elevated cement podium welcoming one and all.

The high scalloped arch of the gateless entrance led through a porch to a large square courtyard with a well in the center. There were three rectangular rooms on the other three sides, which too did not have doors. Unrestricted entry was available to anyone who had renounced worldly life to become ascetic, regardless of his religion or denomination. It was Hira

1

Singh's firm belief that even if one among a hundred thousand mendicants could possibly be like Buddha, Nanak or Kabir, it was worth one's while to offer hospitality to all of them. Sadhus, sanyasis and mendicants would come there at any time during the day or night, but generally in the evening for night shelter. In the morning the servant was required to serve them repast before breakfast was served to anyone in the household. In the evening before the cook retired, he was to make sure that everyone, who came for shelter, had been fed.

After the imposition of martial law and the enforcement of curfew, the police and the army began searching houses for goods looted from the British Mercantile Bank and for those responsible for burning alive its manager and his wife. Fearing search and arrest, scores of persons living in that area had taken advantage of the unrestricted access to the haveli to dump goods stolen, by them, in its well. No effort could make the British sergeant understand that the owner of the house was not responsible for this.

On the other side of the street were standing five young and middle aged persons and an old man. They had been handcuffed. A police sub-inspector and four police constables were keeping guard over them. They were all pleading innocence, excepting the old man, under whose bed bundles of stolen cloth were found on search. When it became known that house to house search was being carried out by the police, he made his sons place all the stolen cloth under his bed in the attic. The old man was leaning on a stick. His head was thrust forward as he glared with left eye. His right eye had the glaze of cataract. All of them were in tears and their face had the shadow of death.

After twenty yards this broad lane turned to the right where it joined Hall Bazaar. Nearby was situated the two storey building of the British Mercantile Bank. It was a massive building one hundred yards on the road-side and twenty yards deep. Built in 1895 of stone slabs, it had Burma teak beams, sleepers and planks for roofs. There was a large shed on back side for warehousing. Almost every thing of daily use and every article of commerce was imported from England during those days. Amritsar was wholesale market for northern and western India for many of these goods. The warehouse and some of the rooms in the main building were piled with boxes, crates and bales containing merchandise of every variety, textile, hosiery, cutlery, sewing machines, cycles, watches, scissors, pens, nibs, needles, paper and many other items. For the last week or so these had remained unclaimed by the indenters due to the previous week's general strike and closing of shops.

As the World War ended, the Home Rule movement had become assertive in many places in India and at some places aggressive. To curb it the Government of India passed Rowlett Act, which empowered the police to make arrest without warrant. Its up shot was countrywide agitation against this and Amritsar, like other populous towns, was in the forefront of this. There was closing of shops and general strike. A protest meeting took place at the boulevard outside Khairdin mosque in the Hall Bazaar where it entered the city. After the meeting the throng formed into a procession and began moving towards the Golden Temple and the interior of the city. As the crowd reached the British Mercantile Bank, they saw the British manager standing near a window. A man in the crowd cupped hands near mouth and shouted anti-British slogans. Soon others began to exhort the people for revenge. In no time a large number of people made a gap in the roadside balustrade of the bank and broke open its gate and doors. Hundreds of boxes, bales and crates lying there and in the backyard were smashed or ripped open. Everyone helped himself with these goods and many came back again and again with bags, sacks and suitcases. Looting and plunder went on till only ripped bundles of paper and match-boxes remained there. Some one ignited bales of paper and similar stuff. Fire soon spread to other rooms containing furniture and files. In matter of minutes, the building with its timbered roof was engulfed in flames.

Next day curfew order was issued and by the evening of April 13, martial law declared after firing at Jalianwala Bagh killed and injured about one thousand persons, who had gathered there for a public meeting.

On April 14 and 15 there was flag march by the British and Indian army units in streets and bazaars of the town. House to house search was undertaken by the police and the army to search for the missing British engineer of municipal power house and to recover stolen goods. These searches were more extensive in this and nearby alleys, because many of the arrested leaders of the Home Rule movement resided here. Those who could not hide the goods stolen by them took advantage of the open access to the courtyard of Hira Singh's haveli. Suddenly men and women carrying stolen goods started rushing in shortly before midnight. In less than half an hour the well there was cluttered with every variety of merchandise. Because of curfew in the city, mendicants or holy men were not there in the ground floor rooms. Before the commotion of the intruders awakened those living in the first floor and the domestic helpers shouted them out, the mischief had been done.

Searches were still going on. Persons suspected of having taken part in the procession and burning of the British Mercantile Bank were being gathered there. Some of them were followed by wailing women with veiled faces begging for mercy. Occasional gunfire made them more nervous.

None was daring to peep out of the windows and balconies. One could hear the muffled sound of weeping from the houses wherefrom male members had been picked up by the police or the army. All the houses were shut in mortally afraid of a knock at the door. The silence had the pitch of death rattle and everyone was benumbed with fear.

Hira Singh was a distinguished citizen of Amritsar. He was a well known practitioner of the indigenous Unani system of medicine and was addressed as hakim ji. He was a man much respected for his philanthropic disposition. This was a time when modern anti-biotic and other drugs had not been discovered. Even aspirin and quinine were not commonly available. Hakim Hira Singh's herbal powders, syrups, electuaries and distillations were, in many cases of common diseases, more beneficial than the medicines available in the allopathic system. Some of them were very efficacious cures for seasonal fevers and digestive problems. Even the Europeans in the town preferred to have treatment from him, when they suffered from these local ailments.

The Unani or Greek system of medicine had been introduced into India by the Muslims and Hira Singh was the only non-Muslim hakim practicing it. He, however, was eclectic in his formulary, just as he was very catholic in his outlook. The population of Sikhs in Amritsar was negligible at that time. He, however, had a large circle of friends and admirers amongst Hindus, Muslims and Christians. As the news of his arrest became known, it created much disquiet in the city.

Many persons had gone up to the roof and were communicating by gestures and sometimes by calling out. The news of the arrest of Hira Singh which was spreading fast from house to house reached Sir Aroor Singh, the most influential resident of the city and also government appointed Supervisor of Golden Temple. Hira Singh was his physician for many ailments he suffered from. Hira Singh's friend and neighbour, Sardar Gurdit Singh was an Honorary magistrate. He could, without difficulty, go to the Deputy Commissioner to apprise him of Hira Singh's arrest by the Army. Having known him personally, the D.C. could understand the rationale of his innocence. He instructed his Assistant Commissioner to go with Gurdit Singh to arrange his release. By the time Gurdit Singh reached that place,

Sir Aroor Singh was already there with Assistant Commissioner of Police and Inspector of the local police station. Assistant Commissioner suggested that Hakim Hira Singh should better be temporarily in the custody of the local police instead of letting the Army take charge of him.

Wearing ghaghra, the ankle-length skirt, and covering her head and upper part of the body by a white chaddar, Hira Singh's wife Khushwant Kaur had come down to that place from the first floor of the haveli. She reminded Sir Aroor Singh that they were living happily in their house near the Golden Temple before the War when he persuaded her husband to buy this house and shift here. That, she bemoaned, was responsible for this misfortune.

A police constable who had gone to the police lines to fetch a prison cart returned before long. It was a large square cage mounted on a four wheel cart driven by a buffalow bull. The Assistant Superintendent of Police suggested that a chair be placed in the cart for Hira Singh. Thinking that the Army Sergeant might take it amiss and might try to prevent his arrest by the local police, it was decided that he should use the bench meant for the escorting police staff.

The policeman on duty in the prison cart declined to sit on the bench beside Hira Singh. It was not because he belonged the low caste chamar but out of regard for him. Hira Singh's main method of diagnosis was to 0bserve pulse of the patient by holding his wrist. This was regardless of the fact whether the patient was a high caste Hindu, a muslim or a low caste. The poor and the low caste often had free treatment. This policeman's father had started working as a gardener when Company Garden was set up in the six hundred acres of land to the north-east of the government civil hospital to commemorate silver jubilee of Queen Victoria. His father had become a Christian and had started sending children to school. This son had become a police constable after passing matriculation examination. His elder sister was a teacher in a government primary school and his younger sister a nursing maid in the municipal maternity hospital. The change in religion had given upward mobility to the family. Hira Singh enquired from him about his other chamar relatives who had not changed their religion. The constable replied that they found that the high caste school staff strongly resisted their children's admission even to the' government schools. He added that one of his maternal uncles had become a Muslim and was able to get his children admitted to the school set up by the Muslim community.

The prison cart moved out of that lane and came to the Hall Bazaar on way to the police headquarters in the Kotwali. The bazaar was deserted and was still cluttered with rubbish. A minor case of breach of curfew was to be registered against him at the Kotwali before he was escorted to the district jail.

CHAPTER TWO

As the string of bells around buffalo's neck chimed, the mind of Hira Singh was crowded with flashback of twenty seven years of his life and recollections of earlier four generations of his family. His maternal grand father's - nana's - ancestors used to live in Lahore and left that city after it was ravaged sixth time by Ahmed Shah Abdali in the later half of the eighteenth century. More he thought of the past, the more he was filled with anxiety and dismay. Beads of perspiration dropped down his face on to the beard. His heart beat fast. He took a long breath and wiped cold sweat from his forehead with a finger. With unblinking eyes he stared into the past. The recent past loomed large before him and he realized how life had been changing before his eyes and changing for the better. A year after giving him birth, his mother died of influenza which ravaged the town in early nineties of the last century. His father died five years later when this town and most of the country were in the grip of plague. The epidemic lasted for almost three years. His entire paternal family perished as did one fourth of the population of the town. These epidemics seldom appeared again with the same virulence.

Having been built on a low lying land, rainwater stagnated in the lanes and the streets of the town. Storm water drains had been laid and flood water now cleared the same day. This reduced greatly the wrath of malaria, cholera and dysentery which were the bane of the town for many months every year. A municipal committee consisting of nominated and elected members did its work efficiently.

Roads, lanes and drains were repaired or laid afresh. Sweepers came to clean the roads punctually, water-carriers came with their leather water bags on time sprinkling water on the road to settle the dust and the postman came to deliver letters at his fixed time. This was how many people kept count of the hour of the day.

As the prison cart moved along the Hall Bazaar, he saw lion-shaped cast iron public hydrants and ornate lamp posts which had been imported from England and put in place shortly before the war. A municipal employee came regularly to light the kerosene lamps at the lighting-up time and to put these out at daybreak.

He had seen Victoria Memorial Hospital, Company Garden, public library, railway workshop, veterinary hospital, primary, middle and high schools, separate for boys and girls, colleges and similar institutions come up in just two decades. As he lived and walked in the city, he noticed new developments in progress. More and cheaper necessities of life were becoming available. Life was more comfortable not only for the well-to-do, but also for the less fortunate. The market was flooded with every variety of imported goods catering to various needs and requirements. There were velvets, georgettes, chiffons, crapes, tweeds, serge and blazers for the better off, whereas there was drill, sheeting and long cloth costing a few pice' a yard which even the poor could afford. Gold was fifteen rupees per tola of twelve grams. A new street of goldsmiths and jewelers had come up on the north-east of Golden Temple. There were new streets stocking and selling goods from Sheffield as there were for textile from Lancashire. There were new bazaars selling sewing machines, cycles, knives, scissors and stationery requirements. Scores of items of daily use were being imported from England and the town had become wholesale outlet for these articles of daily use both luxuries and necessities. Many towns in India had reputation for one thing or the other. Benares was known for its thugs, Lahore for Hira Mandi and other streets of dancing girls and Murshabad for its sorcerers. Amritsar was called: sifti da ghar - abode of virtues. Its traders had the reputation of honesty in their business dealings. This had attracted traders and customers from as far as Kabul and Delhi, making the place grow faster than others.

Railways had made goods from the eastern and western parts of the country plentiful and cheaper. Dry fruits from Quetta, Kandhar, Kabul and Kashmir, mangoes from Maida and oranges from Nagpur were no more articles of luxury. With new tools carpenters, blacksmiths, weavers, masons and other craftsmen were now earning more. There were many new trades and professions, tailors, drapers, watchmakers, cycle repairers, hair dressers and dealers in new merchandise. Not only playing cards -and sports goods of various types and qualities were freely available, playing grounds for cricket, foot ball, hockey, etcetera, came up both in the city and in the civil lines area. Life everywhere seemed to be in upswing. There was a general feeling of well-being and personal security.

The prison cart moved out of Hall Bazaar and passed near the company garden.

He reminisced the mornings and evenings he had treaded the foot paths of the garden, enjoying the soothing sight and the delicious aroma of the flower beds. He had basked in the new light of the rising sun and at nightfall wondered at the twinkling of thousands of fire flies hopping from one flowery bower to the other. The buffalo with its chiming bells reached the jail road. As it started moving towards district jail at the other end of the road, he was downcast. He prayed most earnestly that this well-being of Amritsar should not be short-lived as before and the town would not have again bloodbath and destruction as it had had twice earlier in its short history of a few centuries.

What had made him most happy and was after his own heart was the growth of mutual trust amongst various communities and castes. There used to be a highbrow touch-me-not attitude of the high-caste Hindus towards the low castes. The feeling of seclusion for Muslims was of a different type, resulting from associating pollution with them. These had been abating during the last few decades. There was commingling of communities and castes not only in trades, crafts and professions but in many cases in personal life also. The railway trains, schools, colleges, hospitals, courts and government offices were equally open to all and served as some sort of crucible, remoulding the mind and changing the attitude of the people. He thought with a heavy heart whether this growing affinity among the communities would now come to naught. When he was a young boy he had noticed that persons belonging to various Hindu castes rarely had the feeling of belonging to a single entity. These castes were not only mutually exclusive but in many cases inimical to one another. More than that there was a feeling amongst the upper castes Hindus that the British rulers had not only brought down the edifices of Muslim rule in India but also vouchsafed them an advantageous position, giving them an upper hand. When the raising of a statute of Queen Victoria in Amritsar was proposed on her silver jubilee, the Hindu traders in the town raised the required money in the matter of a few hours. During the last few decades, this attitude of a position more advantageous than the Muslims had largely waned. A feeling was developing, in recent years with much rapidity, that persons of all castes and communities were sons of the same soil, were one people and India was their common motherland. The two communities worked together during the Home Rule movement and agitation against the Rowlett Act. What would happen to that? He reflected in vain for an answer.

The chime of bells around buffalo's neck made it impossible for him to break the thread of these disconsolate thoughts. The street was desolate, completely deserted. The houses and bungalows on both sides of the road appeared to be without a soul. Buffalo's reins having been left loose, the cart was slow in pace, whereas the dismal thoughts whirling in his head were becoming more and more distressing.

For a moment he was stung by deep remorse that he did not resist being pushed into the prison cart and left other innocent persons to their fate. His head throbbed and his eyes had a film of tears. Seldom in his life had he allowed himself to be placed or forced in a position where he would feel cowardly or lacking rectitude. Was it because his wife Khushwant Kaur was standing there weeping and he thought of her and their little son?

The face of the old man standing in the line of prisoners near his house came into focus before him. He was Charan Das or Charan chacha-uncle as he used to call him as a boy. More than twenty years ago he visited his small kiosk for buying parched gram for a cowrie. Cowrie, valued at almost two-hundredth of a rupee was more common currency at that time than these days. For a cowrie one could have so much of parched gram that a boy of his age would have satiety. All the day Charan Das sold parched gram for cowrie and half pice and during the day he would have a sale of more or less one quarter of a rupee. Life was static all around. His father and grand father had done the same business and probably had the same daily income. Now his elder son had a sales agency for Raleigh cycles and his daily sales were hundred times more than his father's. His second son was wholesale supplier of pulses and seemed to be doing even better.

Hira Singh looked at his own life, how it had changed beyond recognition. It was less hard and more profitable than that of his maternal grand father, who had adopted him and made him his apprentice. His nana was a renowned hakim and he invariably had enough persons coming for medical treatment but the payment in those days was in cowrie and pice. The population of the town had been increasing at a fast pace. Horse carriage had replaced bullock cart as a means of transport. More pilgrims and traders came to the town from near and distant places and more often. The railways made it possible to procure the various ingredients of his medicines with much less effort and at cheaper rate. Even lower strata of people were somewhat better off and payment now was in quarter rupee, half rupee and in rupee.

He had witnessed the rise of a generation of men with almost a new ethos, a society with somewhat new outlook, self-possessed, freed from the inhibitions and passions of the past. God had mercifully given the people a span of peace. Was this going to be short-lived? He shuddered as he put this question to himself. He bowed his head; mmersed in melancholy thoughts.

If things turned topsy-turvy again, he thought, the loss he would feel most was that- of books. The most heartening aspect of the new dispensation was the easy availability of books, particularly the imported ones covering various aspects of human life and knowledge. The books printed in India were becoming better and cheaper. Letter presses and lithographic printers had been established in this town as elsewhere. Some of these were small and hand driven, others larger ones working with electricity. There were a large number of locally produced books, pamphlets and periodicals on a variety of subjects. Every week brought a new newspaper, or a periodical espousing a different viewpoint and conveying a new message. These were not only in English but also in Urdu, Punjabi and Hindi, many of these low priced enough for mass circulation. It was a period of the opening up of mind, of contentious exchange of ideas and of religious, social and political controversies. This was a time of change, of searching new vistas and of demurring old attitudes. There was striving for education and for knowledge, though there was in some cases reinforcement of orthodox religious beliefs. A new class of liberal minded and educated elite was emerging, both amongst Hindus and Muslims, who had much in common. An educated mind and a trained intellect had become the new generation's best passport.

When he was a boy of six, nana made him sit before him and memorize the sacred scriptures and later various ingredients of each one of prescriptions for various ailments. Similarly, traditional knowledge and cultural heritage was bequeathed to him orally and he had to learn all that by rote. The printing presses had made much of this available in low price books and booklets. Breviaries were available for a few pice each. Holy Koran, Ramayana and the voluminous Holy Granth were available for a rupee or a little more and were no more the monopoly of priestly class.

The road to Golden Temple passed through a fifty feet high and two hundred feet long archway. On its both sides were large halls flanked at right angle by two storey buildings. One of the halls was the meeting place of the municipal committee and in the other was the municipal public library. The library had over a score steel shelves full of books in English imported from England. Their number had been increasing from year to year. There were also locally made teak shelves containing books published in India in English, Urdu, Punjabi and Hindi. There were also journals, magazines, periodicals and newspapers in English and Indian languages on a large rectangular table in the center which had twenty or more chairs on its two sides. Seeing all those treasures of knowledge in English he had felt like being blind. He had learnt Urdu and Persian on his own. A Muslim primary school headmaster living in the vicinity of his dwakhana - as his dispensary was called - helped him to learn English and made him purchase an English dictionary which gave meanings in Urdu. Before the War started he was able to make use of books in English in the municipal library. Later he began to visit English Book Depot every Saturday, when the bookshop received a new consignment of books from London by sea mail. This opened up before him new vistas of knowledge, a wealth of new ideas which virtually made him a different person. Burning desire to learn progressed in him with a speed that astounded him. He felt that learning was a means by which we acquaint ourselves with the secrets of the past, the hope of the present and the dream of the future. The feeling that all this might end now pained him unbearably. The buffalo cart jerked and creaked as it passed over the curb made with raised stones at the entrance of the district jail to keep out rain water. He composed himself and got ready to alight with the bundle of clothes which Sir Aroor Singh had thrust upon him while pushing him into the prison cart. The more he tried to keep out the apprehensions which had confounded him, the more persistently these scrambled back.

He was placed in class A in the prison. The food was reasonably good but he could hardly eat much As he sat on the wooden jail bed, his mind was again jumbled with fears of the worst type. Destruction and razing of Arnritsar twice previously and tribulation of the populace became so sharply outlined before him that it took his breath away.

Sometimes his nana would relate to-him tales from Sikh history and recount the life of his ancestors. He vividly recollected the details of the life of the earlier generations of his maternal grand father and how they became hakim practicing Unani system of medicine. The father of the first hakim, Dhirat Ram by name, used to live in Lahore. In the later half of the eighteenth century, Ahmed Shah Abdali had raided Punjab again and again, every time leaving behind greater destruction and ruination than did Nadir Shah a century or so earlier.

Invited to fight Maratha army, Ahmed Shah had invaded Punjab with a larger militia on his sixth invasion than on earlier occasions. When he came to know that Maratha army marshaled at Panipat was very large, Ahmed Shah conscripted thousands of Muslim youth in the Punjab, luring them with promises of loot. They kept foraging for grain, cattle, fuel and fodder for dozens of miles along their march looting the populace indiscriminately.

The news of the defeat and slaughter of Marathas at Panipat and later of plunder and carnage at Delhi, Mathura and Agra reached the terror stricken people of Lahore before Ahmed Shah's hordes arrived there on their return journey to Afghanistan.

Rumours had reached Lahore that Ahmed Shah was carrying with him, in addition to vast plunder, several bullock carts containing severed heads of Hindus and was adding to these on his way to Kabul. It was being said that he wanted to construct a tower of skulls in his capital city. The Muslims in Lahore city hid Hindu neighbours in their house. The earliest remembered ancestor of Hira Singh's nana Dhirat Ram took shelter in a Muslim blacksmith's house. They had been friends for long and their sons were class fellows in the city's seminary.

When Ahmed Shah reached Lahore on his way to Kabul, it took his entourage days and days to pass through the city. Ahmed Shah's own loot was loaded on twenty eight to thirty thousand elephants, mules, camels and bullock carts. Every trooper of the Shah was taking with him one and sometimes more horses laden with booty. The cavalry was returning on foot, loading the booty on their charges. The need for transport was so urgent that no horse or camel, not even a donkey was left in anyone's house on the way. Guns had been abandoned and their draught cattle loaded with plunder. There was no count of young girls, artisans and craftsmen, who had been enslaved and carried to Afghanistan. For the many days they passed through Lahore, the whole city and the surrounding areas for miles were stinking with the smell of excrements of over one hundred thousand men and animals.

The need for food, fuel and fodder for such a large cavalcade being most pressing, Ahmed Shah's soldiers searched the houses of Hindus of Lahore and removed all grain, goods, doors, roof beams and every piece of wood and iron they could find there. It was fourth time in Dhirat Ram's life when his house had been ransacked and doors and roof beams removed for fuel by marauders. This time two walls had also been pulled down. When the soldiers thumped these, they suspected them to be hollow; having cavities for hidden treasure. After that Dhirat Ram thought of leaving Lahore and shifting to Kasur a town about hundred miles to the south. The younger brother of his Muslim friend was practicing as a hakim there and he offered to give him a letter of introduction. He himself had been thinking of sending his son to his younger brother at Kasur to get trained as a hakim. After completing apprenticeship in Kasur his son could return to Lahore to practice Unani system of medicine.

When Dhirat Ram with wife, son Fakir Chand and the son of his Muslim friend reached Kasur, he found the town in mourning. A majority of the population of the town consisted of Muslim Pathans, who had settled there during the invasion of Punjab by Lodhis from Afghanistan a few centuries ago. Ahmed Shah's soldiers had come there and drafted for his army all the Pathan youth of the town on the lure of returning with booty from Delhi.

For weeks the two armies entrenched at Panipat faced each other, fighting skirmishes and disrupting lines of communication. Ahmed Shah positioned in the center thousands of locally recruited ill-trained mercenaries and made them attack the Maratha army. In no time the Marathas cut to pieces all the thousands of them and began celebrating their triumph. Thereafter, at an opportune time the regular formations of the army of Ahmed Shah attacked the Marathas from the left and the right and routed them.

Out of about a thousand young men drafted from Kasur for Ahmed Shah's army only three had returned alive. All the three had injuries and one of them in such a serious condition that he died shortly after his return. All available mules and donkeys had been usurped by the Afghan army. The three had trodden their way to Kasur. The Kasur hakim's four apprentices had also been drafted and had fallen at Panipat. The Hakim took both, his brother's son and the son of Dhirat Ram, as his apprentice. The name of Dhirat Ram's son was Fakir Chand. The Hakim wanted him to call himself Fakira, a name that could pass as that of a Muslim when necessary.

Normal trade channels having got disrupted, the Hakim found it difficult to procure the herbs required for his pharmaceuticals. After some training, Fakira was required to travel up to Peshawar and Kandhar in the west and

Agra and Kanauj in the east for these herbs. Life was insecure everywhere and Fakira quite often moved about in the garb of a mendicant. Many villages and forests in central Punjab had been set on fire to hunt out Sikhs hiding there. There was desolation everywhere. Whether he came across Afghan militia trailing Sikhs or Sikh warriors helping villagers to return to their home, as a mendicant Fakira could move about undisturbed. After he had crossed river, Chenab in the west or Satluj in the east, travel became less hazardous. Whenever he met hakims or vaids - practitioners of ancient Indian medicine - he tried to learn as much from them as he could. Fakira had thus become quite proficient in the profession and became the first hakim in the family.   -

Dhirat Ram wanted his son to set up his own practice as hakim. This, however, could not be either at Kasur or Lahore. Dhirat Ram's own hardware business in Kasur was unsteady as the town failed to recover from the decimation of its young men. Dhirat Ram went to Chak Guru, as Amritsar was then called. The place had again come to life but was-still a settlement smaller than Kasur. There could be scope here for his hardware business but not for his son's practice as hakim. The local population was small and the sick came there for treatment through prayers and by the nectar of the sacred tank and not by medicine. Fakir Chand had two daughters only. His wife expired during second delivery. Dhirat Ram prayed at Darbar Sahib, as Golden Temple was called in common parlance, for a grandson when his son Fakir Chand married again. He vowed that he would be made a Sikh and they would shift to Chak Guru.

On completion of a month's pilgrimage Dhirat Ram returned to Kasur. Fakira was married soon after and in less than two years he had a son. When Maharaja Ranjit Singh became the ruler of the Punjab he renamed Chak Guru as Amritsar and the town began to develop fast. Dhirat Ram and his family shifted to Amritsar. His grandson was five years of age at that time. Dhirat Ram took him to Golden Temple, baptized him as a Sikh and named him Kirpa Singh. Fakir Chand started his Unani practice in a street near the Temple. Kirpa Singh became his apprentice after he was five, just as Hira Singh had become his nana's apprentice before he was six.

Kirpa Singh was his nana's grand father and lived for over hundred years. He had become a well known Hakim of the town, which before long was much more populous than Kasur. The sacred tank had been filled up by the Afghan marauders with bodies of butchered Sikhs and debris of the buildings in the town. The tank had been cleared and the shrine in its center rebuilt. Artesian wells in the tank soon filled it with water, held sacred by the pilgrims. Maharaja Ranjit Singh got outside of the shrine gold plated. He also built a rampart encircling the town and a fort outside it to guard it. New settlers came to live in the town, pilgrims thronged it and it was teeming with the bustle of new traders and businessmen.

His grand father was still living when nana became his father's apprentice as a boy of six after receiving some kindergarten learning from the school in the gurdwara. For almost fifteen years he had the privilege of learning both from his father and grand father. His nana had thus become very dexterous in the profession when he took Hira Singh as his apprentice.

The war between the Sikh and the British armies was fought far away from Amritsar and it left the town unaffected. As the railways were laid, the gathering of pilgrims and holy men on the occasion of numerous festivals kept increasing. His nana took Hira Singh with him whenever he met and conversed with these holy men, to find out whether anyone of them, knew about some curative herb unknown to him. He had followed this tradition. His formulary was, therefore, richer than those of other practitioners of indigenous systems of medicine in the town. Sitting and stretching out in the jail cell day after day, his mind became, sometimes a beehive and others hornets' mud daub of these recollections of the lives of his ancestors and also of the capricious history of his community. These social memories flashed before him like a thunderbolt. This made him shiver, as he feared that gory happenings of the earlier period might be reenacted and martial law and the massacre at Jalianwala Bagh could just be the beginning. It filled his mind with deep anguish when he thought that these decades- of peace and prosperity were just a passing phase as before.

At the same time glistened before him thousands of books in the municipal public library, many of which bore evidence of richness of mind and high moral values. He was aware that these were a fraction of the books produced in England. He knew from his personal experience that many of these books dispelled darkness of mind and enriched it. He would contemplate, could the people who created these monumental works behave in the same manner as the barbarian hordes from the northwest. He thought of schools, colleges, courts and equality before law which had come about. He remembered the Englishmen he had occasions to know personally in the discharge of his professional work. However frightening and nightmarish his fears, in the heart of his heart he felt that this was a passing phase and the darkness of the gory past would not appear again.

By the fourth week of April martial law had been withdrawn, curfew had been restricted to a small area and normalcy restored in the town. On second May Hira Singh was made to appear before the District Magistrate who acquitted him on the plea that he committed breach of the curfew orders under the necessity of visiting a serious patient. Sir Aroor Singh's buggy was there outside the court to take him home. On his way he noticed that the movement of people and the traffic were almost normal and so was business activity in the shops. Horse carriages carrying passengers from the railway station to the city and from the city to the railway station were crowding the railway bridge as before. None showed any sign of unease or fear which had haunted him all the days he was in jail.

On reaching home he found that a two leaf gate had been affixed to the entrance porch of the haveli, which was closed. The gate did not cover the whole of the high vaulting porch but was high enough to preclude jumping over it. A servant opened the gate and informed him that his wife had shifted to their old house inside the city.

Before going to his old home, Hira Singh decided to first visit Golden Temple for obeisance and to pray. One of the practices his nana had ingrained in him was getting up before day break. He would have to finish his bath, etcetera, before dawn, and walk to Darbar Sahib in the Golden Temple to offer prayers. He would seek benediction for the patients under his treatment. He had followed this practice all his life.

That was the traditional amavas day,' the last day of the dark fortnight of the moon, a day when people from outside came to the town for praying and for their monthly shopping. There was usual hustle and bustle in the bazaars and outside shops. In the Golden Temple also there was festival-day throng of people. After the unhappy thoughts he had in the jail cell, it was a great relief for him to find that life had returned to normal.

When he reached his old home in Katra Ahluwalia a furlong from the Golden Temple he found garlands of red chillies strung above the entrance door, usually done to ward off evil eye. His wife had never believed in this superstition. She had seen him coming and had come down to the entrance lounge. She fell on his feet and asked for forgiveness for shifting to this house without his permission. When he held her by the arms and made her get up she said that an ogress would come out of the well of that haveli and howl all the night. She added that she got scared because it called for their son Dayal Singh.

Their only son was in his fifth year. According to the tradition of the family he should have been initiated as an apprentice at the dwakhana. The boys

17

and in some cases girls also were now going to school and college. His wife insisted that their son should have proper education before he took to the family profession.

CHAPTER THREE

Living in the interior of the city in that narrow lane was now less unpleasant than it used to be. Despite war-time constraints, the lane had changed radically. Previously, the drain which flowed out filthy water was in the middle of the lane. Smaller drains from each house cut across the lane to join the central drain. Entrance platform of houses were of different sizes, some bulging out into the lane to cover almost one third of its breadth. First floor balconies of some house extended out so much that at places it looked almost like a tunnel. One could hardly move through the lane without soiling ones feet with the drain's overflow as it often got blocked. The municipal committee had disallowed extended platforms and balconies of houses and had got them pulled down. Instead of a drain in the middle of the lane there were two drains along the outer wall of houses. The lane had been raised and was well paved. The side drains were deep so that there was no verflow in normal times. Open drains down upper floors had to be replaced by cast iron pipes which were quite cheap. One could now walk through the lane without the fear of being sprinkled with dirty water. Lamp posts had been installed in the lane as in the streets outside. There was a municipal primary school for girls in a haveli in the beginning of the lane, affiliated to a girls' high school a furlong away.

The platform of the community well had been raised and covered with polished slates. Its pulley and the pulley stand were of wrought iron and not of wood as previously. The area for bathers had been demarcated so that they did not spill water into the well. There was more sense of hygiene and disdain for those who did not show enough concern for cleanliness. Charcoal and coke had replaced wood and cow dung cakes for fuel.

Hurricane and many types of kerosene lamps were replacing mustard oil wick lamps, which left a trail of soot. Imported cloth was cheap, stitching had become inexpensive and the people had enough clothes for a change. Quick lime for whitewashing houses was plentiful, so were bricks and material for mortar. The people were better dressed and better housed. Previously everyone dressed alike. The only way a person demonstrated his prosperousness was on the occasion of a marriage or the death of a kith at ripe age. It had all changed. He almost felt that he had come to a new place and not returned to an old one.

Changes, no doubt, had taken place in the bazaar where his dwakhana was situated and in the wide lane of his previous house. Having happened bit by bit from day to day, these had been imperceptible. Here in this lane he had come after four years and his the urine of those who bathed there. He would say that at least ninety percent of the bathers in these holy tanks or rivers would not help passing water while bathing. He was quite well up in ancient mythological lore and knew something of Greek mythology also. His reference to bastard ancient Indian gods and of promiscuity amongst them had always an element of lightness and sometimes of humour. His jibes such as Draupadi having five husbands would have less of sting when he would point out that in Bible there was reference to a woman with seven husbands who came to see Jesus Christ.

Maulana Asad Ullah Khan, a Muslim religious divine also joined this evening gathering frequently. He was a popular orator and made rabid speeches from the pulpit in the mosque, even though by nature he was very liberal in outlook. He was the first to be arrested when leaders of various parties were rounded up before martial law and the last to be released. As he made light of some of the habits and superstitions of traditional Muslim clerics, he was made to leave their organization. He set up his own organization of the Muslims - Majlis-e-Ahrar. His speeches lasting hours at gatherings of Muslims and elsewhere would seldom refer to the subject of the meeting. It would be laced with satire, pun, Urdu couplets, Punjabi proverbs and light remarks about other Muslim leaders in the town. The audience would roll with laughter, but this often created problem for him. He would come with his problem to the dwakhana, which would provide very light moments to the gathering there. Sometimes a solution would be suggested which would be equally light-hearted. Once, Maulana Asad Ullah had gone to Delhi to attend a conference of Muslim leaders. In his absence thousands of handbills were distributed among Muslims in the town that the Maulana had taken with him a beautiful boy. There were also other allegations about his integrity and personal life. Asad Ullah grumbled about this at the dwakhana gathering. One of those present suggested a solution. There was a boy working as a helpmate to a dyer in the adjoining bazaar. He was very dark in colour with pimples on face. He had a cleft palate, which made two of his upper teeth bulge out. His eyes were uneven and narrow and nose misshapen. His ears were large and of lighter shade which made him look all the more hideous. It was suggested to Asad Ullah that he should take that boy with him when he went for prayers to the mosque next Friday. After prayers when he rose to speak from pulpit, he should show that boy to the audience as the one who had accompanied him to Delhi. That boy would willingly play his part if paid a few pice.

Another regular visitor was Amritlal Gauba. He had done Bar-at-Law from London and was the son of Ramlal Gauba, town's most famous lawyer. Amritlal had married a girl from a Muslim aristocratic family, whom he came to know while studying at Lahore. Even though that woman had adopted a Hindu name and had formally converted to Hindu religion at an Arya Samaj reformist temple, she was never treated as an equal. Apart from the otherness associated with her, many women in the family continued to treat her as impure like the Muslims. Their two daughters were also treated differently. This was quite upsetting for Amritlal and his wife. They were very worried because in the circumstance these girls would not be acceptable in Hindu families. Then there would be problem after death. The orthodox Hindus might not allow his wife to be cremated in their cremation ground in the town and the Muslims were sure to deny her burial in their graveyard.

Mr. Gauba's concerns often came for comment in these gatherings, sometimes casually and at others earnestly. Someone would state that things were bound to change in a decade or so. Another person would suggest that the family should convert to Christianity. To that Mr. Gauba would reply that his wife was cut off from her family and by becoming a Christian he would also be severing relations with his family. That would have an adverse affect on his legal practice in the local courts and the Lahore High Court. Maulana Asad Ullah would advise him to become a Muslim and thus become the most popular Muslim barrister in the town.

Someone else would remark: "What a strange thing is religion. Something that promised wings to man had become a shackle and a millstone." Sardar Gurdit Singh would add sarcastically: "It is something worse. It is a boulder hanging on one's head. One passes one's life under fear that it may fall on the head anytime." Another person would remark: "I wish God will make men of different religions tolerant of one another, at least to prove to atheists like Sardar Gurdit Singh that He exists".

21

Hira Singh thought of his nana who was a deeply religious person. Religion for him was neither a millstone tied to the feet nor a boulder hanging on the head. It was a lamp one lit within oneself to see the righteous path. He felt concerned about Amritlal Gauba and used his friendship with his father to make things better for his wife. He was convinced that these prejudices were bound to disappear as an educated professional class came to the fore in the two communities and there was greater commingling of Hindus and Muslims in trade, business and services. He recollected that when the country became unified under the British rule, the idea that all the inhabitants of this country were one people had begun to override divisions of religion and caste. After the World War this process of commingling of communities received a fillip when there was united support by all communities to the non-cooperation movement of the National Congress, the Khilafat movement of the Muslims and the Akali movement of the Sikhs.

Most of the persons in that gathering felt sad that this progress towards national unity had slowed down as a result of the demand by Muslims for reservations and opposition to it by the National Congress and the Hindus in general. Controversy about reservations for Muslims in services and representative bodies was still raging when all of a sudden Shudhi movement for the conversion of Muslim Rajputs to Hinduism shook north India. These Rajput tribes got converted to Islam long ago during the reign of Akbar and later Mughal emperors. Money began to be collected by Hindus in Amritsar to further the cause of this movement. Muslims in the town, in an attitude of tit for tat started collecting money for sending volunteers to those areas to oppose this. This became a cause of communal tension in the city, resulting in occasional exchange of hot words and bitter argumentation between the two communities. Mr. Gandhi's statement that ban on cow slaughter was as important as the freedom movement came as a shock to the Muslims. He did not reiterate it but Hindu leaders and the Hindu owned Press made it a routine to play it up. The result was that many Muslim who could afford mutton took to taking beef. In areas of Muslim habitation, butchers' began to hang on gambrel stick beef along with mutton in their shop. In retaliation, a section of the Hindus began to insist on playing music before the mosques. These became other sources of tension between the two communities.

Both Hindu and Muslims came to the dwakhana as before. These issues were discussed without bitterness but Hindus and Muslims now often took opposite stand. Those who thought differently with a non-communal point of view were becoming fewer and fewer. When a visitor observed that communal tension was the creation of the alien government in pursuit of its policy of divide and rule, many disagreed. Someone would ask whether Mahatma Gandhi's statement advocating ban on cow slaughter and similar communal statement by other leaders were made at the behest of the British government. Despite all the logic that Gurdit Singh could muster, he failed to convince many Hindus and Muslims gathering there that the British government was only making full use of it and that communalism was the creation of Indians themselves. Maulana Asad Ullah would emphasize that communal tension became endemic only after Gandhi took over leadership of the Congress Party, occupied a position of centrality in national politics and declared anyone who disagreed with him as anti-national. He would say that the violence which Mr. Gandhi's non-violence would touch off could not be imagined at that time.

CHAPTER FOUR

Reports about Hindu-Muslim riots breaking out sporadically in one part of India or the other had been agitating the people in the city for more than a year. In 1924, communal riots acquired the dimension of an epidemic. Never before, were these so widespread and persisted for days together everywhere. These riots were different from the infrequent pre-War communal riots. Those were the work of unsocial elements with little support from their respective community and flared up and fizzled out all of a sudden. These riots now were the work of aggressive and fanatical elements in each community bent upon teaching the other a lesson. These kept raging till the local administration acted firmly to put a stop to it. Perhaps purposefully, the Government seldom did it on time. This had created a tense atmosphere in Amritsar, as it did elsewhere. This was fanned as much by the speeches of leaders as by writings in Hindu and Muslim owned newspapers.

At last, Amritsar became embroiled in a very serious Hindu-Muslim riot. It was as sudden as it was virulent and in no time spread to several parts of the city. It broke out after the match between the Hindu College and the Muslim College cricket teams. The Muslim batsman, whose double century had resulted in the defeat of the Hindu College team, was waylaid by some spectators. This soon became fisticuffs between the two teams and fight between the spectators of the two communities. Some one took out a knife and there was stabbing. Soon wild rumours were spreading fast in the city.

Unlike the earlier riots, the riot in the city this time had wider support in each community and the number of persons who raised their voice against this was not as large as before. In every area of dense population of a community, members of that community gathered in large numbers in the streets, bazaars and road-crossings armed, with whatever they could lay their hands on, bamboo sticks, iron rods, knives, daggers, axes, hatchets, etcetera. They attacked anyone of the other community they spotted nearby. A rowdy hubbub accompanied these gangs, a pandemonium of slogan shouting, battle cries, yelling, howling and screaming. Strange and unknown passions which had lain dormant were now springing to life. Gangs formed spontaneously in various localities and began roving about. While, there hardly was any Muslim owned shop in Hindu dominated localities, there were many of the Hindus in predominantly Muslim areas. These were plundered and where anyone had animus against the shopkeeper he was done to death.

Localities inhabited by the Hindus were generally in the inner part of the city and those by the Muslims in the outer parts. Taken unaware on the first day, Hindus going by horse carriage or otherwise from the railway station to their home inside the city were attacked by sticks and rods and life snuffed out of men, women and children. Sticks, iron rods and axes were brandished wildly and slogans and battle cries were shouted loudly. Gang roamed about, merged and separated and merged again, moving lava of violence and brutality. Perpendicular to Hall Bazaar there was a street mainly of Hindu general merchants. Shops there were looted and put to fire. A cripple sat at the beginning; of the street waiting for alms. One in the gang lifted his underwear, noticed that he was not circumcised and stabbed him. Few Muslim workmen, artisans and craftsmen who had gone to Hindu dominated areas for work could return home. Slogan shouting and howling of battle cries was as delirious in the Hindu localities as in those of the Muslims.

Brass bands consisting of imported western band instruments as vehicles of exuding joy and merriment, especially during wedding festivities, had become very popular, a part of local custom and cultural ethos. The day riots broke out was an auspicious day for marriage ceremony for Hindus. All the professional band masters and bag pipe players were Muslims and dozens of such brass band groups were in Hindu areas when riots broke out. Sensing the danger to them, some persons went round from one marriage party to the other telling them that the death of anyone of the brass band prayers would make the marriage inauspicious. They were thus protected and safely escorted to the Muslim areas when the marriage festivities were over. They were the only Muslims who returned safely from the Hindu populated areas during those riots.

It appeared that the city had been given the license to destroy itself. The district administration hardly noticed what was happening in the city and its suburbs, waiting for the commotion to bum itself out. On the fourth day some eminent citizens of Amritsar hired city drummers, Muslims for the Muslim populated areas and Hindus for the Hindu areas. They went round announcing by the beat of drum that peace-loving citizens would gather at the large terrace around the clock tower. From there they would move in a procession throughout the city to restore peace and harmony. The district administration then moved into action. Section 144 of the Indian Penal Code was clamped on the town, prohibiting carrying of weapons and gatherings of more than four persons.

The day riots broke out the wife of Hira Singh had given birth to another son. In initial phase of the communal riot, Sikhs were not attacked but Hira Singh's worry was that a Muslim midwife was in his house attending on his wife. Not knowing that communal violence was at its height in the bazaars she might move out in that area with Hindu population. She was residing near the dwakhana and her two sons had already come to enquire about her.

Hira Singh sent for a horse carriage with a Sikh coachman from the haveli of Sir Aroor Singh situated at a distance of a few furlongs. He told midwife's sons that he would make their mother stay in his house till it was safe for her to move out. After visiting his home, he went to see some influential local leaders who shared his concern about the communal situation in the city.

The midwife Zeenat Begum belonged to the kanjar clan, a tribe among the local converts to Islam who were hustler by profession. In the Ram Bagh bazaar in which the dwakhana was situated and in the adjacent Katra Ghananya there lived a few dozen women who had their professional rooms above the shops or storerooms in the bazaar. Some of these were dancing girls only and entertained their guests with mujra as their special semi-erotic dances and songs were called. Others entertained their guests in any other manner they desired. Many of these women, with proper make up, would sit in the windows or balconies of their first floor room during the evening to invite customers. Zeenat Begum's mother was a well-known dancing girl of the area. She resided about twenty yards to the right of the dwakhana on the opposite side of the bazaar. Her dancing hall was above four shops. Three of these shops were for different trades and the fourth shop served as an entrance lounge with wide stairs leading up the first floor. More than her exceptional beauty and dancing nuances, she was known for her witticism and pert and entertaining dialogue. Many aristocrats in the town visited her dancing hall to see her mujra. Two or three persons were in love with her. One of them was a Pathan landlord from the adjoining Jullunder district. He had been pressing her to leave the dancing hall and enter his harem. She decided to do so when she was well passed her youth and her daughter and pupil Zeenat Bai became eighteen years of age. She used to keep a box with a slot in the backroom of the dwakhana. Once or twice a week she would come and drop coins in the box. Once she came and emptied the box. She gave key of the box and some money to her daughter Zeenat and left the place for good. Zeenat Bai was more beautiful than her mother and was more selective about visitors and lovers. She came only once a week on Fridays to drop coins in the box. Fridays she spent in prayers and did not allow any customer on that day, keeping closed the shop providing enterance upstairs.

One day, it was just before the World War, she came to push some coins into the slot of the box and sat down near Hira Singh's dais. Lowering her eyes she whispered: "The midwife says I will have twins. Even if one is a son, I will forsake this profession and leave this place. As upper caste Muslims would not agree to a person belonging to the kanjar clan to live amongst them, I would need your help to find a suitable place for me to live with dignity and bring up my sons properly." After saying this she bowed before him with joined hands and left quietly.

She had twin boys and kept her promise. She closed the outer door of the fourth shop and locked it from outside, putting to use the back stairs. She dispensed with the services of all those who were there to help her in singing, dancing and make-up. As soon as she was fit enough to move out, she came to see Hira Singh and waited till he was free. She requested him to arrange a place for her, where her belonging to the kanjar tribe would not haunt her. He advised her to change her name to Zeenat Begum, because the appellation Bai was associated with women of the kanjar clan. He also advised her to buy a house instead of taking it on rent. Once she had purchased the house and it was registered in her name, none could object to her residing there. He asked her to go to the store and bring her moneybox. He weighed it in his hand and asked her whether it had sovereigns also. She replied that there would be more than fifty sovereigns in it.

The box was opened and it contained more than nine hundred rupees in all. He quietly talked the matter with the local elected member of the municipal committee. In Amir Ali Lane inhabited by Muslim Sayyads a house could be purchased for rupees eight hundred. Being next to a mosque, it was available at little less than' the market rate because of noise there. Zeenat Begun was quite happy about it. Her other problem was more perplexing and a chance happening helped in solving it. While living as a dancing girl, her two sons could be without a known father. When she was living like a normal family person, this would place her and her sons in an awkward position.

Two rich hide merchants of the town, a Hindu Krishan Kumar Kalia and a Muslim Mian Nasim Ali had died a short while ago in the Poonch area of Jammu and Kashmir State. They were hide merchants who often dealt with hide of newly born calf or of a calf in embryo, which fetched a high price as calf leather. A week ago their maimed bodies were brought to Amritsar for cremation of the Hindu and burial of the Muslim. Everyone knew that both of them were fond of Zeenat Bai's mujra and were very regular visitors to her dancing hall. Hira Singh suggested that she should claim the deceased hide merchant Mian Nasim Ali as the father of her sons and have this recorded when she reported the birth of the two sons to the municipal registrar of births.

The midwife who had delivered Zeenat Bai agreed to take her as an apprentice so that she was able to earn a living as a midwife. A Missionary Maternity Hospital had been set up that year. Its Matron was coming to the dwakhana for treatment of dysentery, a local seasonal ailment. In her talk she mentioned that women from upper classes of Hindus and Muslims shunned her hospital. Hira Singh told her that it could be because the entire staff was Christian. He advised her to employ a Hindu or Muslim woman as a help-mate and suggested that one Zeenat Begum known to him could suit her purpose.

After a year in Missionary Maternity Hospital, Zeenat Begum started working as a midwife on her own and was a success. Unlike other midwives, she insisted that the lying in woman should have a clean and well-ventilated room and not a dark and dingy one, as was the traditional practice. Zeenat Begum moved about in a burqa, a head to heel veil. If Hira Singh had not prevented her from moving out of his house, she would have been dead. It was not known in that lane till that time th~t communal disturbances were spreading fast in the city.

It took more than a week for peace to be restored and for life, trade and commerce to become normal. By that time over one hundred persons were dead and over four hundred lay injured in the hospital. Most of the dead and injured were poor persons and their families became poorer and more helpless than before. Only those well off persons who were taken unawares fell victim to the riots.

One such person was Gopal Das who was going from the railway station to his home in the interior of the city on the forenoon when communal riots broke out.

As his horse carriages entered Hall Gate and reached Khairdin mosque, a mob started raining sticks and clubs on him and on his wife and two sons with him. His wife and sons died there and then and he survived with a broken arm and swollen back. He came to see Hira Singh for poultice for his swollen back and arm. In addition to two sons his wife had given birth to six daughters who did not live beyond a day. It was generally believed that he ended the life of the new born girl by thrusting through her throat red sulphur tips of match sticks. Match sticks imported from England during those days had red tipping made of some sulphur compound. Hira Singh sympathized with him and gave him the various ingredients and told him how to make the poultice. Gopal Das grumbled that there was no one to look after his house and he would have to remarry soon. Hira Singh remarked that had anyone of his six daughters been alive, he would not have felt so lonely. He advised him to accept as God's grace whether he had a son or a daughter after his remarriage.

It was an unprecedented situation after the riots. However friendly were the relations between individuals, tension between the two communities persisted. It heightened from time to time by reports of minor and major riots, which unfailingly kept erupting in one part of the country or the other. The bazaar in which dwakhana was situated acquired a new look in a month or two after the riots. New shops came up and many of the old shops had new occupants. New trades and businesses were started by Muslims for which they previously depended on the Hindus. In this bazaar there were now Muslim cloth merchants, grocers, goldsmiths, dealers in utensils, braziers, silver-leaf beaters and purveyors of many other trades. The Hindus had similarly introduced in their areas businesses and trades, which were previously with the Muslims. Touching leather was regarded as impure by high caste Hindus. Many footwear shops had now come up in areas of Hindu predominance. Hindus took to manual work and crafts for which they had previously utilized the services of Muslim artisans and craftsmen. Though all this sustained tension between the two communities, personal relations between individual Hindus and Muslims continued to be without any hostility. There were common wholesale importers and stock-in-traders. The new trading relations in many ways brought individuals of the two communities nearer.

Educated and professional classes amongst Hindus, Muslims and Sikhs were becoming closer as a result of their common education and similar professions and working places. A liberal was still a person who tried to understand other's problems and appreciated other's point of view. Books were common source of ideas and more and more books and journals from England and from within the country were available in the book shops and public and college libraries. There were Muslims among the educated classes who felt that there should be a solution other than communal reservations for redressing the grievances of the Muslims. Similarly there were educated Hindus who held that instead of blindly opposing Communal Award, Hindus should suggest how Muslims could get their due in services and educational institutions without reservations. There were Muslim who believed that beef-eating was not an issue on which national unity should be imperiled. All these views often came for discussion at the dwakhana gatherings. Someone would point out that always in India's long history, rulers and leaders of men had given precedence to their individual or sectional interests. The same was the case at that time. Another narrated that immediately before the coming of the British, the Marathas were a great power in central, northern and western India. The Marathas could have united the kings, rajas, and chieftains of these territories against the foreign British power. Instead they rode roughshod over these kingdoms and principalities trying to reduce them to dust. The result was that when Marathas encountered Ahmed Shah Abdali at Panipat, every ruler in northern and western India, whether Rajput, Jat, Ruhela, Gond or Sikh, wanted the Marathas to be vanquished. It was pointed out that the same unfortunate tradition was being followed now. What united the people should have been emphasized, instead of what divided them. Gandhiji and Hindu leaders should not needlessly have brought up cow slaughter just as Muslim leaders should not have raised the demand for separate electorate.

However true it might be that rulers and leaders in India had always been self seekers, Hira Singh had no doubt that this was not the only reason why the numerous domains of this country so easily fell under the British rule. Apart from this flaw in Indian inheritance, there must be some advantage with the British people that made that possible. The books on English history that he generally came across dealt with kings and battles. He had to make special effort to procure books on science and technology to be able to have some understanding of this.

Going through these books he came to know that at the time of the Roman conquest in the eleventh century the British people were barbarians able to cultivate only a small fraction of land in the island. This population of about four million became one half in 1348 when Black Death - plague - scourged the land. The resulting shortage of manpower gave fillip to non-human and non-animal energy. Use of wind-mills and wind-power came into vogue. The new techniques of water and wind power accelerated the development of both mining and manufacturing. Deforestation acquired a rapid pace, as more fuel was needed for growing industries and for making charcoal for the production of iron. This rapidly increased the area of land under agriculture. The shortage of wood became so severe in some areas that mining of mineral coal became necessary. This increased almost ten times in the course of the seventeenth century. Improved farming practices and increase in industry and trade made the people acquire a forward looking and go ahead attitude. It also broke the mould of feudal relations. Reading habit became widespread and universities and seminaries sprang up.

Hira Singh was surprised at the rapidity with which developments took place after that. When in the later part of the seventeenth century, European Renaissance burst upon the British island, there was effervescence of scientific thinking and the emergence of scientists such as Gilbert, Napier and Harvey; and then Boyle, Hook and Newton. The Royal Society was founded in 1662 and became the world center of scientific activity. Each development was a catalyst for many others. Wood and charcoal became very expensive and sulphur in the pit coal continued to spoil the iron. By 1709 Abraham Darby had learnt to rid the sulphur fumes from the coal by a process of preheating converting it into coke. In 1705 Thomas Newman and John Galley designed a steam engine, which could drain water from mines, thus making more coal available. In 1764 Hargreaves invented spinning jenny, a combination of many spindles into a single machine run by a single operator. In 1765 Watt constructed a steam engine, which by 1785 was used to drive both the spinning machines and the power looms. By the beginning of the nineteenth century screw propelled steamboat, the threshing machine and the sewing machine had been invented. Maudslay developed screw cutting lathe which made possible the standardization and automatic production of various engineering requirements. . The development of farm implements, made possible the extension of agriculture to an extent unimaginable before. Better breeding practices doubled the average weight of cattle and sheep. Stethoscope, anaesthesia, principles of hygiene and modem medical practices became more common. Life became better with the coming of railroads, Portland cement, high pressure steam boilers, electric engines, battery, dynamo, telegraph, vulcanizing of rubber, pneumatic tires, cheap wood-pulp paper, rotary cylinder press and scores of other inventions. Side by side the democratic idea of equality affected political scenario. The fusion of reason and pragmatism encouraged a belief in the rationality of man and nature. Literacy, though not education, was so widespread that there were many Sunday newspapers each with a circulation of over a million copies. Women were still auctioned in the streets of London and a man would call his dog dear but not his wife. Universal suffrage and social justice were still distant dreams. However, the trail had been blazed.

As he looked at India's historical past, he discovered a completely different process at work. The second millennium began with repeated depredations of Mahmood of Ghazni. For more than thirty years till his death in 1030 he carried out annually a campaign of loot and plunder in India. From 1030 A.D. to the seventh invasion of Ahmed Shah Abdali in 1764, there had been invasions and continuous wars. Even Mughals did not give the country much peace. During forty years of his rule, Emperor Akbar waged thirty major expeditions. Emperor Aurangzeb spent the second half of his reign in Deccan ceaselessly waging wars. Many invaders took away thousands of artisans and craftsmen as slaves. Their armies foraged for food and fuel all along the route. This denuded the villages and towns of all livestock and every article of wood and iron, thus wiping out productive and other assets.

Thinking of all this Hira Singh came to believe that the coming of the British had done some good to the people of this country. It broke the unending sequence of invasions and wars. Things were no more at a dead end or moving at a snail's pace, to be thwarted again and again. He thought of the changes and improvements that had taken place before his very eyes, political and social reforms and economic progress which had come about. All this came for discussion at the dwakhana gatherings. Many disagreed with him that the coming to India of the British was a blessing. Some would refuse to accept that the assortment of governments and ruling authorities in India before the coming of the British were more evil than rule by foreigners. To him this appeared to be an attitude of the vanquished showing contempt for the victor by refusing to see any virtue in him. When someone in the gathering drew attention to the massacre at Jalianwala Bagh and martial law atrocities, he would point out that during the Great War, Germans killed more Poles than the population of Switzerland and no one was punished for this. In Britain General Dyer was duly tried and punished for the Jalianwala Bagh atrocities. He would state that Gandhi and others could talk of non-violence because the rulers were the British. The non-violent Akali movement for gurdwara reform could succeed only because of that. Another ruler .would have got the non-violent volunteers beheaded en masse just as the Mughal governors of Lahore, Lakhpat Rai and Mir Manu did.

Someone would point out that Gandhiji insisted on being the sole leader of the freedom movement. He treated anyone differing from him, not only against him but also against the Indian nation. This implied an element of violence. Another person would remark that Gandhiji was behaving like a person who saw sundial for the first time and was thrilled by the invention. After all, human society and family life would not have emerged without non-violence appearing in human mind in some form. Human civilization would not have made any progress without non-violence and pacifism played an essential part in the development of human society. Someone would remark that old ideas became new and acquired great vitality when the time became ripe for them. Another would state that non-violence was a form of assertion by the weak against the strong, a manner of saying that if I did not have a gun like you, I had my spit.

He pondered over these issues and thought over the abolition of oppressive Acts including the Rowlett Act, which was never used. There was the induction of more and more Indians in higher services and the Indian Army. The excise duty was abolished and Tariff Board was set up to enable Indian industries to compete with British industries, a demand which was accepted as soon as it was made.

CHAPTER FIVE

After seeing a serious patient in the afternoon, Hira Singh had shifted to the divan and was reading a book when Sardar Gurdit Singh and Maulana Asad Ullah Khan came in at almost the same time and took their seat on the front settee.

A journalist had asked Mahatma Gandhi what he would try to achieve if he was made Viceroy of India for a day. Gandhi replied the he would clean the lavatories of the Viceroy's Lodge. The questioner asked him if he were made Viceroy of India for the second day, what he would try to achieve. Gandhi replied that second day also he would clean the lavatories of Viceroy's lodge. Asad Ullah Khan commented that if a Muslim leader had said this he would have been described as a nitwit but in the case of a Hindu leader these utterances were being described as pearls of wisdom. Before Asad Ullah could say anything more, a robust person dressed in ochre clothes entered the dwakhana. On finding two persons sitting there he retreated and disappeared as suddenly as he had arrived. The three of them were surprised about it and could not guess who he was and why he went back without saying a word. Next forenoon he came again and sat on the back settee. He told Hira Singh that he would explain to him the purpose of his visit when he was free and alone.

It took Hira Singh more than an hour to be alone. During this period he kept sitting on the back settee motionless, most of the time with bowed head. When Hira Singh was free he came and sat on the divan. That person in ochre robe came near him and sat by his side on the divan with his back towards the bazaar. Both of them stared at each other.

Hira Singh could not place him immediately even though something in his features appeared to him familiar. His dark, fatty masculine face with high cheek bones was adorned with high rising crop of curly hair like South India's Sai Baba. The tufts at his temples were white and not gray, which .indicated that he had dyed his hair black. He had the dull round eyes of a bull buffalo. He had little veins in his eyes which clearly were the result, not of drinking, but of smoking chillum, the clay pot with a stem which mendicants used for smoking locally made unrefined tobacco balls. He seemed to be an avid smoker of chillum. His nose was broad and his nostrils were, like a camel's, turned inside out. Hira Singh observed the scar on his chin which was like a cross. This and his nostrils were like that of the son of his former sweeper who had disappeared over fifteen years ago. He was a very active and intelligent boy, so hardy that nothing affected him whether he fell from a roof or slipped into a ditch. Anyone else would have broken his bones, but nothing happened to him. Once he tried to climb up the clock tower by holding on to the cavities on its facade. He fell down from the fiftieth feet. All that he had suffered was a smashed chin, which took several months to heel leaving behind a cross-shaped scar. After that he had enteric fever which kept him in bed for almost a year. He subsisted for over eight months on whey water and distillation of gaozaban plant and had become a bare skeleton. His round buffalo-like eyes and cross-shaped scar on chin stared at Hira Singh whenever he went to examine him and prescribe treatment for him. Typhoid fever had gripped the city in an epidemic form resulting in a large number of deaths and this boy's recovery was almost a miracle. That was the first time he had started adding a few crystals of aspirin to the powder he prescribed for the patients having temperature. This reduced the intensity and pain of fever though its cure took a lot of time and care.

"Don't you recognize me Taooji" he asked in a voice which did not seem to be unfamiliar to Hira Singh. He was addressed as Taooji by the family sweeper and his kith and kin. It had occurred to him that he was the sweeper's son who had run away from home more than fifteen years ago. Even to posit this to a person who was dressed as a high caste religious figure could turn out to be a blasphemy. Hira Singh remained silent indicating by the way of looking at him that he was all-at sea about it.

"I am Jharkoo, your jamadarni Bharpai's son. Don't you remember the scar on my chin for which you gave me green ointment for more than six months? Don't you remember my year long fever for which you treated me with so much love and attention?"

Hira Singh put his arm round him to show how happy he was to see him and greeted him with a smile. The inhibition of a former untouchable got over him and he withdrew but Hira Singh kept holding his hand. He said he was the chief priest at one of the important Hindu religious foundations in Central India which administered many temples. He said that his origin is not known to anybody there and earnestly urged upon him not to whisper about his visit to anyone. He wanted to leave some gold ornaments and some money with him to be passed on to his mother without divulging anything about him. Saying this he took out two bundles from his jhola, the mendicant's bag, and placed these before Hira Singh.

Hira Singh lifted the heavier bag and said: "These gold ornaments must be over twenty tolas and similarly the other bag seems to contain about five hundred rupees in currency notes. Don't you realize that even with a fraction of this gold and cash in the house, the whole family will be accused of theft and arrested. I will not pass these ornaments and money to them. Better take these back. Don't tell me where you are staying here. You should return immediately and desist from coming to Amritsar, because the scar on your chin, your round eyes and upturned nostrils might betray you to anyone who has seen you as a boy. As a matter of fact I had no difficulty in recognizing you. I would not call you Jharkoo. What is your new name? "Swami Gyanendra Pande" he replied unpretentiously.

Hira Singh was silent for sometime with eyes fixed on him. He thought of the rich religious endowment of which he was the head priest. Then he thought of the small thatched hut where he was born and where he had lived before he disappeared. Under the British rule things had changed for the better for most of the communities but not for the sweeper Balmiks. Every morning and evening almost all members of Bharpai's family went to various homes to clean dry latrines there. Every one of them carried on his head an uncovered bucket containing faeces collected from those houses. This was passed on to a male member of the family who carried it in an open hand driven trolley outside the city. All the half a dozen or so members of Bharpai's family together earned rupees five or six a month. Sometimes, a male member of these families got a job with the Municipal Committee as sweeper for cleaning and washing the gutters and sewers in the lanes and street. The work of mopping the dry latrines and carrying the shit on head in open pans or buckets was then mainly done by women, boys and girls. They worked without gloves or masks. The odour of the night soil they carried on their head or in open hand driven carts was so nauseating that men felt compelled to consume country liquor in the morning before they started their work. It was only in this drunken stupor they were able to cope with this work. Women consumed massive quantities of scented betel nuts. Even worse than the work itself, was the way people treated them, as if they were not human beings but effigies made of filth and were stink personified. Cash they gave to shopkeepers was washed before it was accepted. Where the house did not have separate stairs or entrance for them, these were symbolically cleaned by sprinkling water after they had passed through it. They were not permitted to sort out or pick and choose articles they bought and had to accept whatever bad stuff was given to them.

Despite all that, when their young girls reached puberty they became a play thing not only of young but even of older men in the household they served. There was a school not far away from their shanties, but none of the boys or girls of this settlement had ever dared to enter it except to sweep the school compound and to mop the school latrines. Long board with flapper, hung from the ceiling, with string pulled from outside the class room served as fan in summer. Children from sweeper families were not allowed to come so near the class as to hold the string for flapping. When Jharkoo recovered .from his illness and was somewhat fit to work, Hira Singh tried to get him a job in a municipal school for pulling string of the cloth fan. The reply of the school head master was that he was a sweeper's son, how could that be? People would touch a dog, a donkey or a buffalo wallowing in mud and dirt, but not a Balmik man, woman or child. During his illness Jharkoo had to spend almost an year in fresh air and the first day he was made to carry the bucket of shit, he had a vomiting sensation and the bucket fell down. There was an outcry when the contents spread in the alley. Jharkoo ran away from there and that was the day he disappeared from his home."

"Your father Jhangaroo died two years ago" Hira Singh informed him in a voice full of grief, "The Balmiks are not allowed to elect their headman as they used to do. A pliable bad character among the Balmiks is appointed as headman by the high castes. He does not permit anyone to bring beef in the sweepers' colony. Two years ago, they could not afford mutton nor could they bring beef for the annual Holi festivities. They butchered an ass and cooked its meat for these revelries. Your father was among the four elderly persons who died of cramps. When I carne to know about it I went to see him, but it was too late. Your father was at his last gasp and his eyeballs had bulged out of the sockets. He breathed his last in my presence and I could do nothing to help him."

"Does not the Balmik panchayat object to a headman being foisted on them?" Swami Gyanendra wanted to know.

"You have been too long away and do not know the situation. If it has changed it has changed for the worse. The nominated headman gets enough money to have a few toughs around him and it is not easy to raise voice against him. Earlier this year he raped a nine year old Balmik girl. The Officer in Charge of the Police Station refused to register the case. He said that if he were to register cases of raping of Balmik girls he will have to register a case and more every day."

The red veins in Swami Gyanendra eyes began to glow and his face became red. It could be from anger or shame or both. They remained silent for some minutes. Hira Singh could hardly think of something to say to soothe his hurt feelings.

Jharkoo now Swami Gyanendra Pande was sitting by Hira Singh's side as a respectable Hindu religious personality. He wanted to send some gold ornaments and a few hundred rupees to his mother but even a small fraction of that gold and money in that sweepers' house would provide ground for arresting the whole family for burglary. This was a system which dehumanized the whole community so much so that its members could not keep even rudiments of property. As had seldom happened before, great anger swelled in Hira Singh. He strongly felt that the British government in India stood condemned for not doing anything to put a stop to this. It completely nullified all the good that their presence in India might have done.

Hira Singh recollected what Asad. Ullah Khan had mentioned as Gandhiji's reply to the question about his becoming Viceroy of India for a day. He said he would clean the lavatories in the Viceroy's lodge for that day. Fortunately for him these were not dry latrines from which night soil had to be carried on head in an open pan.

Hira Singh remembered Asad Ullah's assertion that Gandhiji always spoke and acted in such a symbolic manner as would get him applause but would not offend the Hindus He would not say that the existing system of scavenging is a crime against humanity, should be done away with and till then people should themselves carry their shit outside the town .Gandhiji would never advise Hindus to be non-violent in word and deed during communal riots but would advise Jews to offer themselves to be shot or thrown into the Dead Sea by the Arabs without raising a little finger against them. He would say that if all the people of the Punjab get killed, Punjab would become immortal but would not advise the Hindus not to mind being killed so that India became immortal. Such utterances would not get him any applause. The beauty of non-violence was that it could be symbolic and selective.

Swami Gyanendra asked, after waiting for sometime for Hira Singh to be attentive to him: "Is there no way for me to send this jewelry and money to my mother?"

Hira Singh regretted: "I cannot suggest anything. The thatched hut has no door. One or two boxes in the hut have ramshackle lock if any. Quite often all the family members are out on work. When a poor person has so much of wealth it shines in the eyes. Even if your mother is not arrested for robbery, someone will steal this money and jewelry in the matter of a few days."

They were silent for sometime, Swami Gyanendra staring at him forlornly.

Hira Singh advised him: "Ujjain has the largest number of rich Hindu shrines in Central India. If you are there you can send by money order five or ten rupees to your mother every month from some other town incognito or in the name of some fake charitable organization. This will, more than double their income. Last year your mother came to ask for some help for the marriage of her youngest daughter. When I advised her not to borrow much for this, she replied that she was marrying her to an elderly person and would not have to spend beyond her means."

Swami Gyanendra got up and took leave with joined hand. Before he left, Hira Singh blessed him by placing his hand on his head and warned: "Even for a swami, mendicant or recluse, it is very risky to carry so much of money and jewelry on his person. You should be careful about it. Don't visit Arnritsar again unless it is absolutely necessary." Before he left, Hira Singh patted him on his back and said that he was very happy to see him having prospered so much.

CHAPTER SIX

The coming of Lord Irwin as Viceroy, Gandhi-Irwin parleys and the visit to India of Simon Commission increased further the distance between Hindus and Muslims as communities. Gandhi's fast against reservations for depressed classes and Poona Pact further alienated the Muslims and filled them with the fear that Upper Caste Hindus were engineering a huge majority to keep Muslims permanently under heel, appropriating seats in legislatures as Hindus of those whom they have never treated and will never treat as Hindus. The communal harmony of earlier days quickly gave way to communal polarization, mistrust, hostility and perpetual tension. The exchange of views at the dwakhana gatherings had now less relation to facts. Facts and truth were .now two different, sometimes opposite concepts. Small events kept honing communal sentiments from day to day. There was imperceptible apprehension and mistrust between the communities in the city, despite some goodwill among Hindus, Muslims and Sikhs as individuals which continued to subsist as a result of their interaction in several aspects of common life. Gandhi's fast against reservation for untouchable Scheduled Castes, however, became a watershed in Hindu-Muslim relations even though it had nothing to do with Muslims as such. The entire non-Muslim General category mentioned in the Reforms Act thus got defined as Hindu identity. This contrived seventy-five per cent Hindu majority when counterpoised against twenty-five Muslim minority filled the Muslims in general with fear and suspicion. Poona Pact thus widened the gulf between the two communities so much so that it became virtually unbridgeable.

Suddenly communal tension flared up again in the town. Amrit Lal Gauba, a well known barrister, had gone to attend a family function with his wife and two daughters. The wife, though born a Muslim, had adopted Hindu religion and had a Hindu name.

She touched, for benediction, some articles meant for worship, as other women present there were doing. There was a hue and cry by the priest and many others present there. The articles touched by her were discarded and new ones used for worship. Gauba protested against this but some others were unrelenting leading to exchange of hot words. Gauba, his wife and daughters left the place in a huff. On reaching home Gauba sent for Maulana Asad Ullah and told him that they had decided to get converted to Islam. Asad Ullah felt that if this took place with enough fanfare, this would help him in his legal practice. He reminded Amrit Lal Gauba about his having told him earlier that conversion to Islam would make him one of the important Muslim barristers in the province. Gauba visited Hira Singh's dwakhana and told him of his intention to become a Muslim, describing to him all that had happened. Hira Singh advised him to think over it again and if he finally decided about it, he should do so quietly. There was already much communal tension in the town and he should do nothing to add to it.

Asad Ullah on his part planned to dramatize it as a big event not for Amritsar town but for the whole of the Punjab province. Anticipating pressure by local Hindu leaders on Mr. Gauba, he immediately converted his wife and daughters. He and some other Muslim leaders exerted pressure on the local Muslim member of the Punjab Legislative Assembly to resign so that Gauba could be elected unopposed in his place immediately after conversion. He was the first highly educated Hindu belonging to a renowned Hindu upper caste to become Muslim in a decade. The Muslims made it a celebration. His conversion ritual on Friday was attended by many Muslim divines who specially came for this from outside. After conversion he was taken out in a procession which was made out as a victory parade.

After that there were processions off and on in the town, some converting a Muslim to Hinduism and others converting a Hindu to Islam. Everyone knew that a Hindu had been given a Muslim name or a Muslim a Hindu name to create hullabaloo of conversion in this game of doing better than the other. As this was escalating communal tension in the town, Hira Singh and some other eminent citizens went to see the Deputy Commissioner and requested him to have these fake conversion processions stopped. The Deputy Commissioner said that he agreed with them but there was a snag. When Mr. Gandhi started his march to Dandi for breaking the salt law, the

Viceroy wanted him to be arrested. The Law Member of his Executive Council, however, advised against it. His contention was that under British Indian Jurisprudence, the mere intention to break law was not culpable. The law had to be broken before the person concerned became an offender and was apprehended. He said that he would contact the Governor immediately and see what could be done to save the situation.

Before the Distract Magistrate could have done anything in the matter, communal riots broke out in the city, more ferocious and more widespread than before. The saner element in the two communities striving for communal harmony had shrunk this time and the number of Hindus, Muslims and Sikhs directly or indirectly involved in the riots had become much larger. This time it was not limited to stray stabbing and killing of passersby. Pitched battles took place between the gangs of the two communities. These flared up with increasing virulence again and again, despite ban by government on gatherings of more than four persons and carrying of weapons of any type. It took ten days for the communal riots to subside completely. There was a trail of misery and desolation in many parts of the town. No one was certain how these riots broke out. The Hindus put the blame on the Muslims and Muslims its onus on the Hindus.

After peace was restored in the town the gathering in dwakhana was for sometime smaller than before. Everyone was sad and Hira Singh was the saddest of them all. His eyes quite often became wet with tears. These tears were not only for the innocent men, women and children who had died but also for the truth that was dead. Each one of the two communities held tenaciously to its own version of truth, very different from that of the other. Each regarded its truth as infallible and that of the other falsehood. What distressed him most was that these two truths were becoming more and more irreconcilable with every passing day. "Were these parallel lines so incompatible that these might not meet even at infinity?" he kept brooding with a heavy heart.

Unknowingly economic recession had hit the city as it did the country and the world at large. Hindu, Muslim and Sikh shopkeepers suddenly realized that they were having less and less customers. Workmen, artisans and craftsmen belonging to all communities found that there was less and less work available for them. More and more persons were looking for job and chances of getting one were becoming less and less. During the last decade or so factories and workshops had sprung up in various parts of the town which had grown into a city with a population nearing one hundred thousand. Railway Axle Factory had grown into a major locomotive workshop. Adjacent to that in the Putli Ghar, a spinning mill, which commencing with the manufacture of blankets, had begun to produce tweeds, serge and carpets. On the other side of the railway line up to the Lohgarh Gate of the city rampart, dozens of workshops and factories had come up manufacturing a large variety of goods which were previously imported. Nearly all these manufacturers had either closed down or reduced the staff and workforce. Hindu businessmen put the blame for this slump on the Muslims and the Muslims on the Hindus. The same was the case with workmen, artisans and craftsmen. This became another factor which made one community feel aggrieved, and quite often embittered, against the other. This created a climate wherein riots between Hindus and Muslims would break out with or without any pretext, in one part of the country or the other. This was a situation in which unhealthy elements in both the communities came to the fore and found ways to run down and hurt the other community.

Miss Mayo's account of India published in her book 'Mother India' received wide publicity through its condemnation by Hindu leaders as a gutter inspector's report. A Muslim owned paper began serializing it which helped it to greatly increase its readership. Another Muslim owned Urdu paper, in order to maintain its position, started publishing extracts from the writings of Dr. Ambedkar and others about sexual life in ancient India and about bastard ancient holy men and demi-gods. In order to retaliate, a Hindu owned paper started serializing blasphemies from history of Muslim countries and another joined the issue by publishing short stories about imaginary life in which a Hindu was always honest and courageous and Muslim invariably a wicked and cowardly person. This resulted in an unending state of tension, a situation in which the city was almost constantly at the brink of Hindu-Muslim riot. Reports of communal disturbances, often of a very serious nature, in one part of this large-country or the other, also kept the situation in the city near a flash point. Persons living in areas of mixed population began to shift to areas inhabited by their community. Entrance of more and more streets and lanes were provided with strong iron gates and where possible other fortifications. Bad characters in each area became leaders of groups of men which were arming and training as if fearing attack from the other community any time.

As elsewhere, the entrance of the lane in which Hira Singh resided was given a strong iron gate with a wicket door. The gate was mostly kept closed and only wicket door was used for entrance and exit. Money had been collected for the construction of the gate and for buying sticks, batons, spears and daggers for more than three dozen persons of the lane who had volunteered to work for self-defence. Two persons in the lane, previously regarded as good for nothing, were in the forefront of this. One was Wazir Chand, a copperware dealer. He came to know that under the British Indian Law, when a person became insolvent, the jewelry of his wife could not be touched, when his movable and immovable property was attached to redeem his liabilities. He bought a two horse carriage, brightened up his house and shop and began to live like a very rich man. He began to flourish long moustache and all the time he was sitting in the carriage he would curl and flick its ends. He had no difficulty in borrowing large amounts from professional money lenders. After two years he applied to the court for insolvency. He had disposed off most of the goods -in his shop and other movable property. The creditors could get only a small fraction of the money they had lent as he had invested the borrowed money in wife's jewelry. He had rented another house in this lane and spent most of the time at home. He was a thickset plumpish man of middle height somewhat dark in colour. He was always talking about witches and wizards. His voice was dull and shaky except when he was talking about magic cure-all and astrology. His wife was tallish, with untidy scanty hair. One of her ears was partly torn off and there was a scar on her forehead which was the result of cut when once he had thrown her out of the window. After insolvency he shaved off moustache. His wife was now finding him less overbearing. Before coming out of the house for the first time in the day he would ask his wife to check that a Brahmin was not passing by, as he regarded this as inauspicious. An old beggar woman - a Brahmin widow - came to the lane trailed by a cat. She always wore woolens and a jacket made of stuffed cotton whether it was winter or summer. She had big muddy eyes and a nose which looked as if it was of cast iron. She treaded leisurely swinging a stick made out of a branch of neem tree. She would knock at a door again and again till she was given something. Wazir Chand would hide himself when she knocked at his door and ask his wife to shoo her off. He had dislike for dogs also. A dog had been coming to the lane daily shortly after noon to pick up leavings. He would chase it with a stick and on seeing him it yelped and yelped. He was the example of a person who could live by doing nothing except eating, by thinking of nothing except ill of others and by believing in nothing except money

The second man was Rulia Ram. He was a man past his youth, of short stature, with wide unequal shoulders, a large forehead and squalid figure. He was in the habit of borrowing money. He spoke to everyone meekly, sweetly and reverentially. He would have a very indigent orphan-like look when he entreated someone for a small loan so much so it would be impossible to refuse him. He would keep borrowing from that person, small amounts, on promise of returning the full amount soon. When the amount was reasonably large, he would invite that person to his home to collect the money lent to him. He would leave him alone with his wife saying that he would go and bring some pure clarified butter sweets for him. His wife was of medium height, buxom and comely. She had big eyes with high cheek bones. A small nose made her luscious lips very prominent. When she moved to bolt the door from inside after her husband left, her large bosoms and robust buttocks swung invitingly. After it was over she would start wailing and beating her breast saying that she would go out like this. She would soon calm down and give that person a light slap and pinch his nose. She would remove his gold ring etc. and empty his purse. She· would open the door and push him out by the full force of her hands, saying: "The account is settled, do not ask for this money again." The wife of Rulia Ram was very free with her tongue and it was as sharp as a knife. None in the lane would whisper about this even though no one approved of what she did.

Rulia Ram had once come to the dwakhana with his problem. He said that he was all right with street girls and with other's wife, but never with his own wife, do whatever she may. He wanted an aphrodisiac for this. In reply to a question by Hira Singh he said that he started visiting street girls when he was fourteen and had been doing so even after marriage eight years ago. Hira Singh advised him to come for medicine four months after he had completely stopped visiting street girls.

The people in this lane, as elsewhere were in many areas, were living in fear. More they feared the other community the more hatred for it they nurtured. Love may not beget love but hatred and fear do beget hatred and fear. The fortified gate at the entrance of the lane, evening parade of the semi-armed volunteers, their watching out at night, occasional raising of slogans to buck themselves up cumulatively engendered an atmosphere of hatred and dread which Hira Singh found very suffocating. More he kept himself away from them the more he got singled out as an outsider and a dark horse. He decided to shift outside the city in the Civil Lines area as going back to the old. haveli was not possible. He had given it on lease to the municipal committee for a school on a nominal rent. He discussed this with Sardar

Gurdit Singh and Sir Aroor Singh. They said that some 'well off businessmen of the city who had built bungalows 'in' the civil lines area were shifting back to their home inside the city for security reasons and it should not be difficult to find a suitable place for him. When he mentioned this to his wife she said that all good men have only one house just as they have one wife, then why did he want two houses. His reply was that while living in the haveli he had only one house never visiting this place and now again he would have one house only. His argument that in the civil lines area, their sons, Dayal and Nirmal, would have better company and better environment, diminished her resistance to shifting.

Suddenly he was made to shift from that lane to a civil lines bungalow. A child widow of a rich Hindu grain merchant in Sialkot city was a devotee of the Sikh gurus as were many other Hindus. She had no children and had converted her palatial house into a Sikh shrine and used income from her properties for running a free kitchen and a school and that gurdwara. When she died intestate in old age, her heirs converted the gurdwara into a temple dedicated to god Shiva and took over her property. The Sikhs in the town did not touch other property of the deceased widow but took possession of the gurdwara. This created tension between Hindus and' Sikhs in the town each using its musclemen to take possession of the area. Soon there were large scale riots and pitched battles between the Hindus and Sikhs in that town. Fueled by some leaders of the two communities and their newspapers, riots between Hindus and Sikhs soon spread to some other big and small towns of central Punjab. Tension gripped Amritsar also. There was apprehension of riots between Hindus and Sikhs breaking out any time in the city. Ram Lal Gauba came to see Hira Singh one morning before he left for dwakhana. He told him that he might be quite safe in the Muslim dominated area where his dwakhana was situated but not in this lane. He was the only Sikh residing there and all the Hindus were orthodox petty traders. He said one of his three bungalows on Dhyan Singh road in the civil lines was vacant and he should shift immediately.

CHAPTER SEVEN

As the economic crisis deepened with the passing years, job opportunities and business possibilities became constricted for members of all the communities, resulting in more tension, conflict and violence. These were exacerbated by the imperatives of representative government with separate electorate for Muslims. The value of everything had crashed down in many cases to less than half. The house or shop one owned and goods stocked in it all tumbled down in value. Many people in the lane and the bazaar became bankrupt, more were on the verge of bankruptcy and reduced to poverty.

Many persons uprooted in smaller towns had also shifted to Amritsar. One such person was Suraj Bhagwan who had come with his wife Ram Ditti and two sons Har Bhagwan and Shiv Bhagwan to Amritsar from Peshawar in July 1932, not only to run away from creditors but also for the education of his sons. Har Bhagwan had an exceptionally good memory. He could hold in his memory anything just by reading it once and had stood first in the Matriculation Examination in the Frontier Province.

When Suraj Bhagwan met the Principal of Khalsa College for the admission of his elder son Har Bhagwan, they were the picture of indigence. He told the Principal that they were very poor and he would not have thought of the education of his son had he not been so brilliant with a unique memory. The Principal put his memory to test and readily agreed to admit him with fee concession and a stipend. Dayal Singh, son of Hira Singh, had also joined the first year of Khalsa College the same year.

Suraj Bhagwan was a prosperous fodder and fire wood merchant of Peshawar. He used to import wood logs from Muree near Rawalpindi and wheat straw for fodder from Montgomery. He had stocked these for winter by getting several wagon loads, when prices suddenly crashed putting him to great loss. Apart from this, he lost heavily in the value of the property he owned. When he borrowed against his property, his debt was a small fraction of its value. After the slump the debt remained the same while the value of property fell suddenly, more than elsewhere, because in Peshawar there were very few buyers. After he had sold all property he was still in debt and decided to leave for Amritsar surreptitiously. Living free in gurdwaras and other religious places and having meals from the free kitchen there, they subsisted somehow. They sold one by one whatever of value they could bring with them and tried to borrow small amounts from persons with whom they could strike acquaintance. Despite best efforts Suraj Bhagwan could not get any work. He wife would break into tears and complain that they would get shelter in a gurdwara or rent a house like saints and leave like thieves. The sons were always famished and shabbily dressed. The younger one avoided going to school but Har Bhagwan took it bravely and did not miss classes. He would frankly admit before class fellows that his father was an invalid, unable to earn anything. He would tell them that one serious disease his father was suffering from was his desire to educate him and his unusual memory had become a curse for the family.

Some class fellow would take Har Bhagwan to the hostel and make him share his food. Dayal Singh many times brought from home for him brunch and sometimes a washing soap so that he could have clean clothes. His shoes were in such a wretched condition that these could not be repaired. His class fellows collected three quarter of a rupee to buy him a pair of good sandals. Many times he would get a lift from college to his place in the city on the cycle of a class fellow and would be saved the trouble of walking home.

One day he was walking from college to his residence in the city when he was accosted from behind by a touch on his shoulder. As he turned, that man looked straight into his eyes and said with an air of superiority: "It is your good luck that you have come my way." He was past his youth and appeared to be a Muslim in the way he was wearing his lungi around his waist. He was tall, slim, with a body as thin as his own. He had big ears from one of which was hanging a brass ring. As Har Bhagwan moved to

48

take his way, he held him by the arm and asked him: "Do you pray to God"

"Why, even cats, dogs and rats pay to God." Pointing to the peepal tree nearby, he added: "Even that tree is praying. Don't you hear the leaves rustling?"

To Har Bhagwan's surprise, he started reciting some shabad from the Sikh breviary and then asked: "Do you believe in fate?"

Har Bhagwan was intrigued by the question and the bewildering way he had asked it. He put him off by the reply: "A rigid unalterable fate is for the animals only. A man's fate is in his hand." Saying this he jerked that man's hand off his shoulder and made a move. He again tried to hold his shoulder but Har Bhagwan took a step back to avert this. He had a staring gaze at him. His clothes were dirty, dirtier than his had ever been. It seemed he seldom had a bath or change of clothes. He was with bare feet and his feet and hands had fissures. His pale and apparently suffering face livened up and he muttered: "Whether you believe in fate or not, it is there. It is born with you and follows you all your life. All thorny bushes do not grow roses and those which do should thank God for this." Har Bhagwan turned to take his way but that man held him by the arm saying: "Give me a rupee, God will give you ten thousand rupees after ten years and ten million rupees in your next life." While saying this that man was looking fixedly at his new sandals.

"I do not have even a cowrie in my pocket." Har Bhagwan replied humbly.

"Where do you live" was his next question.

"We are so poor that we cannot pay any rent and keep shifting from place to place."

"Give me whatever you have" that man urged. When Har Bhagwan shook his head and said that he had absolutely nothing that man demanded: "In that case give me the horse you are riding."

Har Bhagwan could not follow this. That man pointed to his new sandals. He replied that he could not have bought these and were a sacred gift which he could not give to anyone. Saying this he ran off from there at full speed and rested only after reaching home. When he related this to his father, he said that he now knew that there were ill-fated and helpless people in the world more than they were. It was last day of February, 1933. Har Bhagwan hardly had much to eat either previous night or in the morning as breakfast. He had just drunk a few tumblers of plain water in order to feel less hungry. He had attended the first two periods of his class and the third was in a different place. He was slowly walking to it when a class fellow accosted him and thrust a cover in his pocket. Har Bhagwan held his hand and asked him whether it was an invitation to a party. When that person replied not immediately, he asked him to take him to the tea shop and get him something to eat. Only then he would have the energy to read what was inside the cover.

After he had some snacks he took the cover out of his pocket, tore of its side and pulled out the inside sheet. He began reading it: "Good Luck and Good Health. Continue this chain. Make nine copies and send to nine of your most intelligent friends whom you wish happiness. This chain was started in Flanders by a General of the American artillery and must go round the world three times. Forward it, if possible within twenty four hours of acceptance. Do not break the chain. It might bring you bad luck. During the time of nine days you have sent it a happy event is going to take place and fill you with joy. These predictions are always true. If you take this a joke and do not send out copies correctly bad luck will befall you. Mrs. Hasfess of Victoria won prize of $ 3,000,000 in nine days. Leer Dillock's house was destroyed on the sixth day due to not taking notice of this chain seriously. Mr. Dixon lost his only son after receiving the chain and not forwarding it. Mr. Mag Sohaustry won nine hundred thousand dollars and Rola Nigry owns her fortune to having carried out these instructions in the most conscientious way."

Har Bhagwan decided to send out these letters within twenty four hours so as to be sure of this bringing him good luck. He tore nine sheets out of his notebook but was wondering how to arrange covers or buy stamps for sending some of these by post. He decided to do without covers and drop the copies in letter box of bungalows on the Mall Road. While he was just working this out in his mind another class fellow pushed a cover containing the same letter in his satchel. He made eighteen copies in the night and before day break next day went to the Mall Road to drop these folded sheets in the letter box of bungalows there. He could only find seventeen letter boxes and the eighteenth copy he pushed into the pocket of his class fellow Dayal Singh when he met him in the college.

When Hira Singh noticed his son making copies of that letter, he felt amused. He had seen his son raking his brain for hours over cross word puzzles of Illustrated Weekly and other journals, which offered prizes for correct solutions. That required some mental effort. He had often solved the cross word puzzles with one error only and Hira Singh had admired his son's sharpness of mind. He felt unhappy that his son believed that one could have good luck through making copies of a letter.

"Do you think that it is possible to acquire good luck merely by copying and forwarding letters?" he asked his son.

Dayal Singh replied somewhat cheekily: "If there is the slightest hope, what can be the harm in this?"

Hira Singh asserted: "No my son it does great harm, by creating both superstition and illusion. It is just like hoping to catch the moon by grabbing its reflection in water."

Dayal Singh lowered his head and remained silent. His father asked: "Why do you need all this extra money. Cross word puzzles and now this letter chain."

He looked at his father and spoke slowly: "Papa, just as one needs air for one's life, one needs money for one's living. My class fellow who gave me this letter is extremely poor. The family is absolutely penniless. As I watch this class fellow, I realize how penury can grind a person to dust and how impossible it is to have any worthwhile life without some money. This class fellow received two letters in this chain and is making eighteen copies not because he is hopeful of good luck but to avoid bad luck. He said that Dame Luck passes by those who are utterly down and out. If I have some luck in this chain, I will help him."

Hira Singh felt a little reassured on hearing this explanation. He suggested: "If your class fellow is so needy, why do you not help him without waiting for good luck through this letter-chain. We need a tutor for your younger brother. Can he take up this work?"

He replied: "Surely he will. The son of a lecturer in Chemistry in our college has failed thrice in Matriculation examination. This class fellow Har Bhagwan has guaranteed that he will make him pass the examination if he coaches him. He wanted three rupees per month but the lecturer said that he could pay only rupees two per month because he had only recently got the job after working as an honorary lecturer in the college for two years."

Dayal Singh brought Har Bhagwan to the dwakhana the same evening. There were about a dozen visitors in the gathering there, one of them a lecturer in Government college, Lahore. He had come to the dwakhana for some consultation in the morning and had stayed on for the sundown gathering there before returning later in the evening.

Har Bhagwan's was a simple intelligent face. He appeared to be in good spirit, although his yellowish complexion was far from indicating sound health. No one moved out with a bare head during those days and wore a turban or a cap. Har Bhagwan had a kullah over his head, thick felt round cap on which men in Peshawar wrapped the turban, so that it remained set and did not need to be done again and again. It was unusual to have a kullah only, which looked queer without the turban. The gold thread on its upper tip and its velvet were worn out but it was of a very good quality. His shirt and pajamas were of cheap cloth and had many patches nicely done. This showed that his mother was an intelligent person who wanted to do the best for her children. Out of all this evidence of poverty, his face shined promising and bright. He was of the same height as Dayal Singh but thin and famished. His arms and legs did not have sinews normal for his age. Everyone there felt sad to see such a picture of poverty and undernourishment. Hira Singh noted with much satisfaction that the boy had an air of dignity and self confidence.

Hira Singh gestured him to have his seat on the front settee. He sat in a corner. The visitor from Lahore had brought as gift a small basket of andarasas, fried thin rice cakes which were the specialty of the sweetmeat sellers of Lahore. Hira Singh gave him a piece. Instead of eating it he asked for a piece of paper for wrapping it and said: "My father is very fond of these. Whenever some acquaintance went to Lahore from Peshawar, my father would ask him to bring andarasas from there."

Hira Singh took a large sheet of paper and made a packet of half the andarasas in the basket. Har Bhagwan declined to have all these and said that he would have at the most four, one for each member of the family.

Hira Singh complimented him for his sharp memory and said that he too had a good memory but he had to read a text twice or thrice in order to fix it in memory.

Some of those present there found it unbelievable. Hira Singh looked at Har Bhagwan enquiringly. He said that he had come there for a job and not for a test of his memory. He picked up a book lying on the diwan, read a paragraph aloud, closed the book and repeated it from memory.

Hira Singh told Har Bhagwan: "You will have to teach Nirmal Singh, younger brother of Dayal Singh. He has passed out of his primary school this year and joined fifth class. You will be paid rupees three per month. There will be rise of half a rupee every year till the tenth class. I want him to do really very well in the Matriculation examination, better than Dayal Singh."

Har Bhagwan lowered eyes and spoke after remaining silent for a while: "I will charge only rupees two per month. Having agreed to teach for rupees two per month a difficult student of the tenth class, it will not be proper for me to charge-rupees three for a student of the fifth class. I am also not likely to stay in Amritsar beyond my Intermediate, because B.A. Honours in English is not available in any College here.

Hira Singh spoke more politely than before: "I am against underpaying anyone. I will pay you rupees three per month. If you like you can give Nirmal more time. You can also do this tuition as long as you are in Amritsar. You can start your work from tomorrow and fix up the time convenient to you with Dayal Singh."

Har Bhagwan gave his approval with deferential silence and eyes full of thankfulness. Hira Singh asked him in a sympathetic voice: "What is the ailment your father is suffering from? What was he doing in Peshawar?"

He replied sadly: "His knees are swollen and he cannot work even as a labourer. We do not have a house and have to keep shifting, leaving behind every time some creditors. At Peshawar my father was a wholesale dealer in firewood and fodder. Scores of people owed him money and did not pay back but he redeemed his debts as much as he could by selling all he had. When he could not do it in full he left that place saying that a man without a good name was less of a man, with no face to show to people."

His eyes narrowed and darkened and his face assumed a pitiable expression as he continued: "He used to be a man of great energy and very enterprising. Now his back is almost broken and a presentiment of misfortune keeps growing within him all the time. He feels very depressed because his swollen knees do not allow him to earn even as a labourer. He says that he will keep a tray to sell something without the need of moving much. That also needs fifteen or twenty rupees and he has never been able to borrow more than a rupee or two."

Hira Singh asked him: "Bring your father to the dwakhana tomorrow in the morning for treatment of his swollen knees. If fifteen or twenty rupees are all that your father needs to start life again, you can be paid in advance tuition fee for six or seven months."

Har Bhagwan brought his father Shiv Bhagwan to the dwakhana next morning. He had skin drawn tight on his bones with innumerable fine wrinkles etched on it. Hira Singh had seldom seen a face so full of despondency, gloom and remorse. For a while it appeared to be that of a man who expected the destruction of the world not at some indefinite time but at that very moment. Then he was struck by his big brilliant eyes, which one noticed soon after one saw him. These had a touch of pride which at times melted into sweet humility. He had high cheek bones and something in his pale, thin face which fascinated. There was a muffled self-esteem in the ardent glance of his shining eyes. He seemed to be a loving and caring father as his son appeared to be less famished than he. His clothes had more patch-work than those of his son. His turban of special handloom cloth made in Afghan homes meant only to be worn on a Kula-cap had been oddly rapped around his head.

After greeting him with joined hands, Hira Singh felt that he would not feel comfortable standing on road near his dais for diagnosis. He asked Har Bhagwan to help him move up the three stairs and seat him on the bench. He moved to him, counted his pulse, felt and tapped with a knuckle his swollen knees. He had a look at the nails of his fingers and toes and examined his feet. He told him that his feet were not swollen, his nails were normal and he would get well soon.

Hira Singh told him: "A friend of mine owns a caravan sarai. Now that travelers don't move in horse carts, the rooms for stables there are vacant. If you don't mind living there till you can have better arrangement, I will request my friend to make one or two rooms available to you."

He was dumb with happiness. A flood of warm sweet tears rolled down his cheeks. Without uttering a word he raised his joined hand as a mark of thanks.

Giving him medicine for fifteen days he said: "By God's grace you will be all right within fifteen days. After I have talked the matter with my friend I will tell Har Bhagwan when you can shift to the caravan sarai."

Gurdit Singh readily agreed to make two rooms available to Shiv Bhagwan in his caravan sarai. He also engaged Har Bhagwan as a tutor for his daughter. There was a vacant plot next to the sarai. Shiv Bhagwan got logs on credit, on Hira Singh's surety and set up his fire wood business there. Till he himself could axe those logs into smaller pieces for use as firewood he hired cheap labour to do so.

Both Har Bhagwan and Dayal Singh were among the toppers in the Intermediate examination. After going through the question papers for the last few years, Har Bhagwan had prepared a list of twenty questions for each subject which he expected in that year's question papers. He made Dayal Singh also do these thoroughly and most of the questions in the examination papers were from those which Har Bhagwan had guessed.

Shiv Bhagwan continued to live frugally and in penury, though he had added selling hay to his fire wood trade. When he left for Lahore after Har Bhagwan completed his Intermediate examination, he had paid all the small amounts he had borrowed in Amritsar and had some money to start a new life in Lahore.

Har Bhagwan kept coming to Amritsar after two or three months mainly for some medicine for his father. He would come on a bicycle peddling all the thirty two miles between the two cities. It was not difficult for Hira Singh to guess that they were not doing better than their sojourn in Amritsar. Apart from medicine, he would give him used and new clothes for him, his father, mother and brother. With that bundle of clothes he would travel by late night bus returning to Lahore, which charged half of the normal fare of a quarter rupee, with nothing extra for the cycle carried on the roof.

CHAPTER EIGHT

Dayal Singh passed B.A History Honours creditably with high first division. That year one of Zeenat Begum's twin sons Mohammed Munir did M.A Mathematics standing first in the University and got a lecturer's job in the city's Islamia College. Dayal Singh went with him sometimes to the meeting of leftist intellectuals held every Friday at the residence of its Principal, Dr. A. D Taseer. This was noted by the Intelligence department. When the second son of Zeenat Begum was arrested for terrorist activities they found that Dayal Singh was known to him. After the Lahore Conspiracy case, groups suspected of taking part in revolutionary activities were being arrested in other districts of the Punjab and some of them implicated in conspiracy cases. As the police in Amritsar had not been able to work up a similar conspiracy case, it was regarded as a negative point by Mr. Plomer, new Superintendent of Police. The police inspectors and sub inspectors started looking for young men who regularly attended public meetings and other gatherings of youth wing of the Congress or Socialist Parties or who bought leftist papers from the news stands. The second twin of Zeenat Begum Mohammed Bashir had joined service in the Municipal Committee after passing B. A. examination. He often attended these meetings and also regularly bought leftist weeklies in Urdu and English. Once one Police inspector thrust a paper in his pocket and on search found that he was carrying a recipe for making bombs. He was arrested and they found out from him names of his friends, including that of Dayal Singh. The police wanted him to mention all of them as co-conspirators in the making of bombs and in terrorist activities. The police offered to make him an approver, give him a reprieve and thus absolve him of any punishment. He was also promised a reward. When he mentioned this to his mother who came to see him in jail, she firmly told him: "Do not implicate any innocent person in this manner. Let the police punish you even though you are innocent." Dayal Singh was now a leftist and a friend of a terrorist in the police records.

While studying in college, both the sons of Zeenat Begum got married. One Sayyad living in that Amir Ali Lane showed keenness to marry the twin daughters of his sister to the two sons of Zeenat Begun. He was hoping that when left alone she would agree to become his second wife. Zeenat was glad to get her sons married into a high class Muslim family. After the marriage of her sons was solemnized, she declined to marry that Sayyad. By the time the sons finished their education, both had two children each, elder Mohammed Munir a son and a daughter and the younger Mohammed Badshir two daughters The elder son shifted to a Muslim locality near Islamia College after he got appointed there as Lecturer in Mathematics. The road from the house in Amir Ali Lane to Islamia College passed through some bazaars inhabited mainly by Hindus. In view of frequent communal tension in the city, Zeenat Begun also thought it safe for her son to reside near his College.

Dayal Singh wanted to compete for the Indian Civil Service examination. He got the application form from the Federal Public Service Commission and found that it had to be submitted to the Deputy Commissioner of the district who was to forward it to the Commission. When Dayal Singh came to know that his application was not being forwarded, he went with his father to see the Deputy Commissioner.

The Deputy Commissioner Mr. Bozman told Hira Singh that he himself was surprised to see in the police report that his son was a friend of Mohammed Bashir, arrested in connection with the Amritsar Conspiracy case and that he was attending the weekly meetings held at the residence of Dr. Taseer, who according to police record was a leftist.

Hira Singh explained to Mr. Bozman, how the mother of Mohammed Bashir gave up the profession of a hustler and settled down to normal life. He made him understand how they came to know each other without Dayal Singh in any manner being close to him or associating with him in his activities. As regards attending meetings at Dr. Taseer's residence, Hira Singh asked his son to explain it.

Pointing to some copies of Times Literary Supplement lying on the rack near the Deputy Commissioner's table, Dayal Singh asked him: "Sir, have' you not been noticing that someone has gone through the copy and turned the pages before it is supplied to you by English Book Depot."

"Yes, the book seller would be doing it to prepare a list of books he would get from the British publishers. Many book sellers do it."

"No, he does not do it. He gets catalogues from publishers and makes his selection from these. Every Saturday the Book Depot receives two copies of Times Literary Supplement, one for you and the other for Dr. Taseer, Principal of Islamia College and head of the Department of English there. Every Saturday afternoon I go to that book shop and spend an hour or two on your copy. The shopkeeper does not object because my father is a regular customer of his shop. Once Mohammed Munir, a Lecturer in the Islamia College took me to the meeting at the residence of its Principal, Dr. Taseer. He has the reputation of being the most brilliant teacher of English in the Province and also a great scholar and a well read man. Nothing was discussed at that meeting. Dr. Taseer, the host spoke most of the time mainly to display his great learning and his vast reading. I was surprised to note that his knowledge of the books he mentioned was limited to long reviews in Times Literary Supplement. I attended the meetings in his house two times more in order to confirm my impression that he did not read any of the books he spoke about and merely read their reviews in the various foreign journals, which he thought none else in the city read. There was a long article reviewing several books on Greek mythology and Greek civilization. He repeated most of it in his talk. He somehow created occasion to mention Tophet, the shrine near Jerusalem where children were offered as sacrifice to god Moloch. Then he referred, also from that article, to Pygmalion, sculptor and king of Cyprus, who brought to life the ivory statue of a maiden he had sculpted and had fallen in love with"

"Don't they discuss political subjects" The Deputy Commissioner asked.

Dayal Singh replied: "Only once in the three meetings I attended. In the last meeting, there was reference to Amritsar Conspiracy Case. One Muslim whom I did not know pointed out that the Defence Committee for the accused consisted of members of all communities. He mentioned that since 1922, this was first time when all the communities had joined together for a national cause. Dr. Taseer remarked that this showed that communalism was created by the Congress Party's sectarian national movement. Though the government was happy about it, but was not entirely responsible for it. He argued that a strong socialist movement only could unite the people. During the three occasions I attended these meetings, another point not in the book reviews which came for mention was the desire for a long life. When some one recited a couplet in Persian about Khawaja Khizar, the mythical figure who lived for a very long period, Dr. Taseer drew attention to Biblical patriarch Methuselah who lived for 969 years. I mention Bernard Shaw's play on the subject which I studied in my Intermediate class. I had then penned a couplet against such a long life which I recited in that meeting:

> There was a seer who lived for a thousand years.
> First hundred years ancing and smiling, Next hundred
> years pouting and coughing, the rest, lonely, forlorn and
> in tears Umpteen generations passed by
> None recognized him even on the sly.

Dr Taseer liked it very much and when I did not go to the meeting again, he kept enquiring about me from Professor Mohammed Munir."

Mr. Bozman smiled and said: "Now I know the many uses Times Literary Supplement can be put to. Any way I am forwarding your application to the Federal Public Service Commission. You will have to work very hard. Only three posts are to be filled this year from the Indian Civil Service examination held in India. Be careful because the Central Intelligence makes independent enquiry before an appointment letter is sent to the selected candidate."

Dayal Singh worked hard to prepare for the examination. A week before he had to go to Simla to take the examination, Har Bhagwan came to help him. On the basis of question papers during the last six years, he prepared a list of sixteen likely questions for each subject and made him do these thoroughly. There was ample choice and he did well in the examination and later in the interview. He stood second in that examination, the first position was that of a Muslim candidate. Both the first and second candidates in the merit list were not considered for appointment. The Muslim was not selected because his elder brother had been arrested with a dagger while loitering outside the residence of Punjab Chief Minister four years ago. Dayal Singh was left out because, according to communal reservation rules, twelfth post was earmarked for a Sikh or a Christian and last year a Christian had been appointed.

Muslim members from the Punjab in the Central Legislative Assembly raised the matter on the floor of the House. They said that for the last four years a Muslim had not been appointed to the posts reserved for them on the plea that none got sixty per cent marks. Now that a Muslim candidate had stood first, he should not be ignored on flimsy ground. A Sikh member also demanded the appointment of the Sikh who had done so well and said that the communal quota could be adjusted later on. The Home Member did not yield, but promised that these two candidates would be considered for other class one posts.

CHAPTER NINE

Dayal Singh received an appointment letter offering him the job of Assistant Director in the Intelligence Bureau of the Department of Home, Government of India. This was because he could not be considered for appointment in I.e.S., despite high position in the Indian Civil Service Examination. It was a three page letter stipulating terms and conditions which on the face of it looked very stringent. Dayal Singh felt much upset, but was told these were of a routine nature. One was that the appointment was temporary, subject to confirmation only after probation. Dayal Singh wanted to go to England to compete for I. C.S from there but Hira Singh was disinclined because the son of his friend Gurdit Singh had gone to England for this and settled there. He only came once for marriage. Similarly the son of one of the most successful advocates of the city went to England to do Bar-at-Law. He married there and did not return to India.

Hira Singh went to see the Deputy Commissioner, Mr. Bozman to seek his guidance. He suggested that Dayal Singh should accept the job. The Starting salary and annual increment were the same as that of I. C.S., though the grade was unfavourable. He said that an advantage was that the posting was at one place and not transferable from district to district as in the case of I. C.S. He told them that Indians were now having less chance in the London Civil Service examination because there was a prejudice against them after this examination commenced in India. He informed them that he would also be in New Delhi in a few months as he was being appointed as Under Secretary in the Finance Department.

Dayal Singh joined the Intelligence Bureau of the Home Department in September 1937. The appointment letter had mentioned that on joining he would be provided accommodation in the Government hostel in Western Court and if he was in need of family quarter, he could apply for it on joining service.

Before he shifted to Delhi, he got married to Didar Kaur, the daughter of his father's friend Gurdit Singh. She had done that year her B.A. Honours from Kannaird Girls College, Lahore. She was also the most beautiful girl he had known.

Dayal Singh found the job to his liking. The work was light and did not require late sitting. There was another Assistant Director, Robert Mathews. He was a Christian from Mangalore, married to a beautiful Anglo-Indian lady. He also did not belong to the Indian Police Service and was more than fifteen years senior in age. He had come on deputation from the Bombay Presidency Police cadre, after the earlier Assistant Director, an I.P.S officer, was promoted as Deputy Director. Mr. Mathews had been there for about a year. He was tall, barrel-waisted with wide shoulders and a keen handsome face. He had thick eyebrows and grave lines between the brows which subdued the sharpness of his alert blue eyes. Grey spot on his temples made inroads into his hair, which gave him an air of maturity. He would speak in the tone of a person deciding weighty matters. He laughed at the slightest occasion and sometimes without reason. This often frightened people who did not know him.

Another post of Assistant Director had been created as part of large scale expansion of Central Intelligence set up in the Provinces. Dayal Singh had been appointed against that post and was given plans already sanctioned by the Home Member of Viceroy's Executive Council. He was required to assist the Deputy Director to implement these proposals and to arrange recruitment of the staff Federal Public Service Commission had been approached for recruitment of senior staff. Plans were being drawn for the recruitment of the rest. The Provincial Governments had already been requested to suggest names of junior level officers who could be deputed to Central Intelligence Bureau for work in those Provinces.

Dayal Singh was required to correspond with Provincial Governments on the subject and was to have their replies processed and catalogued before putting up to the Deputy Director. The two Assistant Directors were assisted by a staff of one Superintendent, four Assistants and two clerks who did the file work. The Superintendent Mr. Victor Bannerji was a

Bengali Brahmin converted to Christianity and was nearing superannuation. He had carelessly cropped grizzly hair, a face with broad forehead and puffy cheeks. He was in the habit of twirling moustache with the fingers of the left hand while doing office work with the right hand. He had five daughters all unmarried. He wanted his daughters to marry a young man who was a Bengali Brahmins converted to Christianity. As his daughters were less well up in Bengali than in Hindi, the eligible young man was required to be acquainted with Hindi also. His eldest daughter was a stenographer in the Home Department.

Dayal Singh was allotted a room in the Western Court hostel on Queensway the day he joined service and he moved there the same evening. He found that some of the residents in that hostel were couples, only they had to take their main meal either from the hostel mess or from restaurants in nearby Connaught Place. On the very first weekend, Dayal Singh went to Amritsar and brought his wife to New Delhi.

The Works and Housing Department had allotted in a separate area quarters for staff of the Intelligence Bureau. Three D Type bungalows at the end of the Irwin Road had been earmarked for the officers of the Intelligence Bureau. Type E and F quarter in the Albert and Clive Squares in the rear, were separated by an enclosure for the ministerial staff. The idea was that the staff of the Intelligence Bureau should have least possible social contact with others. Dayal Singh was allotted a bungalow on the Irwin Road next to Wellingdon Hospital adjoining that of Mr. Mathews. The rent was five percent of the monthly salary. On the advice of Mr. Mathews, he had applied for a furnished quarter and one per cent extra was to be deducted from his salary for this. Mr. Mathews had arranged that he was given new furniture. Their wives also had become good friends. Didar Kaur took the willing help of Mrs. Helen Mathews in shopping for setting up a house as she was new to the place. Mrs. Mathews, though over forty, dressed and behaved like a woman in her twenties. She was of medium height with heavy breasts, rotund buttocks and shapely waist. Her golden eyebrows lent much charm to her big bright eyes. She looked more like a beautiful English woman than an Anglo-Indian. Didar Kaur was happy to know that she was a good natured person, with a face that did not miss an opportunity to be lit with a smile.

Life in Western Court was enjoyable and western style food in the mess was excellent-and inexpensive. Mr. and Mrs. Mathews and their two daughters loved to be invited to the Western Court and Didar Kaur and Dayal Singh also dined with them many times. After they became neighbours, Didar Kaur and Helen became bosom friends. Quite often the two families had dinner together in one house or the other. Their two daughters Lola sixteen and Zola thirteen began to spend most of the time after school with Didar Kaur, getting help from her in their school work.

The guard outside the bungalow was provided by the Intelligence Bureau and gardener and sweeper by the Public Works Department. They lived in the servant quarters at the back of the bungalow and their wives did household chores in lieu of that free accommodation. Life for Didar Kaur was happy, easy and comfortable. When she wrote about this to her father and father-in-law, they were all very glad about it.

In the office Mr. Mathews and Dayal Singh made a good team and at home Helen and Didar Kaur had become so close as if they were sisters. On Sundays Mathews went to the nearby Church and Dayal Singh and Didar Kaur to Bangla Sahib Gurdwara not far away.

Didar Kaur was a deeply religious person and the nearness of this historic Sikh shrine made her quite homely in New Delhi. In the second month in Delhi she was in a family way. In her seventh month she went to Amritsar with Nirmal Singh who had come to spend a weekend with them. Helen had said that maternity arrangements in Delhi were quite good and she was there to assist and to look after her. The mother of Didar Kaur was insisting that she came to Amritsar, as the tradition required that first delivery should be in parental home.

Dayal Singh went to Amritsar shortly before his wife was due to deliver.
He stayed there for two day only and returned to Delhi immediately after she delivered a son. After that he neither paid a visit to her nor replied to her letters. When for almost two months, she did not hear from him, she wrote to Helen. She replied that she should come to Delhi as soon as she was fit enough to travel alone and that she should not bring the baby.

CHAPTER TEN

Didar Kaur had written to Dayal Singh about the date and time of her arrival in Delhi by Frontier Mail. He was not there at the railway station. Taxis were not common in Delhi those days and she could get one with difficulty. She did not want to take a horse carriage, the common mode then, because she wanted to reach home before Dayal Singh left for office at nine thirty or little later. She reached home shortly after nine. She noted that there was a new nameplate outside the bungalow, S. Dayal in place of Dayal Singh. There was a new guard outside the gate who informed her that sahib had gone to office. He was disinclined to open the gate but she pushed herself in.

The way Lola came out and stood in the veranda, left Didar Kaur in no doubt that she was living there. She was dumbfounded to comprehend what had happened in her absence. Lola stood there with legs apart with self-important look, having the tranquility of a domestic animal. When her mouth half opened it was not a conventional smile but a special smile of triumph. She had all the charms of her mother heightened by her teen age. She had the airs of a proud woman, and was no more an innocent girl as before. A teenager's face and girlish shapeliness of waist made her breasts and buttocks more prominent. A time comes in the life of every young woman when she feels like being the most beautiful woman in the world. The way she stood there with mouth agape and slightly hanging lips, she seemed to be having that feeling. Her hair drawn over ears made her teenager face look more sharp and sensual. She did not utter a word and looked as if she did not want to welcome her. She pushed back a strand of hair which had fallen on her cheek and went inside the bungalow. Didar

Kaur felt a stunning blow, shook her head, heaved a long sigh and staggered out of the bungalow. She limped to the adjacent house. Helen embraced her and wept bitterly. After she had calmed down, they sat on the sofa with Helen holding her hand. She was very apologetic and left her in no doubt that she greatly sympathized with her and totally disapproved of what had happened.

The maid brought tea. Helen started explaining: "After you left, Dayal spent most of the evenings in our house, quite often having dinner with us and helping Lola with her studies as you used to do. He did tutoring before dinner and generally left immediately or shortly after dinner. Lola who never went to the kitchen, now started making special dishes for him and taking more interest in her make up, but we did not attach much importance to it. After a month and half she started taking his help in studies after dinner also. Her examinations were drawing near. We did not take it amiss. Shortly before he left for Amritsar, he took her out in the evening and then to his residence. She returned home quite late that evening. He came back from Amritsar and gave us the good news without any eagerness. By then their behaviour towards each other had changed so much that we could notice it. We discussed this, all the time I was more concerned about you. We started going out in the evenings in order to avoid his dining with us, but Lola would not accompany us. After much thought we decided to take her to our native place and leave her there for some time. Robert applied for leave for a fortnight giving mother's illness as reason lest Dayal guessed anything. We postponed packing her books and other things to the last few hours so that she did not have a hunch. The evening before we were to leave, when we began packing her books and other things she became peevish. When we were getting ready to move out, she quietly slipped out with some of her clothing and went to Dayal in the adjacent house. We did our best to bring her back but she refused. She refused to leave that house even for going to school. On the third day Dayal removed his turban, got his hair trimmed short and shaved. The name plate outside the bungalow changed from Dayal Singh to S. Dayal, so did his name in office"

She was again brimming with tears and sobbing. When she could calm herself, she continued: "We were in fix what to do, all the time I felt concerned about you. In the manner she had solidly installed herself in your house your coming would not have helped even if you were able to travel. We continued to persist in our efforts to bring her back. She was adamant and Dayal was uncommunicative. After sometime, I asked her about her periods. She said that she had missed the periods. I think they became intimate before he left for Amritsar. I have been thinking how I can help you to rebuild your home and to take her out from there. Let us hope we are able to see some light out of this darkness."

Both kept sitting motionless for sometime. While Didar Kaur was sipping tea and thinking over, Helen did not touch her cup, she was so full of remorse. Didar Kaur requested Helen to agree to her staying with them for a day or two till she was able to plan her way out of this mess. Helen agreed saying that she was most welcome to stay as long as she wanted. Instead of making her stay in Lola's room, Zola was shifted there and her room made available to Didar Kaur.

Didar Kaur shifted to the room and began to give serious thought to the various alternatives before her. After much thought she decided that leaving the country and going to her brother in England for further studies was the most respectable course for her. This was how she had planned before marriage. She went to Connaught Place and booked passage with Cox & King by the ship leaving Bombay on the fifteenth of next month. On return she wrote two letters. One to her brother explaining to him why she had decided to come to England and informing him that she had booked her passage by S. S. Devonshire leaving Bombay on fifteen of next month. The second letter was to her father telling him all that had happened here in her absence and about Dayal Singh's apostasy. She knew that her father was an atheist but he was also aware that his daughter was of deeply religious nature and Dayal's apostasy would be an important point for her to take a decision. She wanted to reach Amritsar after her father had received the letter and therefore booked her seat for Amritsar after three days.

She sent a note to Dayal in the evening requesting him to see her at Mathew's house where she was staying for two days or meet her outside if he preferred that. Dayal did not reply. He sent her clothing and other belongings to that house but did not come to see her. The evening when she was to depart for Amritsar, she went to see him in office at about five p.m., shortly before he was due to leave that place. He did not enquire about his son, his parents or any relative in Amritsar. He kept sitting dumb for some time and then whispered: "I have been under a spell and under an irresistible compulsion to do what I have done. I cannot undo it." He was in tears and for a few minutes, she waited for him to say something. He suddenly muttered: "After you left I started helping Lola with home work. In my bed at home I started thinking about her, her face, the expression of her mouth and eyes, the lines of her figure without dress, the motion of her body in walking and dancing. She would flicker before me and hover around me. In my dreams I found her deliciously near me, pressing against me, her delightful body all mine. Then in the moment when she was about to yield herself to me completely, I would awake to find her vanish. That made me a marionette of my emotions." Without turban and beard his face looked smaller. He had back swept his hair and there was a light brown patch in the upper part of his forehead previously covered by turban. He did not have moustaches with tips like a police officer but well trimmed bristles covering most but not all his lip. He muttered something again but she could only catch the word 'God'. She waited for a minute in vain for him to make himself clear and remarked with emphasis: "God will never rob a man of dignity, he does it himself."

The way he was feeling sunk, made a lump rise in her throat. She felt a great pity for him. She smiled at him in order to make him feel better. He smiled back in a lifeless smirk. "Have some water" she suggested. He picked up the tumbler on the table and had a few sips. He straightened himself on his chair. Its high back made him look a pigmy. A smile flashed on his face and disappeared. He gazed ceiling wards and then stared at her blandly. She asked him politely without any regret or bitterness: "Do you want us to separate? Do you want a divorce?"

"Yes", he muttered.

She explained: "Sikh marriages are not registered anywhere though these are as solemn as any other. Would you like to claim that you are unmarried?"

He replied dejectedly: "I cannot do it. On joining service, I put it on record that you are my wife and my nominee and that is recorded in the life insurance policy also." He wished to smile, but do what he would his countenance retained his half dazed look.

Didar Kaur thought for a while as if trying to remember something. She stood up and said in a voice in which compassion, exasperation and incredulity were mixed:

"You can initiate divorce proceedings. I will not contest it. If any statement by me is necessary, send me a copy, I will sign it." She felt blood beating in her ear drums and a great pressure at the back of her head. She kept standing there in silence for some time, trying to control herself. She looked straight at Dayal and in a tone full of grace she explained: "Our two families have been very close to each other and we two have known each other since our childhood. You know that I never thought of marriage and had plans to join my elder brother in England for higher studies. I was a topper in all my classes and further studies, a good career and not marriage was my priority. But your father came to our house and placing his right hand on my head begged me to be his daughter in-law. I became dumb when I saw the glow of happiness on my mother's face, the like of which I had never seen before. You know my father is an atheist. Your father is a deeply religious man and has all the qualities of a saintly person. For my mother, for me and everyone in our family he has been guiding light and a father figure." She stood there for sometime absolutely motionless staring at him with as much love as pity. She raised her joined hands to bid him farewell. While turning to go out of the room she said with a lot of good will: "Good bye, may God bless with good luck and give you strength to do the right thing."

Helen went to the railway station to see her off. On the way she told her that she and her husband have been thinking of various plans to make Lola leave Dayal. She requested her to break the journey in Delhi and stay with her for a day or so to know what they would be doing about it. She said that they were keen that she came back and her life was not upset. Didar Kaur replied that she would not be able to break the journey but would write to her when she would be crossing the Delhi railway station. She would really like to meet her. She advised Helen to keep Lola's future in mind, do what was best for her .and should not allow him to wreck her life also."

As the train steamed out of the Delhi railway station, her eyes brimmed with tears and she felt as sorry for Dayal as for herself. Then she smiled and thought that one should be careful about reading books on happy married life, as these were full of misprints". As she looked back she began to feel that it was all for her good. If a few months service in the Intelligence Department could wipe out in him all the values imbibed in twenty two years, she wondered how he would shape himself after some years in this service. She consoled herself with the thought that the grand son of a noble person would not now grow up in this atmosphere. She did not take the plea that Lola was very beautiful and a teenager. In the bazaars where her father-in-law had his dwakhana, there were always many nymphets and young beauties, but he lived with a dignity which was an example for others. She began to recite from memory Rehras, the evening-time Sikh prayer and steeled in her the resolution that the change will be for the better and to the good of her son.

When the Frontier Mail steamed in the Amritsar railway station next morning, her father was there to receive her. He said that she did not write the day of her arrival and he had come yesterday also. He was in tears when he put right arm around his daughter. A lump rose in her throat but she mustered courage. As they walked out of the railway station, she fell back. On reaching the horse carriage, she told her father that she would prefer to go to her in-laws first. She instructed the coachman to take her to Dhyan Singh Road and after leaving her father at his house he should come back there. She said that she would like to be with her son as early as possible.

Hira Singh received her with great composure and deep sympathy. He said affably: "My dear daughter, it is only in misfortune that a person's inner strength and faith in God is put to test. When your father came with your letter and showed it to me, I was for a moment thunder struck. It appeared incredible to me. I and your father kept sitting side by side. Your father's eyes were lowered and mine eyes and hands raised up wards as if I was asking God what was His purpose in doing this. Then I stood up and with joined hands prayed that God should give you strength and the girl who had chosen to make this home her own should always have good luck." She burst into tears and fell on his feet. When he raised her and made her get back on her feet, he added: "Your mother-in-law has a weak heart and we did not tell her anything but she could guess that something was amiss. She sent for the coachman and went to see your mother. When she came to know the position she fainted. She opened her eyes after two days and only then I could bring her here. She is still in bed, though no more delirious. You should be a picture of fortitude when you go to see her otherwise she might have a relapse. Dry up your tears, look normal and help your mother in law to feel strong."

Hira Singh added: "If you have chosen to go to England, it is all right but you should have waited till the baby was six months old."

Didar Kaur replied: "Before I booked my passage I mentioned this to the travel agents. They told me that they could make suitable arrangement for a three month old baby and I have made extra payment for this while booking the passage. If I delayed going by three months I would miss a year at the university."

Her father felt strongly that she should not leave the country in a huff and should wait and see how Dayal Singh conducted himself. She related to him what Mrs. Helen Mathews, the mother of the girl, had told her. She assured her father that her absence from India would not make any difference. She would remain in touch with Mrs. Mathews and could return if that helped matters. In the meanwhile she would not be wasting time.

CHAPTER ELEVEN

Didar Kaur had to go to her College in Lahore to collect her degrees, certificates and '- testimonials. She got from her father-in-law the address of Har Bhagwan her tutor and a friend and class-fellow of Dayal Singh. She wanted to have his advice about the course of study she should pursue in England. He was always full of ideas, like a bell that rang whenever you shook it. His address was 'Neem Tree Bungalow, near Municipal Toll Tax post, Grand Trunk Road, Lahore'. This was very far from her College or the residence of the friend with whom she was staying. She agreed to accompany her to that place. As an old resident of Lahore, she knew where the Municipal Toll Tax office could be.

When Didar Kaur and her friend reached the Municipal Toll Tax post, persons on duty there pointed to a neem tree about twenty yards down the road from there. It was a massive tree but many of its branches had been ruthlessly removed to obtain twigs for cleaning teeth. Har Bhagwan's father was sitting outside a fire wood stall. Not even a proper hut was there. A mere thatch, one side of which was tied to a branch of the neem tree and the other supported by two bamboos, was all that was there for a bungalow. He appeared to be awfully sick and was all alone. There was a dog lying nearby, in a narrow strip of shade. It was trying to wriggle its body out of the sun but either his head or his hind would remain exposed. In doing so it would be striking its paws at the shadows of flies.

She felt his wrist. He was running temperature. His feet and knees were swollen and his greasy eyes were crisscrossed with red veins. He was shrunk and bony. His dry unkempt hair, were peeping out of his loosely wrapped dirty rag of a turban. His face was thin and brittle as if the skin was dried up

71

and was on the point of cracking. He was not wearing pajamas but only a kachh, loose underwear touching the knees. His muslin shirt was also too big for him and was hanging on his emaciated body. He seemed a mere shadow of his former self. Even his teeth were gone and his gums were black. Excepting his eyes which retained its former sparkle, he seemed drained of vitality and self confidence. He knitted his brows to look at them. He took a minute to recognize that one of them was daughter of Sardar Gurdit Singh. A smile lit his face and he helplessly raised his joined hands to greet and to welcome her. He looked more miserable and was close to tears in a state of abject helplessness. She came to know from him that Har Bhagwan had cooked food for him before he left for work and during the day the municipal employees at the Toll Tax post kept an eye on him. He said that Har Bhagwan was away from morning till late in the evening. First he goes to College and then was busy with tuition work excepting for two hours between one and three in the afternoon. She came to know that he was in Dayal Singh Public Library during those two hours and decided to see him there.

As they were about to leave that place, the father of Har Bhagwan was in tears. His face which appeared to have been carved out of wood suddenly became human as he wrinkled his forehead and wiped his tears with the loose end of his turban. He sighed and begged her to give his greetings and good wishes to her father. She thought Milton, Dante and many others had written in minutest detail about hell in life after death. She wished someone had written about hell in this life itself to which many people were condemned.

Didar Kaur met Har Bhagwan in the Dayal Singh library. He was thinner than before and there was evidence of extreme poverty. His clothes though cheap and clean were not ironed and the cobbler seemed to have used much ingenuity to make his shoes serviceable. Har Bhagwan told her: "When we came to Lahore we could not find any place to live and for our father to do his business. We had perforce to choose this neem tree for our residence and for father's small trade. But it turned out that this place had some disadvantages which we could not foresee at that time. The people living in that suburban area are mostly poor, petty traders, casual labourers and lumpen elements. Business there has largely to be on credit which is seldom fully redeemed at the beginning of next month. If he does not sell on credit there is not much business and if he does so there is much loss. In a way it is Peshawar being repeated. Those who owe him money do not pay in full or on time and those to whom he owes money for the wood purchases have to be paid on demand. This has made me work harder for father has to be kept busy if he is to be kept alive."

She told Har Bhagwan how and why she had to say good bye to Dayal Singh and about her decision to go to England for studies and for a career. He was as deeply shocked as was her father. He said that he was not quite happy about his joining the Intelligence department but could not imagine that he would get derailed in such a short time. Patting her on the back he consoled her: "You are a woman with great courage. I am sure there will soon be a time when Dayal will regret what he has done. Your brother in England is the best person to advise you about the course of study you should choose. History is your pet subject but I would suggest sociology because it is a new discipline."

She asked him: "How is your M.A English .class?"

He replied: "There are thirty two students taking M.A. English examination in the Punjab University this year, only two of them can compete with me for the top position. I can beat them easily provided I can have some time to do my studies. It is not merely time and drudgery which tuition work involves. Walking more than twelve miles every day from home to College and from one tuition work to the other makes me half dead by evening. After reaching home quite late, I have to cook for my father and myself'.

They remained silent for sometime. Didar Kaur was thinking of some words of sympathy and friendship which would give him solace and strength.

Har Bhagwan took a deep sigh and continued: "We have been poorly off always, at Lahore more poorly off than at Amritsar. That is something we have lived with and can live with. Our calamity started six months ago. Our mother's paralytic elder brother was suddenly brought to Lahore by one of her sons and dumped at our home. None of his five sons and six daughters was willing to look after him and he was all of a sudden left in our house. Before we could have a word with his son, he disappeared. He could not do anything himself, not even drink water and for four months one had to attend on him for everything. There were two alternatives, either to dump him back at Peshawar or take him to Hardwar, which sacred city has some charitable homes for such persons. While for us taking him to Peshawar would be a big financial hardship, for his sons to dump him back on us would hardly be any problem. So father persuaded my mother to take him to Hardwar and I found out the address where he could be admitted. I entrained both of them in the Hardwar Passenger train which is cheaper than the Mail train. She was to return after a week, but did not. After five weeks I went to Hardwar to find out what had happened to her."

His eyes brimmed with tears and he remained silent for a minute or so. In a voice soaked in grief, he continued: "At the charitable home where my maternal uncle had been admitted I was informed that on the second day my mother went to the Ganges for her morning bath but did not return. Some other inmates said that they went there with my invalid uncle but there was no trace of her. None of the morning-time bathers were there from whom they could enquire. When I went to the ghat, as the terraced bank of the river Ganges is called, I found that the current of river-flow at that particular point was very strong but for the safety of bathers, ropes and iron chains had been fastened to the bank. The bather held one of these while dipping into the waist deep water near the bank. It might be she did not take this precaution while getting into the river. It could be, she wanted to save herself from the shame of not being able to support her brother through this martyrdom. She could also be seeking salvation, a happier life in her next birth by consigning herself to the holiness of river Ganges, for which she was unlikely to have another opportunity."

They were standing near the porch of the library hall. They walked to the corner of a small patch of green outside the building and sat on a bench. He continued:

"On my return to Lahore I was not inclined to tell my father that my mother was no more. Telling him that she was alive and not coming would only complicate matters as he was sure to insist on being taken there. I had returned without her. That itself told him everything but he showered on me questions day after day to find out what had happened to her. I told him what I had learnt there. The shock of her death became a terrible blow as he felt guilty about it. This aggravated his ill health. There was another shock for him and a misfortune for me. There was a Muslim workman from Kashmir who helped my father to axe logs into small pieces for fire wood. After my mother left us, he began to live with us and did cooking for himself and all of us. In the last communal riots in Lahore a gang of Hindus and Sikhs, looking for Muslims to kill, came to our shed near the neem tree. My father embraced that Muslim workman to prevent them from killing him. His left arm was outside the embrace. One in the gang held it and turned and twisted it on and on till it cracked and went out of socket. My father wept for weeks, not because it had made me cook for him morning and evening but because that workman was an exceedingly honest person and had been living with him like a son. That Kashmiri workman did not

74

want to return in that state to his village near Gandharbal in the Kashmir valley. My father gave him a letter for a Muslim friend in Peshawar and sent him there with most of my monthly earnings". After a deep sigh, Har Bhagwan added: "Since then my father's health has been deteriorating. The father of a Muslim class fellow of mine is Professor of Medicine in the Medical College. He came in his car and took my father to the College hospital. All the tests were done free and he gave medicines from the samples he had. There is only very slight improvement."

Har Bhagwan said that he would come to Amritsar to bless her son and to see her before she left for England. He offered to go and see Dayal but Didar Kaur advised against it. She wished him to see him after six months or more, as doing so at that stage could be counter-productive.

Har Bhagwan said gravely: "The brook of my life is overgrown with thorny weeds more than ever before. Every time I try to cross to the other shore the weeds catch me and hold me back. Even if father's stall is to be closed I will have to continue living there because I cannot afford to pay any rent. Many on the staff of the Municipal Toll office, though low paid, are very humane and take care of our hut and my father during the day. One of the peons there has agreed to do the cooking for us. You can write to me at this address and if there is any change I will let you know. I have your brother's address in Edinburgh." He suddenly had a hearty laugh and remarked: "I live in a bungalow on the bank of depression. It has a garden of poison flowers which dodge anything lucky trying to intrude."

Didar Kaur decided to return to Amritsar by ordinary bus spending quarter rupee on it instead of by first class in Frontier Mail. She kept a rupee for herself for the journey and gave all the money she had to Har Bhagwan. She said that her father would send him money by postal money order at his college address for the treatment of his father. The bus stand was on the Railway Road about two furlongs from there. Har Bhagwan accompanied her to the bus stand and saw her off, wishing her the best of luck.

Before she was to leave for Bombay, Hira Singh took Didar Kaur and the child to the Golden Temple to give the boy a name. When the sacred book Holy Granth was opened at random the first letter on the left page was Panjabi equivalent of A. They decided to name the child Amrit Singh.

Har Bhagwan came to see her a few days before she was to leave for Bombay. He told her that his father passed away two week after she left Lahore. With tears streaming down his face, he bemoaned: "One evening when I returned home it was already quite late. It was a dark night. The sky was full of stars which were shining brighter than ever. My father was reciting prayers. Seeing me he raised hand to beckon me to his side. As I sat next to him he said that he was going to die after two days. It was the day when the anniversary of the martyrdom of Guru Arjun Dev was to be observed by his followers. During the reign of Mughals, the Governor of Lahore had made the fifth Sikh guru sit in a cauldron containing mustard oil and fire was lit under it. He was roasted alive, because he had become a rallying point of opposition to his oppressive rule. It seemed my father willfully chose that historic day to die. All the night my father kept sitting, reciting prayers. Next morning he sought help to climb up a heap of fire wood and sat on it. He could not sit cross legged because of swollen knees but he sat with raised head and straight back occasionally taking water only. All the time he was reciting prayers with closed eyes. Next day he wanted to be bathed with a splash of water while sitting there. Soon after that he breathed his last." Har Bhagwan began weeping bitterly like a child. Didar Kaur holding back tears, tried to console him.

Suddenly Har Bhagwan stopped weeping and said with a deep sigh: "There cannot be an oppressive system worst than the one which chains you to poverty so strongly that you cannot break out of it. I too want to fight against this oppression and am prepared to make, greater sacrifice, but do not know how to do it." His dejected face which depicted wretchedness more than words could utter, again became sober and graceful. He promised to come to see her father and father-in-law whenever he could find time. He took a photograph of the child with his name on the back and said that he would show it to Dayal Singh when he went to see him after a few months.

Helen had come to the Delhi railway station when Didar Kaur traveled to Bombay. The train had an hour long halt there. She told her: "We have decided to somehow separate them but not let Dayal guess it in any manner. We will rather give him the impression of our acceptance of their relationship. After her seventh month, I propose to take her to Bombay for delivery. We will hand over the new born child to a convent and marry Lola to a distant relation of mine who has been in love with her and with whom she also has been very friendly. It will be a Catholic marriage and even if Dayal wants she will not be able to break out of it."

Didar Kaur said in a cordial tone that they should do what was in Lola's best interests. So far as she was concerned she had no plans to return to India without completing her education. "Let Dayal experience all the delectation of a free life", she said sadly.

Helen concurred: "That is how we too have been looking at it. If he can leave a beautiful and highly talented woman like you for a semi educated youngster, he can do that again. After all, Lola has to grow up and there will always be a younger woman available if one is fascinated by teenage only. In the mental state Dayal seems to have placed himself, one is soon exasperated by the ugliness of familiar beauty. We do not want to wait till that happens." There was silence for sometime. Helen added: "We feel that when you saw Lola in the verandah on return to Delhi, you should have gone in and thrown her out instead of quietly leaving that place to her."

Didar Kaur replied: "My mother also thought like this. I told her that for this she should have brought me up differently. I had grown up in a home in which none spoke at the top of his or her voice or shouted."

Helen had brought some nice frocks for the child and had made a small nice cap of velvet with gold thread-work on it. She also presented Didar Kaur with a South Indian silk sari. She said that she seldom puts on a sari. Many had been gifted to her and this was the best among them.

Didar Kaur noticed that Helen was not the same person she had known as a neighbour. She was no more trying to look a woman in twenties and was having maturity and sobriety of her real age, a woman nearing forty. She had not done her usual make up and was less gaudily dressed. She went out of the compartment and stood on the platform near the window. Mr. Mathews also came there and wished her the best of luck. As the train whistled, she shook hands with both of them. She thanks them for the deep sympathy they had shown in this hour of crisis in her life. She gave Helen her brother's address in Edinburgh and promised to write to her on reaching England.

She looked out of the window waving hand at them. Her mouth opened in a smile. She thought of the happy eight months she had lived in their neighbourhood. She was sure that Dayal was equally, if not more, happy during this period, giving the impression that he was living on the bank of a river of honey. Then she suddenly became sad as she thought about it and reflected on the tragedy which had struck her unawares. She was more inclined to blame Dayal than Lola. If one read advertisements and thought of buying and buying things; it was not the fault of advertisements. No woman could bewitch a man unless he himself wanted to be bewitched. As she brooded over this, her heart became heavy and she wondered whether she will ever again have the same happiness. She picked up the child in her arms and kissed him. This made him feel strong and she resolved that she would help the child to grow up into a person of moral strength, a good doctor who would carryon the tradition of his grand father in a worthy manner.

As the train gathered speed and the serpentine lines of men on the railway platform disappeared, she unwound the tightly rolled skein of memory. She gazed helplessly upon what she had gone through. More the running away of light points in the railway yard gathered speed, faster moved the pictures of her past before her. She held her breath as it neared its tragic climax. She resolved that she would make her and her son's life happy not through what is conventionally termed as 'happiness' but by having a better quality of life, and by contributing her bit to make life around better through the honest performance of her duties as a mother and as a human being.

CHAPTER TWELVE

After the departure of Didar Kaur there were changes in the life of Hira Singh. When his wife Kushwant Kaur came to know about Didar Kaur leaving for England with the child, her condition worsened and she passed away within a month. His second son Nirmal Singh was selected as a cadet for training at the Indian Military Academy in Dehradun and he also left this place. A letter from Didar Kaur in the beginning of every month was a great consolation for him.

Five young men had been arrested in connection with the Amritsar Conspiracy case, four Hindus and one Muslim, Mohammed Bashir, second son of Zeenat Begum. One of them had become an approver. The charge was that they were planning to kill the Deputy Commissioner and Superintendent of Police, both Englishmen. A committee of prominent citizens of Amritsar was constituted to defend the accused. Mr. A. L. Gauba had agreed to become Chairman of this Defence Committee and to fight as a Defence Counsel without charging anything. The case was mainly built on the slip of paper found on the person of Mohammed Bashir when he was searched, which contained a formula for making a bomb. It occurred to Mr. Gauba that the formula could possibly be in the handwriting of one of the police personnel and if this could be proved, the case would be without any substantial evidence. He got it checked with the registers and receipt-slips maintained at the police stations. Mr. Gauba found that the slip containing formula for bomb making was in the handwriting of the Head Clerk at the Kotwali police station, where the Assistant Sub-Inspector who arrested Mohammed Bashir was posted. In the course of trial, as soon as this came to the notice of Sub-Judge trying the case, it was dismissed. After acquittal Mohammed Bashir was able to rejoin his job in the Municipal Committee.

During the period Mohammed Bashir was in jail, he came in contact with Workers and Peasants Party revolutionaries imprisoned there. Every evening they would meet and there would be a discussion and education session. He made up his mind to join them and help them when he was released. When his release became known, he agreed to set up a cyclostyling machine to publish bulletins and other literature to propagate their point of view. The problem was to arrange for a cyclostyling machine, the previous one had been confiscating when the last group publishing the bulletin got traced and arrested. The only business house selling it in the Punjab was Gestetner Company which were required to keep a record of all their sales. This was occasionally checked by the Intelligence Department of the Punjab police. It was because of that the last cyclostyling machine got traced, though it was frequently shifted from one town or village to the other. It was decided that one of their fellow prisoners, who was serving a sentence for many cases of theft and larceny, should apply for parole on some pretext, steal a cyclostyling machine from the office of the distributors, hand it over to Mohammed Bashir and return to jail.

Mohammed Bashir shifted from Amair Ali Lane to a nearby lane and explained to his mother why he was doing so. He did not want his wife to know about the cyclostyling work as she might not be able to keep the secret. He also did not want his wife and children to be in a difficult situation in case the cyclostyling machine was found out. Left alone, ground floor was enough for Zeenat Begum for her residence. Mohammed Bashir placed the cyclostyling machine on the first floor. After discussion with the groups in Amritsar and Lahore it was decided not to distribute the cyclostyled literature in Amritsar so that there was less suspicion of its being produced here. For more than four months this arrangement worked satisfactorily. Unknown men and women, to be recognized by a pass word, came to deliver material to be cyclostyled, to supply blank paper and ink tubes and take away the printed copies. The police was unable to trace the source. It was distributed in most of the towns and large villages in the Punjab except in Amritsar city. This made the Intelligence men consider the possibility of the bulletin being produced in Amritsar. The police knew that those who associated themselves with such work had instructions to keep away from leftist meetings and book shops.

On the basis of past history of some of the persons in the police record, a list of a dozen suspects was drawn up and their movements and contacts began to be watched. The name of Mohammed Bashir was among them. Bashir and some others noticed that they were being followed and watched. The group decided to be very careful and shake off the Intelligence man before anyone of them entered Amir Ali Lane.

The Intelligence men zeroed on three persons and by shadowing them most of the time, Mohammed Bashir became the main suspect. They found out that once a fortnight he went to the house of his mother late in the night and stayed there for twenty-four hours and left that place late next night. In between sometimes very late in the evening, he and sometimes others came there to bring bundles or to take away the bulletin 'Lal Dhandora'- 'Red Trumpet'. This was being produced in Urdu and Punjabi languages. Zeenat Begum had been reading the Urdu bulletin avidly and had become sympathetic to the movement. She was watchful and noticed that a stranger, looking like a policeman in mufti, was spending much time in the adjacent mosque.

The group decided to shift the cyclostyling machine from there and also where to hide it next. It was decided to do so immediately after the next bulletin, the printing of which was in progress. The Intelligence men too noticed that Mohammed Bashir and his companions had become aware that the police had discovered their hideout and might do something to save the situation. A majority of the police staff in the Punjab consisted of Muslims. Sikhs were there more than their share in the population but the Hindus were under represented. A Hindu Inspector of Police, one Mr. Hari Ram Goswami had been posted in the City Police Lines. This was after a long time and the Hindus in the city were happy about it.

Mr. Goswami was in charge of the party of half a dozen policemen who carried out a raid on Zeenat Begum's house in Amir Ali Lane. Warning his son and his friend to climb to the roof and jump over the backside house which opened in another lane, Zeenat came and stood behind the entrance door bolted from inside, refusing to open it. .she entreated that they should come in the morning as she was alone in the house. The policemen pounded the door and shouted at the top of their voice asking the inmate to open the door and do it immediately. Dozens of neighbours came there and began to confirm that Zeenat Begum lived in that house alone and her sons lived elsewhere

It took much time for the policemen to break open the door which had been fastened by a horizontal iron bar from one end of the jamb to the other. There was scuffle as Zeenat prevented their entry into the house to give his son and his friend time to disappear with the cyclostyling machine. In the hand to hand skirmish which followed, the black burqa, head to heel veil, she was wearing got torn. In her bed time underwear she stood there dressed in less than what was proper to the horror of policemen and her neighbours. She started weeping and whooping as she stood on the platform outside the door beating her breasts. Those were the days when police officers did not carry revolvers on their person. Dozens of Muslims gathered there pounced on the police Inspector. Before the few policemen with him could come to his rescue, he had fallen on the ground semi-conscious, bleeding from the nose. Four policemen surrounded him to save him from further attacks and two rushed to the police station to bring reinforcements and a stretcher to carry Mr. Goswami to the hospital. The crowd of neighbours gathered there soon disappeared. Zeenat Begum was left alone stunned and dazed. She went in and dressed herself properly before wearing the torn burqa. Its cap was in tact and it hung on her body despite the tom part. Mohammed Bashir and his friend were able to rescue the cyclostyling machine. They threw some waste material in the drain outside the adjacent lane into which they had descended after climbing to the backside house. His friend took away the cyclostyling machine and he returned to his house. Many had seen him coming home in the evening but none had notice his moving out later in the dark.

After the injured Police Inspector was put on the stretcher and removed to the Hospital, the other Inspector who had come there with reinforcements, asked Zeenat to go in, have a new burqa and give the torn one to him. She was handcuffed and they entered her house. They searched the house and found none else there. In a small store room cluttered with cobwebs they found a few wooden boxes, some with lock and others without lock, all covered with layers of dust. A policeman picked up a large piece of cloth, dusted the boxes and brought these out. The Police Inspector opened them one by one, except one the lid of which was fixed with copper nails and which had copper straps binding it on all the four sides. The other boxes contained old clothes mostly used by dancing girls and courtesans. The box with copper straps was lifted by the Police Inspector and he found that something rattles in it. A policeman went to the kitchen and brought a large knife meant for mincing meat. Straps came off easily and when the box was opened they found a skull in it. On the first floor, they found black patches at a few places which could be of ink. That was the only evidence of that place having been used for cyclostyling work. They took away the box with skull, leaving the other boxes there.

The lane was completely deserted. There was no sound or light in anyone of the houses around. Policemen knocked at all the nearby houses and made all the young men come out and stand in a row. None of them had eyes heavy with sleep or any other evidence of having been made to wake up. The Inspector and Sub-Inspector questioned them with flashing eyes to find out who had attached and injured the Police Inspector and prevented him from performing his duty. Everyone pleaded ignorance. Half a dozen policemen who were with the previous Police Inspector recognized some who were present in the gathering when the Inspector was attacked. Six men were picked up and handcuffed. The Police Inspector went to the roof. One could jump quite easily to the house on the right, left or the back. He made the residents to come up and enquired whether anyone had made his exit through their house. Even the residents of the backside house denied it, afraid of getting involved in a police case. The Police Inspector asked his men to remove Zeenat's handcuffs. She and six handcuffed men were marched to the Kotwali police station. Their names and addresses were entered in the 'First Information Reports' register. There was only one detention room in the Kotwali police station. All the six men were locked in there. Zeenat Begun had to keep standing in the office room. It was already past midnight. When the policemen on duty put their head on the table and began to slumber, Zeenat also sat down, put her head on knees and dozed off. Later the same night the house of Mohammed Bashir was raided and he arrested after some proscribed literature was found in his house.

CHAPTER THIRTEEN

Next morning news spread faster than wild fire in areas of Hindu population that Police Inspector Mr. Goswami, had been attacked by a Muslim job and was in a critical condition in the Victoria Jubilee Hospital. He was a Brahmin of the high Goswami gotra and it began to be spread among Hindus that killing him was like killing a cow. Thousands of Hindus spontaneously poured out of their house into the streets. No body knew how all that happened in the next few hours came about. It was too vast, too violent too sudden and too fast for anyone to comprehend and to recount. First crowds of Hindus; and then of Muslims began to steamroller. Wild, shrilling mobs tearing through the streets gathering numbers and a variety of weapons as they went on, joining other gangs, impelled by the rhythm of their rushing and jumping. If anyone was unable to arm himself with a stick or a rod, he broke a cot to obtain bamboo stick. Some dismantled railings to obtain bars. Many were carrying kerosene bottles, cans and tins. There was a pandemonium of shrieks, shouts and slogans. It seems that gargantuan wild animals, gigantic boars stung by sharp arrows were running amuck in blind, uncontrollable and torrid rage.

By the evenings huge gangs of the two communities returned home, exhausted, their anger deflated. There was more murk in their mind than in the dusk of the nightfall outside. Dozens of houses were on fire, scores of shops had been broken and goods scattered, and hundreds of houses had windows splintered. None knew how many innocent persons had been killed or maimed. The day ended in mutual defeat. Hira Singh and some of his friends were there in the dwakhana all the day. Someone said that the two communities were doomed to live chained to each other for ever. Anything that increased the heaviness of chains was self defeating madness. But madness had its own way of waxing and multiplying itself by twisting facts, fostering illusions and mutilating truth. It can pervert sanity, make sordid look noble, guilty innocent and coward a hero. It can portray disaster as victory, falsehood as truth, hatred as love and enmity as friendship.

Hira Singh was not sitting on the divan but on the front settee with others. All were silent most of the time, some with inclined head others with lowered eyes. There was a feeling of someone very dear passing away. Their eyes were brimming with unshed tears. Hira Singh was suddenly overwhelmed by unbearable sadness. He bowed as if he was a hunchback. His grief knew no bounds as he felt that the ideas, proffered by the two communities as their truth were no more, as he had thought earlier, two lines perpetually running parallel to each other. The two contradictory 'truths' of the two communities were now like railway engines running on the same track from opposite sides. A disastrous collision was inevitable unless something was done to signal a timely halt. He continued to follow the whirlwind of his thoughts. His head throbbed and his eyes had a thick film of tears so much so he could hardly see anything. An idea came to him like a thunderclap: 'This is a flower and the fruit has yet to come. What sort of fruit it is going to be?'

Finding Hira Singh motionless someone held him by the shoulder and shook him. He straightened his back and drew a deep breath. He stood up and looked outside at the road. He saw a boy of five holding the hand of his drunken father and taking him home. On the other side of the street two dogs were fighting for a bone. He saw Bhagatji pass that way. For over thirty years he had been spending his day sitting near the well outside Ram Bagh Gate offering gratis water to travelers and passersby. There were separate brass tumblers for Hindus and Muslims but he kept these clean by washing and cleaning with ash. Many homes kept aside for him the first chapatti baked there and this was sufficient for his two meals. At the end of the day he would walk to the Golden Temple. While going by the dwakhana he quietly turned that side with joined hands without uttering a word or halting even for a second. Hira Singh had been seeing this from the day he became his nana's apprentice.

This thought of the colourless unassuming figure of that man who without demanding anything from anybody, without complaining against anyone served people who were strangers to him. This was truly a noble life. Then he saw Banta sweeper with his dozen or so donkeys, returning after carrying city's refuse to shallow fields outside. The empty sacks were dangling on the sides of the donkeys. Without wanting it, Hira Singh thought that even animal serve people heart and soul without complaining. These were the times, he thought, when a different and more dynamic type of nobility was needed.

What made Hira Singh very ill at ease was that every change in the political scenario made the two communities take a more and more uncompromising attitude, putting all the blame on the other community. Facts had become irrelevant and the two communities had their own version of truth, each staring more and more angrily at the other.

The 'individual civil disobedience' movement of 1936 fizzled out in a few weeks. After the top leaders were arrested, others went into hiding or lay low. In Amritsar as in other cities the name of an 'individual' was announced every day as 'dictator' of the movement and a satyagrahi for courting arrest. This soon became infrequent with the number of those volunteering for arrest dwindling day by day. That provided an occasion to some Muslims to jeer at the Congress and Hindus. The Hindus on their part would dub the Muslims, as anti-national and communal, with bitterness greater than before. Later in the 1937 elections to the Provincial assemblies, the Indian National Congress party managed to secure a majority of seat in six Provinces with Hindu majority, while the Muslim League could win very few seat in the Provinces with Muslim majority. This became an occasion for the Hindus to jeer at the Muslims and thus more and more Muslims veered towards the Muslim League. Neither Congress nor Muslim League made an effort to find common ground. Both rather strove to widen the gulf that had come to exist between the two communities.

Maulana Asad Ullah Khan was now leader of the Muslim League in Amritsar. He enrolled as its members a number much larger than members of the Congress Party in the city and got himself elected as its President. His speeches lasting hours were now not mere rambling to amuse the Muslim audiences, occasionally attacking the clerics. His speeches consisted mainly of attacks on Hindu leaders, how they were trying to enslave the Muslims politically and economically, even in Provinces like Punjab and Bengal where they were in majority. He had become a leader more popular among Muslims than before. In the 1937 elections to the Provincial Assembly he stood as a Muslim League candidate. He was able to collect more funds for his election campaign than he needed and was able to give a tough fight to the most important Muslim in the town who was a candidate of the Unionist Coalition Party ruling over Punjab. Despite the use of government machinery against him he lost by less than a hundred votes only. He preferred to be addressed as Khan Sahib and not as Maulana Sahib as before. He now talked less about religion and more about politics.

He had three sons who had gone to Government school and College and not to a religious seminary. Two had joined the Intelligence department of the Punjab police and the eldest, after his B.A degree, was recruited as a supply clerk for the British Mission in Basra in Iraq. For one and a half year Asad Ullah Khan did not receive any letter from him and then suddenly there was a letter from him which had come via Red Cross in Geneva. He had written that he had gone to Spain a year ago to join the International Brigade fighting against the Fascists and the Nazis trying to overthrow the democratic government of that country. After the defeat of the International Brigade about thirty thousand survivors were put in prison. One thousand of them were being taken out every day, in alphabetical order of the names, and shot dead. His name being Usman his turn would come in the end but there was no escape from death. He requested his father to recite Namaz-e-Janaza - the Muslim funeral prayer - for him three weeks after the date of that letter. The letter had been received four weeks after its date. Asad Ullah Khan, his friends and family members went to the community grave yard and recited the funeral prayer for his son.

There was, sometimes later, tragic death of his second son. In the Intelligence wing of police his two sons were often required to attend public meetings of various political parties incognito for making a record of what transpired at those meetings. Many of these meetings were venues of fiery speeches by their father, the reporting of which embarrassed them. One of his sons got transferred to the Law and Order section of the local police department and the other was posted to the Intelligence department in Lahore.

Being new to the city, the Intelligence department found it possible to make him associate with a socialist and revolutionary group from Bengal trying to set up a cell in the city. His unusual enthusiasm made them suspect him and before long they found him a shallow person, a windbag and possibly a mole. They made him accompany them for a training camp at Cawnpore. During the journey by train they gagged him and threw him out of the train at midnight, when other passengers were fast asleep.

These two tragedies in Asad Ullah Khan's life made him more bitter, not against the system but against Hindus, the Congress and its leaders. He became tireless in organizing Muslim League in various parts of the Province. On every visit to the dwakhana, Hira Singh found him more bitter and uncompromising than before. He would describe Congress Party as a communal Hindu body and Gandhi not a religious but a highly communal-minded person, differing from others only in his method. No amount of arguments on the part of Hira Singh would dilute his bitterness. This made Hira Singh very sad because Asad Ullah used to be one of the most pleasant visitors to the dwakhana gatherings.

Hira Singh had another headache. One of Zeenat Begum's twin sons Mohammed Munir, who was Lecturer of Mathematics at local Islamia College, had taken up tuition work for a Sikh girl, Iqbal Kaur, studying mathematics for her Degree class. He fell in love with her and began to grow beard and wear turban like a Sikh. He started calling himself Nanak Singh. He was already married with two children. This was as embarrassing for the family of the Sikh girl as it was for Zeenat Begum and her daughter in law. Dr. Taseer, Principal of Islamia College took it lightly, particularly when there was no chance of securing the services of another Muslim to teach mathematics in the College. He said that he would take no notice of it despite protests by his fellow staff members and students, as long as he stuck on to his Muslim name in the College. Mohammed Munir was a very popular and successful teacher of mathematics. He had made B.A Honours in Mathematics the most sought after course in the Islamia College which many non-Muslims also joined. On Hira Singh's advice Mohammed Munir's wife went to see that Sikh girl. She told her that her father, who is Chief Engineer in Sind Province, was founder president of All India Ahluwalia Sikh Association. He had fanatical pride in the exclusiveness of his clan. He was dead against anyone in the family marrying outside Ahluwalia clan, even if he was a Sikh. He got his brother-in-law murdered when his sister married a Sikh outside Ahluwalia fraternity. She told Mrs. Mohammed Munir that her husband could become a Sikh but could not belong to Ahluwalia clan, and hence would not be acceptable to her father. She said that she had already told Mohammed Munir that if she broke the family tradition her father would have both of them murdered. She told his wife that she had already discontinued tuitions from him and her father would soon take her to Karachi.

Even before National Congress, Muslim League, Justice Party, Home Rule Party and similar political organizations came into existence, associations of clans, and sub-castes among Brahmins, Kshatriyas, Aroras, Kayasths, Jats,

Rajputs, and various sections of Muslims had emerged towards the end of the nineteenth century. This took place on the substructure of splintered social polity which had existed from earlier times.

With the spread of education in English these sectarian societies became all the more influential as these tried to advance the interests of fellow members of clan or sub-caste in services and business. Kinship as a social phenomenon had become more assertive after it came on the same plane as politics and economy. Not only weddings, communal festivals also became occasions for asserting kinship and caste solidarity. There were separate organizations among Hindu and Muslim of Rajputs, Jats and others. All India Ahluwalia Sikh Association was one such group. The movement for separate sectarian mobilization had become so widespread that even sweepers had their Balmik association, artisans their Ramgarhia sabha and Muslim weavers their Anjuman-e-Ansar. Hira Singh had often thought that this proliferation of sectarian groups had undermined the evolution of homogeneous social life in the country and was thus one of the motivations for the heightening of communal feelings among Hindus, Muslims and Sikhs.

CHAPTER FOURTEEN

Barkat Ullah, the third and the only surviving son of Asad Ullah Khan resigned his job in the Police Department and began to work for the socialist party. He had started writing poems and believed that when poetry captivated and intoxicated a person he became unable to do anything else. He would speak about poetry as a slave talked about his master. To his father he said that a poet could achieve anything only when he was a good man, loved and dear to all. That could not be possible for him in the Police department. He came to the dwakhana sometimes and spoke in a flowery language. He would say: "A poet tills not earth but the sky and reaps a harvest of stars. Common people seek faith and salvation. Only a poet seeks the truth." He would say that he did not know which word or sentence could be spoken with safety. Words and ideas had become like snakes kept in a basket. He would regret that distrust between the communities was now like a vast cloud of locusts which had completely blocked the sun and created darkness all around. Hira Singh remembered that till a few years ago several miles long swarms of locusts used to visit Punjab almost every year and for days there would be darkness for all the twenty-four hours. Even when many of the locust swarms came down on fields and houses, there were still more in the sky to blur the sun. Barkat Ullah had shaved off the small beard he had grown since boyhood. He had big shining eyes, a prominent nose and thick eyebrows; He smiled like an open harmonium and would say that he was afraid of persons who did not laugh. When his father insisted that he got married, he would say that he did believe in marriage because he believed in future but let him first give up walking on a railway track. He had started putting on pant and coat and was the first person in the family to clean teeth with a brush instead of a twig. He was trying to a get the job of a primary school teacher and was making two ends meet by selling journals and newspapers on a pavement.

One day he brought to the dwakhana a middle aged person who was so badly stung by bees that he could not open his eyes. He was feeling great pain. Hira Singh added a few crystals more of aspirin to the powder' he gave him and advised him to apply iced-water swabs on his swollen eyes. When he came next day he was almost cured. He was all in praise of the unani system of medicine and condemned the allopathic system. His name was Dina Nath and he too was a poet. He did not generally write poems but translated or reproduced in his own idiom in Punjabi verse Mahabharata, Ramayana and similar epic tales. He said that unlike other poems, epic poetry belonged as much to the masses as to the educated persons. He was a veterinary doctor by profession and had been transferred as a punishment to the Society for the Prevention of Cruelty to Animals in Amritsar from a similar institution in Lahore which was his home town. Both the dog and the servant of an officer had got injured in an accident. That officer was bothered about the dog but not in the least about the more seriously injured servant. Someone in the veterinary hospital remarked that there should be a society for the prevention of cruelty to human beings, which offended that officer.

Like men of the old generation, talking was Dina Nath's great inexhaustible delight. He had a small grey goatee, high forehead and a small red nose squeezed between two fat cheeks. His two lips did not match. The lower one was thicker which moved awkwardly while talking. He had wide glittering eyes and carried a solar hat often in his arm and sometimes on his balding head. He believed that human heart found peace and pleasure only by returning evil by evil and God should better have stopped evolution at monkeys and chimpanzees. He asserted that man was the only animal who lied and sinned. While relating a story his hands, eyes and goatee would be as much a part of it as his tongue. Hira Singh found that Barkat Ullah and Dina Nath had become good friends but it was a strange friendship. Dina Nath not only believed in ghosts and ogres but relished to talk about them He was against socialism. He believed that there had to be different fate for different men just as there were different features, sizes and heights. He held that diseases and misfortunes were caused by evil spirits. His prescriptions for these problems and afflictions were multifarious, such as feed a bull buffalo with jaggery, offer red garment to Hanumanji on Tuesday, light a mustard oil earthen lamp in Bairon temple on Friday, bum a handful of black til seeds in a black cloth on Saturday, etcetera. Added to this were a large variety of devices like precious stones, fasts or incantations for every difficult situation He firmly believed that if people observed fast on full moon day and if on the fourth day of the dark fortnight of moon in August they threw stones and pebbles to ward off evil spirit and bad luck, they would be free from illness and ill-luck throughout the year.

Later, Asad Ullah Khan and veterinary doctor Dina Nath became good friends, which was less surprising for Hira Singh. Both were avid readers of whatever Gandhiji wrote and whatever was written about him in newspapers and journals. Both disliked him from the bottom of their heart. Dina Nath held that if one was selling vacuum cleaners, one would sell better if there was dirt around. Similarly if one was selling truth, the more falsehood was around the better. Gandhi knows that he would be able to sell non-violence better if somehow violence was in the air; hence the need for communal tension. Dina Nath believed that non-violence was only a state of his mind and not a fact of life. He would point out that in December 1920 Gandhi declared: 'We will use swords when the time will come. He who does not use sword at the proper time is a fool and one who uses his sword at an improper time is also impudent' In August 1931 and even later he asserted that the Swaraj government 'shall provide for the military training of citizens so as to organize a means of military defense apart from regular military forces.' Gandhi read Gita every day which says in one form or the other again and again 'tasmad yudhyasva Bharata'- fight well the battle Arjuna.

Asad Ullah would enquire: "Why should Hindus want to create a brand new god when they already have so many? Only a community without any tradition of equality and fellow feeling can accept heroic leadership or render unquestioning obedience to a leader. In placing their hopes and responsibilities upon a heroic leader, Hindus through that very act lower the moral temper of their personal life and the tone of their intellectual effort. All impractical ideas thrashed out long ago and flung aside like carcass are being presented by Gandhi to the Indian people as something new. Earth quake in Bihar has been described by him as a divine chastisement for untouchability, as if this evil had suddenly appeared on the day of the earthquake. How can you move forward when you have in the driving seat a person who keeps on accelerating without putting the car in gear?"

The dwakhana was now less of an amiable and genial place where the visitors came for chit-chat and expressed their point of view without hurting anyone or without wanting to score a point. Now they stated their fixed ideas and likes and dislikes with vehemence and seldom without bitterness. The minds of the people had got frozen. Previously Hindus and Muslims lived in different parts of the town but now they also lived in altogether different world of ideas. They had lived separately all these years but for the first time there was a feeling of separateness, which was increasing with every passing day. The thoughts and outlook of the two communities had now lost all common ground and were drifting more and more apart. Nothing was more deceptive than truth itself and every successful deception closely approximated truth. Every problem was being stated in wrong terms so that it would baffle solution. The result was that nonviolence was tending to generate what it decried most - violence.

Hira Singh felt very sad that everything that transpired henceforth served to widen the gulf between the two communities. Muslim owned Urdu papers were full of stories how in 1937 the Congress had secured majority in the six Provinces by rigging elections and about corruption and nepotism under Congress rule. Gandhiji's own statement about reports of widespread corruption was repeatedly published by the Muslim owned dailies and weeklies so also poet Rabindra Nath Tagore's statement against some of Mr. Gandhi's policies. Tagore had stated that demand for unquestioning obedience was 'despotism,' surrender of the dignity of man and denial of reason. Tagore's chastising Gandhi for saying that he would become a better poet if he spun for one hour every day was largely commented upon by Muslim owned Urdu newspapers. Everything that Gandhi wrote or said was used by the Muslim owned Press and Muslim public men in their speeches to create fear and distrust among Muslims and to belittle Gandhi. When after the Munich Pact, Gandhi stated that the Czech people should have faced the might of Germany and Italy combined and died to a man without shedding the blood of the robber or when he advised the Chinese to say to the people of Japan to bring all their machinery of destruction we present half our population to you, the Muslim owned Press and public men would again and again appeal to Gandhi to give the same advice to Hindus. This had not only increased feeling of alienation among the Muslims, but also created distrust and hostility.

Rulia Ram of Katra Ahluwalia, where Hira Singh lived previously, had become a rich man. He came often to the dwakhana for the treatment of his and the ailments of his two wives. During the Individual Satyagraha started by Gandhiji in 1936, there was hardly any person volunteering to court arrest after a fortnight. The Congress leaders then started hiring volunteers, which was not difficult because the arrested satyagrahi was sentenced to three months imprisonment only. Rulia Ram was paid rupees one hundred and fifty which he could not have earned in three months. On an amavas festival day when the crowds of villagers thronged the city, he walked through the main streets of Amritsar with neck heavy with marigold garlands and a national flag in his hand. He was arrested before he reached

Queen Victoria's statue at the end of Hall Bazaar. A rich widow belonging to a well known Congress family was also in jail during this period in connection with the same individual civil disobedience movement. Having known many women in his life he was not deficient in art of enticing women. When he came out of jail he visited her daily and after sometimes married her in the reformist Arya Samaj temple as well as in Court because he wanted to be sure of inheriting her property. Hira Singh suspected that he was giving her some slow poison and using the pretext of treatment by him as a cover up. He warned Rulia Ram, after which he discontinued visiting the dwakhana.

During this period Wazir Chand had also become a rich man. His wife's grand father was a village money lender. He, his two brothers and their families were the only non-Muslims in that village in West Punjab with - about four hundred Muslim families. After the-death of his wife's grand father her grand mother continued to do the business and was living alone in a house surrounded by the other two Hindu kin families. There was a marriage in one of these families and Wazir Chand and his wife went to that village to partake in it. They stayed with the grand mother, and came to know about her thriving usury business. They suspected that she was hiding somewhere a lot of gold and silver pawned with her.

They looked around the house, checked the walls, roofs and floors and finally concluded that the trove could be under the red stone slab in a corner of the dry lavatory beside the stairs to the garret. They were to leave for the return journey before day break to catch 6.30 am train from a railway station about five miles away .They removed from the trove after midnight as much as they both could tie around their waist and while leaving before dawn gave a ten rupee note to the grand mother as a token of their affection. The grand mother found out about the missing jewelry two weeks after they left the village. She came to Amritsar with a relative. She found that Wazir Chand had renovated his house and a wall had a new plaster. Wazir Chand denied having touched anything in her house. She wailed and wailed and said that when the Muslims, in her and the nearby villages, were unable to get back their gold pawned with her they would kill her, murder all her relatives and also Hindus in the neighbouring villages. The relative accompanying her threatened to report the matter to the police and have the new plaster removed. Wazir Chand relented and brought before evening the implements with which masons removed plaster. He said that he would take out the gold articles that night and they should think out how they would safely take these back to the village. They had a happy get together with a sumptuous dinner. In the night both grand mother and her relative had many loose motions. A vaid - practitioner of indigenous medicine was called at midnight. He gave them some medicine which was not of much help. Both of them passed away early next day. A priest was called and they were cremated before noon.

CHAPTER FIFTEEN

Hira Singh read in the newspaper that one Professor Har Bhagwan had been arrested and released on bail for writing a book "Real Secrets of Love and Marriage". The police considered the book lewd and indecent and had proscribed it. Hira Singh had been sending someone to Lahore to buy one pound bottle of aspirin crystals. He decided to go there himself and wrote to Har Bhawan to see him in the afternoon at Lal & Lloyd Chemists on the Mall Road. Har Bhagwan met him and told him that he had been victim of a conspiracy. He explained: "I was offered a lecturer's job at a Bombay College on rupees one hundred per month. 1 discontinued all my tuitions and when 1 reached Bombay, 1 was told by the college principal that for the first year's probationary period, they pay the new lecturer only rupees fifty per month. He assured me that my salary would be rupees hundred per month after probation of a year or two. The College authorities were not willing to provide accommodation. Finding that hiring a room and living in Bombay within rupees fifty per month was impossible, 1 returned to Lahore. There was no work for me to do. I started writing books for publishers on any subject they commissioned, at rupee one per page with all rights sold. 1 hired a typewriter and typing with one finger I could write hundred or hundred fifty pages of a book per month depending upon the subject. 1 have authored more than twenty books on Mahatma Gandhi for different publishers almost the same number on Jawaharlal Nehru apart from scores of text books and dozens of books on subjects of common interest such as astrology, palmistry, nature cure, vegetarian and non-vegetarian recipes and many other popular subjects. Some have been published under my name but many more under names of fictitious authors. Last month a publisher gave me ten books on sex and happy married life published in England, with some portions sidelined in red pencil. He wanted a new book entitled: 'Real Secrets of Love and Marriage' to be written mainly based upon portions in the ten books sidelined by him with red pencil. 1 told him that ten per cent alcohol taken out of each of the ten books would make the new book hundred per cent alcohol and very hot stuff. He argued that this was being culled out of standard published works and no one could object to that. After the book was published the publisher himself approached and probably bribed the police to have it proscribed. The result is that despite the sale of the book being illegal it has run into several editions and is selling like hot cake. The publisher has already earned more than twenty thousand rupees for a book for which he paid me only one hundred seventy three rupees in all. He tried to prevent my release on bail so that there was no problem for him or I do not write another hot-selling book of the same type for another publisher."

Hira Singh had listened to him attentively and was sorry to feel that whatever a poor man did to make a living, he was bound to become victim of exploitation and injustice. He remarked: "Seeing so many books on Gandhi and Nehru and the national movement, I was wondering how such a huge crop of authors had suddenly sprouted in the country. They have been exploiting you most cruelly."

Har Bhagwan interjected: "Apart from exploitation, they play silly joke with me. They used to introduce me as a man who made Mahatma Gandhi famous. When I resented this, they avoided saying this at my face but continue to refer to me jocularly among themselves as a man who made Mahatma Gandhi and Pandit Nehru famous."

They were both standing outside the entrance of the shop and talking. The shop keeper urged: "Hakimji why don't you come in and have a seat. I have sent for cold drink for both of you. They went in and sat on two opposite chairs behind the counter Hira Singh said: "Mr. Trevelyan the Deputy Commissioner of Lahore was D.C. Amritsar six years ago and is known to me. I will talk to him and try that prosecution, if any, is of the publisher and not of writer. You might have to furnish an affidavit explaining your position. I will see the Deputy Commissioner today before returning to Amritsar by the Frontier Mail and will write to you from there."

"Has Dayal Singh ever written to you or come to see you. He told me that he had visited Lahore sometimes." Har Bhagwan enquired from Hira Singh.

"No, never," Hira Singh replied and enquiringly looked at him.

Har Bhagwan began to narrate: "I was broke after two weeks stay in Bombay. When I guessed that they would not pay me on the first of the month, I decided to return while 1 still had money enough for the journey back to Delhi because 1 was keen to meet Dayal. My visit to Dayal did not have even a fraction of the cordiality with which poverty-stricken Sudhama of epic Mahabharata was received by Lord Krishna. I was not allowed to enter his house and in office also it was with great difficulty I got admitted to his room. Of course he was somewhat cordial if not warm and asked his peon to escort me to his home, where I stayed for three days."

Har Bhagwan was silent for sometime as if thinking whether to inform Hira Singh of all he observed there. He looked into Hira Singh eyes with the same rapport as on his first visit to the dwakhana and said slowly in a sad tone: "Each and everything that binds a man to his family and all that holds him to his kith and kin has altogether left him. There was nothing he wanted to say to his family, nothing he wanted to know about them or hear about them. For an instance I felt that he had ceased to be a human being and was a mere cog in the government's Intelligence apparatus. I showed him the picture of his son with his name on the back. First he showed complete disinterest but he later took that photograph from me and kept it safely in his cabinet."

They had been too long in the shop and decided to stroll along the pavement on the Mall. Some persons recognized Har Bhagwan and greeted him. Differences in the habits and mores of the people living in the two cities of Amritsar and Lahore have been subject of many mutual quips, puns and epithets as if these were not two cities separated by thirty two miles but were worlds apart. Hira Singh did notice that at least the outer part of the city had a different ambience. The people moved about more freely and more leisurely. The road was wider, better laid and with lines of trees on both sides which were coming up with new leaves after having shed the old ones. This lent an air of freshness to everything. More persons were in western dress with solar or felt hat. It was still afternoon but the shops and the pavements were more crowded than they were in Amritsar. They walked to a small triangular park and sat down on a bench.

Hira Singh said: "I sometimes feel very sad, not because my dear son is of no use to me but because he will sooner or later find life barren and sterile without any fulfillment or satisfaction."

Har Bhagwan adjusted his round loose cap and thought of innate goodness and charity of mind which was Hira Singh's second nature. Scratching his chin he observed: "I asked Dayal about the Anglo Indian girl for whom he had deserted Didar Kaur. He said that the family went on leave when that girl was nearing her term but later the father returned alone. Within a month he got himself transferred back to Bombay Presidency from where he had come on deputation. During the few weeks he was there, he did not want Dayal to talk about it and gave the impression that the girl married an Anglo-Indian pal soon after she was able to leave maternity home. About the new born child he was more laconic, leaving him to guess that it was a still birth."

After a pause Har Bhagwan added: "Alone and poverty stricken as I am, your stamina and fortitude give me much strength." Hira Singh had telephoned the Deputy Commissioner from the Chemist's shop and it was time for him to go. There was a procession winding through the Mall Road and the horse carriage might take more time to reach Deputy Commissioner's office. While leaving, Hira Singh tried to give some money to Har Bhagwan, which he politely declined. He said that the work he did was very disgusting but gave him more money than he had ever earned in his life of poverty.

When Hira Singh returned to Amritsar late in the evening, he came to know that there was communal tension in the city and skirmishes between Hindu and Muslim groups had taken place during the day. The previous night an armed gang of robbers had uprooted the entrance gate outside the Goldsmiths' Lane and looted the house of a jeweler. Even events unconnected with communal issues would many times become pretext for communal skirmishes and riots in the city. Most of the peace-loving citizens felt much perturbed about it. A meeting of intellectuals in the city - teachers in the Khalsa, Hindu and Islamia Colleges, lawyers and medical practitioners - took place in the Town Hall to discuss how cordiality and mutual trust could be restored. It was suggested by some that much of the fear psychosis and distrust had been generated by the building of iron gates and other fortifications outside lanes and by-lanes. That prompted persons living in areas where the two communities had lived together for generations to shift to quarters exclusively inhabited by their community. It was felt by most of the persons attending the meeting that those who had left areas of mixed population should be persuaded to shift back to their earlier house and that Hindu and Muslim residents should be requested to dismantle the fortifications outside their lanes and by-lanes. A committee of College teachers consisting of three from each college was selected to go round the city and persuade people to remove iron gates and help in restoring mutual confidence. Professor Mohammed Munir alias Nanak Singh was to be leader of this nine member delegation of college teachers. Even after the Sikh girl, he had fallen in love with, left the college in Amritsar, Mohammed Munir continued to have a turban and a beard and was not addressed as Professor but as Sufi₁ as was the case with some unconventional religious mentors among Muslims. After his mother's arrest he had shifted to her house in the Amir Ali lane.

When the delegation of College teachers went round the city they were looked upon with suspicion. Hindus thought that it was a conspiracy to disarm them and to place them at the mercy of the Muslims. Muslims refused to do so unless Hindus were ready for it. Wherever they went they were treated with disdain. Somewhere there would a sarcastic remark that these were the chosen few, chosen by providence, chosen by history itself. They met with stone silence at some places at others a rude 'no' would be hurled at them in a voice mingled with anger and exasperation. Somewhere a question mark would appear on the forehead of some one and they would be abused in a tone that was at once brutal and violent: At another place they would be received with narrowed eyes, dark faces and stern expression. None listened to their plea that whatever the religion, a man had to eat and earn a living, which could be better done in an atmosphere of mutual trust and communal harmony.

It was decided to persuade residents of one lane each in the Muslim and Hindu area to dismantle fortifications simultaneously. The delegation of college teachers moved from one area of the city to the other but none was willing to be the first and unless there was the first, there could not be the second and the third. More the effort they made more frustrated they were. People seemed to believe in worst against the bad and not in good against the bad. After futile effort for a few days, when they came to the dwakhana in the evening, they all were in tears. Hira Singh could only say that some other way had now to be found to restore mutual trust and communal harmony.

Hira Singh was in no doubt that it was not religious conservatism that was blocking a solution. Conservatism was there throughout. It was conservatism that made it possible for the society in India to cohere and to transmit their values to future generations. In a traditional society religion was not a separate or distinct compartment of life. It was something that informed and gave meaning and coherence to social life. It was not a thing by itself but was an inseparable part of a whole that encompassed every aspect of daily life. What had come to the fore during the last decade or so had nothing to do with religion or conservatism. It was a hard and cruel situation, augmented by a climate of hatred which was the creation of men and society. It was the result of a feeling held by each and every section of the Indian community that its members had more wisdom and righteousness than others. This made an Indian adhere tenaciously to his own version of truth refusing to believe that there was a reality which continued to exist even when one refused to accept it. None could forsake this reality just as a fish could not abandon water however it might dislike it. He muttered "Oh God give a little light to this country so full of darkness and wind. Let people put the snakes of hatred in a basket and free the future out of the cages of their prejudices."

The trial of Zeenat Begum and others lasted for a year and A.L.Gauba defended them. The prosecution did not accept Zeenat Begum's statement that the box had been with the family in that very sealed and strapped condition ever since their great grand mother left Balanpur State and shifted to Amritsar. They, however, could not provide any other explanation for the presence of the skull in that house. The only charge that could be sustained against Zeenat Begum was preventing the Police Inspector from searching her house and creating a situation which lead to riot and attack on police personnel. Later on the police was able to trace the cyclostyling machine and arrest other accomplices of Mohammed Bashir. They were charged with printing and distributing seditious material and sentenced to two years of imprisonment .Zeenat Begum was fined rupees one thousand and released.

CHAPTER SIXTEEN

After coming out of jail, Zeenat Begum came to dwakhana to see Hira Singh. She was accompanied by a middle aged person who she said was also in the same prison and was released a few days before her jail term ended. He was introduced as Krishan Kumar. His thin emaciated face and dull bulging eyes ill-matched the hectic flush on his cheeks. His curly black disheveled hair would have looked like a skull cap but for a bald patch in the middle. There were bluish shadows under his eyes. The corners of his mouth drooped wearily. "How long were you in jail" Hira Singh asked him.

His face wrinkled, became more somber and a slight smile glided rapidly over it. He coughed, blinked and looked imploringly at Zeenat Begum.

"Tell him the truth. Tell him everything." Zeenat Begum exhorted him. His expression suddenly changed, the pupils of his eyes contracted like a caged bird's. His narrow intent gaze was fixed and distant as if he was vengefully recalling his past. He suddenly looked ceiling-ward. His amber-coloured eyes looked larger and their expression disagreeable. His temples were sweating. Opening his mouth wide he said in one breath: "Fourteen year, full fourteen years."

"Life sentence, Was it for murder?"
Hira Singh questioned him again.

"Four murders" saying this he smiled wryly, his lips shivered and his eyes glittered pathetically. Then he became silent and thoughtful, scratched his stubbly chin with a finger yellow from smoking. He stared at Hira Singh blandly as if making up his mind where to begin.

"Tell every thing. Tell the truth", Zeenat Begum implored him again in a

102

genial and kindly tone.

His face took an expression of deep concentration, his eyes withdrew under his bent brows and he attempted to speak but remained silent opening his mouth in an unpleasant smile. Hira Singh looking at his gingham clothes, thought of his long life in which he was not treated humanely, not even as a human being. He asked him to shift to the center of the settee and as their eyes met, he felt encouraged by Hira Singh's friendliness.

His pale face blushed and he twitched his cracked lips as he spoke: "I belong to Paswan low caste and 1 was the only son born after five daughters. My father named me Krishan Kumar, a name to which the high caste people objected because the low castes were given names like Gheesoo, Gaseeta, Chatkoo, Phikoo etc. They called me Chhika as 1 was the sixth child. My father bought for me kindergarten books and when 1 was five took me to a school for admission. The nearest school was four miles away but its. Brahmin head master refused to admit me. There was another school at a distance of ten miles which had a Muslim as its head master. He admitted me but the problem of a boy of five covering twenty miles every day to school and back was formidable. He persuaded a cobbler in that village to keep me as his helpmate on the condition that he left me free for the school hours.

"No child from the low castes had ever gone to a school and high castes in our village were outraged at my father wanting to educate his son. They scolded and beat him on this score quite often. 1 did quite well in my primary examination and was to join the fifth class. The high caste people insisted that my father stopped educating me further. When my father did not yield, they beat him mercilessly. There were four of them and my father single handed resisted them till one of them hit his back with a bamboo stick with spikes that wrecked his spine. After that he lived for a year all the time shrieking with pain, unable to stand or walk. 1 returned home and became the bread earner of the family. 1 noted down on a piece of paper the names of the four persons who had attacked my father and kept it in a small box along with the blood-soaked shirt he was wearing at that time. A determination steeled in me to kill all the four to avenge my father's death. Though outwardly 1 kept normal relations with them, 1 prayed to God every day to give me strength for this. 1 began to eat horse gram daily and to perform dand, baithak, and other exercises wrestlers did to become strong. After 1 was fourteen 1 began to look for an opportunity to kill all the four together. There were occasions such as holi festival when 1 could kill three but 1 waited till 1 could kill all the four. The opportunity came when 1 was seventeen. The entire village had gathered to see performance by dancing girls on the occasion of the marriage of the son of the Rajput land lord of the village. All the four were sitting close by. 1 could kill them, before anyone noticed what had happened. Someone grappled me, but 1 shook him off, ran fast to the police station and surrendered myself there."

He sighed and continued in a voice mellower than before: "I passed matriculation examination in jail. My father wanted me to become village patwari after matriculation. But I cannot go back to the village. One of the persons killed by me has eight sons and others also have two to four sons. They will have blood in their eyes as soon as they see me. Moreover, my mother is dead. She married or sold my sisters before she died. She had a letter written to me in jail shortly before she died which contained addresses of my two sisters whom she could marry. They live in far off villages."

Hira Singh felt deeply moved by this narration of his past, even though he had noticed every day similar instances of man's inhumanity to man. He asked sympathetically: "Where are you staying here."

He glanced at Zeenat Begum who replied: "For a few days he slept in the mosque adjacent to my house but they discovered that he was not a Muslim. The situation has worsened during the last one year and now they do not trust any Hindu in any manner for anything. He now sleeps under arch below the clock tower. There are many homeless wanting to stretch there for the night. When he does not find any room there he spreads his bed sheet outside on the terrace around the clock tower."

"Has he started doing some thing? What are his plans?" Hira Singh enquired.

Zeenat Begum replied; "The Royal Cinema near the Hall Gate seems to be doing very good business now. About hundred persons come on cycle everyday to see the picture. One of my neighbours looks after the cycle stand there and charges one pice per cycle. When the picture is over, there is much rush at the cycle stand. He helps the cycle stand manager for three hours in the evening and is paid ten pice a day. He is happy to earn about rupees three in a month, which he seldom did before.

His eyes, which at first appeared colourless, suddenly had a curious sparkle.

When he winked, his pupils glistened. His mouth was large for his face. Though he kept his lips obstinately pressed, they seemed to be twitching as his woolly moustache was quivering most of the time he was not speaking.

"For the last ten years in jail I worked as a gardener and produced all the vegetables needed for the jail staff and the prisoners," he said humbly.

"If I come across the job of a gardener, I will let you know". Saying this Hira Singh asked him to shift to the bench near the entrance of the shop. Zeenat Begum reminded him that it was soon going to be time for his cycle stand. He, greeted Hira Singh with folded hands, and departed.

Hira Singh smiled enquiringly at Zeenat Begum and opined: "But for the skull you would have come out of jail early."

Zeenat Begum explained quietly: "That box with skull has been there since the days of my grand mother. She brought it with her when she secretly left Balanpur State and came to Amritsar shortly after this town was free from the scourge of Plague in the end of the last century Photograph of my grand mother was also in the box which they threw away when they took away the box and skull. I had kept that photograph, which helped me to establish that it had been in the box since the days of my grand mother. Zeenat Begum handed over a photograph to Hira Singh

The picture fixed on a card board frame had not faded much but it had lost its sheen. The frame had cracks. The paper used by the box camera to take the snap was of good quality and the features in the picture were still clear and bright. It was that of a woman nearing thirty but who had all the pertness of a teenager. Her brilliant eyes betrayed a touch of pride and more than that of extreme sweetness. Every part of her face was well proportioned and lent a rare charm and beauty to it. The mouth was small, the lower luscious lip projected slightly and so did her chin which gave a peculiar firmness and spellbinding charm to her beauty. Her complexion looked very healthy and fresh.

When Zeenat Begum was handed back the photograph, she remained silent for a minute waiting for Hira Singh to put a question. When she found that he was looking at her enquiringly she narrated: "My grand mother was one of the seventy-seven queens of Maharana of Balanpur, one of the many native States which escaped annexation, because after Mutiny the British Government gave a promise that no further annexations would take place.

This was one of the several dozen States which have continued to subsist in central and western India, as elsewhere in the country. When this Maharana ascended the throne of Balanpur he had two ambitions, to have one hundred queens and to hunt one hundred lions. In his vast palace he had got constructed one hundred chambers for his queens, twenty three of which were still vacant and Maharana's agents were on the search to find more queens for him. He had almost reached his targets of lions he was to kill by using children as tiger bait in his hunts."

Her throat became dry and after coughing and clearing it she continued:

"A perversion suddenly overpowered the Maharana just as it seemed to have many other Princes at that time. Many of them had made a bet among themselves that whoever deflowered the largest number of virgins between Diwali festival in the beginning of November and Holi revelries in the middle of the following March, will be presented a gold crown studded with jewels, rubies and diamonds. Ring in the nose of the girl symbolizing virginity was to be collected as a proof."

"Nose gold rings were distributed by the Maharana of Balanpur among all the female children in the State above the age of five and they were to be brought to the palace by turn. These included female children in the palace itself born to many of the queens. My grand mother also had a daughter six years old and a gold ring was pierced in her nose. Everyone in the State felt outraged but none did anything to stop this. All his crown prince did was to keep a record and provide material to the British Resident so that he deposed his father and installed him in his place. My grand mother made up her mind not to allow this in the case of her daughter because unlike many other queens she was sure that the Maharana was her father. The evening it was her daughter's turn, my grand mother went to the Maharana's room and coquettishly created an occasion when she could thrust a knife in his throat. She beheaded him and put his head in an ornate jewelry box which she had kept in the ante room. Soon after that the crown prince came there and saw his father's headless body. He went to the back side of the Palace where Maharana's younger brother resided. They had almost similar features. He brought him there, cut his head. He dumped his body in a cellar and put the head on his father's body. He had thought that a headless body could create problem with the British Resident and rendered his succession far from smooth."

"The crown prince informed the queens who crowded the room weeping

106

and beating their breast. My grand mother had already planned everything. With some luggage and the box, she went to Delhi where she found that the hustlers' streets were overcrowded. She came to Amritsar and got a room in this bazaar. Her grand mother was called Benares ki Bai, - harlot from Benares -.as she spoke in an eastern Indian dialect. In a few years, her room over one shop expanded to a hall above four shops."

There was dead silence for sometime. Suddenly Zeenat asked: "Is all this going to happen again when the British rulers are gone?"

Hira Singh did not answer but Zeenat kept looking at him questioningly.

After sometime he remarked: "One of the legacies of British rule is the concept of just and unjust which a large number of the people in India now understand and cherish. The type of abominable depravity which your grand mother witnessed has already become a thing of the past in most of the princely States. I do not think such things would ever be repeated but there can be other failings and shortfalls which we cannot fully understand at present. As both the communities are not exhibiting the needed sense of accommodation and respect for the other's point of view, there is the possibility that the communal tension will continue, and perhaps increase, in one form or the other. It is not being realized that the section of Indian society which has got a head start will always be at an advantage in a competition based on merit. Unless this is corrected, this can result in much tension. Then there will be tyranny of wealth and corruption. The administration may become more and more inefficient and make hell of common people's life. Lust for power might make the rulers manipulate elections, and destroy the integrity of administrative machinery and judiciary. It all depends upon how serious and honest our leaders are about their claim to truth, justice and brotherhood."

Zeenat Begum spoke hesitatingly: "I feel that the people will look ruefully back to the old regime of comparative justice, peacefulness and honest administration."

While leaving, Zeenat Begum asked: "Should I apply to the Court for the return of the box." Hira Singh advised: "Do not rake up any such issue. Forget about it unless the Police themselves return the box with or without the skull."

As she turned to go, Hira Singh enquired: "I have not seen Mohammed

Munir for sometime."

"A government college is being set up at Rawalpindi and he is joining there as Professor of Mathematics" Zeenat Begum replied, "Before leaving the place Munir wanted to help his class cover as much of the course as possible. He is in College till late in the evening."

Hira Singh remarked: "This is good because Dr A. D. Taseer is likely to shift to New Delhi and the new Principal of Islamia College might not like Mohammed Munir's antics."

CHAPTER SEVENTEEN

In the worry and anxiety of his personal life and the life around him, Hira Singh received much strength from his love for patients and more than that from his love for books He visited English Book Depot every Saturday without fail. He picked up books of interest to him and treasured them even though he could not scan through all of them. He ordered new volumes of Everyman's Library, Thinkers Library and of the Rationalist and Left Book Clubs. Suddenly there appeared a new series of full length paper back books priced as low as quarter of a rupee. Many of these were reprints of hard bound volumes, available at almost one tenth of their original price. These paper backs were Penguin and Pelican books which virtually came in a flood and were like rays of sun piercing the darkness of his mind. The exchange value of a shilling was less than three quarters of a rupee. A new Penguin or a Pelican book of some hundred pages, priced six pence, was available in India for five annas, less than one third of a rupee.

A pound was worth rupees fourteen. He sent one hundred pounds to Allen Lane publisher of Penguin Books and asked them to send all their paper back books direct to him. After the commission for bulk purchase, he could get four paper back books for less than a rupee. Every Saturday he received by sea mail a packet from London containing Penguins and Pelicans, fiction and nonfiction~ paper backs. There were series on New Writings, and the latest researches in slciences, later on separate series on Physics, Chemistry and Biology After sometime, there were Puffin books meant for children but he found these also interesting. He could hardly scan through a fraction of them but these added a lot of thrill, enchantment and luster to his life. Burning desire to learn progressed in him with a speed that astounded him. He felt that learning was a means one acquainted oneself with the lessons of the past, the hope of the present and dream of future. He had read somewhere that books in the library of Turkish Sultans used to be scented.

Each volume has its particular perfume. A scent master incharge of mixing precious essences decided which perfume could best suit the content and character of the book. Hira Singh felt that, even otherwise, each book tasted and smelled differently and tickled his mind in a different manner. His strong memory helped him to recount and explain to Gurdit Singh what he had read and also about the books which he did not have time to read.

Reading some of the great novels of English and other European literatures, he found that fictional universe was more elegant and well ordered than the human universe made by God. Imagination is creative but a writer cannot create as he desires. He has to follow, more than the Creator, the laws of unity and harmony of composition and of exquisiteness of his cosmos. He has to have strong upright convictions but these cannot have even the slightest appearance in his work, not even as much as God appears in nature. Russian novels enraptured him and he tried to assess the quality which has given the Russian novel its extraordinary eminence. It is not just realism. Besides humanism and realism, there is a lyrical and rhetorical force in Russian novels, something which lifts the realism of the Russian novel a few inches above the rest. It is deep and passionate concern about the fate of Russia and humanity itself. These novels scorch like a blow torch. Shakespeare may have everything great in him but Hira Singh found that his tragedies did not induce similar feelings in him. He did not like Walter Scott. He felt little poetic in-him. He found Dickens clever and original but thought that he had more brains that could be good for him.

He also read other writers who were like mouse before a mountain. He thought that their works failed because of the comparative poverty of the writer's mind and his lack of any concern for the future of man. He began to understand the infinite possibilities of art, that there was no limit to its horizon and that nothing - no method, no experiment even the wildest - is forbidden, but only falsity and pretence. There is no specific and fixed stuff of art. Everything is proper stuff of art, every feeling, every thought, every quality of life and spirit. All that is required is that a writer should call a spade a spade. If words have been made sick by the habits and mores of men outside the realm of art, he should cure them and make them pristine and meaningful again, because these are his artifacts, his weapons, his soul, very sinews of his creation. He began to believe that literature properly employed can be a means of liberating the reader from the murkiness of the atmosphere around him in this country. A good writer takes up as his task to dispel inertia, ignorance and false ideas.

He compared the world of Indian politics with the world of art. While in the world of art the artist keeps searching, discovering and utilizing unlimited possibilities and avenues for his work, the Indian politician is unwilling to search new possibilities to solve his and the country's problems. Instead of thinking out new options, he tries to close as many options open to him as possible. While the artist has to be completely absent from his work, the politician must remain in the centre of it. Not only that, he is most disinclined to share space in the center with anyone else. He felt that the problems of this country would have not been so baffling if God had given India more poets like Tagore instead of politicians like Gandhi.

His strong memory enabled him to discuss some of these books with his friend Gurdit Singh and some others who came to the dwakhana in the afternoon. Gurdit Singh was now more vehement in his belief that the advantages of British rule far outweighed its disadvantages. He would say: "Those who criticize British rule do so because they find that the British rulers did nothing to turn the Indian desert into a garden. They did not come to India to replicate British standards of life here. The chief reasons for the economic stagnation of India were present before the British arrived and remained in place during the British rule. They were unable to do anything about it because after Mutiny they would do nothing that the upper classes would resent. Even tax effort necessary for any development was kept at the-minimum Is it not enough they gave a government more equitable than has' seldom existed previously, an administration very much better than any .in the' princely States subsisting side by side with British India? When small British forces came to India, they could not have imagined that the whole country, one principality after the other, would be presented to them on a platter in the manner it did. As had happened earlier in Indian history, when they fought a feudatory, half a dozen others came to help the foreigners to destroy him. Because of the social hierarchy created by the caste system, most of the people were then as indifferent to the change of a ruler as were the animals and insects sprawling this land."

There were more persons now, particularly among the Muslims, who shared Gurdit Singh's views. One of them pointed out: "Railways, telegraph and postal service came to India before most of the European countries. Many progressive measures' were introduced in India by the British Government even before they were in Great Britain.

Swami Vivekanand pointed out in his Chicago speech that India had women graduates much before the portals of Oxford and Cambridge were opened to women. It is said that English language was introduced to create babus and clerks. Are not doctors, engineers, teachers in the colleges and schools and writers and journalists several times more than the babus? They say that railways were brought to India to serve their military purpose. Look at the map of India... Can you think of any other intelligent route? They had conquered India without the railways and they could very well have remaremained on the top without railways. " .

Hira Singh would add: "Education in English has been a blessing greater than the idea of patriotism, nationalism and freedom. It is the fountainhead of all other blessings of British rule. All the men we see today on the stage of Indian history are its creation. Education in English has given birth in India to an intelligentsia on par with that in England. When India becomes free we might have intelligent people more than today but not an intelligentsia of this type."

Gurdit Singh was more convinced than ever before that the freedom movement launched by Gandhi was unnecessary. It rather created rather bad blood between Hindus and Muslims which never existed before. He would assert that inevitable forces have sealed the fate of British Empire and now they are working out how best to get out of India.

A few decades ago the position was altogether different. A Briton belonging to Indian Civil Service posted as Deputy Commissioner in a district was responsible for the well being of a vast region. Years spent on endless grinding, moving on horse back from village to village, inspecting facilities and settling disputes could be rewarding for a single Briton in that district, only when he had the willing cooperation of hundreds of Indian government functionaries and the goodwill of the people. He read every official paper, knew all the facts and took personal interest in the smallest detail of administration. His life was strenuous, increasingly exhausting and endless typhoon' of" tasks. His sense of duty and the loyalty of his staff was the result of the belief that British government stood for justice and was working for the good of the people. The British people it seems now know that this belief has got undermined by many trends and occurrences and the Indian Empire can no more be maintained by the manpower that a small island in decline can spare."

After a short pause he continued: "Some of the Deputy Commissioners posted in this city were highly educated, broad minded and good-natured. One of them was the brother of a Labour Party Member of the British Parliament and his father was a well known Trade Unionist. When I came to know about it, f asked him why the British people had put a stop to the good they could do here. For example the whole district had only one Government High School, while for the same population in Britain there would be at least twenty. He replied that undoubtedly, every Indian District required at least twenty government high schools and more than one hundred primary school. There was need of ten times more hospitals and hundred times more roads. But this required money which could only come from taxes. After Mutiny there has been a policy of keeping the taxation effort and interference in social mores at the minimum. There would be hue and cry against even marginal increase in direct or indirect taxes. The common salt was .cheaper in India than elsewhere in the civilized world. The demand should have been not for the abolition of the salt tax but for its slight increase so that primary schools could be set in thousands of settlements where sweepers and other deprived sections lived. He confirmed my view that the British had necessarily to quit this country because of the changed situation in Great Britain and the world. He only wondered how this would come about, while retaining the unity, peace and modern education which were the blessings of the British presence in this country. He was only afraid that Indians would throwaway the baby along with water in the bucket. While we were talking over this matter his familiar face .of the district head had vanished and in its place had appeared a very gentle and human face, a face full of compassion and friendship for the Indian people."

Many contested Gurdit Singh's view that communalism was the fault of religion itself and whatever the believers might profess, a religion, necessarily promoted exclusiveness and hatred. Hira Singh would rather argue that the' question whether a religion is good or bad was not relevant. In traditional societies religious beliefs and practices encompassed every aspect of daily life and were very sinew of social life. Instead of finding fault with religion as such, what needed to be thought over was how to make use of the potential which religions had of instilling goodness in society and goodwill among men.

More Hira Singh thought of his life and the times he had lived through, the more he was convinced that goodness was not a thing by itself which could be thrust upon a person or which he had on birth. Thinking, no doubt, was innate in man like hunger and sexual urge but not right thinking. Conscious effort had to be made to create the habit of right thinking and of goodness in individuals and consequently in a society. He remembered how diligently his nana sawed out his bad habits and grafted good ones. How hard he was to ensure that fullest attention was paid to each and every patient and the poor received at least as much attention as the rich. How angry he would become when he found him even slightly inept in selecting and measuring ingredients of various medicines. How rigidly he insisted that there should not be any dilution in discipline or rectitude in day to day life. Even the slightest departure from this called forth nana's wrath. He remembered that when he once picked up a ten rupee currency note lying unclaimed at the Rego Bridge, his nana asked him again and again what he would do with this. When he told him of the various ways he could spend it, he received a scolding the like of which he had never received before. Nana said that he wanted to keep the money which he had not earned and which he had no right. Nana went with him to the place where he had found the ten rupee note and made him place it back there.

Someone in the dwakhana gatherings said that had Mr. Gandhi been born in a Muslim family, he would have been as fanatic against ban on cow slaughter as he was new in favour of it. This half truth showed that communal prejudices could not suddenly be thrust upon a person but were the product of the social environment in which he had lived since childhood. Hira Singh affirmed: "The sanctity of the cow, the merits of the" caste system, the supremacy of the Brahmins and the pollution imputed to the Muslims are the ideas which most of the Hindus imbibe with mother's milk. Similarly the prejudices which Muslims have against multiplicity of gods and other Hindu beliefs get into their psyche in childhood itself. Any effort to eradicate communalism has to start by consciously creating atmosphere of religious tolerance and harmony in homes and by the education of the child in moral and social values that can bind the two communities into close friendship."

CHAPTER EIGHTEEN

Dr. A.D. Taseer, Principal of Islamia College came to see Hira Singh to bid farewell and to get from' him Dayal Singh's address in Delhi.' He said: "Full scale broadcasting services are being set up under the Home Department of the Government of . India. Mr. Fielden has been brought from London to organize the whole set up. I came to know him when I was studying in England. He has directed· the government to appoint me as his Deputy in the new All India Radio outfit. Dayal Singh is one of the few persons in Delhi whom I know. I will like to seek his help in fixing up a residence for me." Hira Singh advised him to write to Dayal care of the Intelligence Bureau, Home Department of the Government of India.

The afternoon gatherings at dwakhana had .lost their vivaciousness and equanimity. The conversation would sooner or later drift over to deteriorating Hindu Muslim relations however they might try to avoid it.

Quite unexpectedly there happened a way out. One Pandit Nand Lal Pani was brought to the dwakhana by a local resident. Pandit Pani was a head master in a high school in Kheora, rock salt town In Jhelum district and had left that place with other non-Muslims because of the communal tension and insecurity there. He described in verse his illness and also the rugged beauty of that town of rock salt mines. He claimed that he was rendering into Panjabi poetry the 'sacred four Vedas. Finding him unusually interesting Hira Singh suggested to him to come to the dwakhana in the afternoon to recite his rendering of the Vedas.

He was short statured and had a white turban over a head somewhat smaller for his body, sharp long nose an a small dark face in which eyes were very prominent. He wore a long coat and narrow pajamas. He had an altogether different way of looking at things. Even though he was a victim of communal situation in west Punjab he exhibited no ill will against the Muslims and was least interested in communal matters. He had a queer way of injecting a folk tale or a mythological reference into a subject under discussion, which would be often interesting and sometimes laughable, such as his explanation why orthodox Hindus eschewed eating of garlic and onion. According to him, during Vedic times onion and garlic grew out of the body of a ritually sacrificed cow.

Relating a story he described that during Satya Yuga, the first of the four yugas of Hindu cosmology, Vedic rishis were performing Gomedha, sacrificial slaughter of a cow, for the welfare of the community. A cow would be cut into pieces with the recitation of mantras and placed on the sacred fire in an urn. After that some other mantras would be recited and the cow would come back to life, as good as before. Once, the rishi who was performing gomedha had a pregnant wife. Unable to resist the urge to eat meat, she stole a piece. When mantras were recited to bring the cow back to life, the rishi found a part of the cow missing from the left side. The rishi went into meditation and found out that the missing part had been stolen by his wife. Realizing that her pilferage had been discovered she threw that piece of meat in the nearby field. Due to the mantras recited by the rishis that piece of beef had become active, bone turning into garlic and flesh into onion. Because of this Hindus do not eat garlic or onion. While relating a mythological tale, he would straighten his back, raise his head and have an air of solemnity as if he was uttering a gospel truth. According to him every thing in ancient India was superior to elsewhere in the world. He believed that India was the fountainhead of all learning and everything ancient Indian was perfect and unique. He would quote Shri Aurobindo who had said that 'India is not a piece of earth, she is Godhead.' Asserting the superiority of the script for the Sanskrit language he related a mythological tale regarding one primordial rishi Rishabha who according to him lived for eight million years and was five hundred poles tall. Pandit Pani credited the invention of all the scripts' to this primordial rishi Rishabha, who bestowed this knowledge to his daughter Brahrni asking her to choose the best script for Sanskrit language. The script she chose is thus called Brahrni. He would describe with full conviction stories like that of rishi Sagara, who did not have any children. By undertaking long penance he was promised progeny. His second wife Sumati gave birth to a gourd containing sixty thousand seeds. These seeds rishi Sagara placed in a vessel of milk and in time each seed became a son.

Pandit Pani believed that none should himself kill anyone and thus be responsible for committing a sin. The person to be killed should be put in a bag and thrown into a river. The time of death of everyone was fixed by God at the time of his birth. If the man in the bag was not destined to die, God will save him. Even without any context he related with relish stories of ghosts, demons, ogres, witches and various evil spirits. Or recited

Sanskrit shlokas, explaining their meanings, such as putting faith in things of the world is like crossing a stream in a clay boat, to soothe lust by satisfaction is like tethering a raging elephant by the hair of a tortoise, the mind during meditation should be like a lamp in a windless place where the flame does not flicker, a wise man is like a blacksmith's anvil on which many experiences are hammered out without change in the anvil itself, etc.

Suddenly he started relating tales about the adulterous life of some gods and ancient rishis and munis. How god Indra fell for every beautiful woman and various ruses he tried to achieve his purpose. There were tales of Draupadi and Kunti, of saints Drighatamas, Uddalaka and many others, of Lord Krishna's escapades with young milk maids and about his seventeen thousand wives. One day he shook hands with everyone present there, instead of saying goodbye with joined hands as he did earlier. After that he did not come to the gathering. They came to know, a few days later, that he had eloped with the teen-aged daughter of a neighbour, leaving behind his wife, four grown up daughters and heaps of debts.

CHAPTER NINETEEN

Dayal invited Dr. Taseer to stay with him till his own accommodation was available. Dr. Taseer had written that he would have to shift bag and baggage from his residence in Islamia College. Dayal informed him that his house was big enough to spare a room to store his effects till he had a bungalow of his own. He wrote to him that he would try to get him suitable accommodation as early as possible.

The Home Department was against the appointment of Dr. Taseer as Deputy Director, All India Radio, because Intelligence reports from Arnritsar and Lahore described him as a person with strong leftist leanings and a fellow traveler of the banned Communist Party. Director, Intelligence Bureau put up a letter for the Home Member of the Viceroy's Council to Mr. Fielden informing him that Dr. Taseer could not be appointed as his Deputy. The Home Member returned the letter unsigned with remarks on the file: "Mr. Fielden comes from an open and liberal society and the plea that Dr. Taseer is a communist fellow traveler will not carry any weight with him. It was proposed to Mr. Churchill soon after he took over as Prime Minister that the British Communist Party should be banned. He enquired: Are they not Britons? When replied in the affirmative, he said that there should be no ban. Mr. Fielden and His Majesty's Government are not likely to accept this proposal. The broadcasts Dr. Taseer plans and schedules will be an open affair and should be monitored for any leftist slant. If necessary the matter can be taken up with Fielden at that stage. In the meanwhile his contacts and movements in Delhi should be watched." Mr. Dayal was made overall in-charge of this. When he received letter from Dr. Taseer he was very happy and was eager that he stayed with him on arrival in Delhi. This would enable him to establish good rapport with him.

The Intelligence Bureau had much expanded and Dayal had become Additional Deputy Director. There were now four Assistant Directors at the headquarters and. more than double office-staff. There was an Assistant Director in each Province with a unit in each District which worked surreptitiously from an inconspicuous place - from the back rooms of a business house or a shop or store - without the slightest indication to the landlord or anyone outside as to the sort of office it was weekly and monthly reports were being received regularly from the Provincial units. Every week there were reports of Hindu-Muslim riots, major and minor in some part of the country or the other, more so after the Congress lead governments were formed in the Hindu majority provinces in 1937. There were reports of power hungry cliques being organized in various Provinces and the manner in which those who were not to Mr. Gandhi's liking got sidelined. It was reported that most of the Congress Chief Ministers and ministers in the Provinces were Brahmins. Mr. Sri Krishna was made Chief Minister in Bihar by overriding the claim of a very prominent Muslim leader. Pandit.B.G Kher was made Chief Minister of Bombay despite the seniority and long service to the country of Mr. Nariman who was a non-Hindu and non-Hindi speaking. In Central Provinces and Berar, with capital at Marathi speaking Nagpur, the claim of a senior. Maratha leader was ignored by Gandhi and Pandit Ravi Shanker Shukla was installed as

Chief Minister against wishes of a majority of Congress legislators. Some reports described this as Mr. Gandhi's Hindu-Hindi obsession and some mentioned that Mr. Gandhi's preference for Brahmins was the result of his innate Hindu orthodoxy which mandated paramount position of Brahmins. This further heightened communal feelings among the Muslims. Apart from detailed reports of corruption and nepotism, Mr. Gandhi's statement about corruption and favouritism by Congress ministries was also received. It was brought to the notice of the Home Member that Mr. .Gandhi did nothing about it after issuing the statement. When a Minister from a Province, accompanied by orderlies in red brocaded liveries, came to see Mr. Gandhi, he lost his temper but the Minister stuck to his point and said that no one would take him for a . Minister if he did not have these orderlies. Reports were received that when Mr. Gandhi told Mr. Jagjiwan Ram, a low caste Congress leader that he, at least, should lead a simple life. His reply according to the report was 'Bapu you want me to remain a chamar - a cobbler, all my life'

When the War broke out in 1939 detailed instructions were formulated for the staff in the Provinces. As the German and later Japanese armies achieved one victory after the other, reports were received that a majority of members of the Congress Party in the country expected the axis powers to win the war. The caucus around Mr. Gandhi held the same opinion.

According to the reports this was the reason for the resignation of Congress Ministries in the Provinces and of the unwillingness of Congress leaders to have a settlement with the British Government. Detailed report was received of discussions among Congress leaders after which Mr. Gandhi described Mr. Cripps proposals for constitutional reform as a post dated cheque on a sinking bank. There were reports from the Provinces of 'left wing pressure through the labour and peasant movements on the Congress itself. Later the Provincial units were directed to send names of leftists who should be put behind bars.

There was general impression from the reports that most of the Congressmen did not want another movement. Not only because they were tired men but because they felt this served no purpose other than that of strengthening the Muslim League. Copy was received of Mr. Mahadev Desai's letter to Mr. Birla dated May 15, informing him that "from the time of Holland's surrender Hitler's stocks are steadily rising in his {Gandhi's] eyes." Birla replied: "Bapu unfortunately took it for granted that Britain had lost the War" On May 23, Mr. Gandhi wrote to Rajkumari Amrit Kaur after the bombing of London: "Why should you feel depressed? The Allies seem to be losing ground everywhere ... The slaughter is awful but it is part of the game." Reports were received that at a meeting of Sewa Sangh, Mr Gandhi was eloquent in praise of Hitler and of Hitler's 'unclouded and unerring' intelligence. Reports were also received about Mr. Gandhi's and Nehru's belief that British imperialism was 'drowning', 'tottering' and that it was a 'sinking ship' Reports of discussions at a Congress working Committee meeting stated that there was a general feeling that the British power had begun 'to crumble though it might take time to disappear.'

There was a belief among many sections of Hindus that Germans built their superior weapons on the information provided in the Vedic texts. Apart from the Sanskrit texts published by Max Muller and other Germans, it \vas believed there were other works, mainly in manuscript, which they stole from this country. Ever since the start of War, Intelligence Bureau had been receiving reports from Magh festival at Allahabad and other religious festivals and congregations of the Hindus about what epitomized the orthodox Hindu attitude towards Hitler. It was repeated there that many German scholar spoke fluent Sanskrit and that Sanskrit was a compulsory subject in German schools. Nazi symbol of swastika, held sacred by orthodox Hindus endeared Hitler to them and despite what the Press was saying against him, he was held to be a rishi, almost like an avatar. He had never married and many of them considered him a visual incarnation of Aryan tradition. Intelligence reports were also received from the United

Provinces that a short play in Hindi written by Pandit Mahan Das Dube was being staged in Banaras and other places. It was not printed but its hand written copies were being freely circulated. The plot was quite directly the destruction of British Raj by Hitler. The drama was modeled on Ramlila as performed in the region. It ended with the conquest of Britain, the burning of London on the model of burning of Lanka caused by Hanuman, and the reinstatement of rishis in India and Germany. These reports made the British government suspect that many Congress and other Hindu leaders might act as a fifth column at the time of crisis.

The Intelligence Bureau was of the view that the Congress was playing a double game. Anticipating victory of the axis powers they wanted to keep up the pretence of opposition to the British government and some facade of anti-British struggle. Side by side the congress wanted to avoid creating misgivings in the mind of the British rulers. When Mahadev Dev Desai, Gandhi's secretary met Tottenham, Additional Home Secretary or Laithwaite, the Viceroy's Private Secretary, he asserted that 'we don't' prevent those who want to pay for the war fund or those who want to join as recruits. When Laithwaite asked Desai: 'If you think that your propaganda does not have any effect on the war effort why pursue it', Desai replied; 'For our own existence. On the one hand there is little affect concretely on war effort and on the other if we do not exercise the right, we smother ourselves.' Mahadev Desai repeatedly complained that it was 'a libel', 'a gross and ungrateful libel' to say that the Congress was hindering War effort. In a letter dated December 2, 1940, Mr. Gandhi wrote to the Home Member of Viceroy's Council: "Duty has enjoined upon me a seemingly opposite course. I take comfort in the fact that though seemingly in the opposite camp, I work for the same end as is declared by the British Government". In reply Home Member wrote: "I am glad to know that you are only seemingly in the opposite camp and that your end is the same as ours." When copies of these and similar letters were received in the Intelligence Bureau, Dayal was not surprised about it.

As Dayal was supervising Intelligence reports from the Province, Mr. Puckle, Director General of Intelligence, discussed with him the report he had prepared on the basis of material supplied by Provincial Intelligence chiefs. He agreed with Dayal that Gandhi would initiate some token political struggle so that some of the leading Congress figures were put in jail. Dayal explained: "This will have two advantages. Firstly, if the Axis powers win, as they are expecting, they will come out of the jail with laurels, without the blemish of having fought against the Japanese. If they are out of jail they may have to pretend to do so. Secondly greatly weakened by

War as Great Britain will be, the British Empire is unlikely to survive in its present form. When the situation in Great Britain makes it incumbent upon the British Government to grant home rule or some sort of Independence to India, the Congress leaders can then claim to have made sacrifice for it and get credit for it."

Dayal added: "There is a snag in it. Previously when Mr. Gandhi thought he was doing something to bring about Hindu Muslim unity, actually that divided the two communities more and more. Now also his strategy can have the opposite effect. All his life he has managed to remain in the center of the Indian political scenario, sidelining everyone else. Now when he and other Congress leaders go to jail, Jinnah and the Muslim League will strive to occupy as much political space as possible. Jinnah will have a field day and when Gandhi comes out of jail, he will find to his consternation that Jinnah and not he is in the center of the stage and that key to India's future is no more in his hand."

What Nehru had recorded in his diary in the prison was brought to the notice of the Intelligence headquarters. Nehru had written about Gandhi in his prison diary:

"With all his great qualities he has proved a poor and weak leader, uncertain and changing his mind frequently. How many times he has changed during the last few years since the War began. It is very very sad deterioration of a very great man. The greatness remains in many ways but the sagacity and intuition of doing the right thing are no more in evidence." Nehru again wrote in his prison diary: "What I may do outside after my release, I do not know. But I must break with this woolly thinking and undignified action, which really means breaking with Gandhi. I have at present no desire even to go to see him on release and discuss matters with him. What do such discussions lead to.....I suppose I shall see him any how? On Muslim - League 1940 resolution on Pakistan, Nehru wrote on December 28, 1943: "Instinctively I think it is better to have Pakistan or almost anything if only to keep Jinnah far away and not allow his muddled and arrogant head from interfering in India's progress."

Intelligence reports about other Congress leaders showed that they were as frustrated as Jawahar Lal Nehru. The advice by the Intelligence Bureau that Quit India movement might be allowed to simmer in areas where it did not affect War effort had the benefit of preventing the emergence of revolutionary secret cells like those in Bengal earlier in the century and in the Punjab and northern India in the twenties and thirties. Reports were that Achhut Patwardhan and many other radical nationalists who partook in the Quit India movement began to believe that it was a disaster and it was totally unnecessary because Britain had no alternative but to leave India after the war. Even Gandhi felt sorry that some have "taken fancy to guerilla warfare. But I have no doubt that it will be a nine day wonder. It will have no affect."

CHAPTER TWENTY

As the belief gained ground that the British Government would inevitably have to quit India after the War, both Hindus and Muslims began to prepare, it seemed, for an Armageddon. This resulted in much additional work for Dayal and the Intelligence Bureau. Reports began to be received from the Provinces of semi-military formations coming up in the two communities financed by urban commercial classes and rich landlords. Even many Hindu and Muslim Princes of the native States were having a hand in this. In most parts of the country, over a hundred thousand branches of Rashtriya Sewak Sangh of Hindus were-having their gatherings every morning where the members were given Para-military training and indoctrination. On the same lines Muslim National Guards, Ahrars and Khaksars had been set up by the Muslims and were similarly being trained and indoctrinated. Hindu and Muslim Princes in many cases had begun to augment substantially their military resources and armed might hoping to take advantage of unsettled conditions that could possibly come about after British departure. Muslims at many places had begun to collect funds to send religious mentors to northwest tribal areas, Afghanistan and central Asia so that armed Muslim hordes could be summoned from there in the event of a civil war in India. Dayal had brought these facts to the notice of Viceroy and His Majesty's Government.

Dayal found in the files of the Intelligence Bureau of the earlier period that even though only freedom struggle had been highlighted in the Press, there was a subterranean movement of Hindu consolidation which was the main stimulus and focus of mind of the Hindus. As the freedom struggle became more and more Hindu centered, quite a large number of leaders of the nationalist movement became forerunners of Hindu revival. When separate electorate for the Muslims divided the people of India into two segments - Muslim and General - determined efforts began to be made to categorize everyone in the General category whether he followed Hindu practices or not, as a Hindu. Mr. Gandhi's fast against separate electorate for untouchable Scheduled Castes was according to some Intelligence sleuths motivated by the same desire of Hindu consolidation. Unhappy are the people who do not have a hero and more so who did not have one for many centuries. Some British Intelligence Officer had recorded that the time was ripe for Mr. M. K. Gandhi to be made into such a hero and worshipped as a Mahatma, who also made every effort to fit into this mould. The analysis of those officers was that de-secularization of freedom movement had injected communalism in every facet of national life, which could be of much use to the government.

Intelligence reports again and again mentioned increasing social breach between Hindus and Muslims. Note had been made in relevant file of Mr. Nehru's statement in his book 'Discovery of India' that "Indian nationalism is dominated by Hindus and had a Hindu look." Everyone had become narrow minded and narrow minded people are more likely to be untruthful and violent. It was held by many in the Intelligence Bureau that Hindu Muslim relations in the country were fast drifting to a vanishing point. Relations between Hindus and Muslims had already reached a point where the two communities would not trust each other while living in the same town. Where it was possible, strong iron gates and other fortifications had been erected outside localities to ward off attack by the other community. A withdrawal by leaving a vacuum was likely to unleash a civil war extending not only to hundreds of towns and villages in British India but also to one and half thousand native States pockmarking the entire subcontinent. It could result in carnage.

The Intelligence Bureau received reports of Mr. Gandhi saying that if blood bath was necessary it would come in spite of non-violence. In his note of conversation with Mr. Gandhi, Major Wyatt recorded: "He thinks that there may be blood bath in India, before her problems were solved." Lord Wavell noted that M. Gandhi seemed quite unmoved by the prospect of a civil war. Pyare Lal, Mr. Gandhi's secretary had recorded that Sardar Patel, Congress Home Minister in the interim government, thought in terms of reciprocity in the matter of communal riots in Bengal, Bihar and elsewhere.

Before the Cabinet Mission arrived in India for a solution of the Indian Home Rule problem, Dayal had prepared a report for the Viceroy and India House., London. According to feedback by Provincial units, majority of the Congress leaders were willing or half willing to accept Pakistan in a modified form. Mr. G. D. .Birla, the industrialist whom Mr. Gandhi treated like a son, had been since 1938, working behind the scene for the partition of India on communal lines, before the Muslim League adopted the Pakistan resolution. On January eleven 1938, he had proposed to Mr. Gandhi, the partition of India into two federations, one Hindu and the other Muslim. In December 1939, he recommended to Sir Stafford Cripps the division of India as the only solution of the constitutional problem. In reply to Mr. G. D. Birla's letter of July 14, 1942, arguing in favour of Pakistan, Gandhiji's secretary replied on July 16, "Bapu (Mr. Gandhi) has given it careful attention. The question is not of Pakistan or separation as such but the real contents of these conceptions {sic]". On July 20, 1942, Mr. Gandhi wrote to Fakir Nasir Khan that he was agreeable to Pakistan on certain conditions. The same year Mr. Rajagopalachari put forward a formula supporting Pakistan which many believed had the blessing of Mr. Gandhi.

While it was tactically rejected in All India Congress Committee session at Allahabad in May 1942, a majority was in favour of it.

Mr. V. P. Menon, Reforms Commissioner to the Viceroy had recorded that shortly after the Congress leaders joined Interim Government Home Minister Sardar Patel had signified his acceptance of Pakistan. There wee reports of Mr. Patel sending signals to Mr. Jinnah about division of Punjab and Bengal also on communal lines. After joining the interim government in 1946, both Prime Minister Nehru and Home Minister Patel had, according to Intelligence reports, begun to support the division of the country with the zeal of new converts. Nehru's letter to Mr. Gandhi in reply to his letter was brought to the notice of the Viceroy. It stated categorically that "this is the only answer to partition demanded by Jinnah." On March 9. two weeks before Lord Mountbatten arrived, Congress approved a resolution which envisaged a division of Punjab and Bengal.

His Majesty's Government, Mr. Dayal reported, should not expect any serious opposition to the partition of the country from Hindu and Muslim leaders, if on arrival in India Lord Mountbatten could find no other solution. There would not be any problem from Mr. Gandhi, who had been long enough in politics to make an about turn without losing his sheen as a Mahatma. On arrival in India Mountbatten found these reports had more or less correctly assessed the ground realities. His main worry was about the people of India. Mutual hostility between the two main communities had been aroused almost to the flash point by the leaders. Feeling of opposition to the division of the country among the Hindus and the need for a viable

Pakistan among the Muslims had been stirred up to hysterical frenzy. Any reasonable solution based upon the division of country was bound to leave both the communities dissatisfied and could immediately ignite a communal holocaust. Reports were that unrest among the Muslims was increasing day by day because of the general impression that the new British Labour Government was partial to the Hindus. Mr. Jinnah's letter to Mr. Winston Churchill which was brought to the notice of Viceroy had stated: "The Muslim League was progressively betrayed by the Cabinet Delegation. When the Secretary of State for India and the Viceroy finally disclose their hands, undoubtedly there can be only one result and that is general revolt against the British." The new Viceroy had therefore to keep on the process of negotiations for some months so that the minds of the people got ready for an unpleasant solution and it did not come to them as a sudden unbearable shock.

On the basis of feedback by the Intelligence Bureau and discussion with Provincial Governors and Army Commanders, Lord Wavell had conveyed to London that an immediate solution was necessary as India had become a 'running sore' and that British rule in India should demit by the middle of 1948 at the latest. He had stated that governing India by force would not be liked by British Parliament and would be unacceptable to the British public. In view of that 'some imaginative and constructive move 'needed to be taken immediately'. On February 20, 1947 the British Prime Minister announced that power would be completely transferred to Indians by June 1948, and that a new Viceroy was being appointed to effect peaceful transfer in the best manner possible.

When Lord Mountbatten took over as Viceroy in March 1947, the ghastly Calcutta slaughter had taken place, followed by the killing of Hindus in Noakhali and other eastern districts of Bengal. Soon after he arrived equally ghastly attempts were made by Muslim armed gangs in western districts of the Punjab to wipe out Sikhs and Hindus. Intelligence reports hinted at the possibility of such flare up in many other areas, if not in most parts of the country. Intelligence reports particularly mentioned such preparations in many native States with the connivance of the ruler where British control was now not possible. It was therefore felt that if power could not be transferred to a single entity, it could not be to more than two, forcing the responsible for the safety of the inhabitants of native states to one unit or the other. From the Intelligence reports it was clear that there was a possibility of communal flare up even before June 1948, the date fixed by the British Prime Minister for the transfer of power. Watching the situation worsening day by day, Lord Ismay concluded that it was electric and may go off any time. Lord Mountbatten also began to feel that the people were sitting on a time bomb or a volcano and that taking no decision would be worse than taking a wrong decision.

When Lord Mountbatten consulted the Commander-in-Chief and other Indian Army Generals, they agreed with him about the grimness of the situation. The Director General, Intelligence Bureau, asked Dayal: "Do you think Partition of India could be avoided. Not only most of us here and most likely the British Government also are of the opinion that it is madness from every point of view political, economic and strategic."

Dayal replied: "Partition is not inevcitable but these are big 'ifs' of the contemporary Indian history. Firstly, if Partition of Bengal had not been annulled in 1911 against the strong opposition by the Bengali Muslims, the demand for Pakistan might not have arisen. The position of Muslims in Bengal would have improved as markedly as that in the Punjab. In the Punjab and to some extent in Frontier and Sind also Muslims had reached in professions and education a position almost equal to that of the Hindus. In these Provinces parties hostile to the Muslim League were in power. These could stand against Mr. Jinnah's pressure to the very end till, division between Hindus and Muslims became absolute and total. Secondly, if Gandhi had not sabotaged separate electorate for scheduled castes, there would not have been any demand for Pakistan. There is unmistakable evidence that Jinnah would have readily accepted fifty-five percent caste Hindu majority in a United India."

Dayal added: "More relevant question is whether in view of total mutual mistrust and belligerence between the two communities any solution other than Partition is at present possible. I do not think so. The determination of everyone in India to whichever community he may belong from the highest to the lowest in the land, to regard the opposite religionist as devil incarnate makes any solution other than Partition out of the question. I am not sure even Gandhi and Nehru are completely free from this prejudice. They characterize Muslim League's non-acceptance of seventy-five percent Hindu majority at the centre as negation of nationalism and democracy but both of them are opposed to Hindu's in Bengal and Punjab accepting fifty-five percent Muslim majority. I also do not think that Partition of the country is a calamity or madness or an impractical proposition as is made out. After all, East Bengal had a separate existence, and the annulment of the partition of Bengal was rather a calamity for Bengali Muslims. The figures quoted by Bengal Muslim League indicate that among those studying in Bengal schools only twenty percent are Muslims even though their population in the Province is fifty-five percent and in services and professions their position is no better. As regard Punjab Maharaja Ranjit Singh's realm was mainly beyond river Beas. As Pakistan, it will be a very much bigger state with Sind, Baluchistan and large tribal areas added to it. There might be migration and transfer of population and possibly mayhem and bloodshed in some places. Alternative seems to be an unparalleled civil war throughout the country.

Dayal told the Director General: "The Home Minister has been sending for me, wanting me to find out what happened to rupees seventy thousand crores which the Indian National Army were believed to be having when they surrendered to Mountbatten at Singapore. Mr. Nehru was also in Singapore at the time of surrender. I do not know what to do in the matter. The Home Minister also desires the Intelligence Bureau to keep an eye on relations between Mr. Nehru and Lady Mountbatten. I told him that Mahatma Gandhi was as touchingly fond of her as Mr. Nehru. If he had been of the same age as Nehru he would have been a serious rival. Already the Mahatma had declared that she was born in India in her previous birth and her name was Mira."

CHAPTER TWENTY ONE

After he was separated from Lola, S. Dayal did feel lonely sometimes. Occasionally he went to Bombay on official work and met her father Robert Mathews. Mr. Mathews never invited him to his house nor did he allow him to enquire about his wife or Lola. There was a new gardener from the Public Works Department, who was living in the servants' quarters on the back side of his bungalow. As was the practice, his wife came for domestic chores. She was a buxom woman less than forty. In the evening when he was at home, she brought her teenaged daughter with her to do the chores. The girl was studying in the tenth class and was perhaps slightly older than Lola as her breasts peeping out of her low shirt were better formed These were also more seductive so much so Dayal became obsessed with breasts and when he came across a woman, he would first look at her breasts and not at her face. He became very cautious when he came to know that an Assistant in the Home Department had to marry the daughter of his washerman when he got involved with her. The way she brought her adorned daughter only in the evening whenever he was at home left him in no doubt that she was doing it purposefully. He got the gardener replaced which made him feel all the more lonely.

He could think of no other women except Rosy Bannerji, the daughter of his Office Superintendent Mr. Victor Bannerji. From a stenographer she had become a Senior Personal Assistant, working with a British Deputy Secretary. She quite often came in the evening to take her father home. Their eyes met sometimes and she never missed an opportunity to wish him. He rang her up one day and invited her to dinner in a Connaught Place restaurant. She declined the invitation for dinner but said he could meet her at 6 p.m. at Army and Navy Store in the Regal Building.

When he reached Army and Navy Store at five minutes to six, Rosy was already there leisurely moving in front of counters. They greeted each other and moved out. He held her hand and helped her to cross the road to the inner circle. He talked appreciatively about her father's efficiency and devotion to duty. He remarked: "The files put up by him are meticulously referenced with various slips. The day I joined office I got confused by slips like PUC, DFA and others pinned to the top of papers in the tile. For a day or two I wondered what it could mean. Then I sent for Mr. Bannerji, bribed him with a cup of tea and biscuits and requested him to explain to me what these slips meant. I could not restrain my laughter when he told me that it meant' Papers under consideration' Draft for approval', etc. Mr. Bannerji has been in the Intelligence Bureau for almost three decades and has virtually become indispensable." By then they had reached Wenger's Corner in the inner circle of the Connaught Place. He bought some pastries, patties and other snacks from Wengers Confectioners and suggested: "Let us go home. I have told the cook that I will dine out and that he can have off."

He parked his car in the porch of his house as near the entrance door as possible and they moved in. They chatted leisurely and enjoyed nibbling tidbits they had brought. He enquired about her sisters. He knew that all of them had married non-Christians and two of them a non-Bengali against the wishes of the father. She said that they were more or less happy with children and write to her regularly. Dayal asked her:

"When are you going to disappoint your father?" No, never, he will have heart attack if I follow my sisters", she said with a smile.

The curtains were already drawn. He went and bolted the two drawing room doors from inside. She was waiting for him to take her in his arms. He had always felt that more than seventy percent of sex was above neck and just below it. Both relished it. Her eyes began to twinkle like stars and her brownish face acquired the sheen of gold. Positioning her on her back on the sofa, he cheerfully remarked: "This sari is the greatest invention of our Kam Sutra civilization. One can share happiness with a woman without actually undressing her." There were drops of blood. He laughed and whispered: "I could not have imagined that you would be a virgin at thirty." "I am thirty eight my dear", she cooed sweetly. "So much the better", Dayal murmured. After they had been caressing each other for a while she suddenly made effort to get up and said softly: "I am getting very late,"

As she stood up and gazed at the stain on the sofa, Dayal remarked: "Do not worry about it it is synthetic leather. What' about your sari?" he asked. Reassuring him, she replied: "It is crimson in colour. My father does not wear glasses after dinner. I have told him that I will be late in office and not to wait for me for dinner."

She put her arm around him again and remarked with a smile "You are a tiger." He kissed her cheeks and whispered in her ear: "Thank you for this happiness. This is much more than I ever had from Lola. She was always in a hurry. She was like grapes and not even grape juice and you are heady like wine. Why not stay here for the night? She clasped his hand firmly and said: "I will never be able to stay here for the night except on rare occasions when it can be possible to pretend being on tour. I do not want to upset my father in any manner." He entreated: "Let us meet daily for a few times and then once a week." Rosy replied: "No, it can be at the most once a month. A prohibited deed has to be done carefully and intelligently. Gossip is the most ubiquitous mill in this country and I do not want to provide grist to it."

She tidied up her dress and got ready to leave. She kissed him as they went out and whispered: "AII the time I knew you would call me up one day." Dayal took her in his car to a point quite near her home. On return he made a cup of coffee and finished the remaining snacks. He had never before felt so hungry for everything in life.

After that Rosy Bannerji did not come to take her father home. Whenever they passed by each other, she would lower her head or look the other side.

During those days a British I.P.S. Officer from Bengal, one Mr. Maurice Cornforth, joined the Intelligence Bureau as another Joint Director. He was of medium height, cold and matter of fact type. His assignment was to appoint, guide and motivate agents who would help in pushing up recruitment to Army in various parts of India, particularly in the Punjab, Frontier Province and Western United Provinces.

Mr. Cornforth was a very clever and disagreeable person, but tried to cover this up with simulated politeness. Soon there would be scowl on his face as he talked in his harsh manner. There was a sneering trait in his character and he hardly looked straight at anything. He rather took pride in thinking differently from others and more brutally he expressed his adverse opinion the happier he felt. Unlike most other Scots he had raven hair. He was meticulously dressed and talked in a loud voice. Soon Dayal discovered that the best course would be to listen to his eccentricities patiently without betraying any reaction to them.

Mr. Cornforth had an extraordinarily good understanding of the Indian situation. When he came to know that Subash Chandra Bose, a Bengali radical Congressman antipathetic to Gandhi, was planning to go to Germany via Afghanistan, he made sure that the Intelligence Bureau was completely nonchalant to it, so that he did not get cautioned and changed his mind. He felt that his going away would prevent him from creating any mischief in India. More than that, his becoming Germany's and Japan's showman for war against British India would make Gandhi less enthusiastic about Axis victory. Mr. Cornforth firmly believed that from the very beginning of British presence in India annexations of Indian domains and taking over of any territory under direct British rule should have been forbidden. The interdiction against annexations after Mutiny should have been there from the very beginning ever since the days of Clive. In that case there would have been more than two thousand self-governing native States under indirect British rule. Residents and his British officered troops, paid for by the native States would prevent tyrannical and plunderous rule under the overall guidance of a Viceroy in Calcutta. Thus governing India would not have cost the British exchequer anything and at the same time we would be ruling over a vast empire. The various native rulers would not have an army of their own, ensuring that there were no more aggressions, internecine wars or extension of territories. The Khyber, Golan and other passes in the West should have been walled up so that invasions or raids from the West were made difficult. We should not have introduced railways, hospitals, modern education, modern machinery or English language. Internal peace and freedom from raiders from central Asia would have brought about prosperity and created a good market for machine made, cheaper and better British goods. The native people would have continued to live as they had lived for centuries, only a little better and more peaceful life.

Mr. Cornforth was a bachelor. He claimed to be a celibate, which appeared to be true because of his skeptical stance towards marriage and sexuality. He held that God, while blessing man with a thinking brain and a mind, had also cursed him with unbounded and unrestricted sexual disposition. The result was that the main thinking man did was about sex, which dominated his art, literature and even day to day conversation. He believed that human race would never advance to next level of evolution unless some asexual method of procreation got developed or at least till man acquired biological clock of seasonal sex like other animals. He held that India was world's most sex obsessed country.

One evening, when Dayal returned home, after a harangue by Mr. Cornforth, there was a telephone call from Rosy Bannerji. After a short, polite tête-à-tête he put down the receiver. Then he regretfully recollected

133

that it was exactly a month since they had met. After that whenever he rang her up, she would put down the receiver on recognizing his voice.

CHAPTER TWENTY TWO

Communal tension kept escalating in Amritsar as elsewhere in the country except that in this city a major confrontation between the two communities was kept at bay through the intervention of some well-meaning citizens. The Muslim League declared that Muslims in the country should observe March 23, 1945, as Pakistan day. The Muslim League in Amritsar took out a procession on this occasion. It appeared that almost the entire Muslim population of Amritsar, men, women and young boys and girls had come out to join it. There had never been such a big procession in the history of Amritsar city. Suddenly a rumour gained currency that the procession intended to pass through the streets inhabited by the Hindus. Thousands of armed Hindus gathered in Chowk Chabutra and adjoining streets to block their way. Barkut Ullah, Asad Ullah's son gathered his socialist colleagues, informed Hira Singh, Dr. Saifuddin Kitchlu and others about the likely confrontation between the two communities. Passing through some alleys and by-lanes they reached the two hundred yards of buffer area between the Muslim and Hindu groups. Maulana Asad Ullah who was leading the procession of the Muslims told Dr. Saifuddin Kitchlu that they earlier had not the least intention to pass near the Hindu areas but now that they had been challenged they would do so. After much effort it was possible to persuade those leading the procession of the Muslims to proceed along the route they earlier intended to follow. When the Hindus were informed about it they refused to disperse saying that it was a subterfuge. The peace loving people kept standing there till the mile long procession of the Muslims had passed through the road west of Jalianwala bagh away from the Hindu dominated areas. After that, a majority of Hindus gathered there, went back brandishing weapons and raising slogans as if it was a victory parade.

Between Pakistan Day observed by the Muslim League in 1945 and their Direct Action Day in 1946, there were a few localized skirmishes between Hindus and Muslims in the Amritsar city but no major communal conflagration as was happening in many parts of the country. Peace Committees consisting of small influential groups had come up in many

135

areas. These were useful in thwarting the attempt to foment or to spread communal riots but were ineffective in instilling mutual confidence or in mitigating hatred between the communities which was spreading by leaps and bounds in the city as elsewhere in the country.

As Mahatma Gandhi cast himself in the role of sole and supreme champion of patriotism and nationalism, painting everyone else as anti-national, the Muslims became increasingly hostile to him and his demands. Hira Singh and many others who came to the dwakhana in the afternoon often concluded after discussion that this could be avoided if Congress could understand that democracy was tolerance, if not respect for the other point of view. The more Jinnah was demonized, the more Muslims flocked around him.

In 1947 gangs of armed retired Muslim army personnel began to move about in Rawalpindi and other western districts of the Punjab to cleanse those areas of Sikhs. As there were many mixed Hindu and Sikh families a large number of Hindus also were killed. Even from the standard of the Punjab where communal riots had been endemic, these massacres were unprecedented. Though more than half the Hindus and Sikhs in these areas were protected by their Muslim fellow villagers or helped to move out to safe places, this did not prevent terror from spreading to other areas. Hindus and Sikhs living in other districts of western Punjab and in Frontier Province and Baluchistan began to move out. Most of them migrated to Amritsar waiting for things to settle down. In a month or so the population of Amritsar rose from less than one hundred thousand to over three hundred thousand. They had left behind all their belongings hoping that they would go back when things calmed down. They became desperate when division of the country and the creation of Pakistan began to be considered seriously.

By the beginning of May, it was clear that the Congress and Muslim League leaders were inclined to accept the division of the country in which case there would be division of Punjab also. Everyone was sure that Amritsar will stay in India. This sense of safety did not lessen the desolation and desperation of those who had migrated here. Muslims living in Amritsar who previously constituted almost half the population of the city were now a vulnerable minority Their nervousness and sense of insecurity went on increasing by leaps and bounds as Hindus and Sikhs from west Punjab and Frontier began to pour into the city like a flood. All the schools, colleges and public places even of the Muslims had been occupied by the new comers. Thousands of tents and sheds had come up in parks, gardens and all other open areas in the city and the civil lines. The face and mind of the city had changed altogether. There were many areas and lanes inhabited by the Muslims in the exterior parts of the city within its rampart. Many Muslims living in these areas felt insecure, locked their houses and shifted to a dozen suburban colonies of Muslims. There the fortifications were further reinforced and more arms were collected for defense .Some of the Muslims there began to shift with bag and baggage to relatives and friends in western districts of the Punjab. This further increased the sense of insecurity among Muslims. There was consternation among the Amritsar Muslims as some Hindus and Sikhs from western Punjab and Frontier began to break locks and move into houses from which the Muslims had shifted.

Mohammed Munir came to see Iqbal Kaur, the Sikh girl whose part-time tutor he used to be and with whom he had fallen in love. He had then kept unshorn hair and beard and had begun to wear a turban like a Sikh. He knew that Iqbal Kaur's mother went to Golden Temple every morning at daybreak and returned at near about 9 a.m. He had therefore come to see Iqbal Kaur at 8 a. m. She received him in the porch somewhat indifferently. Instead of inviting him to the drawing room, she requested him to have a chair. She dragged another and sat down. opposite him at a distance of a few feet.

Mohammed Munir was wearing a dark suit and a tie and was holding a felt hat, which he placed on the ground near the chair. His beard and moustache were now short and nicely trimmed. He looked a person quite different from the one in Indian dress who was a reader in local Islamia College. He noticed that Iqbal Kaur looked slimmer and was unfeeling and statuesque. He had his eye fixed on her. She had lowered her eyes raising these once or twice avoiding meeting his eyes. Mohammed Munir's lips were shivering as if making up his mind how to come out with what he intended to say.

Iqbal Kaur broke the ice: "It is more or less four years since you left Amritsar. Have you not been coming here at least to see your mother?"

"Very rarely", he muttered. Raising his voice a little he explained: "Soon after I joined Government College in Rawalpindi, the Punjab Government decided to constitute a Provincial Education Service on the lines of the Indian Education Service. As I had been appointed a Professor, I was given the senior grade on a salary more than ten times I was getting in Amritsar. It was a bonanza which I was sure to lose if the Government came to know that I had any contact, whatsoever, with my mother and younger brother who had been to jail for anti-government activities." After a pause he added: "When the War ended, I began to plan going to England for higher studies in Mathematics, for which facilities were not available in this country. Dr. Taseer suggested that I should prefer Cambridge University, where he had studied. He gave me a letter for the Dean there. It took much time and labour to prepare synopsis for three projects, for which material was not available at Rawalpindi or at Lahore. I was keen to send synopsis for more than one project so that a single project did not get summarily rejected. Last year I submitted my application with the three projects, my biodata with letter from Dr. Taseer. Early this year the Cambridge University informed me that they were ready to admit me on the basis of the first project for which I had indicated preference. I wrote back thanking them and requesting them for some stipend so that I could support myself. I was informed that I would get a bursary on admission to Tripos. As their mathematics faculty was short of suitable junior staff, I would get some allowance if I could do about a dozen hours of teaching per week. I have to join there on October 1 and will be sailing from Karachi on September 12." "It is very good" Iqbal Kaur smiled and remarked: "So you have come to say good bye to your mother".

Mohammed Munir cut in: "I will presently tell you the purpose of my coming here. As regards my mother you know the position of Muslims in this city has become most insecure. With lakhs of Hindu and Sikhs from west Punjab having taken refuge here, there is every possibility of partial or whole scale massacre of the local Muslims any day. My mother, therefore, wants to shift temporarily to her mother in a village near Jullunder which, like the neighbouring villages there, has exclusive Muslim population. Her Pathan husband is reaching here much before dawn tomorrow morning and they will leave for Jullunder before day break otherwise it may not be safe. She has written to me that unless I reach in time to take my wife and children to Rawalpindi they will accompany her to Jullunder. I am taking them to Rawalpindi tomorrow morning by Frontier Mail. I have told my mother that the way most of the Hindus and Sikhs in west Punjab are packing and leaving their hearth and home, the situation in other towns in east Punjab may become similar to that in Amritsar and that she better come with me. As my younger brother has refused to leave Amritsar, she does not want to shift to west Punjab."

Iqbal Kaur said in a feeble and sad voice: "What I see around leaves me flabbergasted. I am completely stunned. I find this deluge of hatred unbearable. Amritsar has become a city quite different from the one in which I was born.

Mohammed Munir's tone was sadder: "I shiver when I think of the shape things are likely to take when partition of country actually materializes. To me it bodes very ill. I am already feeling suffocated." He closed eyes for a few second and then looking at Iqbal Kaur suppliantly added: "Let me tell you in confidence that I do not propose to return to Pakistan after completing my Tripos at Cambridge and will settle down in England. I am not taking my wife with me and am leaving her in Rawalpindi."

"Why should you be so unfair to your wife and children?" Iqbal Kaur admonished him.

"I will give them a life very much better than they have in Amritsar. I have bought a house in Rawalpindi from a Sikh colleague who has opted for India and has been posted to Government College, Ludhiana. This is a local family which built this palatial house in 1934 at a cost of Rs. 1,800 and he has refused to charge me anything more. Even if my wife gives half the house on rent she will have enough to live comfortably. More than that the Education Department has sanctioned me study leave for two years and I will get half my salary all of which will be available to her. When I finally divorce her; I will have no regrets and she will surely not resent it because we have not shared a bed since I fell in love with you."

Iqbal Kaur sat tight-lipped, motionless with her hands on knees as if she was indifferent to what he had spelled out. Failing to gauge her reaction, Mohammed Munir looked at her blandly for a little while then affirmed: "You know,' I love you. All these years my hungry soul has been thirsting to blend with yours. I solemnly assure you this places you under no obligation. I am not prostrating before you though sometimes I feel strong urge to do so. I want to touch your beautiful hand but be sure I will restrain myself from doing it. All this does not prevent me from thinking of what is good for you and of suggesting it to you. However, I want you to take the decision coolly, only thinking of what is best in your own interest. I have come to suggest to you that, without the slightest obligation or commitment on your part, you come along with me to Rawalpindi and then move with me to England where you will be entirely free to decide where and what to study and how and where to live. Of course, I will help you financially as long as you need. Even though I do not want it, you can take all that as loan. After becoming a British citizen I will decide whether to become Nanak Singh or remain Mohammed Munir, but you will be quite free to remain unconcerned with this. For the two months you will be in Rawalpindi, I have arranged your stay with Saulat Rehman who has been your class fellow at Kannaird Girls College, Lahore. She told me that she had occasionally been corresponding with you and had written to you after she became lecturer in the Rawalpindi Government College. In Pakistan you will become from Iqbal Kaur to Iqbal which name will easily pass as that of a Muslim. There surely will be no nikah but necessarily you will go to England on a Pakistan passport as my wife, which becomes irrelevant when you reach England. There you will be free to choose your own life and use the name Iqbal Kaur which is on all your certificates and college testimonials. If you do not want to settle in England after completing your education, it will not be difficult for you to have an Indian passport as you were born in Amritsar, India."

Mohammed Munir uttered all this in one breath. He stared at her to watch her reaction. Iqbal Kaur continued to sit tight-lipped, motionless, with hands on knees. Once or twice she became thoughtful but soon relapsed into unconcern. Mohammed Munir's voice was entreating when he started speaking again: "All religions degrade women. After the Partition of the country, there will be greater bigotry and religiosity in both the countries, both men and women will be worse of, women more than men. I have made you an offer. If you want, you can choose a life of freedom not only from the narrow minded world of communal hatred but also from the drudgery of a house wife. Communal fanaticism is like a ball of snow. It has been set rolling, has been gathering more and more of snow and has already become an avalanche. God alone knows what dimension this will take after Partition of the country. The freedom we are getting is going to be devoid of liberty, enlightenment and fellow-feeling. In our country even the wisest are not wise enough." Mohammed Munir became silent again and after clearing his throat he added: "I have booked my and my family's seats in the General second class compartment and for you in the ladies second class compartment. On reaching Rawalpindi railway station, I will first take you to Saulat Rehman's residence and then go home with my family. The Frontier Mail steams off the station at 8 a.m. I will wait for you at the station at 7.30 a.m. If you choose not to come I will cancel your seat."

After saying all this in one breath, Mohammed Munir felt somewhat relieved. He sank into silence, sometimes fixing IiWo!t eyes on her. Abruptly she tilted her head backwards staring at the roof. After a while she bent her head, rubbing the forehead with right hand. As she sat straight, her eyes had a glint and her right hand had tightened into a fist. She shook her head as if trying to shake a storm there. Suddenly she again became cold and her cold eyes sank deeper. Mohammed Munir felt deep compassion for her. He said very calmly: "I have placed all the cards before you. Do as you think best for you, not only today, but also tomorrow and day after."

All of a sudden she no more had a look of uncertainty. She seemed to be thinking hard to make up her mind and her eyes were no more ambivalent. She rubbed the tip of her nose which had become red. "Is it sure that I will not have to stay with you either in Rawalpindi or in England." She asked emphatically.

Mohammed Munir replied calmly: "I have told you that on reaching Rawalpindi I will first take you to Saulat Rahman's residence before I take my family home. There is no doubt that immediately you step out the ship in England you will have absolute freedom to decide about yourself."

She got up, went inside the house and came back holding the Sikh book of prayers. She calmly sat down. Placing the Sikh breviary in her lap she prayed with folded hands and then lifting it, opened it at random. She looked at the first verse on the left page and smiled. "After some silence she asked: "I have my own personal savings and some personal jewelry. Can I start meeting my own expenditure from the very beginning, from Amritsar railway station onwards?"

Mohammed Munir picked up his hat and before he stood up he said that he would agree to it if that helped her to come to a decision. As he turned to leave, he said:

"I look forward to meeting you tomorrow at 7.30 a.m. at the railway station."

CHAPTER TWENTY THREE

Ram LaI Gauba, along with his Muslim son A. L. Gauba, came to the dwakhana. A. L. Gauba did not want to migrate to Pakistan. Both of them were wondering how and where he could stay till things settled down. There was no doubt that even after the formation of Pakistan, hundreds of thousands of Muslims would continue to live in India. Various alternatives were examined. Ram Lal had some Muslim clients in Delhi whose property suites he had pursued in the Lahore High Court the jurisdiction of which then extended up to Delhi. It was agreed that he should write to those clients if they could help in the matter. It was felt that Delhi will always remain free from communal riots of the type which were prevalent elsewhere. Ram Lal wrote to three of them who were well off. One of them. Hajji Barkat Ali, a Sadar Bazar merchant, replied back immediately welcoming his son and stating that Bara Hindu Rao the area in which he lived had hundred per cent Muslim population and was the safest in Delhi. Next day A.L Gauba left for Delhi.

Suddenly Hindus and Sikhs in western Punjab and Muslims in the eastern districts of the Punjab started packing and leaving their ancient home for the other side. In the western Punjab it was first from the districts sure to be included in Pakistan and later from the other districts of central Punjab. It was as though some frenzy, an overpowering furor, a terrifying cataclysm, some great upsurge had suddenly seized the entire region. A section of the society was leaving for good its ancient home, at some places without ill-will, at others under the threat of death for avenging unknown coreligionists killed elsewhere. Revenge can sometimes be a delight and a glory. Where the persons belonging to the minority community in a particular area were in sizeable numbers, they gathered together, packed their bullock and other carts, loaded their cattle, carts, cycles, etc. with possessions they found possible to carry and started marching towards the border. In-many cases such processions were miles long. In cities they took refuge in schools, colleges and places of religious worship, wherever they could defend themselves and wait till rescued. Danger lurked everywhere and was oppressive and pitiless. Not that death was everywhere on the rampage. If at one placed Hindus and Sikhs were tied around a haystack and set on fire, at many more places they were hidden in haystacks and barns to rescue them till they could leave safely. There was looting and killing at scores of places but not many attempts at a general massacre. There also echoed among the common people a voice of friendliness and neighbourliness, a human voice side by side with the mayhem which was more eye-catching.

Communal frenzy was worst in the Amritsar city, because many of the over two hundred thousand Hindus and Sikhs from western Punjab who were sheltering there had lost their all and many also kith and kin. There was more bitterness among the Sikhs and Hindus from Rawalpindi who had come here in March after the massacre by Muslim retired army personnel. They had left everything behind in the hope of going back and were now very frustrated. Communal hatred can be a devouring flame. They were determined to kill and loot the Muslims in the city, who had all shifted to the fortified colonies in the suburb. Old residents were now much outnumbered but were making every effort so that the Muslims were able to leave peacefully and safely. It became known that thousands of armed refugees were planning to attack Sharifpura, the largest and the most prosperous among the suburban Muslim colonies. Sardar Gurdit Singh did his best to prevent Hira Singh to join those who were to go there to persuade the refugees from Pakistan to let these Muslims leave' peacefully and then take over their property. Gurdit Singh personally went to Chheharta about six miles from the city on the road to Lahore. He met the Border Security Force officers overseeing there a transit camp for Muslims and urged upon them to come to the rescue of Muslims in the suburbs of the city before midnight. They came with a part of their army unit just after 10 p.m. and evacuated to Chheharta Muslims livings in these colonies. Next day there was bitter fight among refugees from west Punjab to occupy the vacated houses and to grab the property there.

Letter received from A.L.Gauba was very disquieting. In a scribbled note he had written: "The situation in Delhi is much worse than that in Amritsar. Muslims are much more scared here. I moved out only on the first day of my arrival here, went to the local courts, Chandni Chowk and nearby places and was advised not to do so again. The entire surrounding areas are full of rustic Hindus and Sikhs from west Punjab. They have occupied every nook and corner, all foot paths and every public place. It is very unsafe moving out of Muslim localities. Muslims living in areas of mixed population have moved to exclusive Muslim localities. Our house here has also three such families, in addition to mine and Hajji Sahib's own. We cannot sleep at night, because of fear of an attack any time and have to be on the watch. Many Muslims have been arrested on flimsy grounds and let off only when they agreed to move to Purana Qila where a camp has been set up for Muslims intending to migrate to Pakistan. Most of the telephones in this area, including ours, have been disconnected. Hajji Sahib has written to Janab Rafi Ahmed Qidwai and if the telephone is restored I will talk to Dayal, otherwise I will write to him. One is not sure about letters. None comes to collect letters in the postal boxes in our area and it is not free from risk to go outside to post letters."

At Amritsar, after all the Muslims were cleared out of the city, attack on Muslim convoys and trains going to Pakistan increased, till these were fully protected by personnel of the Border Security Force. The thirst for revenge of many Hindu and Sikh refugees remained unquenched. Soon they started quarrelling about the distribution of spoils. Persons who could occupy shops vacated by the Muslims were doing business better than they did in their small villages, to the envy of others. Those who had occupied commodious houses of Muslims resisted sharing extra space with other refugees. Few wanted to share what they had grabbed. Schools at various levels had been set up for refugee boys and girls in various areas. Books in Urdu were set on fire. This was the medium of instruction in Punjab schools before Partition. The other language which used to be taught in schools was Punjabi in Gurmukhi script.

Suddenly there was procession in the city of Hindus both refugees and others, which had placards and were raising slogans that Hindus should refuse to study Punjabi as their mother tongue was Hindi. The slogans were in Punjabi because Hindu refugees from Pakistan had never read or spoken Hindi or Shastri as they called it. This created insipient tension between Hindus and Sikhs and there were a few cases of exchange of blows. Men of good will were many and they calmed down the rival groups. The problem did not become critical because the refugees' immediate concern at that moment was problem of Livelihood.

When Gurdit Singh became aware of it he commented that religion must necessarily divide people, but Hindus and Sikhs should better wait for the present wounds to heal before they started inflicting new ones on themselves. He told Hira Singh: "Only religion and politics divide the people, while everything else is the same and is shared by all. Everyone is lamenting about the barbarity of the other community. I look at it differently. I remember you once old me how Christians and Muslims wiped out the other community in one fell sweep in Eastern Europe after the defeat of Ottoman Turks in the First World War. Just think in the Punjab more or less two million people are crossing the borders safely one way or the other, most of them with much of their wherewithal. Number of those killed may just be more than double the number killed during four days of riots in Calcutta in 1946. I remember you told me a story about Eastern Europe after the First World War. Once, a Christian Slav met a Muslim going on the same side on a road, which passed through a thickly wooded area and was particularly dangerous. They had not known each other previously but thought it safe to travel together. The Muslim was obviously a peace loving family man. On the way they offered each other tobacco and chatted in friendly fashion. Traveling through the wilds the men grew close to each other. The road skirted a little stream where they enjoyed together the fresh coolness of the brook and shared whatever Tiffin they had. From here their journey' parted. As he shook hands with him and was about to take his way, the Slave took out his revolver and shot the Muslim dead. He thought, he would otherwise be cursed by everyone of his community for sparing the life of a Muslim. In the Punjab such an attitude is unthinkable. "

Gurdit Singh remained lost in thought for a while and continued: "Last night I saw in a dream both Gandhi and Jinnah. Between them lay an abyss of blood and hatred. I asked Gandhi you wanted to make omelet without breaking the egg. Before you took over as the most important leader of the Congress in 1922, Hindus and Muslims had no enmity. Social separateness which existed in a section of the upper strata was without hatred and hostility. After you took over reins of the Congress, there were more and more Hindu Muslim riots which increased in virulence year by year till inter-communal hatred became a devouring flame. Tell me how it all happened. Gandhi pointed his finger at Mr. Jinnah." Gurdit Singh took a sigh and added: "Then I reminded Jinnah of his speech recommending secularism for Pakistan and assuring safety for all non-Muslims there. I told him 'you are learning traffic rules after the accident. You were a paragon of nationalism in 1913 when a hall in Bombay Congress building was named

145

after you. It was a unique honour never before conferred by the people on their leader. Then you became a demon, an evil incarnate and a monster of negativism. Tell me how all this happened?' Jinnah pointed his finger at Gandhi and said that this little man cast a very long dark shadow over events. Both of them had their fingers pointing at each other with eyebrows knit, when I awoke from my dream."

Hira Singh kept silent for sometime and said slowly and thoughtfully: "Our's has been a great friendship, a friendship full of contradictions and irreconcilable differences. Intellectually we are completely different persons but this does not even slightly harm our friendship because both of us believe in a common truth and common human values which we continually test on the touchstone of human life. We know that a man can regard himself as truthful only when those who differ from him regard him as truthful. Both of us have believed that truth is not a parrot put in a cage to repeat whatever we fancy to be true and that the acid test of truth and morality is the attitude you adopt towards those who differ with you."

Both kept silent for sometime looking at each other. Hira Singh informed Gurdit Singh: "Barkat Ullah one of the few Muslims left in the town has been killed. He tried to prevent the burning of Urdu books mainly poetical works. Young men in the anti-Punjabi procession urging upon Hindus not to make their children study Punjabi, attacked him when he tried to pick up some Urdu books after a Hindu Pathan saved a copy of Koran by a leap through fire. That Hindu Pathan also rescued a bundle of papers in Barkat Ullah pocket containing poems. When I came to know about it I arranged Barkat Ullah's burial with the help of that Pathan who could recite Namaz-e-Janaza, the Muslim funeral prayer. "

Gurdit Singh felt very sad about it. Hira Singh deliberated: "Freedom is not rabble-rousing passion. It requires self-control and circumspection. Only then it can be mother of a better future. Otherwise freedom would become fountain-head of regression and oppression. If in any country someone is declared a superman, he not only becomes smaller in that attempt but also makes others still smaller. Germany was free and it elected Hitler in a free election. In India we are prone to similar hero worship. We know from our experience of the last few decades that a charismatic leader would not like anyone to disobey him and therefore to think freely. Difference of opinion is one crime which a supreme leader cannot forgive. In such a climate the human heart can find pleasure only in returning evil by evil. I have been wondering what would be the force that will bring about change. It is now an altogether different city, new people and a new country. Something new is taking birth in me and giving me a new strength. Never before had I such an urge to serve people and to lift them out of their sloth and subservience, out of their present atmosphere of hate and greed. Real love of the country and its people consists in attempting the renewal of the present thus making better the time to come."

Gurdit Singh held Hira Singh's hand and said with the warmth of old friendship: "I have often chided you of being an equatorial African praying for snow, of wanting to roll up the sky so that paradise descends on earth. Freedom, commonweal and goodness are not easy to achieve. The process through which these and other values will get ingrained in human nature and society will be a very long one. This is the lesson of history. Despite millenniums of evolution man yet remains essentially small. Every man however eminent and renowned he may be, is essentially small. It is a long uphill march before all men become fully humane and society completely just and benevolent. We need today more men who want to become better than others and who want to make the next generation better than the present one. Without that talking of non-violence will only generate violence and talking of love will only tear the people apart."

CHAPTER TWENTY FOUR

Ram The banquet hall of the Viceregal Lodge was reverberating with chitchat of over a hundred British officers who had trooped in an hour ago for an audience with the Viceroy. They were to entrain for Bombay next day on way to their home in Great Britain. Divided into several big and small groups they were having vivacious exchange of views on their years in India and about their own and India's future. In the cocktail of their conversation on diverse subjects and varied reminiscences there was much mood swing from euphoria to melancholy and from talk-big to sheer talkativeness.

This cacophony of high 'pitched to low toned sounds was occasionally intermingled with distant staccato of dusk-time howl of half a dozen terriers which had come to New Delhi with Lord Mountbatten.   .

All of them were Indian Civil Service, Indian Police Service and British Indian Army officers from the Punjab, Frontier Province and Upper Sind. They were directed to hand over charge to their Indian or Pakistani counterpart a few days before the transfer of power ·and move to Simla, the summer capital of the Government of India which was more or less free from the communal disturbances ravaging the whole of northern India. Two Gorkha platoons had been billeted there for their safety. Two days ago a train carrying the Muslim staff of the Simla Viceregal Lodge was stopped half way near Ambala and all of them were butchered. The British officers in charge of the Gorkha platoons did not agree to their making the journey to Delhi at night or by train. Even during the day travel was not uneventful.

After they had come down to the foot hills, S. Dayal, Deputy Director,

148

Intelligence Bureau joined them. His police transport vehicle with a dozen fully armed Sikh constables, was equipped with machine-guns, wireless sets, etc., to ensure their safe journey to Delhi. He had arranged a repast for them in the Panjore Garden of the Mughal period which the road to Delhi skirted. There was surfeit of sandwiches, buttered toasts, omelet and cutlets. They were not only to have their fill but also to pack the leftovers for the journey because they were not to stop before reaching the Viceregal Lodge in New Delhi, where an audience with the Viceroy and dinner had been arranged for them.

When Dayal found that the British Officers were relishing the refreshments served in that garden guest house, he informed them that these victuals had been prepared by the policemen who had come with him. He told them: "All the cooks, bearers and gardeners at that place belonged to the Muslim community and have migrated to Pakistan that is why this beautiful garden is in such a God forsaken state. I have come here after a few months. When I arrived here this morning, the place reminded me of a young comely girl who had become a widow."

One of the military officers asked: "Did they get murdered near Ambala as was the case with Muslims belonging to the Simla Viceregal staff."

Hindu Manager of the guest house replied: "No, over a dozen Hindus and Sikhs working in the nearby canal department of Punjab government, are escorting them to the border. They are avoiding the main road to Pakistan via Amritsar and are taking the longer route along the Himalayan foot hills. They would help them to cross over to Pakistan somewhere north of Gurdaspur." An Officer who was Deputy Commissioner of Ludhiana in East Punjab said that in his and the adjoining districts also the Sikh villagers escorted their Muslim fellow villagers safely to the border. They needed no threats to leave their homes when it became evident to them that transfer of population was inevitable.

One of officers remarked that it is incredible that none of the Indian leaders; Hindu or Muslim could foresee this, knowing fully well that Hindu Muslim relations throughout the country had reached zero point. Most of the towns and settlements had become battle grounds with Hindus and Muslims living in separate fortified areas.

A Military Officer remarked: "Men never do evil so completely and with a feeling of righteousness as when they do this with religious convictions".

Another officer said in a bass voice: "I have often wondered why the Indian leaders could not comprehend that what they were saying and doing would inexorably lead to the present imbroglio.

Another officer uttered with a cackle: "To me Gandhi's philosophy appears to be , like a swinging rope: You can move as fast as you want, without going anywhere".

What surprised Dayal was the belief among all of them that the present communal massacres have been minimal because of the British presence and that British rule in India had been for India's good. Another belief held by them surprised Dayal more. Almost all of them believed that because of caste stratification and social injustice deep-rooted in India, democracy might turn to be sham and after becoming independent Indians might have less freedom and justice than before.

They got ready to move. They climbed into the four military vehicles. One Gorkha squad in a jeep was in the front and another at the end of the convoy. The police bus with Mr. Dayal and armed constabulary was leading the convoy. There were road blocks at a few places which the Gorkha soldiers and the constables cleared in no time. In a road side farm they saw a Persian wheel turning out fresh water from a deep well where they stopped for a while for refreshments. It was nightfall when they arrived at the Viceregal Lodge. They got down and had waited for a while when the A. D. C. came and guided them to the banquet hall. Ennui and fatigue were written large on their face. After drinks were served they felt a little better.

During their stay together at Simla, the journey down to Delhi and in the animated chitchat in the banquet hall, they had reflected over all they had gone through sometimes thoughtfully and at others cursorily and casually. They had discussed their own past and future and of the country to which they had given the best part of their life. The present and the future were uncertain in their case and appeared much more uncertain for India and Pakistan. An officer with a broad flat face and short moustaches, remarked: "What is happening is horrible and most ghastly. I am thinking if this can happen after the British Government have solved the Indian predicament in one and the only manner it could be done, what would have happened if we had pulled out of India without any settlement, as Gandhi had repeatedly demanded. Revenge is an overpowering and consuming fire. It flares up and bums away every other thought and emotion." After a short

150

pause he added: "There is no limit to human stupidity and depravity, as is shown by what happened in Poland after First World War. The Versailles Treaty which created Polish State included within its eastern boundary more than ten million Lithuanians, Ukrainians and other non-Catholics. Their persecution, expulsion, extermination and expulsion went on for more than a decade.

An I. C.S. officer, who was a tripos from Cambridge, whose, wide-open 'eyes gave him a serious look, said: "In India there'" is "ample' evidence" of unbroken succession of gory massacres, of wiping out of whole communities, particularly the entire male population of the conquered principalities and tribes. The seraglios of many kings and their princes in ancient India, consisting mainly of women of the conquered tribes, resembled large townships. Mahabharata describes how sage Parasurama rid the whole earth of Kshatriyas in the course of twenty one expeditions against 'them.' Later Sudra king Nanda carried out similar exterminations, so much so that the Puranas lamented that all future kings would be Shudras." Another officer butted in: "It was the traditional duty of Hindu monarchs to perform ashvamedha yagna. A ceremonial horse was "set free t6 wander about. The territory through which the horse passed was attacked and conquered. This was done again and again because the Puranas had ordained that any mortal king who performed one hundred ashvamedha yagnas would become supreme and immortal like god Indra."

"I do not agree with this juggling with this history" another officer sitting near the wall remarked: "All I know is that we are not leaving India with a solution but with problems. It is not a victory for anyone; it is a disastrous defeat for ' everybody."

They had been in the hall for more than an hour waiting for His Excellency. First they were told that Lord Mountbatten was waiting for the President of the Constituent Assembly. He was to bring the unanimous resolution of that Assembly requesting the Viceroy to become the Governor General of the new dominion when the sovereignty of British Parliament over India ended at midnight. Later they were told that the Prime Minister designate was expected with a list of ministers to be sworn in next day when the first government of the new dominion was to be constituted.

They got all the doors and windows towards the Mughal Garden opened. Even the wire gauze shutters were unlatched. A gentle breeze soon filled the Banquet Hall. Lady Mountbatten had entered the Hall unnoticed.

Moving from one group to the other she was trying to make out what was uppermost in the mind of these officers. In a shining white dress one could see the outline of her robust body. The smile gleaming from her lips gave the impression that it was as permanent part of her complexion as her charming eyes. Only half the chandeliers had been put on. She got the others lighted. This made her shining dress more dazzling. It also made more prominent the places in the walls from where the large portraits of nineteen former Viceroys had been removed earlier that day.

Some officers had begun to saunter by her side or behind her. One of them said with a sly smile: "Should I suggest whose portrait can best adorn the empty spaces on these walls."

> "Please don't"
> Suppressing her giggle, Lady Mountbatten said in an
> appreciative tone.

One of the officers had gone to the Darbar Hall where Lord Mountbatten and members of his staff were lounging. When he tried to enquire how long more they would have to wait for the Viceroy to see them, Lord Mountbatten instantly came to the Banquet Hall. The entire retinue of military secretaries, private secretaries, Press attaches and others followed him. Chatting, arguing and deliberating amongst the various groups, into which the British Officers had split, ceased and they all stood up. Dragging their chairs towards the dais where the Viceroy had seated himself, they all crowded around him. Those who did not find a convenient place for their chair stood behind others.

An Officer whose pinkish complexion heightened the blueness of his eyes and who was sitting nearest to the dais, broke the ice: "Your Excellency, none else in known Indian history had created so much of chaos in so short a time."

Before Lord Mountbatten could flash his eyes and react vexingly, he realized that he was face to face not with Indian leaders but British officers. An unhappy smile made him look sallow. He was clearing his throat to speak when an officer with a thick goatee and black frame eye-glasses rose up in the third row. In a grim voice he said:

> "Your Excellency this is not a time for a chat or a speech. We have specific questions and would be grateful for precise answers. These questions are not about future of the officers here, whom you did not mind

leaving in the lurch. These questions have a bearing on the very honour and dignity of the British people."

One of the Military Secretaries stepped forward and addressing the officer with a goatee he enquired: "What is the problem."

Adjusting glasses on his conspicuous nose that officer said: "First tell us what to do with the secret papers. Most of us have brought with us confidential records from our districts. These are about Congress and other political workers who were acting as informers. Then there were written apologies and undertaking for good conduct by leaders of different parties to secure release from prison. In some cases there is record of undesirable activities by distinguished citizens which we were directed to ignore. In Simla we put these in eight bundles which we have with us here. Are these to be handed over to you?"

Pat came Military Secretary's reply: Half raising his arm in disgust he said: "His Majesty's Government has solved this problem for us. Sir Conrad Cornfield, Viceroy's Secretary for Indian States had received from the Residents of all the hundreds of Indian States, big and small, their confidential records which almost filled two rooms. These contained reports, files documents and other evidence, recording horrid details of the unrighteous lives of five generations of Indian Princes. Not merely of 565 members of the Chambers of Princes but of hundreds of others, whose territories, all together, pockmarked more than one third of the Indian sub continent."

The Military Secretary took a long breath. Glancing furtively at the faces of the officers opposite him, he wiped his nape with a handkerchief. In a slightly lowered voice he added: "It was suggested that these records should be sent to London by a specially chartered steamer. His-Majesty's government on the contrary decided that these records should be reduced to ash and in no case passed on to the new government of India. Two large furnaces have been set up at the western end of the Viceregal Estate where these records are being burnt out. Mr. Nehru did not want these papers to be destroyed. Another furnace might have been added in the afternoon because this work has to be completed well before midnight. .'

The Military Secretary ordered four Beldars to come immediately with their cycle. He directed them to take the eight bundles to the furnaces and stay there till these were consumed by fire. Addressing the officers he

153

commented:' - "This 'building has more or less four hundred halls and rooms with long extensive corridors. The peons here have, therefore, been provided with cycle otherwise papers do not move swiftly.'"

An officer stood up in the second row of chairs. He was of medium height, stoutly built with broad shoulders which did not go well with his small head. With a loud chuckle he said; "On coming here we have come to know that there are some boxes containing works of pornography which the British Customs Officers adjudged unsuitable to be allowed into a spiritual country like India. Why not give us some of this reading material for our long journey? This will help us feel young at heart when we reach home."

There were supportive sounds, giggles and guffaw. Before the Military Secretary could get over his own laughter, the Viceroy beckoned him. A cover had been received from Mr. Nehru on which, apart from address, was written in bold letters 'List of Council of Ministers'. The Military Secretary opened the cover, took out the folded sheet and handed it over to the Viceroy. It was blank, completely empty without even a dot on it. Lord Mountbatten was dumbfounded. To their surprise the officers noted that the Viceroy was squirming and rubbing his forehead .as if deeply perplexed. After showing the blank paper to Lady Mountbatten, he gave it to a Private Secretary asking him to inform Mr. Nehru about this inadvertent mistake .. He asked him to advise Nehru to send the list by mid-night positively.

The swearing in was to take place at 10 A. M. next day. The Viceroy would normally have waited to become Governor General before he bothered about the list. However, there were a few knotty issues in connection with the list of ministers of the new government which he wanted to be sure that Mr. Nehru had tackled intelligently. The first was that Mr. Gandhi did not want Education portfolio to be entrusted to Maulana Azad. Azad on his part was adamant about it and had stated categorically that he would have education or stay out. It was hinted to Lord Mountbatten that in such an eventuality it could not be altogether ruled out that he would leave the country. The hunch was that if a much flaunted nationalist Muslim who had been President of the National Congress Party many times forsook India, millions and millions of Muslims in India would feel insecure and· start leaving the country: What was happening jn the two Punjabs could then replicate in the two "Bengals: Lord Mountbatten knew that it was not because of Mr. Gandhi's visit to Noakhali ·or Calcutta that Bengal had been peaceful. Mr. Jinnah and the Muslim League had hoped, till the end· that Bengali Hindus ·would opt for a United Bengal, for which· they had so vehemently fought after the division of Bengal in the beginning of the century. That hope had not materialized. Now even small cinder could ignite a conflagration in Bengal and elsewhere in India.

Another problem was that Mr. Nehru did not want to include eminent scheduled caste leader Dr. Bhim Rao Ambedkar in his cabinet of ministers. Lord Mountbatten made Mr. Nehru do so, by convincing Mr. Gandhi of the desirability of this. Dr. Ambedkar was offered an inconsequential Law Ministry, which he was most unwilling to accept, because he had held an important portfolio in the' Viceroy's Executive Council. He believed that Law Ministry would virtually render him ineffective in the functioning and policy-making of the government. When Lord Mountbatten tried to allay Dr. Ambedkar's misgivings by saying that a new constitution was to be framed and the Law Minister would thereby have an important position in the Cabinet. Dr. Ambedkar simply laughed at it and said that Government of India Act, 1935, was a God sent gift to Mr. Nehru. Visualizing a powerful centralized government with all powers in his hand, he would adopt it with minor additions and modifications British Parliament's 1935 Government of India Act. Because of these reasons the blank sheet received from Mr. Nehru had given the Viceroy cause for worry.

Lord Mountbatten recomposed himself and sat down facing the British officers as if he was ready to hear what they had to say.

Some officers raised their hand, seeking permission to speak. An officer in the front row stood up. Raising his hand he gestured to others to let him speak. He had a stern face, typically British blue eyes and thick silky eyebrows. He was tall like Lord Mountbatten but less stoutly built. His nose quivered and his eyes began to gleam as he said: "Your Excellency, during the few days we have been together we have been looking back thoughtfully over British Parliament's governance of this country for over a century and its demission or denouement today. It is not the time to dilate on this. I will only bring to your attention two issues which have been agitating and perturbing us most." Straightening his back, lifting his chin and raising his voice he affirmed: "Your Excellency not only we here but the entire British nation will feel outraged by two statements which are being repeated in India ad nauseam. We are surprised that Your Excellency has chosen to remain silent about it and has done nothing to clarify the position of British government and the British people. The first is the assertion, both explicit and implicit, that world's mightiest empire has been made to lick dust by the power of non-violence. The writings in the Indian Press and speeches

155

by Indian leaders unmistakably give the impression that we are running away like a beaten dog with tail lowered between the hind legs." The quivering of his nose and glint in his eyes had become more pronounced and his stern face had more redness in his cheeks. After a minute's pause he added: "The second is the outrageous assertion that British government deliberately created, promoted and magnified Hindu-Muslim differences and the communal feelings to: further the policy of divide and rule. It is even being said that British Government is creating 'Pakistan as an imperialist stratagem. Hindu-Muslim animus has been there for. centuries even when ·Hindus lay prostrate during Muslim rule. Did we teach· Hindus not' to· eat anything ·touched by a member of the Muslim community? Did we tell Gandhi to bring in cow and Ram Rajya into the Indian polity? Did we tell the majority community to do nothing to allay the fears of the minority community? Much before Hindu Muslim tension acquired cyclonic momentum making the division of this sub-continent inevitable every town in India had Hindu and Muslim segregation, separate habitations of Hindus and Muslims in the same town. But for this India would have got before the World War' what it is getting today."

The breeze outside was imperceptibly turning into wind. The rustling of leaves in the Mughal Garden was creating the simulation of the flight of millions of birds. There was muffled whispering and slight shifting ·of chairs. When Lord Mountbatten appeared making a rnove as if rising to speak, that officer made him hold off by uttering firmly: "Your Excellency I have a few more word to say, let me finish." In a voice which had as much grit as anguish, he resumed: "Your Excellency, the national movement of India is now imagined to start with Mutiny, forgetting all the time that India as we conceive it today is a post-Mutiny concept and nationalism, even in Europe, is a post Napoleon phenomenon. There was much greater support for the British troops than for the mutineers. Throughout India an overwhelming majority, of the people, not yet calling themselves Indians, did not want the Mughal rulers of their Hindu or Muslim feudatories to come back. Had they in their history ever fought for freedom as we understand it, they would have realized how puerile the 1857 Mutiny was. It solidified an unjust social status quo and condemned one third of India's population to the tyranny of Indian Princes because of stoppage of further annexations. In Poland with almost one twentieth of Indian population, one hundred· thousand people died in the insurrection against Czar in 1831 and their 1863 struggle lasted for as many years as the months of the Indian Mutiny."

That officer halted for a few seconds and took a long breath. Adjusting again glasses on his nose, he started speaking more vehemently: "How much patriotism the people had is apparent from the Jalianwala Bagh firing. All the hundreds who died there had bullet mark on their back and not a single one on his front. In none of the noncooperation movements those who went to jail exceeded one ten-thousandth of the population of India. The 1942 movement fizzled out in a few days after the top leaders walked to the comfort of British jails. By then the possibilities of any freedom movement had completely disappeared because of the certainty of its getting drowned in ferocious Hindu-Muslim riots. In the circumstances to say that we are running away because of the power of non-violence is a perverse travesty of truth."

Hearing the words, "Please cut short" from one of the military secretaries that officer began speaking fast, without making one word run into another. He continued: "I will not take long on the second point that we followed a policy of divide. and rule. Brahmins and other high caste Hindus have always held that theirs is the best, the .greatest and the highest civilization· in the world. They regarded Muslim invaders ·as malechh - beef-eating unclean people. Muslim invaders, on their part, came with the ·intoxication of having conquered half the known world and with the conviction that their religion was far superior in every respect. Their small bands could easily defeat large local armies. This further reinforced their feelings that the people they were subjugating were only worth looking down upon. A head that bows before you is not cut but is treated with disdain. This inevitably resulted in mutual aversion. When the edifice of Muslim rule collapsed with the coming of the British, this antipathy for the Muslims burst forth in upper caste Hindus. The entire Bengali, Hindi and similar literatures of the nineteenth century and the writings in papers like Hindu Patriot conclusively show that Hindu-Muslim schism was there when British entered the Indian scene." ,

Lord Mountbatten beckoned one of his military secretaries and whispered something to him for a minute or two. As the Military Secretary stood before the gathered officers ready to address them, there was complete silence in the hall. He was a tall, well built and tough looking person. He seemed to have been gifted excess of every thing, excess of fat, thick cape of hair, big bulbous nose and big second chin. He began to speak in a sonorous voice: "His Excellency has directed me to throw light on the problem referred to here and to explain why a particular course had necessarily to be followed and why no other alternative had remained open.

My task has been made easy by what my brother officer stated so cogently. We do not have a situation in which we can· say what is right and what is wrong, what is true and what is false. It is said that tragedy is not when truth is pitted against falsehood but when truth contends against another truth. Right now we have a tragedy which is absolute and irretrievable. Here is a case of holding the truth in one's hand but pressing the grip so hard that it becomes lifeless. The two sides uncompromisingly swearing by their own lifeless truth have created a situation in which the British government finds itself helpless in bringing about even a modicum of compromise."

The military secretary looked at the Viceroy and noticing his approving looks, continued in a slightly slower tone: "The Cripps and Cabinet missions sought to maintain the unity of the country and to put the two parties on the path of reconciliation.

After the unfortunate failure of these two efforts, His Majesty's Government invited Indian leaders to London on December 3, 1946. The Labour Government was convinced after talks with those leaders that India was on the brink of a ruinous civil war. So that Indian leaders cease dillydallying about mutual settlement, the transfer of power was fixed for June 1948. When Lord Mountbatten was appointed new Viceroy by His Majesty's government, he was assigned two tasks. Firstly, in the obtaining situation bring about transfer of power with the least possible conflict. Secondly, to leave behind in good shape the rich legacy of the last hundred years of rule by British Parliament."

The Military Secretary noted that the officers were listening to him with rapt attention. He cursorily glanced at the Viceroy again and continued: "When Lord Mountbatten arrived here he did not take long to realize the perilous dimension to which mutual fears and hatred had got worked up. This grim situation left him in no doubt that Partition was inevitable and delaying it to June 1948, could spread the gory killing of the· minority community to large parts of India, even worse than what happened in the western districts of the Punjab immediately after his arrival in India. His Excellency took the decision to advance that date by almost a year after fully consulting you. When he called Indian Police Service officers and asked them whether they could take responsibility for maintaining law and order, their reply was: 'No, Your Excellency, we cannot.' Field Marshal Auchinleck, Commander-in-Chief of the Indian Army and other Army Commanders affirmed the same. The Governors of the Punjab and other

Provinces concerned reported complete break down of law and order and the difficulty of preventing arson, looting and killing, particularly when police and military personnel of the two communities had begun to actively take sides. To say that because of the power of non-violence we are transferring power is mindless craziness. Similarly to say that we are creating Pakistan for' our own reasons is shutting eyes to facts. The sincere concern of His Majesty's Government to maintain the unity of India is clear from the sponsoring of Cripps and Cabinet Missions plans. Jinnah was the first to accept the Cabinet Mission Plan ensuring undivided India and later the Congress Party accepted it only to repudiate it. Similarly Partition announced by His Excellency was first accepted by Congress Party, leaving no other course to Jinnah. It was open to them to reject this plan just as they had vetoed the earlier ones. It is not non-violence but horrifying communal violence that has hastened our departure from this country and has prevented us from doing so peacefully with great benefit to the people of India. Though we are leaving the country divided, the two parts are more united and integrated than ever before in Indian history. This is because of His Majesty's Governments decision that with the demission of British sovereignty, Indian Princes cannot go back to pre-British position and have to merge with one State or the other. Thus the two countries will have a singularity more authentic than British India when more than fifteen hundred big, small and tiny principalities pockmarked this sub-continent. We are leaving behind administrative, legal and educational system the like of which has never before existed here. We are bequeathing an intelligentsia superior, greater and more heterogeneous and heterodox than ever in long Indian history. I hope the new governments will be different from the tyrannies from which we liberated the people and also from the dishonorable practices of contemporaneous Princely States the record of which is on fire just now."

The Military Secretary kept standing motionless for sometime. He glanced meaningfully at the officers whose silence was less spellbound than before. Haltingly, he said in a voice more sharp than before: "What I am going to say now is my personal opinion and not that of the Viceroy or His Majesty's Government. When we came here the common people of India were as unconcerned about the change of one ruler by the other as were the ants in this land. At best they helped the new invaders to conquer others in the country. Patriotism and nationalism was something unknown till we came here. There was no idea of citizenship, much less of any pride in this. The idea of rule of law did not exist at all. There were castes and sub-castes, indifferent if not hostile to one another. Hindu distinctiveness as projected today embracing every indigenous belief and practice did not exit before we carne here. We have been accused of creating Muslim communalism. The real truth is that our coming here gave birth to Hindu consciousness soaring above the previously dominant castes and sub-castes. We gave them a sense of singularity and dignity. If educated Indians are today claiming moral superiority it is because of that, eyen though this claim of moral superiority against' the West is a pathetic attempt to seek an illusionary compensation for what India lacks 'in various' spheres. We made-'these people 'conscious of their history, jurisprudence,' literature ' and their: archaeological heritage. The first history of India was written by an Englishman, so were dictionaries and anthologies in most of the Indian languages and works' on ancient Indian literature. We sowed in the minds of the people here the seeds of freedom and democracy. We, brought 'here modern inventions and discoveries even before they, reached many European countries. British rule marks the dividing line between the immense expanse of essentially static society and a narrow strip of time in which efforts were made to introduce modicum of dynamism in this society. This was, done in a halting and half hearted manner because of the fear of another Mutiny. British India was, not only much more prosperous than the parts which remained under the native, States, but it ' also enjoyed a much larger measure of liberty, justice and egalitarianism. 'The few thousand officers through whom His Majesty's Government ruled scores of millions of the people of British India were nearly all honest, dedicated, discerning and austere, like of which one does not come across anywhere else in the world. When the Indian people look back at their past after a century or two, I have no doubt that this century of rule by British Parliament would stand out as the finest period of Indian history."

The Military Secretary halted for a few seconds and continued "Less than hundred years ago when the British Minister in Bolivia attended an official function without his family, a seemingly discourteous act, the Bolivian President had him tied to a ' burro, a small donkey, facing the tail an~ paraded ltim through the streets. The news reached London. "Where on earth" asked Palmerston "is Bolivia?" Ruling out stern action he said: "Replace him by a shrewd Minister. Let us not lose our sense of humour." Friends let us not lose our British sense of humour while reacting to bragging by Congress leaders about the power of non-violence and else.
After a brief pause, the Military secretary continued: "Long ago, Cicero writing to Atticus said: Do not get your slaves from Britain, because they are so stupid and so utterly incapable of being taught. They are not fit to be part of Athenian household', A few centuries later the British people were

attributed quite different traits.

"Mutational flux is incumbent upon human life. The Indian leaders who are taking over power today are indeed different from those who ruled the various parts of this country before we came here. Some of them, thanks to modern education, are amongst the great men of today. We wish them every success in providing their people with good government and just society."

The direction of the wind had changed eastward. Mild smoke from the smoldering furnaces had entered the Hall and they could smell it. Dinner was to be served to them in this Hall. Three large rectangular tables had been placed on one side and covered with spotless white sheets. Lord Mountbatten had got up to move amongst the officers. A military secretary tiptoed in and informed him that separate rooms had been fixed for Mr. Nehru and Pakistan Prime Minister Mr. Liaqat Ali Khan, where they will peruse the Radcliffe maps and Award. They would come separately to 'see the Viceroy after that and to hand back the Award, which was secret for another twenty four hours. Mr. Khan would come first and arrangement had been made to fly him to Karachi immediately after that.

Lord Mountbatten moved amongst officers. One of them asked him: "It is said that every Englishman who comes here changes one way or the other. What has been the change in you?"

Lord Mountbatten replied: "I might have added more muscles to my torso. In one of Balzac's novels a woman carried her sorrow in the bags of her eyelids. I had to ·carry the burden of my responsibilities upon my shoulders and my chest."

Another officer standing near him remarked: "It is much more honourable than carrying your responsibilities in the lower part of the body as many great men do." There were some chuckling and Lord Mountbatten could not muffle his.

CHAPTER TWENTY FIVE

It was a night hot and stifling just like their tears, a night when bats flew low under the trees. They were full of sorrow and writhing in agony. They had been through hell. They had the feeling that they were jetsam which the skiff of Indian freedom had thrown overboard to be able to reach the shore. For them freedom was not rising sun spreading wide its rosy dawn but a butchered animal hung on the gambrel stick of their blood stained lives. They could hardly feel that they were living beings with roots in the land where they were born. It appeared to them that they were grains of sand blown helter-skelter by the tornado of the country's partition. These thought were working up a whirlwind in their mind as they trudged to the center of Tis Hazari refugee camp, where a mid-night meeting was to take place to celebrate the birth of free India.

As they gathered under the only tree in the Tis Hazari ground, the mid-August night appeared to them more oppressive and black. The street lights burned dismally in the dusty atmosphere. This deepened their depression. Two gasolier lamps had been lit at the two ends on the western side of this twelve acre plot of land to provide light for nightlong work on huts being built for refugees. The sound of shifting of corrugated sheets, of churning with feet of mud for mortar and of the laying of bricks was music to their ears. Two rows of huts, already completed, had been occupied by refugees who had arrived here yesterday. A third row was in the making.

Not far away in the north-west an electric bulb was shedding its dim light on the top of a tower, a church-like spire, situated on the adjacent ridge. This was built after 1857 Mutiny to commemorate the victory of a regiment of Bengal grenadiers over thirty thousand motley soldiers of the Mughal army brandishing swords in the rear of a few dozen musketeers. As Tis

Hazari - thirty thousand - soldiers had camped here for sometime, this area began to be called Tis Hazari, which then extended to Kashmere Gate, a furlong away. The last battle was fought at Kashmere Gate before the British army captured Red Fort, the seat of the Mughal Empire. A refugee camp was now being set up here for thousands of displaced persons from Pakistan seeking shelter after losing every thing except their fortitude and hope.

As mid-night neared, about twenty odd men had gathered there waiting for the zero hour, when in New Delhi the reins of the government would be handed over to Pandit Nehru and free India would have its birth.

That gathering of hapless persons had more pride than joy. They were trying to be firm on their feet and brave in their heart. In midnight murkiness they were like silhouettes, charged with more hope than dismay. Many of them stood silent and motionless as if praying. A dozen black birds began soaring through the sky above them. Someone shrieked:

"These are kites: a bad omen."

Another silhouette commented: "This is dark fortnight of the moon when it is inauspicious to begin anything." His was a large body and his shadow was darker than those of others.

A boy was asked to climb the tree and tie the national flag as near the top as possible. When the hooter sounded they stood silent and motionless for two minutes. Someone began to sing the national song. After a few words he felt choked. Facing the huts under construction as he did, one could see in the glimmer of gasolier lamps, his jaws move but few words coming forth. Suddenly his voice began to shiver as if holding back tears. As they were about to move one of them stepped forward and with folded hands asked everyone: "If anyone of you is from Chakwal or Jhelum district please let me know. My parents and all relatives lived there and I have no news about them. I am Shiv Shanker Kohli who came to Delhi from Chakwal some years ago."

One of the persons there said: "1 come from Chhapoke, half way between Chakwal and Jhelum city. So far as I know, all Hindus and Sikhs of Chakwal, except some old men and women, left for Jhelum city in the last week of June and were staying in Khalsa High School in the heart of the town. In the beginning of July there were reports of pitched battles taking place there. This went on till soldiers of the Boundary Force rescued Hindu and Sikh survivors and moved them to Lahore. In the case of my village Chhapoke, it seems, fellow Muslim villagers provided full protection and most of the Hindus and Sikhs stayed on. When in the beginning of August roving bands of Muslim ex-servicemen attacked the village, Muslim villagers hid Hindu and Sikh families so cleverly that the first few search parties did not find anyone. They camped in the village for five days and searched houses again and again. Even then they could drag out and kill less than half of them. As soon as the Muslim villagers came to know that a military convoy was passing through the Grand Trunk road, a short distance away, they entrusted the surviving Hindus arid Sikhs to them. Shiv Shanker wanted to know his address so that he could contact him again. He laughed bitterly and said: "What address, I arrived here today. My name is Chanan Mal and I am hoping to get a shack in this refugee camp in a day or so." Shiv Shanker told him, after some hesitation, that he lived above a shop in the nearby Mori Gate bazaar. He requested him to let him know in case he came across someone from Chakwal. He moved with Chanan Mal nearer light, wrote his address and gave it to him.

Chanan Mal had arrived in Delhi the same afternoon. He had set himself up on the foot path across the road opposite Tis Hazari ground where camp for refugees from Pakistan was being set up. The footpath was on a very busy road and had on the other side an eight feet high iron palisade which demarcated it from the railway yard and siding. If the flow of traffic on the road was ceaseless, there was seldom a break in the locomotion of trains and the shunting of wagons and engines in the railway yard. Chanan Mal was unable to decide which din was less nerve raking, whether of the road or of the railway yard. Tarpaulin sheets, wooden planks, card board, gunny cloth, etc., had been kept in heaps in the Tis Hazari ground just across the road. Between two shanties on the foot path Chanan Mal and his sister built one for themselves, making best of the available material. They had made sure that they were not far from the place where new huts were under construction.

In the light of the gasolier lamp, he had tried to have a full look at Shiv Shanker. He did not notice any friendliness or goodnature in his looks. He shirked meeting his eyes. There was something in his bearing which made Chanan Mal feel discomfited. He, however, felt that having the address of a local person could be of some help as they both were from the same district in Pakistan.

When he returned to the shanty on the footpath, his sister Lal Kaur was waiting for him anxiously. On her left knee was her four year old daughter Bachni and on the right her two year old son Buta. She would rock Bachni and pat Buta whenever they got disturbed in their sleep by the hustle and bustle of the road. Chanan Mal's sister was six years older than he. She became a widow three days ago. Her husband got killed, not in Pakistan but in Amritsar. In these three days she had aged and thinned. Her voice had become sore. The smile which always lighted her eyes had disappeared. Her full face had lost is chubbiness. Chanan Mal sat near his sister as he went in. He rubbed his neck which had become freckly and dry. In a day or two his neck had become crisscrossed with veins and his Adam's apple had protruded. His hair used to be soft but had now become rough and dry. Not the slightest softness was left on his body or in his life.

Lal Kaur moved away from the entrance and lay crouched in a comer with a child on each side. Her elder daughter Chunno was reclining near her feet. Chanan Mal had shifted to the entrance of the shanty and was staring at the Tis Hazari crossing and beyond toward the wholesale vegetable market. In this dusty and smoky haze, the naked bulbs of the municipal lamp posts frightened him as if these were fiery eye balls of fiends. It was long past midnight. The rush of pedestrians, carriages, mule-carts, etcetera had only slightly lessened. Sometimes the headlights of trucks, carrying fruits and vegetables to the market, lighted up the pedestrians and they would become walking shadows again.

Chanan Mal felt overawed by the endless rush on this crossing and on the three roads that joined here. How vast and hurly-burly a city this was. It was nine hours or so since he arrived here. Leaving his sister here he had sauntered around in the neighbouring areas in search of a niche for the family which was now his responsibility. He was keen to take up some work and do it with zeal more than ever before. He felt nonplussed because in this labyrinthine city he was without money, without any special ability and without any acquaintance.

Gradually Chanan Mal was lost in the thoughts of his past, in the sweet memory of his village. The very thought of his native land made him restless, as if it was mother from whom he had been separated. The memory of the village made alive before him the picture of an evergreen and ever-growing life, a life which was like verdant trees with cool shade and deep roots. Man is not a tree which would wither away when uprooted, he assured himself. Unlike a tree man has dreams and a vision. If uprooted he has to strike roots again and never shrivel. His small double storey house

165

became alive in his memory. Every part of his body began to have the feel of that house. His hands and feet felt the touch of its walls and floors. He could feel the places from where plaster had fallen and the wooden board had become loose. The peculiar sensation of the eleven steps of stairs became alive in his mind as if he was coming down those stairs. His hands felt the wooden lattice of the ground floor windows and recalled the places from where pieces were missing.

Chunno had by then spread-eagled herself and had fallen asleep. Lal Kaur recalled the sound of breathing of her children when asleep. She could recognize each one of them by his or her breathing. Chunno went to sleep immediately she lay on the bed. Her breathing was heavy and deep and after every four nasal breaths a sound of phew came out of her mouth. Bachni's one breath was heavy and the second light. This continued alternately throughout the night. The youngest Buta was asleep immediately after dusk and a gurgling sound kept coming from his throat, side by side with irregular breaths. Suddenly the breathing of her late husband became alive and thumping in the mind of Lal Kaur. While asleep his breath would be heavy and forced, each breath would for a second halt near his nasal bone, swell his nostrils and eject with a whistling sound. When her husband returned from the factory very tired, his sleep would have one long heavy and three short light breaths alternately. This got interrupted for a while when his one nostril closed and the other opened. The upheaval of the last few days had tumbled her life. Her children also had changed, but each one in a different manner. Chunno had hid herself in a serious exterior. She had suddenly begun to behave like a grown up person. Her loquacity, it appeared, was meant to console her mother and uncle. She had begun to add honorific 'jee' to every sentence she uttered. Buta used to keep smiling all the time. As was the custom in west Punjab, he called his father 'chacha'. The moment his father returned home he would monopolize him. He had now become peevish and kept muttering 'where is chacha'. Bachni who was always anxious to run out of the house and play around, now hid herself in the shawl of her mother.

They had come safely from Lahore and it was in Amritsar her husband Jagat Singh lost his life. She could not even have last look at his dead body nor could his last rites be performed. He worked in the railway workshop in Mughalpura, Lahore" and used to live in Singhpura, a colony of the Sikh employees of the workshop. Till the very end complete peace prevailed in Singhpura and the surrounding colonies of Hindu and Muslim employees of the workshop, despite widespread communal disturbances in other parts of Lahore. Jagat Singh had opted for India like other non-Muslim employees of the government's Mughalpura workshop. On August 12, Muslim employees of this workshop safely escorted them to the border town of Wagah. From there they took a horse carriage to Amritsar city.

On reaching the outskirts of Amritsar they found the whole city crammed with refugees from west Punjab. Everyone was crying for the blood of the Muslims. About half of the original population of Amritsar consisted of Muslims. They had assembled in half a dozen of their colonies in the outskirts of the town. These had been fortified and barricaded and there were occasional pitched battles. Dr. Saifuddin Kitchlu, a Muslim nationalist leader, whose arrest in 1919 had lead to Punjab disturbances and Martial Law, had been shifted to the safety of the Golden Temple of the Sikhs along with some others. However, all efforts to provide the Muslims living in Amritsar a safe passage to Pakistan were being frustrated by refugees from Pakistan. Fires were raging in some parts of Amritsar. Bombs, hand grenades and swords were being freely distributed. Thunder of explosions could be heard time and again. It appeared that city had become a slaughter house. Trains to Pakistan would be halted before these reached the railway station and attacked by refugees armed to the teeth. Trains from Pakistan would many times empty or with mutilated bodies and corpses. The odor of blood was hanging over the city like a canopy.

Leaving his family with Chanan Mal in a refugee camp near the railway station, Jagat Singh went to the railway workshop at Putlighar about a furlong from there. All the Muslim employees of the workshop had taken shelter inside the workshop. Built in the last century, even earlier than the Mughalpura workshop in Lahore, it had an eight feet high palisade made with thick iron sheets. The attackers had been unable to dent it. Five fellow employees of the Mughalpura workshop had accompanied Jagat Singh. Seeing the mood of the armed crowd outside the workshop, they thought over the problem and concluded that unless Muslim railway men and their families holed up there were rescued that night, there would be great danger to their life. They collected as much of material like bombs, hand grenades and swords as they could and went to a deserted portion of the palisade. They lightly tapped the palisade till someone from inside responded. Rising above on a colleague's shoulders, he gave them a slip of paper containing their plan and also passed on the material to raised hands on the other side. The slip explained to them the gravity of the situation outside and informed them that they would knock at the gate of the workshop at 10.30 p.m. sharp which they should open for half a minute to enable them to rush in. After midnight, they would lead them to Chheharta about four miles away where a transit camp had been set up for Muslims migrating to Pakistan and which was under the protection of the security forces.

They and some Sikh students and teachers of nearby Khalsa College unsuccessfully tried to persuade the armed crowd to let the Muslim employees of the workshop move out safely as had happened with the Hindu and Sikh employees of Lahore Railway Workshop. Somehow, they managed to move the crowd a little away from the immediate vicinity of the entrance gate. They knocked it at 10.30 p.m. Jagat Singh and a companion rushed in, quickly bolting the gate from inside. The Muslim employs there had on their own thought similarly but had felt that 1 or 2 a. m. was a better time to sneak away. All of a sudden there was pounding on the gate with sledge hammers. After half an hour of hammering, the gate gave way. In the meanwhile they had taken shelter in the main three storey building built with stone.

They barricaded the entrance and got ready for defense One of them had a firearm. Volley of bullets and hand grenades drove the crowd back. They were getting ready· to dash off when the crowd returned in greater strength fully armed. They rained the building with hand grenades and bombs. One of them removed the barricade, entered the ground floor and set it on fire. It had Burma teak roof beams, wooden paneling, file racks and furniture. In no time this raging fire swallowed the upper floors which also had similar teak furniture and beams. The sky high inferno continued for a few hours till the building tumbled down to smoldering rubble.

The building was still in flames when Lal Kaur, Chanan Mal and children came there next morning. The falling stones had reduced the mortal remains of most of the persons there to smithereens. They could do nothing except shed tears and recite the sacred gurbani they had learnt by rote. As living in Amritsar would have been very painful, they decided to leave the city. The train into which they could push themselves with great effort brought them after almost twenty hours of tiring journey to Delhi railway station. Outside the station trucks were waiting to take refugees to different camps. The truck which picked them up brought them to Tis Hazari ground.

Within an hour of living in that improvised shanty, Chanan Mal's head began to whirl. He sometimes felt the whole world going in a spiral. It took some hours before his head and ears became habituated to the commotion and cacophony of the road and railway yard. Much before day break he was suddenly shaken from sleep by din in the shanties to the left and the right. Breathing the fresh air of the early hours, he realized that they were moving towards the huts. He, Lal Kaur and children also rushed to the Tis Hazari ground and occupied a hut the roof of which was still being put in place.

By evening five rows of forty huts each had come up and the community kitchen became fully operative. This was a world as much of despair as of hope, as much of sorrow as of anticipation. Outside huts, shacks, shanties and elsewhere refugees would gather and recount their tales of woe, sometimes to this person, another time to some one else, often again and again amongst themselves. As soon as they woke up, this recounting of the past and worrying about the present and the future would commence. The shadows would become short and long again but their tales would go on, sometimes a yarn of hope would be added to it. Inside the hut and outside, moving from place to place their mind would be honeycomb of-thoughts, sometimes dry and shriveled and at others buzzing with hive of ideas.

Someone would heave a deep sigh while telling his account, the eyes of another would brim with tears. Someone or the other would start crying loudly or sobbing bitterly till he was interrupted by someone else's narration told in a sadder tone. In between another person would emit mournfully: 'Hey Ishwar, almighty father, did we commit so many sins in our previous life'. Another would grumble woefully: 'Oh God, are you not beholding all this?' There were those who would recount in detail the gory killing of Muslims in east Punjab in order to anaesthetize the agony of their own laceration. All of a sudden a person would shake himself off his dismal brooding and grunt: 'So far kings, chieftains and maharajas only had come and gone. Now the people have been uprooted, whole villages and communities have been pulled out of their habitation like carrots and radishes."

If love is blind, hatred has a thousand eyes. With thousand eyes of hatred, each one of them ruminated on his past, present and future differently. Chanan Mal noticed that they were as busy in recounting what had happened to them as in conjecturing all that would have happened had they not succeeded in escaping to India. As they masticated the provender of such thoughts, their reaction differed from person to person. Chanan Mal noticed that there were some who had lost almost all their kith and kin, each and everything that they possessed, but in whose heart the beacon of goodness did not become dim. They remembered long years of camaraderie

169

with Muslims while thinking of the last few months of bitterness. There were others who had come out of Pakistan safely, with all their belongings and kith and kin intact and were only slightly less well off than before, but whose hearts were brimming with hatred for Muslims. Whatever the trepidation their mind felt, they mostly looked forward to tomorrow with anticipation and hope.

Future is a sun that never sets. When it begets beclouded it tends to glitter from one corner or the other giving a silver lining to the cloud. If someone attempts to shut his eyes to future, it somehow reaches his soul. It was always so and had made human beings take step after step forward and onward. Like the act of breathing the perception of future is both the symptom and concomitant of human life. It may be possible to turn back a river but not the spur of man towards future albeit he may be shattered and devastated like these refugees.

CHAPTER TWENTY SIX

In his state of helplessness Chanan Mal again and again thought of Shiv Shanker whose address he had kept carefully. Both came from the same district in west Punjab now in Pakistan. Chakwal, the place to which he belonged, though a small town, was the main grain and cattle market of the area and was less than an hour's journey by bus from his village Chhapoke. There was a possibility that there were persons in the two places known to both of them. He had said that he came to Delhi about four years ago and should be in a position to help him. But whenever he recollected his face he had feeling of mistrust. and wariness

During four years Shiv Shanker has been in Delhi he did nothing and did it very well. He had taken up no work or employment. Despite that he was able to have a good life. He claimed to be a poet and had given himself the pseudonym lohar Chakwali, Chakwal being the place of his birth and, according the practice among Urdu poets, had to be added to the assumed authorial name. Though he was not able to compose even a couplet or two, his behaviour and mannerism was that of a great Urdu poets. He was unhesitatingly accepted as such by other Urdu poets among whom he moved about. This could be because his method of making money effortlessly and of spending it recklessly had all the bohemianism of a poet.

The outline of free India that had taken shape in his mind from the speeches of the Congress leaders and the writings in newspapers had filled him with foreboding. The pattern of his life during the last few years hardly fitted into it. Four years ago when he arrived in Delhi he had no job and no money to stay even in a third rate hotel. Looking for a cheap sarai, he reached Lady Harding Sarai, near New Delhi railway station, where the charges were half a rupee for the room per night. The snag was that in this boarding place one could stay for one night only and the stay could not be extended. Tired as he was, he paid half a rupee to the supervisor of the sarai and took a room for the night.

The day was far advanced when he was woken up by the hullabaloos of recitals and peals of laughter in the adjacent room. Putting on his shirt he entered that room diffidently, hoping to find out from them particulars of some other cheap Sarai. Six young and middle aged men were there, four reclining on bolsters and two sitting tailor style on a mat. In a comer near the door three bolsters lay piled up. Without caring to notice the intruder, one or the other kept reciting Urdu couplets, snippets of a verse or a joke, the more smutty it was, the greater was the clapping and laughter. He soon got engrossed in that laughing and clapping like the others. In a brief respite, one of them asked him: 'What are you doing and to which religion you belong?' .Shiv Shanker straightened his back and replied pertly: 'I do nothing and I have no religion, absolutely none". It was, however, clear to them that he was a Hindu.

Shiv Shanker soon became aware of their problem. One could book a room in that sarai for one day again after a week. There were seven persons in that room and had managed to stay on permanently, each one of them booking this room once a week. For this a bottle of country liquor had to be given to the supervisor every Saturday. One of them had left on getting a job outside Delhi and they were worrying about the consequent break in their stay there. Shiv Shanker offered to become the seventh member of that group. They readily agreed when in the course of mutual introduction he told them that he too was an Urdu versifier and his pseudonym was Johar Chakwali. He immediately shifted to that room and a bolster and the corner near the door was earmarked for him. Four of them Shamim Panipati Josh Rampuri, Sahir Allahabadi and Muztar Jalandhari wrote talks and skits for Hindustani program of All India Radio on all subjects including those relating to science, health, women and children. Akhtar Ambalvi worked as a store keeper with Hamdard Pharmacy and the sixth Niaz Shahjahanpuri was an assistant in the office of the All India Association of Muslim Divines. He also acted as a stool pigeon for government's Intelligence Bureau. He was the only one amongst them who sported a beard and did not appear to be badly off. During the War years American GIs stole typewriters from their office and exchanged these with Niaz Shahjahanpuri for bottles of Indian country liquor which they thought had better kick, than their rum or whiskey. Typewriters in the English language were in great demand during those days and Niaz had made a lot of money through these deals. Shiv Shanker soon came to know that two amongst them were Hindus, both Brahmins. The features of all of them were no doubt different but they were all cast mentally in the same mould. Their conversational style, manner of speech, general behaviour and habits of eating and drinking were identical. Shiv Shanker, in no time, became like them in every manner.

All he had held sacred became profane. They all dined together at the Kashmir Muslim hotel opposite the sarai. When he came to know that the big kabob available at half the price of the smaller kabob was not made of mutton, he felt no compunction. He rather wondered why God had burdened man with a conscience when he can jettison it so easily. Shiv Shanker's pocket was emptying fast. His day long effort to find some work in the business centers of the city were of no avail. An Indian merchant from Iran came to the sarai looking for someone who had helped him during his last visit to get permit for export of sugar bags to Iran. After finding the manager of sarai unhelpful he enquired from Shiv Shanker about his earlier contact. He could only inform the merchant from Iran that no one could stay there for more than a day. From the accent of Shiv Shanker the merchant guessed that he belonged to Jhelum district of western Punjab, the district to which he also originally belonged. To the Iranian merchants many questions, Shiv Shanker replied that he was a Kohli from Chakwal. The merchant's ancestral village was three miles from Chakwal. He seemed to know all he five Kohli families of Chakwal and gave him details of all of them. That merchant did not know English nor could he properly speak Hindustani. He requested Shiv Shanker to accompany him to the office of the Controller of Exports and Imports and help him in filling various forms and in other formalities. Last time he got permit for export of fifty bags of sugar and this time he would like to have permit for more bags. On the way the merchant told Shiv Shanker that if for this some one's palm needed to be greased, this could be done.

As Shiv Shanker thought that his palm was dry and was also in need of grease, his mind set working. He went to the reception counter and got the application which was free of cost. The merchant's last contact had charged him rupees ten for this. Making the merchant sit in the reception lounge, Shiv Shanker entered some room on one pretext or the other, mainly to find out which one had an exit from the other side. He picked up some papers containing instructions for imports and exports and came out with a long face. He accompanied the merchant to his hotel near Lady Harding Sarai and told him:

"Quota for export of sugar for the current year has already exhausted and new permits are not available. I coaxed the babu concerned to do something as a special case and after much effort he agreed to do something but he said that the officer concerned would have to be paid under the table rupees two hundred per bag. I urged that babu to have the amount reduced to rupees hundred per bag and he promised to let me know the position tomorrow." When the merchant told him that he had paid rupees fifty per bag on the last occasion, Shiv Shanker snapped: "In the absence of a quota the position is different now."

Next morning they reached the office of the Controller of Exports and Imports soon after it opened. The merchant gave him rupees five thousand for permit for fifty bags of sugar. This time he took him inside the office and made him sit on a bench outside a room. After entering that room and staying there for a while, he came out and entered the room which had second exit on the other side and disappeared from there.

He bought some cotton, bandages and a walking stick. He bandaged his right knee so tight that he could hardly bend it. With the help of the stick he climbed from the back side stairs of the room above the wine shop in New Delhi's Gol Market where a tailor known to him lived. Both of them had been buying country liquor from the same shop below that room and had had drinks together many times. The tailor did not mind Shiv Shanker extending his stay from day to day because he was procuring food and drinks not only for himself but also for the tailor. The tailor was not doing well and wanted to migrate to England where his brother and some friends from his village had already gone. His problem was that he had not been able to save the needed money. Shiv Shanker offered to pay for his entire passage and for two or three sets of European dress with shirts and matching ties. He told him he would in addition pay him some money in lieu of letter to the New Delhi Municipal Committee transferring the tenancy of the room to him. He removed the bandages after three weeks when he thought it would be safe to move out to nearby Connaught Place for a short while. He booked the tailor's passage for England through a Connaught Place travel agent and bought a suit case and the promised dresses from a well known draper there. Office of the New Delhi Municipal Committee was also nearby. It took no time to have the tenancy of the room transferred to his name when he pushed a ten rupee note in the pocket of the clerk concerned. After enough money had been given to the tailor for the train journey to Bombay, he was quite happy to go to the railway station on his own to entrain for Bombay.

While lying bandaged in that room he had drawn up a list of twelve offices which issued permits, quotas or licenses. He decided that he would play his confidence trick only once a month and would not visit the same office before a year. After one or two tries he could spot out his victim without much difficulty and later on with canny accuracy. This arrangement worked to his entire satisfaction and the delight of his friends till the end of 1946. Shiv Shanker's bad days returned because the functioning of the various departments of the Government of India had virtually come to a standstill. There were widespread communal disturbances in the country and the demand for Pakistan was becoming irresistible. Even where the offices were partially functioning none came to Delhi from outside for permits or quotas.

He subsisted for sometime by selling curios and other expensive articles which he always collected when he had money to spare. Later he started getting food, drinks and other necessities on credit, which source also soon dried up. Niaz Shahjahanpuri now known as Maulana Allauddin Khan used to lend him whenever he had lean period but, during those days he was seldom in Delhi. Shiv Shanker was getting dejected and demoralized as he came to realize that a trickster could have no future in a free India. He was down with viral fever for almost the whole month of June 1947. The sweeper who came to clean the room and with whom he had been quite generous, brought him some victuals, medicine and also the news that there would be freedom and division of the country on August 15 and that Pakistan· had finally been conceded. This demoralized him further. When he was free from fever and could sit up, he sent for the manager of the wine shop below. With folded hands he beseeched him to come to his succour. He promised to pay him back manifold once his hard times were over. The manager of the wine shop agreed to help him. He provided him with two meals a day during July and one meal a day after that. His weakness escalated his pessimism and depression. He could hardly stir out of his bed, much less go out.

When Allauddin came to see him on August 12, the door was closed though not bolted from inside. He knocked at the door again and again. Finding no response he pushed it open and went in. The room was absolutely bare, full of dirt and trash. He saw Johar Chakwali reclining on a cotton bedspread. He appeared very week and listless. The only parts of his languid body which reminded Allauddin of him were his penetrating eyes. It did not take Allauddin long to guess that it was a case of starvation and possibly also of dehydration. "Johar Chakwali, what have you done to yourself," Allauddin cried in anguish.

Allauddin did not have his flowing beard. He was clean shaven and in place of his earlier finely trimmed moustache he had grown it thick. With a Gandhi cap on, no one could have the slightest inkling that he was a Muslim. Shiv Shanker took some time to recognize him and then with much effort he put forward his right arm to half-embrace him. Allauddin brought for him a large pot of tea and a full meal. When he was able to get up, Allauddin helped him to bathe. He did not have a change of clothes. Allauddin had come there on a bicycle and within half an hour he brought for him, from nearby Pahar Ganj market, three sets of white collarless shirt, pajamas, Gandhi cap and Nehru style jacket. He made the restaurant boy clean the room when he came to collect cups and plates. A fill of food, clean clothes and the look of a respectable Congressman instilled some self-confidence in him. Allauddin told him that he had come there to request him to go and see their common friend Bashir Ahmed at his Mori Gate house as he needed some help. He had been there once or twice earlier with Allauddin.

Shiv Shanker reached Mori Gate next morning. He took a seat in the buggy plying to Delhi railway station and from there walked less than a furlong to Mori Gate bazaar. Standing on the elevation of the railway bridge he surveyed that hundred yards long bazaar sloping from the bridge till it ended at the Mori Gate. Groups of refugees were moving one way or the other in that bazaar. All the shops there were owned by Muslims and were closed. Where the platform of the closed shop was large enough, refugees from Pakistan had found a shelter. On the roads towards left and right the foot paths had been occupied by the refugees. He reached the centre of the bazaar, where on the right side above four shops was the palatial house of Bashir Ahmed. All the windows were closed, were without curtains and over laden with dust. These did not seem to have been opened for months and gave the impression of the house being uninhabited. The stairs from the bazaar had its door locked from outside and both the lock and the door, covered with dust and cobwebs as these were, gave the "impression of having remained unused for a long time.

Shiv Shanker recollected that there were also stairs up from the back lane for the use of the menials. As he turned back towards the bridge and entered the back lane he found that refugees were thronging everywhere.

He located the back stairs without any difficulty and climbed up. Even when he repeatedly knocked the back door there was no response. He had done it lightly so as not to attract attention. When he thumped it once with his fist, an old woman's voice was heard: "Who is there?" In a reassuring tone he replied: "I am Johar Chakwali, a friend of Bashir Ahmed." The old woman answered:

"Bashir Ahmed no more lives here." He persisted: "I am Johar Chakwali, Bashir Ahmed's friend. He wanted me to see him. He sent the message through Maulana Allauddin Khan."

Shiv Shanker noticed that some one was peeping through the chink near hinges of the door. Thinking that Bashir Ahmed might have some difficulty in recognizing him because of his present dress, he said somewhat loudly: "Bashir Sahib, adab arz. Yesterday Maulana Allauddin requested me to see you. So I am here at your service." After exchange of a few courtesies, when Bashir Ahmed was sure that the person on the other side was Johar Chakwali, he half opened the door and closed it immediately he stepped in. Fear and anxiety had changed Bashir Ahmed's voice which was piteous and distressful. A sense of insecurity had lengthened his face. His lusterless eyes had a glint of fright. Cold sweat burst out of his forehead and temples as he mumbled in an effort to say something. Shiv Shanker looked around. Six terror stricken faces were staring at him. The seventh person in that room, a woman past her middle age, was sitting with bowed head on a string stool. On his earlier visit he had been introduced to the men folk only. He was seeing these women for the first time. The young lady was apparently Bashir Ahmed's wife. She was a woman of great beauty with big magnetic eyes. The shriveling of her Pathan face had made her eyes look bigger and heart rending. Bowing and raising his right arm in the traditional manner, he saluted adab arz to everyone. In reply they made hopeless gestures and smiled sadly. As they sat on seats without cushions, one middle aged lady whose eyelashes were quivering, said in a shaky voice: "Hundreds of refugees have crowded around. The worst can happen any time."

Consoling them Shiv Shanker said in a sympathetic tone: "Gandhiji is coming here in a week or ten days. Everything will be all right soon."

Bashir Ahmed cooed: "Johar Sahib we want to go to our village in Moradabad till things settle down here. We do not have suitable dress for moving out. Buying tickets at the railway station can create difficulties. Would you kindly help us?"
Bashir Ahmed gave him two hundred rupees and requested him to buy

three plain simple saris with full-sleeve ladies short shirts, like those which lower middle class orthodox Hindu women wear and three white Gandhi caps. They did not want the ladies to wear choli or blouse normally worn by Hindu women of their status, which leaves the hip uncovered. They felt it safer for these ladies to look like orthodox Hindu women. In a cowering voice, Bashir Ahmed suggested: "Across the railway bridge, there is Sita Ram Bazaar where you will be able to buy these things. Please make haste so that we are able to catch 10.50 a.m. train to Moradabad."

Shiv Shanker came back with the things required by them in less than half an hour and handed over these along with the balance of rupees seventeen. He had on his own brought three dhotis for men and taught them how this three yard long piece of cloth Hindus wear round their lower bodies, how one end of which is passed between the legs and tucked in behind. Soon the ladies came out in full sleeve short shirts and saris worn in the orthodox style which left more cloth for covering the head. The men had shaven clean and Gandhi cap fitted well on their skull. The girl wore salwar kameez with matching head covering. They had already packed up the boxes and were ready to move.

Before Shiv Shanker went down to fix up two horse carriages for them, he got from them key of the front door. They also gave him two thousand rupees for seven tickets to Muradabad and for the upkeep of the house during the period of their absence. He told them that he would get the carriages halted as near the door as possible at 10.15 a.m. sharp. They should be as quick as possible to get into the carriages with their luggage. He tallied his watch with that of Bashir Ahmed.

Shiv Shanker hired two horse carriages on the clear understanding that they were to go to Purana Qila via the shorter railway station road route and, under no circumstance, were to slow down, much less halt their carriage outside the Delhi railway station, whatever persons seated in the carriages may say. There were rufugees everywhere along the route. One or more refugee trains had arrived at the station and the refugees from Pakistan were pouring out of the station gate like a dam-burst. They just managed to move out quickly before the flood of refugees deluged the road outside the railway station. Badshir Ahmed and some others in the two carriages raised their voice and waving their hands pleaded something but they were too horrified to act. After crossing Harding Bridge, Shiv Shanker asked the driver to move fast to Purana Qila and waved to the carriage behind to pick up speed.

When they were made to alight at Purana Qila near the camp of Muslims going to Pakistan, they all were struck dumb. They were so shocked that they could hardly stand on their legs. They all flashed angry glances at Shiv Shanker which were like burning coal. The women sat down with their hands on their knees as an expression of despair. Bashir Ahmed was trembling as much from anger as from helplessness. His face became more pallid and freckled and wet with cold sweat. Suddenly everything appeared to him as black as coal. Johar Chakwali gave him an affectionate pat, put his friendly hand on his left shoulder and lamented in a sad voice: "Thank Allah you are all safe. Allah alone knows what would have happened even on a minute's halt there. Stay here, refuse to move to Pakistan. As soon as Mahatma Gandhi reaches Delhi, Insha Allah I will come to take you back. He had already paid off one carriage. He took his seat in the other carriage and returned to the Mori Gate flat. He decided to stay there but keep everything as before for some weeks at least. He cleared the front side stairs of the clutter put there to block the passage .

When he came to his Gol Market room in the evening to collect essential requirements for living in the Mori Gate flat, he found a paper wrapped round the lock. It was a letter in Urdu from Josh Rampuri, his close friend of the Lady Harding sarai days. He had written that he desperately needed his help and would come next morning again at day break, because the movement of Muslims during day time was not quite safe. He decided to spend the night there. Next morning Josh Rampuri was there before sunrise. After a few minutes of courtesies, Josh entreated: "Johar Chakwali sahib Muslims from various parts of Delhi have taken shelter in our Kucha Kadir Yar and are in need of help. Only good men like you, who are above communal feelings, can save India now."

Shiv Shanker went for a bath and when he emerged from the bath room in white khaddar dress, Gandhi cap and clean shaven grinning face, Josh Rampuri felt somewhat perplexed. He put a Gandhi cap on Josh Rampuri and they left for Kucha Kadir Yar. When they stepped into the lane bowing through the iron wicket gate, he noticed that an atmosphere of terror and hysteria pervaded there. They all had the fright and helplessness of a sacrificial lamb. It was a heart-rending spectacle of nightmarish dread. Grim specter of insecurity and helplessness was haunting everyone. Every whiff of air conjured threat to their life. Whole atmosphere was soaked with fear. Danger was dropping from the sky, panic was sprouting out of the ground and terror was peeping into door and windows shut tight. He had seen fear, anxiety and calamity writ large on the face of refugees from Pakistan. Here he saw, in utmost rawness, the dread of extermination and dishonour difficult to imagine.

Josh Rampuri led Shiv Shanker to the triangular open space at the end of Kucha Kadir Yar. Josh Rampuri had already spoken to the people there about his friend Johar Chakwali but the picture he had painted about him was altogether different from the person they saw now. He appeared like any other communal Hindu. Seeing Josh also in a Gandhi cap they felt a little less disconcerted. Johar Chakwali greeted everyone with adab-arz and salam-ul-lekam. He embraced affectionately those in the front row. The first repast of the day was ready and they requested him to join them. One of them offering him a separate plate, said: "Johar sahib, please have your pick before we all start eating together from the common dish. Declining the stainless steel plate with thanks, he joined them and began having his share, like others, from the three feet wide circular dish full of rice cooked with mutton. This was the first time they saw a Hindu having his meals, not along them, but sharing the common dish and tumbler. This was very reassuring to them and confirmed what Josh had told him about his friend.

They were sitting on a large brick platform around an old peepal tree. Only the trunk of the tree was left, after all its branches had been chopped off for fuel. A large sheet of cloth tied with long strings to nearby balconies serveral as a canopy for a part of the platform. After Shiv Shanker had accepted a betel leaf and a cardamom or two, half a dozen elders gathered round him. One of them speaking in a very sad voice beseeched:
"Johar sahib, when we took shelter here some weeks ago, we came with the barest essentials. We left behind everything hoping to go back to our home. Now this seems most unlikely. We have been advised not to venture there even to collect our valuable belongings. Josh mentioned that you are a very large hearted person without any communal prejudices and that he would request you to help us in salvaging some of these."

Looking around he replied: "It is my duty to help you and I will do my best but there are more than· fifty families here". Someone interrupting him said: "Forty eight." Shiv Shanker lowered his head as if lost in thought. Raising his head, he remarked: "I have only a week to be of help to you. After a week, when Gandhiji arrives in Delhi, either you will be able to return to your home or I also will be unable to help you. In a week I will be of assistance to seven or at the most ten of you, depending upon the areas I have to visit. When we were having our repast someone had mentioned about arranging air passage to Pakistan. That also is possible for six or seven persons only." Someone entreated him to make the number of homes to be visited for collecting valuable to two per day. They took some time in confabulating amongst themselves. In the meanwhile Josh Rampuri and Johar Chakwali talked about their good old days in Lady Harding sarai. They called Josh also, who joined them in their deliberation. After some time, they came to Johar Chakwali and most earnestly urged upon him: "Please make two houses a day which means fourteen houses for this week. We will arrange them in such a manner that you can conveniently do so. We will give a short list for each house indicating the exact place so that you will not have to waste any time. Similarly arrange air passage for eleven persons; these are two families which cannot be split."

They took two hours to decide which fourteen houses should be selected for this week, to list articles to be collected and exactly where these would be found. Johar Chakwali entreated them not to insist on paying him for visiting their houses, which would be a labour of love. He was paid rupees twelve thousand for as many air tickets to Lahore or Karachi as he could arrange. He was also given fourteen bunches of keys along with fourteen lists, which he scanned and asked a few questions for clarification. They also gave him 'an elegant leather bag in which all these had been properly arranged and safely kept under a zipper.

He left that place in the afternoon, after profuse adab arz and salam-ul-Iekam and many many embraces. When he bowed out of the iron wicket gate, he was so elated that his feet hardly touched the ground. He felt self confidence surging within him as it' had seldom done before. He was no more pessimistic or apprehensive about his future in Independent India. It had begun so well. He will have to develop the intelligence of an owl, the sharpness of an eagle, the sprint of a leopard and the ruthlessness of an amphitheater bull, he resolved in all earnestness.

On his way back from Kucha KadirYar, Shiv Shanker got a nameplate painted 'Shiv Shanker Kohli - Congress Leader" and fixed it outside the entrance of the Mori Gate house.

CHAPTER TWENTY SEVEN

Chanan Mal had no difficulty in locating the residence of Kohli in Mori Gate bazaar. Almost in the centre of the bazaar on the right side were stairs, bigger" and better 'than those to other flats. The door was open wide and on one side was fixed a freshly painted plate on which was painted in two lines: 'Shiv Shanker Kohli - Congress Leader'. The persons moving about on the road were refugees only. Some of them had occupied Front-side of closed shops where there was enough space for a temporary shelter. Chanan Mal climbed the stairs and found the door at the upper end of the stairs also wide open. He knocked a few times at the open door. Shiv Shanker came there and greeted him with a smile. They went in and sat down on a sofa. The cushions were of different colours but looked almost alike because these were dust smudged. The cushions had been used along with other articles to block the stairs by the previous residents and Shiv Shanker had not yet had time to dust these properly or to have these laundered. Chanan Mal enquired from him about his family. He replied that he was son of Tirath Ram Kohli and lived in Mohalla Rezgaran of Chakwal. Chanan Mal interrupted him: "Grand son of Jharoo Ram." Shiv Shanker nodded in affirmation. Chanan Mal told him: "Your grand maternal aunt was married to my grand uncle. Soon after marriage she was hit by the hind leg of a cow while milking it. This broke her hip bone and she became unfit to bear children. She went back to Chakwal and my grand uncle, despite the opposition of entire family brought home the daughter of low caste barber as his wife. Kohli remembered that his grand aunt, though above ninety, was still alive when he left Chakwal. Her legs had shriveled and she hopped around like a frog.

Shiv Shanker put on his Gandhi cap. Family links established Chanan Mal, requested him to help him in finding a job or some other work. He was lost in thoughts but kept looking fixedly at Chanan Mal. When Chanan Mal repeated his request, he muttered in a sympathetic tone: "In Delhi no one can get a job without greasing the palm of the officer concerned. I do not know the present rate, now that there is rush of job seekers. I think at least two thousand rupees will have to be paid."

Chanan Mal broke into mirthless laughter. When Chanan Mal looked askance at him and their eyes met Shiv Shanker began to blink. Before Chanan Mal could say anything, there was a knock at the door. Shiv Shanker went there and brought in a person whose hand he was holding in a friendly manner. They sat on another sofa side by side. Shiv Shanker patted him and remarked: "Maulana, you look young and smart without your beard."

Allauddin beseeched: "Please do not call me Maulana unless you want me to be murdered I am Shastri, not Alluddin Shastri, but simply A .D. Shastri. Anyone can call himself Shastri but I am a genuine, fully qualified Shastri. When I was young there used to be debates and arguments between Arya Samaj votaries and Muslim divines in Azamgarh as to which religion - Hinduism or Islam - was superior. After I learnt Sanskrit and passed the Shastri examination, I could give the Arya Samajists tit-for-tat." Remembering all that, he laughed heartily.

Shiv Shanker stared at Allauddin. Clean shaven with moustache like that of a Hindu and two ends of a white scarf hanging from his neck on his chest, he would be mistaken for a Brahmin by anyone. Allauddin advised him: "It is good that you have thought of becoming a leader, but as a Congress leader you can not have smooth sailing. So far as I know you are not a Brahmin. It is not fortuitous that all non-Muslim ministers in most of the Congress governments after the 1937 elections were Brahmins. Don't you note that Congress leaders not only at the top but at lower level also belong mostly to the Brahmin community? Looking intently at him to assess his reaction, Allauddin added:

"Congress leaders are now multiplying like mosquitoes in monsoon. The people coming from Pakistan are at present leaderless. Surely there will be greater scope as their leader."

Chanan Mal supported Allauddin's suggestion and added: "The refugees do not know anyone here and are feeling helpless. If some one can assist and guide them he will surely win over their confidence.

After a brief pause, Allauddin disclosed: "Yesterday I went to see some Muslim divines who are bidding their time in hiding, because they do not want to remove their beard like me. They are yearning to go to Pakistan but have no face to do so having vehemently opposed Muslim League all these years. They are now critical of Gandhi and have a good word only for Nehru." His face suddenly looked flushed and remorse was apparent in his eyes. Speaking slowly he added: "The Muslim clerics played the fool before Independence in the hope of gaining paradise, but now find themselves almost in a hell. I did a little plain-speaking to them. They did not like my telling them that Nehru would now need Muslim quislings even more than before the Partition of India."

For sometime Allauddin kept sitting motionless with bent back and lowered head. Even his ears became red. He became shuddery sometimes which filled Shiv Shanker with pity and fellow feeling for him. It took him some time to raise his head and to meet Shiv Shanker's eyes, which he found full of friendship and reassurance. Recovering some of his old self, he exclaimed: "I told those crest fallen Maulanas two things. Gandhi had with him solution to the constitutional problem India was facing before Partition, but did not have political sagacity to put it forward at the proper time. He had been advocating for decades the need for small, self sufficient communities as the cornerstone of his conception of Hind Swaraj. This would have made a short shrift of united India vis-a-vis Pakistan controversy. If with less than half of India's population, United States of America can have about fifty states each having its own constitution, this country could be constituted into over a hundred self governing units and evolve, in view of historical factors, better methods of knitting them together." After a brief pause he continued: "The second point I told Maulanas was that they should have no illusions about Nehru. A successful politician in power must perpetuate himself and that a centralized parliamentary. state which Nehru was visualizing was as capable of tyranny as a totalitarian state. I told the clerics that the lust for power of a successful politician and the ego of a successful mahatma should not be underestimated."

The three looked at one another. Only Chanan Mal gave the impression of a clear reaction. Shiv Shanker had shifted Gandhi cap a little lower on his forehead and Allauddin failed to surmise whether his reaction to what he had said was positive or negative. He recollected what one of the Muslim divines had told him. When people had beard of one type or the other, it could be possible to guess what was in their mind. Now that everyone shaved and could smile like Mona Lisa it had become difficult to hazard a guess.

Shiv Shanker introduced Chanan Mal to Allauldin and said that he was a recently arrived refugee from Pakistan and that he had come there for help in getting a job. How could one arrange a job without greasing the palm? He would have to make much effort to get him a job for a paltry sum of rupees two thousand as he had promised to do. Showing his indifference Shiv Shanker turned his face toward the window. Allauddin took this opportunity to give a wink to Chanan Mal to signal a warning. Catching Shiv Shanker's attention again, Allauldin remarked: "Kohli sahib if he had two thousand rupees he would not have come to you. He is an educated refugee and if you are going to be a leader of refugees he will be of use to you."

Chanan Mal got up to leave. Shiv Shanker offered him one hundred rupees currency note which he refused in a courteous manner. Allauddin now seated himself opposite Shiv Shanker and glanced at him enquiringly. He noticed that his face was not wishy-washy as before. He had more of self-assurance and seemed to be thinking over something. Allauddin preferred to sit quiet, waiting for him to have his say. Shiv Shanker got up and opened the wire gauze shutters of the windows. A few flies rushed in and started buzzing. A rat or two which were moving around the corners created the sound of nibbling at something. Shiv Shanker fidgeted his nose, a line or two appeared on his forehead. His lips quivered as if making up mind to say something. Abruptly he uttered: "No doubt it can be very useful to have a name which is like that of a Brahmin but how can one suddenly change one's name."

Allauddin's looks, always sharp and far sighted, now had the feeling of astuteness. Without his beard he looked more resolute than before. His cheeks appeared more round than they did when partly hidden by a beard. There was slightly more flesh on his left cheek than on the right, which made his appearance quite canny and impressive. He stared at Shiv Shanker and advised: "Becoming a Shastri is not difficult but if you are going to be a refugee leader you better drop Kohli from your name. Luckily you do not have a typical Punjabi name like Chanan Mal. Shiv Shanker seems to me to be a name that can pass as one of a Brahmin. The world in which you were known as Johar Chakwali or Kohli Sahib is dead. The new world in which you are going to live and thrive will get accustomed to whatever name you give yourself. I think the refugees will have less misgivings about being led by a Shiv Shanker than by one of the Kohli's among them.

They walked to Kasmere Gate market and had a good repast. Thereafter they looked up a painter to have a name board instead of name plate. Both of them preferred something that immediately caught attention. They thought of many alternatives and 'decided that the sign board should have in English and Urdu: "Shiv Shanker, President, All India Refugees Welfare Association." The refugees were familiar with Urdu only and not with Hindi language. Allauddin again stressed upon him not to mention Kohli with his name even by mistake.

Before returning to Mori Gate Shiv Shanker bought two bottles of rum, which he knew Allauddin liked more than the country liquor. A bottle of rum and two bottles of whiskey were there in Mori Gate house wardrobe but he did not want to touch these for the present. He had left hanging on the wall the picture of a middle aged bearded person at the bottom of which were printed the words 'Sir Syed Ahmed Khan' .The only change he had made in the house was removing cushions, bolsters, mattresses, stools, tables, chairs, portable bamboo piles, etcetera, with which the front side staircase was cluttered to block the entrance to the flat. Allauddin helped him to better arrange the furniture and to dust the cushions, bolsters, etc. so that these looked less unclean.

Shiv Shanker told Alluddin: "When I reached the Delhi railway station, along with Bashir Ahmed's family, the whole place thronged with refugees. The situation became really terrifying as torrents of refugees were pouring out of the railway station, a few trains carrying them having arrived a while earlier. I could not dare to take them inside the railway station. The driver of the horse carriage confirmed that there was no normal timing now for the trains. Many had been cancelled because of the rush of refugee trains arriving at all hours. I too was aghast and was at my wit's end. I could think nothing safer for them than to rush them to the Purana Qila. We will bring them back from there if and when the things improve." Allauddin agreed that leaving them stranded at the railway station without knowing when they will be able to board the train to Muradabad would have been very risky. He also felt that bringing them back to this house could not have been less risky in view of the refugees crowding around. All the shops in the area were closed and most of the Muslims had deserted the area. Bashir Ahmed could not have ventured out even for daily necessities.

Allauddin noticed that Shiv Shanker did not now exhibit diffidence or a sense of insecurity or anxiety. He never before had such a placid and confident look. Breaking the ice Shiv Shanker remarked: "It is good that India is free. Now there will be freedom and greater opportunities for everyone." Allauddin remained silent for sometime, he grimaced. After a short pause he quipped: "Truly speaking, Gandhiji is not just a product of the climate of India. He is more the creation of the changes brought about by the British in India. But for the coming of British he would have been whiling away his time somewhere near Porbander his native principality, one among, over a hundred in Kathiawar., In fact there had "been no India for him to think about because India as we understand it today is the consequence of the coming here of the British. Now Gandhi says that we were slaves under British and flee before that. It will be worthwhile to understand the freedom the people here had before the British came."

Allauddin paused a little, stretched his right leg and continued a little less vehemently: "After Shivaji, the Marathas, under Peshwas, left a trail of desolation and destruction wherever they went. Contemporary record speaks of them as slaughterers of children, slayers of women, robbers of the poor, abductors of chaste women. Then one among the Mughal twilight kings of Delhi was Mohammed Shah, who like the nawabs of Lucknow and elsewhere led a life of uninterrupted gaiety. He came to know that one of his senior wazirs Kanmuddin had seven hundred twenty concubines only. He sent two hundred eighty more to his harem because a minister of his status should have at least one thousand slave girls. Then a few decades earlier there was the procession of Banda Bahadur being brought to Delhi in an iron cage followed by long entourage of Mughal soldiers carrying on bamboo poles heads of mutineers, followed by bullock carts piled with more severed heads. As all the carts were not full to the top, they on their way to Delhi, beheaded passers by. When the procession reached Delhi on March 5, 1716, the carnage of other arrested Sikh mutineers started. Opposite the chabutra of the kotwali in Chandni Chowk, one hundred were executed every day for weeks. Then there was jazia tax on non Muslims and the levy of chauth by every foreign or Indian invader. There were in addition Pindaras, thugs and freebooters of several varieties. It was commonly said at that time that "what a man had in his stomach was his, the rest belonged to the raider".

Shiv Shanker felt perplexed by what he heard and the rhetorical manner in which Allauddin said it. Allauddin took a sip of rum diffidently. Shiv Shanker decided to make him drink more so that he became less excited. In a mellow tone he continued: "I wish the British had jackboots like the Portuguese or Nazis. Then there would have been no Gandhi or Jinnah. Jackboots were needed to crack the religious orthodoxy of various Indian communities and to crack the rigid structure of Indian caste system. Thus the benefits of British rule would have percolated to lower classes. So far only upper strata of Indian society has been beneficiary of their rule."

Shiv Shanker interjected: "You know too much. Is it necessary to know so much in order to live? All I know is that marriage with history cannot be a happy marriage for every country. India was raped by some, kept as a courtesan and added to the harem by some more and made to live the life of a pathetic widow by some others. India was maid-in-waiting for the British. It is difficult to say whether this is a curse of destiny, fault of Indian geography or some failing of the Indian people." Saying this Shiv Shanker gasped and had a few gulps of rum from the bottle.

They both got up, searched for nails and hammer so that the new sign board could be put in place above the entrance of stairs in the street.

CHAPTER TWENTY EIGHT

In a few weeks the refugee camp in the Tis Hazari ground began to bustle with life, as if dry twigs, dead branches and stunted stems planted there had put forth shoots, leaves and buds. Human life is an ever flowing river. If it is hindered, it has to find a way to flow on. When the previous life of these refugees was scotched by the depredation and affliction of Partition, they searched and found new ways of living. Their misery filled them with courage. It gave them the grim determination to leap on every opportunity. Sorrow could change even a good-for-nothing to a solid person and a lazy one to hardworking. It gave them the persistence of a wood-pecker which heaved down trees with its chattering teeth. It was a misfortune which turned simpletons from villages to wise men of the city.

Every day crowds upon crowds of refugees had been pouring into the city like the muddy waters of a river in flood. There was hustle and bustle of their crowding every nook and comer. They were jostling every where and coming into collision with everything. They had built shelters and shanties of every shape and pattern. No open space, whether footpaths, grounds or parks, had remained unoccupied. They had started living under the arches and parabolas of the Mughal times and in the cellars of the city ramparts and gates. Railway platforms and goods sheds were full of them, so were dharamshalas, temples, gurdwaras, schools and colleges. Some of them had started living on the platform outside closed shops and houses of Muslims.

Rows of huts had come up in the Tis Hazari camp with just walking space in between. The whole ground was buzzing with the commotion of refugees. It was no more the dreary world of a few days ago. Chanan Mal now noticed that there was hunger for life and will to strive among most of the refugees. The road and the goal before them were still hazy. However, there was inclination among most of them to get back on feet and to find a way to move forward. Chanan Mal beheld a new man, quite different from the one who came here a few days ago. He thought to himself whether it was upheaval of partition that gave these people so much strength or was it some inherent human quality which made them shore up their life and to renew it with so much fortitude, effort and courage. He thought of a spider energetically weaving its cobweb after it had been destroyed and of an ant persistently towing away a dead beetle.

It did not take the refugees long to get used to the atmosphere and the mores of the city. They would crowd around the bazaars and outside the shops there. Sometimes they lost their cool and equally often the local residents lost their patience. They were all trying to become a part of the city and to adjust themselves to it. The affect of the city on their mind differed from person to person. The city was a crucible for some in which their personality melted and took a new shape. A few were reduced to ash but a majority was smelted and purified. Hardly, there was anyone who had remained as before.

Chanan Mal noticed that most of the people were not just waiting for others to help them but were trying to find some way of helping themselves and to be of assistance to others. There were a few whose perspective remained limited to self-interest which they sought to advance by hook or by crook. There were many more whom the new situation and the new challenges made more humane and who seldom hesitated to show fellow-feeling. Overriding all that was the desire to be up and doing, to secure some livelihood and to settle down. Only through the daily struggle for existence could the past be forgotten and future rendered secure.

In an atmosphere in which most of his fellow refugees were up and about, Chanan Mal was also spurred to finding some way of making a living for self and the family which was now his responsibility. After visiting Shiv Shanker he knew that he will have to help himself and was thinking hard how to do so. Many refugees became hawkers or sat on the roadside with their wares in improvised baskets to vend something. They took up unhesitatingly whatever work was available. The wife of an advocate from Attock, the western part of the Punjab, began to do household chores in the house of local residents, a work which she never did before. There was no limit to the ingenuity people exhibited in their effort to make both ends meet. A young man who was a college student before Partition and was now the main bread winner of the family bought watch repairing accessories from a Muslim watch maker migrating to Pakistan. All the time he was most carefully removing parts of a watch, noting down and drawing which part fitted where and how. Then he would put these parts back He kept doing it again and again on various types of time pieces he had. After he acquired dexterity in this, he would take up the business of repairing watches of others. When a problem arose in the refugee camp they did their best to solve it themselves. Women started taking turn in the community kitchen so that it served them better. Water hydrant was making a pool where they filled buckets or washed clothes. There were volunteers to dig channel to the roadside drain with rods and iron pieces as spade was not available.

Chanan Mal saw a young refugee sitting downcast near the community kitchen. When Chanan Mal urged upon him not to be downhearted like that, he replied that he was thinking of his mare in the village. It was a beautiful mare unmatched in its gallop.

He said he felt sad because its new master might not keep it as lovingly as he did.

Further he was thinking of the neem tree under the shade of which he" and his mare rested during noon. He was also thinking of the pure sweet air of the village and of the shining brightness of stars at night there. When a day after he again saw him sitting there sadly, Chanan Mal again advised him to get over his sad thoughts. That young man replied, it was a different worry that day. He had offered to buy a horse carriage from a Muslim coachman intending to go to Pakistan. That man was willing to accept payment in the form of his watch and two gold rings but wanted some cash also. He was thinking what articles to sell to raise the required cash and how best to do so. A majority of the persons there, despite their personal problems, extended a helping hand to others. Some like Baba Nihal Singh, who was perhaps he oldest man in the camp, did it more than others. He was the only survivor of his village in the Montgomery district after it was attacked by Muslim ex-servicemen. He was tied to a tree and made to witness the killing of all the two hundred ninety eight villagers, Sikhs and one Muslim family. The Muslim blacksmith chose to die with his fellow villagers and did not disclose that he was Muslim. His beard and turban were not different from that of a Sikh. Boys and girls who were studying in Pakistan started going to schools in the nearby areas. Others and those who were too young to go to school began to be taught alphabet and figures in the camp itself. If there were no slates or paper, etc., they learned by writing with sticks on the ground.

Chanan Mal had beautiful handwriting and knew Urdu very well. He bought pen, ink pot and paper from a Sadar Bazar shop nearby and sat on the pavement to write letters for nominal payment. Every morning and evening after the news bulletins, All India Radio announced the names of persons looking for their missing kith and kin. A little away from the railway bridge there was a tea shop of a local resident. Chanan Mal noted down there the names of missing relatives and of those who were in search of them. He would write these neatly on a sheet of paper district wise and display it on the iron palisade of the pavement where he had begun to sit. Refugees came flocking there and where necessary they had letter written by him. Soon Chanan Mal had a busy time writing letters and did not have a minute free from morning to evening.

There were many difficulties which the refugees in the camp encountered. Water hydrants and other conveniences were not enough for the number now living there. Not only government agencies but some private organizations were supplying household effects, clothes, provisions, etc. for those living in the Camp, almost half of which did not reach the refugees. Milk was received enough for children but many did not get it and those who got it found it watery. Distribution of bed sheets, clothes, blankets, etc, was not impartial. Some of the Hindu owned Urdu newspapers of Lahore had started publishing from Delhi. Chanan Mal wrote to these newspapers about these problems of the Camp. Sometimes these were published in the form of letters to the editor and sometimes attributed to the paper's local reporter. As a result of Chanan Mal's reports in the newspapers, efforts were made to remove grievances and to improve services.

Not only fellow residents but also those managing the camp began to give him special attention and show him much consideration. Refugees began to come to him also for writing every sort of application. Someone wanted a quota for sugar for opening a sweets shop, another wanted license for a ration shop. If someone was a municipal employee in Pakistan, he wanted to apply for job in the municipal committee. Another one wanted to apply for the post of a teacher. All this gave Chanan Mal a lot of self-confidence and a sense of importance and usefulness. He was fast recovering some of his old self. He looked less lean and thin, His voice which had become screechy was now normal.

A few more letter writers had taken up the same calling in nearby areas. One of them had his seat not many yards away from where he worked. Chanan Mal had also begun to contemplate that sitting by the road side and writing letters for a few pice each could not be a permanent career. A

Hindu owned Urdu paper Desh Bhagat had continued to publish from Lahore after Partition. After August 15, it had started attacking India putting all the blame for the Partition on Gandhi and Nehru. As his entire family and all his relatives had left for India he was not fully trusted. As soon as he came across an aristocrat from Delhi who had property there more extensive than he had in Lahore, he struck a deal with him and quietly shifted to Delhi. He began to bring out Desh Bhagat from Delhi and needed some sub-editors. Chanan Mal went to the office of the newspaper and met Acharya Ram Krishan who was all in all, proprietor, editor, publisher and printer of the paper. He gave Chanan Mal a news item from a daily in English language for rendering into Urdu. Finding that the translation was satisfactory and language racy, he employed him as sub-editor on rupees fifty per month. Chanan Mal soon discovered that even calligraphists working for the paper were getting higher emoluments. Chanan Mal decided to mark time, till he had gained some experience.

The daily Desh Bhagat had from its very first issue in Delhi, begun to attack Pakistan and Muslims more vehemently than the other Urdu daily newspapers. Finding that the paper was becoming more popular among refugees, the others adopted the same tone and policy. First thing Chanan Mal learned in the office of Desh Bhagat was that a heading to a news item need not be in accordance with the text of the news. Not only the heading but the news item has to be rewritten to conform to the policy of the paper, even if it sometimes acquired an altogether different purport. In a day or two Chanan Mal became aware that if he was to retain his job, he had to publish a news report not as received but as Acharya Ram Krishan desired. An appeal by Pandit Nehru for communal harmony had to be given a banner 'Nehru's scalp itches again', Statement by Mahatma Gandhi that Muslims should not be evicted, would have to carry the banner 'Gandhi hugs Muslims, frowns at refugees'. Even an assurance by Mr. Nehru that all the refugees will be properly settled would appear under the heading 'Nehru brags again'. Every day a news item had to be there in the paper about the killing and looting of Hindus and Sikhs in Pakistan. In case no item was received it had to be prepared at the desk on the basis of earlier reports. Whenever a new report about the killing and looting of Muslims in trains passing through east Punjab was received, it was necessary to mention that Muslims were carrying arms and ammunition or that they tried to kidnap a non-Muslim girl from the village. Suddenly Acharya Ram Krishan would come to the news desk and would want a story to be written under the banner 'Muslims burn crops in east Punjab villages on way to Pakistan' or 'Muslims in Delhi stockpiling arms: attack on refugees imminent'. As sales of Desh Bhagat climbed up, other Urdu newspapers would not be left behind, though the latter could not be equally ingenious. Acharya Ram Krishan might not have been encouraged in this by those in Government but Chanan Mal was sure that he was not being discouraged at all. In fact many important political personalities began to curry his favour as the sales of daily Desh Bhagat increased by leaps and bounds.

A former sub-editor of the Desh Bhagat began to publish a tabloid 'Azad Bharat' from Delhi. The very first issue front paged the story with full page banner 'Pakistan's plan to extend its boundaries near Delhi' When Chanan Mal enquired from him about its source so that he could follow it up, editor of Azad Bharat, pointing finger at his head replied: "This is the source. It is more fertile than that of Acharyaji, only I am a poor man and cannot make full us of it". The Azad Bharat began to publish everyday on front page news about the death of Hindus in one part of Delhi or the other. One day it would be six Hindus died in Daryaganj and on another seven Hindus met with their death in Sadar Bazar and soon. Acharya Ram Krishan was angry with Chanan Mal and blamed him for missing such an important news item. Chanan Mal made enquiries and found that the editor of Azad Bharat was merely picking up figures of normal deaths in those areas from the municipal record and front paging the news without mentioning that these were normal deaths. The way he displayed these news items created the impression that it was otherwise. All this made refugees and a large section of Hindus in Delhi feel insecure and full of anger, with the result that there was a demand that all Muslims should be driven out of Delhi, subdued in some places and vocal in others.

CHAPTER TWENTY NINE

In As the clock struck midnight, deafening sound of bomb explosions and intermittent firing rent the air. It appeared to be from Pul Bangash, Phatak Habash Khan, Sarai Rohela, Roshan Ara Road and other nearby areas inhabited by the Muslims. As time passed this din became more and more resounding till it seemed to be coming nearer and nearer. All the refugees in the Tis Hazari camp woke up. They had read or had been told about reports in newspapers that Muslims in Delhi had been collecting arms and ammunition and about their programme to commit aggression .Many of the refugees dressed up and got ready to move out if need be. The only place they thought of for hiding was the kikar thickets in the woodland on the long ridge beyond Victory Tower. For the last two or three days they were noticing ex-servicemen and servicemen in mufti moving about in the city bazaars. They were wondering why they could not provide them security.

During the last fortnight, Shiv Shanker had tried to win popularity among refugees mainly by distributing clothes and other used things from the· houses of Muslims, the keys of which he had. The sign board outside his residence was too prominent to be missed. The refugees had noticed it and taken it seriously. Friendless as they generally felt, they had begun to expect much from him. At about 2 a.m. some of them noisily thumped his door and when he opened it rubbing his sleepy eyes, they explained to him the situation. He came with them to the surrounding refugee shanties and then to the Tis Hazari camp. He was no more looking older than his age. Wrinkles and crow's feet, which had appeared on his face due to constant privation and insecurity, had disappeared and he was looking an amateurish youth of twenty four. This became more noticeable because he was feeling lost in the absence of Gandhi cap which he forgot to put on in a hurry. Refugees who had gathered around him were much older than he. They watched his bland face and his eyes which were not yet free from the heaviness of sleep. One of them shouted: "Pradhanji tell us what to do".

Shiv Shanker was titillated by being addressed as pradhan - president - which set him thinking hard. He suggested:

"Across the railway bridge there is Sita Ram Bazaar, a fully fortified Hindu area. I will get its iron gate opened and take women and children to the safety of that place."

It was already past 3 a.m. Din, clatter of bombs and shooting was gradually becoming less and less. By the time some young women and girls got ready to shift it had become sporadic and appeared to be dying down. For another half an hour Shiv Shanker sat there on a string cot and dozed. As others went back to their hut Shiv Shanker also returned to his house.

It was a sullen dawn. As the first rays of the sun touched the city, an endless file of Muslims began to move along the road from wholesale vegetable market towards the railway bridge and the city. They were all haggard, battered, distraught, disheveled and smeared with blood and dirt. They were limping, straggling and walking haltingly. Most of them were in rags. Some had improvised bandages wrapping one part of the body or the other. There was not a man, women or child who was normally dressed. Many women did not have enough clothes to fully cover their bodies, even the long veil on some women was not without slits and stains. Shortly after day break the single file of dispossessed Muslims swelled to two or more rows. Sometimes a family was moving huddled together. Many of them now were less decrepit, their clothes less soiled, stained and niggardly and they were carrying a bag or two. The terror of a single night had taken out the very essence of their life and destroyed every component of their being. Their faces were smudged with terror and misery as if they were all wearing a mask of gloom. Many of them walked with raised head and blood shot eyes. None looked right or left. It was such a picture of wretchedness and devastation that they seemed to be apparitions driven out of some nether world of persecution and torture.

As the sun went up, some refugees from Tis Hazari camp and elsewhere made a line on the other side of the road watching glumly the ebb and flow of this brook of misery, carrying the flotsam of wanton destruction. By afternoon scores of columns of smoke which had arisen skyward in the south west had thinned, so also the moving line of Muslims. Refugees from Tis Hazari remained standing on the roadside at some places in twos and threes and at others in larger numbers. In the beginning, if anyone tried to have a fling at the Muslims on the other side of the road, he was snubbed and sent away. Though many of them had gone through even worse, their hearts became full of compassion and sympathy on seeing again mayhem and bloodshed in raw and in flesh. While refugees from the camp were coming and going, baba Nihal Singh remained standing there throughout the day, a picture of dejection and sadness. In the morning when he saw a young girl in tatters he wished to offer his turban to her but he knew that she would not look at it. Some of them wanted to offer them water but knew that it will be treated as adding insult to injury. They knew from their own experience that even when a man loses every possession, there is some thing more precious than everything else which clings to him and sustains him.

There is another instinct greed, slightly less innate than the first which also subsists in man. As the refugees became aware that Muslims have been compelled to abandon their home, those in the camp and near about became anxious to go and occupy these before anyone else. However, the trickle of Muslims going to Jama Mosque or to the Purana Qila had continued even after dusk. They were still hesitant to go there after nightfall. From early next morning Hindu and Sikh refugees living in the Tis Hazari camp, on foot paths and elsewhere began rushing to the streets, lanes, by-lanes and suburbs from where Muslims had been evicted the previous day. Everyone was in a hurry to occupy whatever he could, before others did it. There hardly was a house in proper shipshape, with doors and windows intact. In any case walls and roofs were there and accommodation was more. The rest could be attended to when they started living there.

Chanan Mal sent a word to his office that he would be late for his afternoon duty as he had decided to look up' a suitable house for himself even though his sister was disinclined to take advantage of this tragedy. After crossing the ice factory and Pul Bangash, he walked over two miles of the area crisscrossed by a maze of lanes, by lanes, streets, sub streets, alleys, bazaars and bastis. Every entrance had a strong iron gate, built during the last decade when communal tension in the city had reached a pitch. All these had been broken with the help of steel cutters, saws, hammers, massive rods and pulleys. Where all this did not succeed in smashing the gate, the walls into which these had been built had been demolished. The doors of almost every house had been smashed before the residents were made to leave or killed.

There was a lane which seemed to be inhabited by a better class of Muslims. Its gate required so much of force and demolition for its dismantling that the adjoining buildings were full of cracks and the entrance was cluttered with rubble so much so that it was not easy to enter it. Not many refugees had come to this side. This neatly tiled alley had patches of congealed blood at every step. Broken furniture, splintered china ware, mangled picture frames, school and other books and household effects were lying helter-skelter.

There was a house slightly better built than others in the lane, with Muslim sacred figures '786' etched in the plaster above the entrance. The door was open and intact, so were the windows though many of the glass panes had cracks and chinks. Entrance lounge had every sort of knick-knack cluttering the floor. On one side was a beautiful shelf with glass shutters. It was full of books, many of them nicely bound. There was a writing table next to it in which someone had made a gape with a hatchet. Door next to it was half open, Chanan Mal pushed open the other half and went in. Under a white bed sheet lay two dead bodies. He felt nausea and was shocked and dazzled. He had no inclination to lift the sheet and see who they were. The stairs on one side of the lounge had been broken so thoroughly that none could climb up. He came out with the thought of postponing, if not giving up, the quest for a house. His sister had already urged him not to make her live in a house wherefrom Muslims had been evicted.

From there Chanan Mal went straight to his office. As soon as he took his seat another sub-editor Mela Ram began to scold him for being late. From yesterday his name had begun to appear on the paper as its editor. This newspaper was attacking the government most rancorously and inciting communal passions more than any other paper. Acharya Ram Krishan thought that if the Government decided to take action against the paper, it would be the editor who would be hauled up and not the proprietor. Hence he decided to print on top of front page the name of Mela Ram as editor, and also discontinued putting his name at the end of editorials, as had been the practice in Urdu newspapers throughout. The appointment of Mela Ram as editor also relieved Acharyaji of the onus of enforcing discipline and of making the staff work after duty hours.

Associated Press of India in his report of the Delhi riots had merely stated that Hindu Muslim riot suddenly erupted in some parts of the old city, despite Government's best efforts to prevent it. As a result of them many Muslim families felt it safe to shift to Jama mosque or to Purana Qila, The news agency had added that there were reports of two Hindu girls missing and it was suspected that some Muslim young men had seduced them.

When Hindus went to enquire about it and meet the girls, free fight started which soon developed into large scale Hindu Muslim riots, one of the bloodiest in Delhi's history. Acharya Ram Krishan scanned this news agency report and threw it in dust bin. He gave a banner for the news item, which was to cover full front page. It read: "Delhi saved. Attempt at insurrection by Muslims foiled." Acharya Ram Krishan asked Chanan Mal to write the news story on these lines and gave him some points.

Chanan Mal wrote the news story as desired by Acharyaji and added that there was such an extensive use of arms and ammunition by Muslims that by the time riots were over arms, etc, were not found on search. He further stated that Muslims followed a scorched earth policy, wrecked and rendered unusable everything, doors, windows, furniture, household effects, etc. Chanan Mal concluded the story by the remark that after defeating the Marathas when Ahmed Shah Abdali entered Delhi he' massacred half its population. It could have been worse this time but for the vigilance of the refugees.

After Chanan Mal had written this story and passed it on to Acharyaji, he was overpowered with loathing and contrition. What he had actually seen gnawed his mind. There was a lump in his throat and a few unshed tears blinded his eyes. He was unable to get over the shame and guilt of it. Suddenly Acharya Ram Krishan walked to him with the news report in his left hand, patted him with his right hand and said: "From today you are made an assistant editor, you have earned your promotion."

CHAPTER THIRTY

After communal rumpus in Delhi, Mahatma Gandhi announced his decision to return to Delhi and stay here till the Muslims driven out of their home were able to go back. This came as a great relief to the Muslims who had shifted to Jama Mosque or nearby areas instead of going to Purana Qila for migrating to Pakistan. Both Hindu and Muslim Congress leaders had visited the Jama Mosque area and had assured the Muslims who had sought shelter there that the Government would compensate them for their losses and ensure return to their home.

This was a God-sent for the three organizations which had begun to work among the refugees from Pakistan. These were merely small groups, set up only for personal benefit. These insignificant organizations now acquired importance as their statements against Gandhiji's visit to Delhi began to be displayed prominently by Urdu newspapers. Unmindful of these controversies, most of the refugees were settling down in their new home and in their new livelihood, some with long strides and others limpy.

They had held that men, like birds, should go out in the morning and return home at dusk, bringing back something for their children. They believed that little happiness that was destined for them lay in the small world of their families and in remaining engrossed in the earning of bread. They were afraid of getting involved in bigger issues which confronted them sometimes. They wanted to keep away from the problems which were not directly connected with their struggle for existence. They mostly came from villages where life was stagnant and motionless. Whatever the difficulties there, these were the same as faced by earlier generations and had the same tested solutions. They knew that the city had much to teach them. Everyone of them was learning it in one's own way and in one's own time.

Many people and organizations would come to them to render some help, to give advice or to provide guidance in something of concern to them. If someone would help them to obtain ration card or to fill claim form for property left behind, they would welcome him. If volunteers came to distribute some articles, they would express their thankfulness. However, most of them would be circumspect when issues not immediately concerning them were raised. Someone would say that Gandhiji should not come to Delhi otherwise refugees would become homeless again. Someone else would try to convince them that Gandhiji should be heartily welcomed because he had as much good of refugees at heart as that of the Muslims. Most of them avoided taking sides and did not get distracted from their daily chores. In the evening sitting outside their hut, they would be asked to join or support one association of refugees or the other. They would evade the issue by looking at one another till someone replied: "You all are educated people, unlike us. Why do not you get together and decide what is good for us, so that we all can follow it."

As life moved forward, for some smoothly and for some other roughly, they became increasingly engrossed in the daily struggle of existence. Hard Work made them set aside the past as much as possible, to hope and to aspire. The various facets of human life inevitably came into play. Here a child was born and there were felicitations, there someone passed away and there was mourning. If at one place a minor scuffle between two urchins led. to fight between two families, at another place a person would go out of his way to help the .other or to foil any harm to him. Going unobtrusively to their work in the morning and returning quietly at or after nightfall, they chose to lose themselves in the big world of their small homes and in the love of their wife and children.

While much was changing their diversions and superstitions remained the same.

They talked about women, some naively and some salaciously. When a smart attractive woman passed by, they would exchange glances, if not a remark or two among themselves. If someone cared to listen, one of them would relate his own adventure. If on any day, business was less than expected, he would try to recollect whether he came across a cat or a Brahmin on his way to work. On Sankranti, the first day of the traditional month, he would go to a temple or a gurdwara to pray, so that the whole month was blessed. He would have special prayers on the full moon day and observe ritual fast on the dark night before the new moon. Previously in the village if his field became less fertile, it was because of the railway line laid nearby. Now if the business did not make satisfactory progress it was the fault of public hydrant across the road opposite the shop.

Each one of them had begun to live life in his own manner, but they all knew that the sorrows of the world could be assuaged by taking the children in one's arms and that the fatigue of hard labour could be relieved with the love of one's wife. What a pleasure it was to love dear ones and to live for them. How consoling was the warmth of friendship. Reports in the Urdu newspapers which they read or heard did upset them sometimes, but they wanted to be mindful of their own affairs and to get fully on their feet as soon as possible.

Most of the Urdu newspapers were publishing statements by individuals and organizations against Mahatma Gandhi's visit to Delhi. Excepting a few these were different in various newspapers, because these were mostly cooked up. Many public men whose name had been included in such statements would know next day on reading the paper that they had made the statement. Normally such statements were included in a single news report, excepting where Acharya Ram Krishan specifically desired that· the statement of a particular public man should be published separately in a box.

A separate report about a statement on Gandhiji's coming visit to Delhi by Shiv Shanker, president, All India Refugees Welfare Association, appeared in the paper on front pager. On seeing this Mela Ram editor of the paper came to Chanan Mal, the local reporter and asked: "Tell me honestly how much were you paid for this?" When Chanan Mal denied having received any payment, Mela Ram asked him whether he had given him a dinner or some gift. When Chanan Mal denied this also, Mela Ram chided him:
"This news item covers two and a half column inches and as per advertisement rates you are giving him the benefit of rupees sixty without any gain." Chanan Mal came to know from Mela Ram that most of the persons whose statement appeared in the paper were making regular payments to Acharyaji and publicity was given to them according to the amount they paid.

Mela Ram suggested to Chanan Mal that Shiv Shanker should invite him to dinner so that he could advise him how to get better publicity.

CHAPTER THIRTY ONE

Chanan Mal brought Mela Ram to Shiv Shanker's house for dinner next evening. He had informed Shiv Shanker that Mela Ram was a voracious eater and the dinner had to be non-vegetarian. In view of that Shiv Shanker bought double the number of plates of chicken, mutton and fish from the Kashmere Gate restaurant he patronized. The yearning with which Mela Ram had his drinks and gluttonously he swallowed plate after plate seemed unusual to Shiv Shanker. Mela Ram was a thin person with shriveled face which gave his· nose the appearance more of a beak. He had dry skin and a sunken belly. His thin protruding lower lip was all the time quivering except when he was munching. While eating he filled his mouth, chewed for sometime and swallowed hastily. After every morsel he would open his mouth wide, sometimes uttering 'ha' 'ha'. He would reveal his uneven teeth and lick his lower lip He sipped his drink with closed eyes, a little at a time, as if it was not iced whiskey but some hot drink. By the time he finished eating, his eyes brightened up. Hearing the rustle of a rat or two moving in the comer of the room, he said: "I like rats because they move about noiselessly and create sound only when eating."

Mela Ram's face had begun to appear less shrunk and eyes less immobile. He had red veins in his eyes as if from chronic insomnia. A wasp was beating against the panes and he found it absorbing. Shiv Shanker noticed his somewhat worn out shirt which was made of cheap off-white cloth. He went to the side room and returned with a silk shirt from the stock collected from the houses of Muslims. He asked Mela Ram to try it. After he had put it on, he chuckled and bowed low to see how it looked on him. He turned his head left and right and chuckled again. The sleeves of the shirt were a little short. Mela Ram said that it was really good because these would not get dirty while working in office or wet when washing hands. Shiv Shanker had thrown the old shirt in the dust bin. Mela Ram picked it up and wrapped it in a sheet of paper to take it home. He had taken out a packet of cigarettes from the old shirt and lit one. Leaning on the chair and narrowing his eyes, he said: "I must wear this old shirt tomorrow, when report about you appears in the newspaper, otherwise Acharyaji will smell a rat." Chanan Mal was surprised when Mela Ram lit the cigarette but did not put out the match stick and threw it on the floor. He picked it up and placed it on the ash tray. Shiv Shanker, noticing that he was smoking a cheap variety, offered him a better one from the packet with him. Mela Ram took out as many cigarettes from that packet as his fingers could hold, put these in his pocket and continued to smoke the one he had lit.

Mela Ram had been staring at the expensive articles in the room. Blowing at the smoke from his cigarette he said: "You seem to be a rich man; you should become a great leader." To emphasize his point, he raised his hand quivered the fingers, dark yellow with excessive smoking and said: "At Lahore we had a jolly well time. Many landlords, lawyers, politicians, nawabs, rajas, maharajas and other well off persons paid Acharyaji rupees fifty to one hundred per month and to me rupees ten regularly. Some of them did it so that their name appears in the paper from time to time. Others did it to prevent any scandal or adverse news-report appearing about them. In Lahore's Hira Mandi where dancing girls and courtesans had their room, Acharyaji had his arrangement with pan sellers and night-time vendors there. He would know which Raja or nawab, important politician or eminent lawyer had visited that street and which courtesan he favoured. When that news appeared in the paper, that person started paying regularly to Acharyaji, so that he could without worry visit those places in future.

Mela Ram himself suggested that Shiv Shanker should not bother about Acharyaji but pay him rupees twenty per month. In return he would have his name published in the Desh Bhagat at least once a week in dak edition of the paper distributed outside the city. Acharyaji scanned only the morning city edition of the paper. Mela Ram got up to leave and while shaking hands with Shiv Shanker he proffered both hands joined together. He went out so noiselessly that there was not the slightest sound of his steps.

Next day a news item appeared on the front page of Desh Bhagat that Shiv Shanker, President, All India Refugees Welfare Association, had announced that one lakh members of his association would join the demonstration against Mahatma Gandhi when he arrived in Delhi. A smaller figure would not have justified putting this news item on the front page and Acharyaji would have his suspicion. Shiv Shanker was nonplused on seeing this news report on the front page of Desh Bhagat. As he thought coolly he would not be able to collect even ten persons. He felt the ground slipping from under his feet. He worried if anyone enquired about it, how would he explain it? He spent the whole day, smoking, drinking and worrying. The following day reports in other papers made prominent mention of it. Acharya Ram Krishan appealing to Mahatma Gandhi not to come to Delhi editorially referred to this.

Shiv Shanker was surprised that instead of realizing the unreality, if not absurdity, of this make-believe, few doubted it. Many were greatly impressed by this news item and began to regard him as a very important person. He had got up late and had just dressed and washed down the hangover of the previous day, when some Congressmen came to see him. They argued that Shiv Shanker should join in welcoming Gandhiji with all his members and not be a part of the demonstration against him. They felt that in the existing circumstances Mahatma Gandhi might not be able to do much for Muslims, but surely, he could be of help in properly settling the refugees from Pakistan. They suggested that if the refugees welcomed Mahatma Gandhi wholeheartedly, they would be able to seek his help to make the government do the needful for them. The picture of a person with beard was hanging on the wall. Thinking that it was that of Karl Marx, one worker suggested to Shiv Shanker to become a member of the Society of Friends of the Soviet Union. Shiv Shanker asked him to come again for this when he was free from Gandhi's visit.

Shortly afterwards a group of members of Hindu Suraksha Samiti - Hindu Defense League - came. They urged upon him to take over the leadership of the demonstration against Mahatma Gandhi. He explained to them: "The news report in the Desh Bhagat does not state the actual position. One lakh and even more members of my Refugees Welfare Association are spread over the whole of northern India, wherever they could find a place for a shelter. Calculating at the lowest minimum each person will need rupees ten for coming and returning to his place and rupees ten for two days stay in Delhi. It means calling ten thousand persons from outside will cost at least rupees two lakhs. Before I agree to take over complete charge of the demonstration tell me how many men you want to be brought from outside and how much you will pay for them in advance. Only when you let me know this, I can talk further in the matter."

In the afternoon half a dozen refugees from the Tis Hazari camp came to see him. They had brought with them a fellow refugee from the camp, Feroze Chand by name. He had refused to accept and accommodate his daughter who had been repatriated from Pakistan and had come to Delhi the same day. He had argued that she had lived with Muslims, shared their food and was not fit to live with him or being treated as a daughter. He wanted her to be sent to the home for unattached refugee women. An elderly lady checked and confirmed that she was a virgin. After that the whole camp was up against Feroz Chand for not accepting his daughter.

Feroz Chand used to practice as an advocate at Sargoda town, now in Pakistan. He was a criminal lawyer with a good practice and had built a palatial bungalow there. During War-time boom in the price of agricultural products, landlords in that district had become rich and had begun to acquire property in Sargoda town. Many months before Partition, he had sold his bungalow at a very good price. In view of the prevailing communal tension he temporarily shifted to his younger brother, a Defense Department employee at Ambala in east Punjab, bringing with him everything of value. When after Partition it became known that refugees would be given a plot of land or evacuee property in lieu of property lost by them in Pakistan, he shifted to the Tis Hazari camp' in Delhi, bringing with him the papers about his bungalow in Sargoda without the sale deed. Feroze Chand's only child, a daughter Sumitra, was studying at Government Girls College in Lahore and was residing in the college girls' hostel. As it was quite safe there at that time, she continued to study and live there. Shortly before Partition, the situation in Lahore also became very grave, with communal riots spreading to all parts of the city. A Muslim class fellow of Sumitra took her to her home. She had to stay there till September, when her uncle from Ambala could reach the Lahore railway station and safely take charge of her. He brought her to Ambala and told her why her father had shifted to Delhi where she reached the next day.

Feroz Chand was not popular in the Tis Hazari camp because of the way he moved about and passed remarks. If the trouble was between a Sindhi and Punjabi, he would say that if you came across a Sindhi and a snake, kill the Sindhi first. If the problem was between a Sikh and a Hindu he would say that if you met both Sikh and a snake, kill the Sikh first. Similarly if the dispute was between a person from Lahore and one from Rawalpindi, he would advise that if you met a person from Lahore and a snake together, kill the one from Lahore first. About women he had convoluted ideas which he often repeated, such as: "From a woman you get nothing except lust for woman", "Men are butter oil and women are like fire and these should not get mixed. The way he stared at women in the camp he was nicknamed 'Jhakoo'- goggler.

Feroz Chand was sitting in a chair, surrounded by others from Tis Hazari camp. They were mostly standing by his side or behind him. He raised his eyes sometimes to stare defiantly at Shiv Shanker. Suddenly Shiv Shanker splashed a frowning look at him, bared his teeth and shouted angrily: "If you do not keep your daughter I will throw you out of the camp. No, no, I will ask my men to pack you and send you back to Pakistan My men will break your legs so that you can do nothing there except begging." Shiv Shanker told the men standing there to take him back and let him know if he still dares to refuse to accommodate his daughter.

Shiv Shanker knew that he will now have to make speeches, but was at his wit's end how to learn to do so. From the speeches by well known leaders, he knew that even the best among them sometimes rambled and fumbled even though as newspaper reports these speeches appeared well worded and consistent. He tried to recollect all the couplets, ditties, snippet of poems, snatches of songs, anecdotes and patches of allegories which used to reverberate in their room in Lady Harding Sarai. If these could be tied up with something concerning refugees, or life in general, he thought, it could keep his listeners enthralled. He recollected a song based on a story that once upon a time it was ordained that the first person who entered the city gate on a particular day should be made a king. Accordingly a village cobbler was set on the throne. He was carried in a procession on a decorated elephant, chaperoned by damsels and treated with elaborate ceremony. He was so frightened. that he got out of wits and made an escape to his village.· The song the villagers sang on his return was full of music and resonance. Its opening lines 'char paon ka thambak thamba' began to resound in his mind. He thought that this story could be used to teach the audience not to aspire very high. The beat of the accompanying song would keep up their interest in his speech. He remembered the quip with which they used to tease the two Brahmins among them: "The lion's mane, jewel in the snake's head and a Brahmin's wealth no hand can ever reach till they are dead." He knew about the Punjab villagers' dislike for greedy Brahmins. Shiv Shanker also tried to remember the Urdu couplets ridiculing leaders and parodying English education, which would be music to the ears of these persons from villages.

CHAPTER THIRTY TWO

Next forenoon he was recollecting and noting down points for a speech, when one Trilochan Shastri came to see him. He had taken his residential address from Mela Ram, after reading the report in his paper that Shiv Shanker was president of an organization which had more than hundred thousand members. Entering his room he hawked: "I am Trilochan Shastri and have come to greet you as a friend and brother." He shook Shiv Shanker's hand with such aplomb that the latter stared at him with disdain. Curtly pushing his hand back, he asked him mockingly: "Are you a Shastri because your neighbour is a Shastri or you have passed the Sanskrit examination for Shastri diploma?" Trilochan Shastri confessed: "In my case it is slightly different. We had a tenant for ten years who was a qualified Shastri and everyone in the house began to be called Shastri, even though none except my father had studied Sanskrit in school."

Shiv Shanker suddenly became grave and looked at him straightly as if he wanted him to come out with the purpose of his visit. Trilochan Shastri slightly loosened the knot of his tie and reassuringly remarked: "You are a great man but the country at large is not aware of it. I have come because I want you to be better known in the city and outside. I organize procession of an aspiring leader with as many persons in the procession as he wants. He can be on horseback like Jawaharlal Nehru, on a chariot like Lord Krishna, on an elephant like king Porus or any other way that person desires. I also arrange public reception to honour a budding politician which will be attended by important and well known personalities of the city and neighbouring Provinces. In your case a procession on a horse or elephant can be later. To begin with you have a reception in your honour. It has really to be a big reception if it is to have the needful impact."

Trilochan Shastri glanced at Shiv Shanker, to measure his reaction to his suggestions. He found the latter's face blank and failed to notice any particular reaction. He continued more reassuringly: "Firstly we have reception in the best hotel in the town where people would feel tempted to come. Invitation will be issued on behalf of important leaders, politicians, advocates, doctors, businessmen, presidents of various religious, social and cultural organizations in the city. The invitation card begins: "Eminent citizens of Delhi, listed on the reverse, invite you to a reception in honour of such and such ... " More or less a thousand persons in the city are anxious to be listed among eminent persons but the reverse of the card can accommodate only ninety. Invitation is sent to all those aspiring eminent persons and most of them come to the reception in the hope that the next card will include their name among eminent persons of the city. In the main text of the invitation it is specifically mentioned that important minister of the centre and the provincial governments are expected to attend. This makes many ministers attend the function so that they are not taken for unimportant. The Chief Ministers and ministers in the neighbouring Provinces welcome the invitation because it gives them an opportunity to come to Delhi on official tour. So my friend it is no problem making the function a resounding success."

After saying this Trilochan Shastri did not look at Shiv Shanker to gauge his reaction. He got up and began to amble in the room as if he was on a. pavement. He lit a cigarette and puffed clouds of smoke. His pensive face had grown darker He was a man of genteel appearance. His face was slender and sallow in which his bright shining eyes were very noticeable, adding much weight to his personality. He stood erect for a minute or two as if there was a vessel of water on his head. Then he bowed and sat down, not in the same chair but another. Putting more motivation in his words, he suggested: "If you try to peep into your future you will realize that the next step or leap in your life is not possible without a grand reception." Making his voice more persuasive, he added: "You are young. If you do not take the bull by the horns now, you will not be able to do so later in life."

Shiv Shanker looked at him with full attention which he had not so far given him. He began to roll in his mind the suggestion he had made. Compared to the gentleness of his face, his body was burly. He did not have much of neck. Unless, he was looking sideways his head seemed to come directly out of trunk. He was wearing an elegant brown suit. His shoes were equally expensive but had not been polished for sometime. His colourful necktie did not look smart due to overuse.

Shiv Shanker walked to balcony, clapped a few times to draw the attention of refugee tea shop on the other side of the street and raised two fingers.

He returned to the room and sat near the centre table. Trilochan Shastri kept silent wishing to give Shiv Shanker time to think. Looking at his face again Shiv Shaker felt impressed by it. His broad forehead imparted purposefulness to his looks. He appeared to be less than forty but looked older because of receding hair line. The boy from the tea shop brought tea for two and some snacks, which he placed on the centre table. Passing a cup of tea to Trilochan Shastri, Shiv Shanker remarked: "Your suggestion is very plausible and does appeal to me. Let first this hullabaloo in connection with Gandhi's visit to Delhi be over.

Trilochan Shastri giggled. He lit a cigarette again and helped Shiv Shanker to light one. Blowing the smoke in circles, he sermonized: "Gandhi thinks that as he steps into Delhi, communalism will disappear. He would have been wiser, if instead of three monkeys, his ideogram had been three men appropriately pictured saying: 'none is more blind than the man who refused to see, none is more dumb than the man who refuses to speak and none is more deaf than the man who refuses to hear.' He puffed hard again and again till a stub was left. He got ready to light another cigarette but changed his mind. In order to divert Trilochan Shastri's attention away from Gandhi, Shiv Shanker asked him: "Do you belong to United Provinces?"

"Yes I belong to Gonda district in eastern U.P. If anything changes there it is for the worse. My Province needs and deserves an upheaval much greater than the present one in the Punjab. I belong to Ghoria a village between Gonda and Faizabad. I had to leave my village because of local landlord who also happens to be the biggest tough and money lender of the area. He is a Brahmin and his father was donated a piece of land by the local feudatory to ward off an ill omen with which he believed the family was jinxed. The feudal landlord was asked to fast on purnima full moon day for a year, eat only fried barley for a year on amavasya, the last day of the dark fortnight, and donate land and two cows to a Brahmin. The estate of this Brahmin priest's son has been mysteriously expanding and he is now a big landlord even though he never bought any land. The feudatory landlord was reduced to poverty and he emerged as the richest man in the village. Another Rajput in the village having fields in between his land, did not surrender his holding to him He got it requisitioned for building houses for untouchable in ·the village, which were never built and the land became part of his farm. When a Muslim family hesitated to surrender his fields to him, he got the whole family murdered and police records show that they had migrated to Pakistan. One low caste boy doing forced labour in his household was suspected to have stolen some grain and clothes. Afraid of being thrashed he ran away. The landlord's goons attacked their colony where they could not find the boy. Since men folk had fled away they attacked women and children, raped some girls. I was in the village during those days. I went with low caste fellow villagers to register a case at the police station more than fifteen kilometers away. The sub-inspector in-charge of that police station refused to register the complaint. The landlord's henchmen searched me there to kill me. Noticing a gang coming, the sub-inspector locked me in the store room and kept me there for two days. In the early hours of the third day the. sub-inspector took me in his jeep to Monghyr from where I took the train which brought me to Delhi in circuitous route reaching western U.P. first. The police sub-inspector had advised me not to take the usual route to Delhi."

Both kept sitting quietly for sometime. Trilochan Shastri stared at Shiv Shanker as if he was expecting him to put a question. Shiv Shanker got up. Offering his hand to Trilochan Shastri, he said offhandedly: "I am grateful to you for all that you have suggested. Only after Gandhiji's visit I will decide whether to have a procession, or a reception or both."

Moving to the door and raising his hand to bid good bye, he muttered: "If you meet Gandhi, ask him where is the rat which wanted to bell the cat. Now the cat believes in non-violence and is waiting for the rat."

CHAPTER THIRTY THREE

An interesting occurrence introduced Chanan Mal to a new way of adding to his income, which proved very useful to him later in life. Outside the hut of Salig Ram, he picked up a hand bill which had been swept there by wind. This hand bill contained an appeal for fund on behalf of 'Refugees Service Society' and was signed by Bhagwati Devi 'former president, ladies committee, Indian National Congress, Lahore'. This hand bill gave details of work allegedly done by Refugees Service Society for the benefit of refugees, such as the upkeep of refugee orphans, marriage of refugee girls whose kith and kin could not be traced, rehabilitation of refugee widows, maintenance of old and infirm refugees, etc. The Society claimed to be the main succor in Delhi of all refugees rendered indigent and helpless by Partition. Bhagwati Devi was wife of Salig Ram. Chanan Mal now understood why and where she went every morning, returning in the evening.

Salig Ram and his wife had come from Lahore. They were in jail for two months only during the 1931 civil disobedience movement. There was speculation about why they were the first to be released, immediately after the movement fizzled out. Salig Ram always had a Gandhi cap on and Bhagwati Devi invariably wore a white sari of coarse hand spun cloth. Both claimed to be freedom fighters and staunch Gandhians. They often reminded people that they had gone to jail and made other sacrifices, thus winning freedom for all of them.

When on August 12, 1947, the Cotton Thread Market residential area of Lahore was attacked by armed Muslim gangs, its entire Hindu population shifted to DAV College refugee camp. While Bhagwati Devi, her three sisters and their families traveled to India with other refugees by train, they decided that Salig Ram should make the journey by air with the gold ornaments of all of them, because the trains were being looted before crossing into India. When Salig Ram reached the air port to emplane for

Delhi, he was searched and was not allowed to carry any money or valuables with him. The rest of the family reached India with everything safe and. intact. This made everyone very unhappy, Salig Ram more than others. All the time he had a hunch that others might be thinking that he was playing a subterfuge. Salig Ram had always had contempt for the poor. He had always thought that a poor man did not deserve any respect nor could he be trusted. Now that he was without much money, he felt broken down. Even unintended remarks by relatives who had entrusted valuables to him appeared to him taunts, which further added to his misery. He avoided speaking to anyone and generally remained lying inside the hut. Bhagwati Devi got shops· and houses allotted to her relatives through her contact with Lahore Congress leaders now in Delhi. Salig Ram had, however, continued to live in that refugee camp. After Bhagwati Devi returned in the evening and they had counted and safely kept the money, Salig Ram would come out to make sure that none was watching.

After two days effort Chanan Mal could know how the collection was made by Bhagvati Devi and her associates and the manner of its distribution. As leader and the only person with credibility in that group, Bhagwati Devi kept half the collection and distributed the other half among the other four or five women who accompanied her. Chanan Mal prepared a news item about it and gave it the heading: 'Fraud in name of the refugees'. After Salig Ram had finished his; dinner and was resting outside his hut, Chanan Mal went to see him. He sat down by his side on the string cot. After some small talk he lighted a torch, which he had with him, and made Salig Ram read the news item. He told him that this news item had been brought to him by the Paper's local reporter. Instead of publishing it he had put it in his pocket, telling him that Bhagwati Devi was the wife of his neighbour and friend, Salig Ram, a well known Congressman of Lahore. On reading the news item Salig Ram began to shiver. He became so nervous that he could hardly speak coherently. Chanan Mal thought it better not to pursue the matter further at that time. While getting up from the cot he remarked: "That reporter said that he has a follow up story also. Bhagwati Devi and other women can be arrested. I am trying to stop him but he can go to the editor and even to Acharyaji. Best thing is pay him some hush money."

For a few days after that Salig Ram and Bhagwati Devi came to see him after he returned from office. Chanan Mal every time told them that the reporter concerned was insisting on a hush money of rupees two hundred per month, because their income from this racket was more than two hundred rupees per day. Finally the deal was settled at rupees one hundred per month, which was to be paid to that local reporter of the paper through Chanan Mal.

Gradually Chanan Mal got distanced from his sister and her family.

Sometimes he felt that he was not residing with them but in some different place far away. A philanthropic organization was distributing sewing machines to refugee widows. Lal Kaur was able to get one. Slowly and steadily she was becoming less and less dependent on Chanan Mal. Out of half a dozen organizations which were visiting the Tis Hazari camp to provide some service to refugees or to solicit support for their activities, Democratic Women's Society was the only one which appealed to Lal Kaur. She felt attracted toward this society mainly because its member believed in Hindu Muslim harmony and did not make unkind remarks against the Muslims. Government had provided assistance for the education of refugee children. Lal Kaur had put both her elder children in a nearby day school, which gave her more time to attend to tailoring vocation. When workers of Democratic Women's Society and Democratic Refugee Association came to know that her husband died in India while fighting to save Muslims, they began to take more interest in her, though they found it difficult to involve her in their work in the Camp and elsewhere.

Most of the girls, who came to see Lal Kaur in connection with the above progressive organizations, were not refugees. They appeared to be well educated from prosperous families. Chanan Mal was thrilled by these smartly dressed girls with serious bearing. sumitra's features had also acquired an intelligent and earnest look. She was short in size but had an unusually graceful carriage. Her face was shapely with every part delicately featured and innocent eyes made her focus of attention. Though Feroze Chand agreed to her living with him, he had always given the impression that she was unwelcome. Sumitra, therefore spent much of her time with Lal Kaur. Chanan Mal was attracted towards her. However, the look of a clever fellow that he had acquired and cunningness which his eyes flashed, kept her away from him.

At the end of the row of their huts, lived Laj Vanti a woman in her thirties but who looked younger. She had come from Bahawalpur. The Nawab of Bahawalpur had provided safe shelter in the spacious compound of the government college to all Hindus and Sikhs who felt unsafe in Bahawalpur town or in their Village in the State. However, their number grew so large that there was extreme overcrowding. Indian army took weeks to come to take them safely to India. In the meanwhile many of them died of dysentery. Laj Vanti's husband was one of them.

Laj Vanti made her son an apprentice in one of the Sadar Bazar shops nearby.

After finishing house hold chores in the forenoon she would loiter about in the Camp. Suddenly she began to show much interest in Chanan Mal, though she was more than ten years older than he. She was always anxious to do small things for an unwilling Lal Kaur. Chanan Mal did not pay much attention to her but in the evening, she would keep sitting there talking to him and inviting him to a game of cards. She would say that women were fond of flattery and what a man was he, who did not understand this. While talking to Chanan Mal, her pink cheeks became red and she would moisten lips again and again with salivating tongue. In between her talk with Chanan Mal or his sister she would mention with a sigh that she sometimes thought of committing suicide. .

Laj Vanti did not commit suicide but Chanan Mal was soon rid of her. After his daughter Sumitra began to live with him, Feroze Chand began to vent_ anger on his wife. He was always scolding her and beat her often. One day he hit her back and it became so painful that she had to be hospitalized. When Feroze Chand's wife along with Sumitra returned from the hospital after a fortnight she found that Laj Vanti was living in their hut with her husband. Feroze Chand had styled his hair like Chanan Mal and was wearing pantaloons and shirt like him. Even his footwear was brown pump like Chanan Mal's. The registration papers of Sargodha Bungalow were in the name of the wife and not in that of Feroze Chand. He therefore was very apologetic and cordial. Without any fuss, he shifted to Laj Vanti's hut allowing mother and daughter to continue to live there.

Shiv Shanker came to the Camp many times and stood at the corner of open space near the community water hydrants and attempted to make a speech. It attracted a passerby or two and few took notice of his public address. Whenever he met Chanan Mal he was almost in tears over his inability to attract even a few persons much less a crowd with his lecture. He even said that because of that he would fail to become a· refugee leader. Chanan Mal had notice a twelve year old refugee boy who could sing very well and who played on a cymbal like contrivance very harmonically. He could also snap fingers of both hands and clap in such quick succession that it became mellifluent. Chanan Mal introduced him to Shiv Shanker, who agreed to pay him rupees five every time he sang and played on his cymbal to attract crowd before Shiv Shanker began his speech.

Within five, or ten minutes of that boy's singing, clapping and playing the cymbal, a small crowd would gather there. Shiv Shanker had learned by' now which quatrains by Akbar Allahabadi caricaturing political leaders and ridiculing western education went well with the refugee audience and which couplets by Nazir of Agra praising common folk, the people enjoyed, Then there were a few stories and anecdotes which the refugees had liked and which he repeated at every gathering. The story of ancient rishi Atri, whose wife Anasuya was regarded as unique in her piety. Mischief maker rishi Narada went in turn to goddesses Lakshmi, Saraswati and Parvati extolling her extraordinarily virtuous life. They burned so much with envy that they forced their lords, gods Vishnu, Brahma and Shiva, to go and tempt Anasuya. In the garb of

Brahmin mendicants the three gods went to Anasuya and wanted to be served food. When food was ready they refused to accept it unless Anasuya served the food undressed. As letting the Brahmins go away hungry would be a great sin, Anasuya consulted her husband rishi Atri, who gave her charmed water which when sprinkled on the three Brahmins would turn them into babies. After turning them into babies, Anasuya served them food undressed, thus fulfilling. their condition. Shiv Shanker would conclude the story, to the refugees' great delight, by remarking that now Lord Mountbatten had turned our leaders into babies while serving them freedom.

His citing example of a crow was much liked by the refugees. He would say in a raised voice; "When a crow is injured or is in danger, hundreds of crows gather there and their cawing would rend the sky. Refugees should also rush to help one another like this. One thing more refugees should learn from the crow. When water is low in a vessel and the crow is unable to sip it, it puts stones in it, one after the other, till water level rises and it can sip a drink. Likewise refugees should not get disheartened and should continue to strive till they succeeded." He had arranged with the singer boy to raise slogans and prompt others to join him, whenever there was a pause in his speech or when he gave him a signal by raising hand towards him.

Leaders of the Hindu Sewak Sangh were noticing that the refugees were not evincing much interest in a demonstration against Mahatma Gandhi on his arrival at Delhi railway station. Having come from remote villages they were more curious to see him. They, therefore, were worried that their much hyped demonstration against Gandhi would turn out to be a flop. They went to Shiv Shanker to seek his help. He repeated his earlier statement that most of his members were outside Delhi and each would need on the average ten rupees for travel and another rupees ten for food in Delhi. He assured them that would get as many persons as they were willing to pay for in advance. After much confabulation among themselves and discussion with Shiv Shanker they decided that Shiv Shanker would arrange five thousand demonstrators, and for that fifty thousand rupees would be paid to him immediately and balance fifty thousand soon after the demonstration. He also assured them that his local members also would partake in the demonstration without any extra charge.

Before leaving the Hindu Sewak Sangh leaders urged upon Shiv Shanker that their organization and his Refugees Welfare Association should join together in opposing and exposing Gandhi.· One of them said: "Gandhiism is emasculating Hindus. It is a camouflage for pusillanimity. When you do not want to die for your country, how else can you keep face and flaunt as a great patriot? Only by making noise about non-violence this could be done." A young man among them remarked: "India had been sliding down the centuries but during every period they were men, however few they might be, who showed determination of an animal who leapt on the hunter. Gandhi's non-violence ruled that out in British India." Another person, the eldest among them observed: "It is unfortunate that Gandhi and Nehru have allowed themselves to be led by the nose by Mountbatten. If transfer of power could be advanced from June 1948 to 15th August 1947, why could not they insist that it should be advanced or postponed by two weeks, so that the inauguration of Independence did not occur during the inauspicious dark lunar fortnight?"

They were all standing. Shiv Shanker had counted the bundles of hundred rupee notes and heaped these on the table. Offering to discuss all this with them after the demonstration was over, he raised his hands, both palms joined, to salute them arid to bid them farewell. Their talk left a bad taste in his mouth, though he was quite elated by the money he had received from them. He had a mouthful of rum and got into a mood of introspection. He decided that he should use part of this money to have a reception arranged in his honour by Trilochan Shastri. He made up his mind to have a procession and reception on the same occasion, now that he had enough money. He was quite enthused by the idea of a thousand important personalities of the ·city waiting for him at the venue of the reception when he arrived there majestically on an elephant surrounded by some other important citizens. He will make Trilochan Shastri live up to his promise regardless of the cost.

Mahatma Gandhi's arrival in Delhi enhanced Shiv Shanker's reputation. When Gandhiji arrived at the Delhi railway station a crowd of several thousand men, women and children had gathered there. Besides the men and women of the local Congress Committee, there were refugees curious to have a look at him for the first time in their life. The railway authorities had arranged that the train bringing Gandhiji should steam in at platform number one and the large third class compartment in which only he and his few companions were traveling halted nearest to the exit gate. Hindu Suraksha Sangh was able to collect only a few dozen anti-Gandhi demonstrators. Police rounded them up in no time. They saw Shiv Shanker moving about with some helpers carrying thousands of black buntings flags and hoardings. He had told the Superintendent of Police on which side of the platform he would be so that they could confiscate the black flags and hoardings. About fifteen thousand persons who had gathered there jam-packed the small .space on the platform and area outside the exit gate. Pell-mell of the crowd subsided when the police rounded up a dozen anti-Gandhi demonstrators who had managed to sneak in. When the train arrived and Gandhiji stepped down on the platform with a cherubic smile, the air resounded with 'Mahatma Gandhi ki jai' and nothing else could be heard.

There were over a hundred policemen in mufti who surrounded Gandhiji when he started to fend his way to the exit gate through that surging crowd. This made it difficult for people who had come there to have his glimpse. Their rush created unceasing jostling and commotion. This made-Gandhiji smile more conspicuously. It took him more than an hour to wade his way through the crowd and to get into the waiting car. All this time, he continued to respond to the crowd with an unending smile and slogans like 'Mahatma Gandhi ki jai' kept becoming louder and louder.

Chanan Mal had, in his news report for his paper Desh Bhagat, given a figure of ten thousand black flag demonstrators. Acharya Ram Krishan changed it to one hundred thousand. This and other anti-Congress papers had added that the slogan 'Gandhi go back' could be heard for miles. In view of that Hindu Suraksha Sangh could not complain that Shiv Shanker did not fulfill his promise and they could not resist his demand for balance of the money.

THUS CAME THE DAWN

CHAPTER THIRTY FOUR

The reception held in his honour was more successful than Shiv Shanker had even dreamt of. He had made his own arrangement for an additional quantity of marigold garlands and rose petals. Not only was the elephant fully covered with marigold flowers, there were two or three marigold garlands adorning all the two hundred persons who preceded or followed the elephant. Boys had been hired to shower rose petals on him and the procession throughout the route. Part of the route was through crowded streets, where there were many lines of spectators. He had also arranged cameramen to record all this. Trilochan Shastri had fixed procession and the reception on the first day of the bright fortnight of the moon in traditionally auspicious month of Ashvin, beginning in the second week of September. The earlier dark fortnight of the moon devoted to annual shradha, libation to ancestors, was considered inauspicious for social and business functions and even for inessential shopping. This, therefore, marked not only the beginning of Dusehra and other festivities but also of the shopping season.

One Chief Minster and seven Ministers from the neighbouring Provinces had come for the reception with their wives. When welcome address printed in golden letters was presented to Shiv Shanker and he was garlanded with garlands made of gold and silver threads, everyone joined in giving him a standing ovation. After the reception Shiv Shanker lavishly entertained many of the Ministers specially those from the Punjab and gave presents to their wives from the stock he had. Some of these wives stayed back because Shiv Shanker wanted to help them in shopping. Shiv Shanker had photographs taken not only of the procession and reception but also with the Ministers and their wives.

All this enormously swelled Shiv Shanker's self confidence. There was something new in the circulation of his blood. His way of talking and his gait became altogether different. There was hauteur in his tone and alacrity in his steps. If a woman begins to bloom and brighten up according to the cajolery showered on her, a man without any difficulty gets molded into the setting in which he is launched. Shiv Shanker felt that he need not now look for people he can take for ride. They will come on their own.

Chanan Mal had made progress as a journalist by leaps and bounds. Acharya Ram Krishan had been greatly impressed by his manner of presenting news and giving their banners and headings. Pandit Nehru's speech explaining the Indian position on Kashmir would be given the banner: "Nehru ready to hand over Kashmir to Pakistan" When results of general elections in France were received from a news agency stating that communists had won two hundred out of five hundred seats, Chanan Mal would give the heading "Communists defeated in three hundred seats" Acharya Ram Krishan made him joint editor and Chief Reporter, on a salary of two hundred rupees. Normal practice in this paper was that an employee was required to sign a receipt for double the amount he was paid. Chanan Mal now insisted that he was paid the amount he signed for.

Soon after Chanan Mal became Chief Reporter, he came in contact with many organizations some of which paid him money to get publicity in his newspaper. One of these was Society for Cultural Freedom. He received an invitation from that Society for tea party at the well known Glamour Restaurant to meet the delegation of the Moral Rearmament movement on a visit to Delhi. Members of that delegations had plans to stage their plays in Delhi to spread their message of moral and spiritual rearmament The actors for these plays belonged to various nationalities and countries The plays intended to show that peace and goodwill in the world could only be achieved by individuals acquiring moral strength and collective action of any nature and by any party should be opposed. They had booked accommodation for about thirty persons in some of Delhi's expensive hotels. They had also booked for four days the hall of the Paramount Cinema, the biggest and the best in the city. The admission to their plays in that cinema hall was to be by complimentary passes, freely distributed. They wanted a grand show. The tea party had been arranged because they wanted to seek the help of local elite and wanted to discuss with them how to go about it so that the function was a great success.

Two years ago when they staged their plays in Delhi, the hall was half full on the first day and almost empty during the next three days even though there were no charges for the shows. This was despite their spending a lot of money on Press advertisements, distribution of hand bills and display of posters. The tea party was attended by representative of some social and cultural organizations and important men in the educational and literary spheres. Many off- the- cuff suggestions were made by some of those enjoying the lavish party but none of these seemed to click with the members of the delegation. Among the delegates only one Professor Goldstein spoke. The main point he made was that war was not yet over, its flames could be seen in one part of the world or the other. More or less the same amount of armament was being manufactured by various countries as during the war. This was because moral armament has yet to prevail upon the armament race. He explained that there was a little white bud in every heart and the Moral Rearmament movement intended to make it blossom into a flower. He added that only moral rearmament could put an end to two evils in the world today, the antipathy against the rich and solicitude for the poor and the down-at-heel. He said that he liked India because here one' saw in plenty beggars with outstretched hand. This reminded one of charity.

When the tea party was over, about a dozen guests stayed on. Chanan Mal was in a hurry to go but Shiv Shanker held him back. Trilochan Shastri was also there and was trying to engage in conversation with one delegate or the other but none of them was paying any heed to him. It seemed, on the last occasion, Trilochan Shastri had been entrusted with the job of arranging audience for the plays. He had taken a large amount from them. Despite that the shows were a failure and they were very circumspect this time.

There were eight members of the delegation, seven foreigners and one Indian, the younger brother of a well known Congress Party leader. Of the seven, three were Americans. One of the Americans was introduced as an eminent clergy of United States, second as father of a United Sates billionaire and the third, an old lady, as a descendant of Abraham Lincoln. At the start of the tea party she was using hearing aid, the plug of which she removed from her left ear soon after the party commenced. The remaining four were a Negro from Honolulu, an Egyptian prince, a Burmese bikshu and an Austrian count. The Egyptian, Burmese and the Hawaiian were partly in their national dress, so also the Indian who had a turban in the Air India maharaja style.

Father of the U.S. billionaire Maxim Goldstein was the leader of the delegation. He was somewhat' spindly. The impression of elegance and gentleness which he gave disappeared immediately he started talking and emphasizing each and every word in his husky voice. The Negro was tall and lean. His multi-coloured jacket was studded with glass beads in rainbow colours and his crimson shirt had small prints of flocks of doves. The Egyptian like Austrian was in European dress with a bright bow adorning his neck. Only his headwear was in Arabic style.

There was a branch of the Society for Moral Rearmament in Delhi. Many well known industrialists and businessmen were its members so also some important lawyers and academicians. All of them were very busy persons and had never shown any .interest in it except lending their name. The delegation was in Delhi to make sure that the shows this time were a success. More these shows succeeded the greater was the success of their fund-raising efforts in the Unites Stats and elsewhere.

Chanan Mal introduced Shiv Shanker to Mr. Sanyal, Secretary of Delhi branch of the Society for Cultural Freedom. He hinted to him that Shiv Shanker is likely to suggest a solution lotthe problem which they were finding so baffling. Shiv Shanker was no stranger to Sanyal. He had been invited to the public reception held in his honour and was one of the eminent men chosen to garland him. Shiv Shanker told him that he would like to help the Moral Rearmament delegation in arranging viewers for their shows. Shiv Shanker-.' was introduced to Goldstein and his colleagues by Sanyal eulogizing him as a writer, social worker and leader of over a million refugees from Pakistan. Shiv Shanker enquired from Goldstein when they proposed to have their shows in Delhi. He replied next month. Shiv Shanker advised him to have the plays in a week or two and in any case before the end of October otherwise Dusehra and other Hindu festivities would come in the way of their success. Goldstein explained to him that for the four days the plays were to be staged in Delhi, they wanted all the nine hundred seats in the hall to be full. Advising him to have the shows for three days, Shiv Shanker admonished him: "I am sorry for you. If you want only nine hundred persons for nine hundred seats, I will keep out of it. I never do anything on a small scale."

Goldstein was taken aback He could not comprehend what Shiv Shanker meant. In a confused state he blinked and stared at Sanyal to know the exact purport of Shiv Shanker's remark. He pleaded with Sanyal to make clear to Mr. Shanker that he wanted the hall to be full on all the days and no seats should be vacant. Shiv Shanker rocked with a hearty laughter as if deriding Goldstein, which further nonplussed him. Shiv Shanker pointing to the comer said: "Let us sit there so that I can explain." He did not let

Chanan Mal go and made him sit next to himself. Fixing his eyes on Goldstein he emphasized: "First it settled that the show will be within the next ten days and will be for three days only"? Sanyal dragged more chairs towards the corner and invited the other delegates to come and join the discussion. They confabulated among themselves for a while. Goldstein asked Professor Sanyal whether the booking for the hall can be advanced to next week Friday, Saturday and Sunday. Sanyal affirmed that was possible.

Shiv Shanker made a sign advising the American lady to put on her hearing aid and with his hands gestured others to come closer. Adding a commanding tone to his words, Shiv Shanker pontificated: "Unless you are all blockheads, you should understand that nine hundred persons for nine hundred seats would mean nothing. A few feel interested and clap, more feel bored, yawn and quietly slip out. That does not make news. If that is what you intend, you are just wasting your money and I am really sorry for you."

There was an uneasy pause. When the Negro looked the other side, Shiv Shanker said brusquely: "Mr. Hawaiian, please look this side." He continued more affirmatively: "If nine thousand persons come for nine hundred seats, ten persons jostling for each seat, there will be tremendous rush, pell-mell, rather a stampede. There will be nine hundred persons inside the hall and almost nine thousand outside, creating uproar, pandemonium, hoopla. If you like there can be a riotous situation, jamming of traffic, breaking of glass panes and the summoning of police. This would mean that not only in this country but throughout the world news would be splashed of the popularity of moral rearmament movement in this country. You can send for cine cameramen, Press photographers, news reporter, etc. from New York, London and other places to record and chronicle this great scene." When Shiv Shanker concluded his voice had become more assertive and he surveyed with self importance the Moral Rearmament delegates.

They were all bewildered. Mr. Goldstein's eyes widened so much that these seemed to fill his face. He appeared less lanky. There was complete silence for sometime, the delegates looking at one another The American lady did not seem to have followed despite hearing "aid, exactly what had made them mull in this manner. Goldstein ignored her query and her face became less wrinkly as she tried to elicit more information: "If last time there were not even two hundred persons for nine hundred seats, how can you now manage such a huge number."

Chanan Mal wondered how Shiv Shanker would respond now. He looked at him. The muscles of his face had stiffened and he had acquired the furtiveness of a spider about to throw itself on a helpless insect wriggling in its web. He said coolly: "There will be nothing hanky-panky about this. I will give a receipt for the fee I charge, which will specifically state that if the entire house is not packed on all the three days, the money would be refunded in full. More cannot be stated on such receipts." Shiv Shanker looked at the delegates. They had shifted their eyes from him to one another. To assure them further Shiv Shanker added: "I had promised to arrange five thousand volunteers for black flag demonstration against Gandhi. Mr. Sanyal will confirm that according to Press reports the actual number was ten times. The police station was piled up with the black flags and hoardings they carried."

There was much whispering among them. It seemed they were making up their mind, somehow, to probe Shiv Shanker not only to appraise him, but also to be sure that his attitude to various issues was not at variance with the tenets of their movement. Goldstein shot at him the question: "Don't you like Gandhi?" Shiv Shanker was still brooding what to say to these foreigners about India's national leader, when Chanan Mal interjected: "We are not against Gandhi but only against a few facets of Gandhiism. Gandhiism like Tolstoyism is backward looking though Gandhi does not stand for return to a pristine state like Tolstoy."

The Austrian count suddenly asked him: "What about China?" Shiv Shanker replied with the same alacrity with which the question was asked: "Of course china should be of high quality. I personally do not enjoy tea, lunch or dinner unless it is served in the best quality of china ware." The Chinese communist armies having captured Peking were advancing towards south China and every day newspapers carried reports of their victories. The intention was to find out Shiv Shanker's reaction to the communist advance and to communism. Shiv Shanker's reply amused them so much that most of them broke into laughter. The old lady had not followed it and when it was explained to her, she warmed up with a smile.

Goldstein was not yet clear about Shiv Shanker's way of thinking, whether it was in harmony with the ideology of moral rearmament movement or not. He thought of asking a direct question. He asked Shiv Shanker: "What do you think of communism." Shiv Shanker had by this time guessed what they were aiming at. He replied:

"Communism is communism and whorehouse is whorehouse,

whatever name you give it." This answer was as unspecific as his reply to earlier questions. Goldstein bowed his head and seemed to be thinking hard about this. He raised his head and asked: "What do you think of Soviet Russia?" Shiv Shanker wanted to be included in the delegation of the Friends of Soviet Union which visited Moscow every November 011. the anniversary'6f the October revolution: He was in a fix as to what to say. He was rolling one or two alternatives in his mind when Chanan Mal came to his rescue by putting to Goldstein the question: "Do you want Russia to give up communism? "Yes, yes" Goldstein and another delegate muttered. Chanan Mal replied: "Most of you are more or less double my age. I am very diffident to teach you wisdom. Do you think that a patient lying on an operation table can throwaway his chloroform mask? Goldstein and others were tickled by Chanan Mal's remark. Noting their questioning eyes, Shiv Shanker introduced him as his secretary. Goldstein showed off: "I always had a damsel as my secretary, and changed her after a year or two." Shiv Shanker confessed: "As soon as women secretaries are available in India, I will surely follow your example."

Professor Sanyal left the place and came back with a bearer carrying a tray with a bottle of whiskey and six tumblers. It seemed some of them did not drink. Whiskey and soda water was poured into glasses and ice cubes added with a tong. There was more than half a bottle of whiskey left. Shiv Shanker picked it up, uncorked it and putting it to his mouth drank it up in one go. They were all looking at him in wonderment. One of them stood up and clapped. What amazed Goldstein was that he was as normal as before and was not even slightly tipsy.

Shiv Shanker stuck on to his fee of rupees twenty thousand and firmly said: "There will be further expenditure more or less up to the same amount on advance publicity in Press and otherwise and on printing of tickets and their postage. All this will have to be paid for separately. All this expenditure will be duly receipted except for items of editorial support, for which newspaper cutting will be furnished." He was again and again pressed to reduce his fee. Shiv Shanker did not budge and assured them that these were concessional rates because theirs was a good cause. Professor Sanyal paid him the amount. Shiv Shanker wrote a receipt stating that the amount will be refunded in full if all the seats in the hall were not full on all the three days. It was also added in the receipt that all expenditure in connection with these shows would be paid for separately. He made them promise that they would not let anyone know before the shows that he was making these arrangements.

Shiv Shanker decided that he would make utmost effort that the promised number of spectators turned up for the shows. He was a public figure now and could not afford to have the reputation of an outright cheat. He felt that it would serve him better if he earned his fee by doing the job to the entire satisfaction of the moral rearmament delegation. The very next forenoon he went to see Trilochan Shastri. In the course of his conversation, he came to know that on the last occasion one common complimentary invitation was printed and distributed to a thousand persons for each show. There was one Press advertisement before the show and one on everyday of the show. Hand written posters were displayed in university area and in college premises saying that free passes could be picked up from the college canteen and some other places.

Shiv Shanker decided that instead of issuing general invitation cards, he would issue tickets as given to-customers in the cinema hall and the tickets would have seat numbers like the cinema tickets. The words: "Complimentary - Not transferable" would be rubber stamped on these tickets. For each seat nurr1ber he would get printed eight to ten tickets. Tickets with the same number would be posted to different areas of Delhi so that there was no confusion before show days. This arrangement would be for two days and the third day would be reserved for diplomats, foreign residents in Delhi and Central Ministers and high officials.

The drama troupe arrived in Delhi on Monday and their group photograph appeared in the newspapers on Tuesday. On Wednesday there was a paid news report about the moral rearmament plays in it which was mentioned that for the shows on next Friday and Saturday complimentary tickets were being issued to eminent writers, intellectuals, doctors, lawyers, other professionals and well known citizens and these were not transferable. The shows on these two days were reserved only for those whom tickets with seat numbers were being issued and were not open to the general public. Sunday show was reserved for diplomats and foreign residents in Delhi. Dates for shows for the general public were to be announced later. Tickets for the Friday show were posted on Tuesday and for the Saturday show on Wednesday. With the tickets was a note on a slip saying: "Two tickets are for you and your wife and are not transferable. Please do not bring children or any other member of your family."

On Friday there were hardly many people outside the hall half an hour before the time of the show. Goldstein and others became nervous. Shiv Shanker also started worrying but thought that, tickets having seat numbers, those invited would normally come on time. At 6.10 p.m. there were enough persons to fill the hall and Goldstein took a sigh of relief. At 6.20 p.m. people were streaming from all sides towards the cinema hall. By 6.30 roads became jammed and cars had to be parked hundreds of yards away. Before people crowding there became restive, Shiv Shanker rang up the police station. A posse of policemen arrived and forestalled pell-mell and a riotous situation. When it was noticed that many persons held ticket for the same seat number, Shiv Shanker explained that after the advertisement restricting entry, either the employees of the cinema or someone else has cashed on the popularity of the plays. It took the policemen more than half and hour to bring about some order inside the hall for he play to start. As Goldstein had his doubt, he had not invited Press photographers, etc. from outside India. Local cine-cameramen and press photographers did an equally good job to the great delight of moral rearmament delegation.

CHAPTER THIRTY FIVE

A few days after Shiv Shanker had a procession and reception in his honour, an office bearer of the Society for Friendship with the Soviet Union came to see him. He was Chaturbhuj Bajpai poet in the Hindi language. He asked Shiv Shanker whether he was also a poet as mentioned. in the address presented to him at the' receptton. Shiv Shanker replied: "1 have not made up my mind whether to be a poet, novelist, a short story writer or a playwright. What do you think is more worthwhile?"

Bajpai was a slim, clean shaven man with a bald crown. Growth of hair appeared to be very profuse above ears and temples and he had combed these in a manner which partly covered his baldness. Assertive eyes lurked under black bushes of eyebrows. He explained politely: "Please do not write novels unless you want to do nothing else in life. Obsession with the novel makes you a good for nothing person. Your kith and kin, your friends and neighbours are no more men and women but mere feed for your novels. Novel is your double and not a shadow. It walks with you, eats with you, sits by your side when you talk with a friend and sleeps with you. So much so you cease to exist, become vehicle for novel, generator of novel. It is easy to write poetry, particularly free verse."

Shiv Shanker agreed to become a member of the Friends of the Soviet Unipn Society. He was informed that one Comrade Abhyankar was its secretary. He requested Bajpai to bring Comrade Abhyankar for breakfast next Sunday when he would become member of the Society and also provide other help.

Comrade Abhyankar came for breakfast the following Sunday along with Mr. Bajpai. He had brought current issue and some back numbers of Indo-Soviet Journal and also samples of some Soviet periodicals. These were all low priced publications and Shiv Shanker readily paid subscriptions for all of them. Abhyankar could not hide his happiness at Shiv Shanker doing so without any canvassing. Bajpai asked Shiv Shanker:

"Do you read so much?"

"No", Shiv Shanker replied: "I may not even tear the wrappers of these, I am subscribing to all these in order to indicate my full association with you. If I have time I read poetry. I have been attempting the writing of poems, but have so far failed miserably. I think poets are born. Probably I am not born with this gift."

"If poets are born, it will be good argument for birth control." Bajpai said with a smile, "As a matter of fact poets are made. Unfortunately few poets understand this otherwise they will not shirk the literary discipline and intellectual endeavour that the craft of a poet demands from them. They think that poetry is not a harmonic device but a grass mower or a hedge cutter. Every poem, worth its name, is a living entity pulsating with vivacity and sparkling with vision. It is not a cut and paste or chisel and carve work." After a brief pause Bajpai continued: "Coleridge said that no man can be a great poet without being a profound thinker. Our poets do not understand that they have first to study patiently, meditate deeply till they begin to acquire richness of mind and a prophetic vision. Only then poems come as naturally to a poet as leaves sprout on a tree."

There was a sudden change in Bajpai's appearances. His eyes brightened and his face acquired great affability. He did not seem to be above thirty-five. Shiv Shanker noticed that maturity and dignity shining in his features was of a person much older than his age. He remarked with a grin: "If writing poetry requires all that, I will never be able to become a poet."

Bajpai replied: "You need not a perfectionist in the manner I suggested and you need not take poetry as seriously as I do. There are several dozen well known poets in the city, who though mere versifiers are regarded as good poets. A moneyed man, as you are, you can be counted among the top dozen. However, one· does not require all these attributes to be a successful politician. Dash and thick skin of a rhinoceros are more than enough. You believe in public service, better give all your attention to becoming a leading politician. It is wrong to say that in politics blind men lead the blind. It is rather the wise who mislead the wise, though the net result is the same. Unless you believe yourself to be an epitome of wisdom and make your followers believe this in all honesty, you cannot get to a higher point in politics. The desire to get to the top by all means, and to stay there under all circumstances, turns a politician into a predator and therefore an adversary of freedom. With your momentous achievement at such a young age, you can be sure of succeeding as a politician in the present condition of Indian politics."

Mr. Abhyankar was listening to all this amusedly. Without much winking he was watching thoughtfully how Shiv Shanker was reacting to Bajpai's elucidations. He said calmly: "In India today your being a poet is not enough. A poet in order to succeed has also to be a politician and like a politician carry a hidden dagger, not for enemies but for friends and companions."

Bajpai informed Shiv Shanker: "Mr. Abhyankar was an officer of the Provincial Judicial Service. The whole social system and the entire administrative machinery is fully geared against the poor is quite obvious, but finding that the judicial system also is very heavily weighed against the poor and the dispossessed, appalled him.

He left his job and as communist party was the only party claiming to be working for the poor he began to participate in its activities. In no time he became such a devoted and popular labour leader that senior old-timers in the communist movement felt jealous of him. Some even whispered that he had been planted by the government. He was shunted to two side-shows of the movement, Progressive Writers Association and Society of the Friends of Soviet Union. He is now frustrated because he finds the purpose for which he quit his job nullified. He is in search of a village inhabited by poverty-stricken people belonging to a low caste, where he can live and help those people to better their life."

Before Bajpai and Abhyankar left, they requested him to join the delegation of eminent Indians which would be visiting Soviet Union in connection with the anniversary celebrations of the October Revolution on November seven. He said that Justice Shokhla would be leading the delegation this year. When left alone, Shiv Shanker gave serious thought to the distance he should maintain from the "Communist Party and its peripheral organizations. He did not want to be called a fellow traveler or a sympathizer of the Communist Party. It will not be enough to be Nehruite socialist, though the communists were less against them than against other brands of socialists. He decided to hang around half way between a Nehruite socialist and a Party sympathizer.

He became more careful when he later saw both Sumitra and Lal Kaur being sucked into the communist movement, Lal Kaur a little less because her children made it impossible for her to get fully involved. Democratic Women's and similar organizations attracted both of them because their workers talked about Hindu-Muslim amity. With the help of Chanan Mal and Shiv Shanker, Sumitra was able to secure the job of a teacher in a school in Dariba bazaar which was not far away.

CHAPTER THIRTY SIX

The Communist Party functionaries had gone into hiding. Sumitra being unknown to the police, they found that in her new position, she could be a good cover for their clandestine work. She began to be used by them as courier of messages from one secret cell to the other.

In the course of her work for the Communist Party, Sumitra came to know that the Secretary of Democratic Women's League Miss Usha Sharma and another communist worker Vijay Gupta had fallen in love. Mr. Gupta was a married man with three children. Through subtle inducement Mr. Vijay Gupta's wife Nibha Gupta was being put in a frame of mind where she would wilt and die without actually committing suicide so that Vijay and Usha could marry without the Party getting a bad name. After Mr. Vijay Gupta went into hiding, his wife was shifted to the house of a Party sympathizer who had been given long leave by his employer, Delhi Cloth Factory, because he was in an advanced stage of tuberculosis. She did not take long to become tubercular and was declining to have any treatment. Sumitra came to know Miss Usha Sharma as Secretary of Democratic Women's League. It was she who had introduced her into the Communist Party and was her main contact in Party's underground work. A few times, Sumitra tried to talk the matter over with Usha but she would always brush her aside.

Both Lal Kaur and Sumitra sometimes attended the meetings of the Democratic Women's League, where Usha would suddenly appear if the place was safe. She also sometimes came to Lal Kaur at night and left communist literature which Sumitra read and explained to Lal Kaur. They had now begun to view not only the political problems but most of the human relations altogether differently. This isolated them further from their neighbours and friends. Party literature talked about revolutionary fervor among the people. Even though they did not notice it anywhere, they began to believe in it. All the people around lived in an atmosphere of euphoria at the achievement of freedom and there was utmost adulation of Congress leaders. For them Indian independence was a unique achievement and end of the road. Despite that Sumitra and Lal Kaur got infected by the make-belief that a revolution that will bring real freedom was at hand, because it was affirmed with so much vehemence at the meetings they attended and in the Party literature they read. This illusion received a boost 'as the armed struggle in Telangana, a part of Hyderabad State, gained momentum. Rapid advance of communist armies in China also gave a fillip to this fallacy. This make-belief gave them an ardor, a redemptive hope to which they tended to cling despite all evidence to the contrary. Sumitra's work in the school was very heavy and many times she brought home note books of the students for correction. Lal Kaur's children also needed help in their studies. This did not leave much time with her for reading the Party literature which was given to her or sold to her.

After getting the job she had written to her friend Salima in Pakistan. She had given her address care of Lal Kaur and had written how her husband died in Amritsar after he safely came from Pakistan. Sumitra wrote to her friend that her earlier letter was tom by her father as it was from Pakistan and was not shown to her and her new address was quite safe. She informed her friend in Pakistan that she felt suffocated by the atmosphere of hate prevailing here and that the memory of their goodness was what gave her strength. The reply was from Salima's father. His letter was brief and said that atmosphere there was no better. Salima had chosen to marry a Foreign Service officer so that she could go abroad and did not have to breathe the vitiated air.

Among the communists Sumitra met sometimes, she found much hatred, sharp like a sword. What made her unhappy was that this sword did not have the hilt of rectitude. Hatred for the oppressor could become the mother of right action only when the oppressed were fired not only by valorous courage but also by moral stamina. Without that iron would not enter the soul of those who are fighting for social justice.

One of those small gatherings of Democratic Women's League was held in one room house of a Hindi writer who was a renowned journalist and was once on the staff of the most widely circulated Hindi daily newspaper. As he avoided giving anti-muslim and anti-communist slant to news items, his services were terminated by that paper. He was convinced that revolution would take place in two years. He decided not to take up any job and to live during this period on rupees six hundred which he ~ received as gratuity from his previous employer. He spent only rupees twenty-five per month on himself and his family, the wage given by the Communist Party to its single whole-time worker. His two sons gave up going to school and he was giving them education at home. There was a stamp of poverty, deprivation, and malnutrition on everyone in the family so much so all women who had come to attend the meeting were deeply touched by it. Whatever he wrote was published in Party journals and Party publishing house, for which he received no payment. One of the women present asked his wife why he does not write for non-party papers also. First she kept quiet but when similar questions were repeated, she replied: "How does it matter if he does not now earn anything. Does not the widow whose husband dies without leaving anything manages somehow? I am in a better position."

As Sumitra had begun to act as an undercover contact between various communist leaders in hiding, she was asked not to attend such meetings, or visit a leftist book shop or to accost a known communist sympathizer whom she might come across, She was also asked not to betray in any manner her sympathy for communist cause in her conversations. This also restricted Lal Kaur's participation in these meetings. As Chanan Mal's visits became infrequent, looking after children became their joint responsibility, more of Sumitra's because she had to assist them in their studies. Whenever Chanan Mal came to see his sister he always advised her not to get mixed up with Democratic Women's League or any similar organization.

Lal Kaur received a message that there would be a massive demonstration outside the United States Embassy at Bahawalpur house and the demonstrators would gather at the Ladies Park at the beginning of Darya Ganj road. The Party weekly in its appeal to women to join the demonstration in large numbers, created the impression that the demonstration would cause a stir, if not shake the whole of Delhi. A woman came to guide Lal Kaur to Ladies Park. They reached there when the procession was about to start. There were nineteen women in all including them, eleven of them with banners and rest with red buntings. A young girl held more buntings for those who may join onthe way. They passed through crowded Darya Ganj bazaar, with passers by amusingly looking at them. They moved out of Delhi Gate by then their slogan shouting had become somewhat muted. By the time they reached Hardinge Bridge for turning right for U.S. Embassy in Bahawalpur house, five women had slipped away. The road had been completely barricaded. There were more than hundred policemen and women and half a dozen police vans. As the women in the procession tried to push themselves through the barricades towards the road leading to the U. S. Embassy, they were all arrested and made to get into a van. The van drove for a few hours in an unknown direction and as the sun was setting they were dropped in a jungle. Their names and thumb impessions were recorded in a register by the accompanying policewomen .Their purses and whatever of value they had was taken away.

A younger woman among them climbed a tree and told them that a small village was a mile away. By dusk they reached that village. They did not have money to buy anything. The villagers gave them jaggery, roasted gram and whey and told them that the nearest railway station Hapur was five miles away. They explained to the villagers who they were and all that had happened to them. The villagers discussed this among themselves and asked one villager to take them to the railway station in his bullock cart so that they could catch the night train to Delhi. Some employees at the Hapur railway station belonged to the Railwaymen's Union. They collected money to serve them dinner and to arrange their return to Delhi.

When Lal Kaur returned to her Tis Hazari hut next forenoon, she was running temperature. She was in bed for two weeks. After school, Sumitra had to spend most of her time with Lal Kaur and her children. She curtailed her Party work to one daily trip on cycle between two cells. Some packets and covers would be left at Lal Kaur's hut very early in the morning when it was still dark and she was required to cycle to the code address indicated and deliver it there after nightfall. During this period she went to see the parents of Mrs Nibha Gupta. She had once gone to that place to deliver papers to her husband Comrade Vijay Gupta who at that time was hiding there. She explained to Nibha's parents that she would not recover from her illness where she was staying and that they should arrange for sending her to a sanitarium. They told Sumitra that they were very keen to have her home or to send her to a sanitarium, but Vibha does not want to leave that place.

One aftermath of her visit to Vibha's parents was that she was spotted by the Police and began to be followed by an Intelligence man in plain clothes. She sent word about this and also that she was discontinuing her work for sometime. She received instructions that she should carry on with her work and dodge the shadow before reaching her destination, even if she had to circumambulate on cycle for some time to do so.

One evening she had to take some papers to the unit secretary, Comrade Aftab, who was overall in charge of labour front supervised by Vijay Gupta as well of democratic women's movement of which Usha Sharma was the leading activist. Leaving her house on cycle soon after dusk with the papers left at Lal Kaur's hut in the early morning hours, she soon spotted the 'shadow'. She cycled aimlessly for two hours but could not dodge the policeman in plain clothes cycling at a short distance behind her. She was in a fix and after taking left turn towards a lane went into a soda water fountain, ordered a cold drink and rested there for about twenty minutes. When she came out the 'shadow' was still there. Thereafter she took another turn went inside an iron gate of a bungalow and sat in the cabin of the watchman for half an hour. This time when she came out she did not spot the 'shadow'. It was ten-thirty and she had to cycle for another half an hour before she reached her destination. The traffic had thinned by then and she could make sure that she was not being followed. She called at the place where Comrade Aftab was living incognito. It was ten minutes past eleven. She was dead tired and breathless. She was not supposed to give her real name at places she visited and to have a new name for each place. Here she was known as Tara and this was her second visit to this place.

The house had a large open veranda with a wide wooden bench. There were interconnected two rooms, both having exit door and a window towards the veranda. The right side room was used by the family as living room and the second to provide shelter to a communist in hiding. It seemed the guest kept changing because last time she had come here to deliver papers to Usha Sharma. The house belonged to an assistant in a commercial house. He was under strict instructions not to associate in any manner with the employees union or to visit a leftist book shop or coffee house. Sumitra had brought some papers for Comrade Aftab this time and this was the first occasion she was seeing him. Comrade Aftab was a person of average height. Between his high cheek bones protruded thick nose with round tip and broad nostrils. On his upper lip nestled a well trimmed moustache. The glance of his enquiring eyes often fluctuated. Sometimes it would be soft and another time hard like that of an overbearing leader, when his broad forehead would have a wrinkle or two. Shaking hand with her he said: "You are really quite late." Sumitra replied: "I left home immediately after dusk and have been trying to dodge the shadow for four hours. Only now I could be sure that I was not being followed." Handing over the packet of papers to him, she said: "I will leave immediately otherwise my people will start worrying."

He replied with a smile: "We are your people now. It is very late and I cannot agree to your going at this hour." He asked the host to bring a cup of tea and biscuits for Tara and also leave cotton matting and a sheet for her to spend the night there. Sumitra explained her keenness to leave saying that Lal Kaur, with whom she was staying, was unwell since she took part in the women's demonstration against U.S Embassy and she was looking after her children. Comrade Aftab repeated more firmly: "It is almost midnight and I cannot agree to your going out so late."

Comrade Aftab was seeing Sumitra for the first time though he had a dossier about her on the basis of information furnished by Comrade Usha and others. He-sat on the only cot in the room and asked her to take the chair. He had a full look at her from head to foot. She was elegant with distinctive refinement and self-assurance. Her eyes had fearless modesty which was emphasized by her satiny brown complexion and the way she had plaited and arranged her hair in a bun at back of neck. Red in her cheeks had appropriate dimness. Her well formed teeth were strikingly visible between her thin lips, as if trying to suppress a smile.

They began to discuss women's demonstration at the U.S. Embasy. Sumitra gave him Lal Kaur's version. She was surprised that he had an exaggerated account of the demonstration, even about the number of participants. Darya Ganj always had a rush of pedestrians. That was described to him as a sympathetic public lining up of the route. Sumitra told Comrade Aftab that the version she had given him was of one of the participants. and she was one person who would always speak the truth. Comrade Aftab did not seem to react to this remark favourably and grimaced. Sumitra had felt so strongly about it that she could not help remarking: "However much one may play up, the demonstration was a small one, starting with nineteen women and finally only twelve were left when the police arrested them. It does not seem to be correct to nurse the illusion that revolution is across the comer when none in the public at large feels any urge or possibility for it." Comrade Aftab was taken aback. He retorted: "When the Chinese communists started from north China they were not many and had not much support but by the very act of keeping up and escalating the revolutionary struggle they became magnet for hundreds of thousands of Chinese people." He sraightend his back and asserted: "Indian working class is taking the shortest route to emacipation, short but very difficult"

He lighted a cigarette and offered one to her. Pushing the smoke away with both hands, she firmly declined it and asked: "Does Comrade Usha Sharma smoke." Comrade Aftab replied: "She does not smoke in my presence but Comrade Vijay Gupta is a chain smoker. It might be she is not able to say no to him."

Moving her eyes away from Comrade Aftab's stare, Sumitra observed somewhat diffidently: 'Now that there has been mention of Comrade Usha Sharma:," I want to entreat you to do something to save the life of Nibha wife of Comrade Vijay Gupta. She should be prevented from courting death in the manner she is doing. if Vijay Gupta and Usha Sharma are in love with each other and feel that their relationship should have the seal of marriage, why should it be necessary for Vibha to die in order to facilitate it? I understand that Vibha was a member of the Party before Vijay Gupta joined it. A way can surely be found for Vijay and Usha to marry while Vibha lives on to serve the Party. Even a desperate solution of both becoming Muslim to marry would be better than making Vibha suffer the torture of slow, devouring death.

As Sumitra said this, Comrade Aftab fixed his stem and vexing eyes on her. Her ears became red. Though it was not an occasion to smile, she tried to mollify Comrade Aftab with a friendly look and a subdued smile which created tiny affable wrinkles on her cheeks. There was silence for sometime. Comrade Aftab's disconcert showed no sign of abating. His attention was diverted by two flies which had entred the room and after flying around for a while sat on each other in the middle of the pillow.

In the commandig tone of a leader he said abruptly: "What you call courting death or suicide is a supreme act of revolutionary heroism on the part of Vibha Gupta in the service of the Communist Party of India. She knows that both of them will serve the cause of communism better when they start living as husband and wife." Sumitra felt this elucidation as a blow to her good sense. She crossed her arms on her bossom, placing her palms near her bony shoulders which raised her head, and disagreed: "What you say is beyond my understanding. This is a human problem and needs an equally human solution. Why do you look at it dogmatically only?" Comrade Aftab affirmed: "Nothing is more human today than that serve the cause of communism and brings nearer the emancipation of the people of India. Marxism is my guide to action. Do you read the works of Marx and Lenin?"

Sumitra replied: "It cannot be even a fraction of what you seem to do. During Partition riots in Lahore, a Muslim class fellow of mine rescued me from my hostel and I lived with her family for sometime. Her grand father was among the Punjabi Muslims who tried to go to Turkey during the Khilafat movement in support of the Sultan in 1918. Soon after they reached Afganistan, there was Ataturk revolution and sultanate was abolished. He returned and was jailed for a few years in Peshawar. He used to say that when one's belief in social justice and moral values is from books, whether religious or others, it remained in one's head. If you are inspired to it by love of the common people and the desire of their welfare, it goes to your heart. He believed in a world without poverty and tyranny and also one.in which compassion, charity of mind and moral excellence would prevail. He believed that this was communism and did his best to sub serve it. I do not think that you attitude to Vibha Gupta conforms to this humane aspect of Marxism." Interrupting Sumitra Comrade Aftab affirmed: "Everything has to be viewed in the perspective of the struggle of the Indian working class for communism."

In a measured tone Sumitra expressed her surprise: "I do not know what you imply by the struggle of the Indian working class for communism. .Do you mean only working class, which is fast becoming part of the upper half of the Indian society and many sections of it are in the upper twenty percent. In that case, the communist party is another upper class party. India's bottom twenty per cent people are the world's most oppressed, the most starved, the most wretched and the most accursed people. They possess virtually nothing and own neither their labour, nor their life and children. Even rudimentary effort to improve their condition will be resisted by the Indian elite with all the instruments of oppression which they have perfected over years. A revolutionary struggle for the empowerment of these oppressed zeros of life can have chance of success only when those who spearhead it cultivate unprecedented heroic valor and the highest level of moral excellence. I therefore appeal to you not to overlook moral aspect of issues you face.

This upset Comrade Aftab and an angry look that her plain speaking gave him was obvious to Sumitra. In a voice brimming with displeasure he roared: "Do you want to teach me Marxism? Do you want to order the Communist Party what to do?" She bowed a little and lowered her head as if she did not want to pursue the matter further. She had already decided not to spend the night in that room alone with Comrade Aftab. After sometime she quietly picked up he floor spread, tiptoed to the door and unlatched it. She spent the night on the bench in the veranda. Half an hour before day break she cycled back to the hut of Lal KauL

Chanan Mal was there in the hut and informed her that police had been there an hour ago in search of her. There was a garret in Shiv Shanker's Mori Gate flat. Chanan Mal arranged for her hiding there for a few days till he could find out the nature of police case against her. The news of the arrest of Comrade Aftab from his hide out the same morning complicated matters for her, as Chanan Mal suggested to her that Communist Party was likely to hold her responsible for disclosing it. Sumitra requested Chanan Mal to find out the residential address of Professor Saraswat of Reori Mal College. He was married to her neighbour and class fellow in Sargoda. On the third day Chanan Mal brought the address and also informed her that the Communists were greatly upset at the arrest of Comrade Aftab. He told her that she had got herself in a wrench. The police regards her as an important communist while the communists suspect her as a police mole. Late same evening she shifted to Professor Saraswat's house in Regharpura in Karol Bagh area. Both her friend and her husband welcomed her.

Sumitra gave a detailed account of all that had happened to her. Professor Saraswat agreeing with Chanan Mal remarked: "You have placed yourself in a very puzzling predicament. The safest course for you is to surrender to the Police already in search of you, but this will confirm the suspicion of the Communist Party that you are a mole. The longer it takes for the Police to arrest you, the more they will think that you are a hard core communist. After your release you will find that a person once branded as a communist does not get a job easily. The door of the communist party is already half if not fully shut to you. Another course is that you leave Delhi but you will all the time live in fear of being arrested." For a few days various pros and cons were examined threadbare. Professor Saraswat informed Sumitra that while at Benares Hindu Univesity he and one Mr. Lengdu from Sikkim became good friends and ,had since remained in touch with each other through occasional exchange of letters. In his letter received last month he had stated that he was principal of a high school in northern part of Sikkim and that he was facing the problem of shortage of staff. Sumitra liked the idea of staying for some time in Sikkim. Professor Saraswat gave her an introductory letter and she left for Sikkim.

Shiv Shanker went to Moscow on November 4, as a member of the delegation of the Friends of the Soviet Union to partake in the annual celebrations of the Russian revolution. Immediately after the main celebration on November 7, Justice Shokhla returned to India and Shiv Shanker became the leader of the delegation. One of the functionaries of the Communist Party of India who was shepherding the delegation had notes for speeches ready for all occasions and all places they visited. Shiv Shanker was quite happy with the importance he got and the Communist functionary was also happy because he most willingly followed his guidance. There was enough to eat and drink and more accolades than he had ever received. When persons with worn out clothes, full of patches were pointed out to him, he described this as glory of simple living and high thinking. Only problem was a young woman attending to their rooms in the hotel. She had been married for seven years and was without a child. She said that her husband always came home drunk and would drink more till by the time of going to bed he would be completely besotted. She behaved as if she wanted his help to have a child. He was not only the youngest among the delegates but appeared to be least drunk in that group.

On his return to India Shiv Shanker was asked whether he would like to write a series of articles or a book on his experiences during visit to the Soviet Union. To shelve the matter he said that he would like to write a book when he found some time. After about a month the Party functionary who had accompanied the delegation to Moscow came with an Attache of the Soviet Embassy. They showed him the manuscript which could be published in his name provided it was to his liking. Shiv Shanker agreed to this without any hesitation because when the Attaché was taking out the manuscript from the hand bag, he saw bundles of currency notes lying there. They gave him a typed letter addressed to the Cultural Counselor of the Soviet Embassy in whch he agreed to bestow all rights of publication of the manuscript including the right over transactions, for an outright payment of fifty thousand rupees as one time royalty. The Soviet Attaché took out money from his hand bag and handed it over to the Indian Party functionary who explained to Shiv Shanker: "The Soviet Union does not subscibe to the Copy Right Convention and normally does not pay any royalty to outside authors. Out of this amount of fifty thousand rupees you are to donate twenty-five thousand rupees to the Party. Would you like the receipt to be in your name? Normally we make the .donation anonymous unless the donor is closely associated with the Party." Without waiting for Shiv Shanker's reply he wrote the receipt for rupees twenty-five thousands by an anonymous donor and handed over twenty-five thousand rupees and this receipt to Shiv Shanker,

Shiv Shanker looked straight at the Party functionary as if he was greatly offended and said curtly: "This is not a correct way of soliciting a donation. As regards copy right this is an altogether a different case. The Soviet Public Relations set up will be using my name for views which are theirs and might not be mine. If you attended the reception held in my honour by the eminent personalities of this city you will realize that fifty thousand rupees is a small sum in view the position I have." Saying this he angrily snatched the balance of twenty thousand rupees from Party functionary and gave him back the receipt.

The Party functionary was flabbergasted as if he had slipped on a banana peel.

Perplexedly he fell back on the chair with closed eyes. Opening his eyes he gazed at Shiv Shanker formidably. Suddenly. he leaped at Shiv Shanker like a panther and snatched three bundles of twenty five thousand rupees from him. Swiftly he handed over the agreement signed by Shiv Shanker to the the Soviet Attaché, threw the receipt at Shiv Shanker and walked out roaring: "You used to behave like a circus bear. Do not play fast and loose like this."

Before Shiv Shanker could recover from the stunning jolt, the Party functionary had already dragged the Soviet Attaché down the stairs.

CHAPTER THIRTY SEVEN

When Chanan Mal was appointed as Chief Reporter and Joint Editor of Desh Bhagat, Acharya Ram Krishan advised him: "Your name Chanan Mal does not appear to be that of a first class journalist and seems more the name of a village shop keeper. You should add your caste Chopra to your name. In future your news stories will appear under the name 'C.M.Chopra'." He announced on the front page of the next issue that a well known journalist C. M. Chopra has been appointed the Special Correspondent and Chief Reporter of Desh Bhagat and that the paper will be more up-to-date wth news than before.

To buttress his announcement Acharya asked Chopra to front page in the same issue a news story under the banner: "Frontier Gandhi Khan Abdul Gaffar Khan on death bed." An Urdu newspaper received from Pakistan had carried an appeal by lawyers in Peshawar for the release of Khan Abdul Gaffar Khan in view of his old age. Acharya wanted this information to be twisted into a news item conforming to the banner suggested by him. Chopra wrote a story how early in the morning Khan Abdul Gaffar Khan had pain in his right shoulder. Despite repeated urgent requests medical help was not made available and by noon he had paralysis of the right side of the body. He could neither lift his right arm nor open his right eye. His speech had also been partially affected. Next day a doctor examined him and advised his shifting to a hospital. To date the Pakistan government had not done anything. There was immediate denial by Pakistan government that Abdul Gaffar was in any manner indisposed. There were diplomatic exchanges which made Chopra feel important.

A few scoops of this type made Chopra rise to an eminent position as a journalist. Before long he received an offer from National Times as their Special Correspondent on double the salary he was receiving at Desh Bhagat. The paper also arranged for him accommodation in Constitution

House hostel at Curzon Road on concessional rent. This cluster of three storey barracks was built doing War years by U.S. Army as G. I. hostel and consisted of about five hundred suites and cubicles. After the World War it was taken over by the Works and Housing Department of the Government of India. It began to be called Constitution House because members of the Constituent Assembly, not requiring family accommodation, were provided free lodging here Arrangement had also been made here for high class catering at reasonable rates. Some rooms were reserved for senior government officials awaiting regular allotment and about half a dozen cubicles were earmarked for senior journalists. Some of the members of the Constituent Assembly had passed on the accommodation to their friends or rented out to others

Chopra found that it was a strange world of small men with great plans and of great men with small minds. There were men here who could make mountain of mole hill and others who like monkey god Hanuman found a mountain lighter than a mound. It was a world of dreamer and of schemers. It was a playground of carpetbaggery and skulldruggery. It was a free-for-all for leg pullers and headhunters. It was a heaven both for the brainy and the moronic. There were persons living or spending most of their time here, who were preparing to contest elections to the first Parliament of India. There were others waiting for their turn to become a Minister in the Central or some Provincial government. There were Khadi clad persons who claimed that they could manage any work in any Ministry or Department of the Government of India There were others who made a comfortable living by professing that they had access to officers of the government and were much sought after by agents of some embassies. There were not a few men and women moving around here who proferred permits, quota, licenses etc. from government departments. Equally active here were those who made a comfortable living by contriving liaison for favour-seekers with Ministers and high officials. Chopra met highfalutin persons here who were associated with one shady foreign agency or the other. Chopra also came across here person who boasted to be the greatesf. Titer or the greatest artist or the greatest philosopher of India.

Shiv Shanker was in need of a telephone connection. He had seen many times the Contract Officer of the Telephone Department who had promised to provide him with a telephone as soon as possible. There was War-time shortage of telephones and he was unable to to get a connection despite months of effort. Chopra came to know about a person in the Constitution House who traded in this and got Shjv Shanker a telephone in two days. Because of Chopra he got it on concessional rates but even then it was not a small amount. He was told that most of the amount will be paid to a member of the Legislative Assembly close to the Minister concerned.

After Chanan Mal Chopra shifted to the Constitution House, Shiv Shanker began to visit it often. Here he met Professor Hiren Sanyal whom he had come to know during the visit to India of Moral Rearmament delegation. Professor Sanyal introduced Shiv Shanker to Miss Bhavana Shreekant, Director of the Indian branch of the Society for the Promotion of Democratic Freedom and to Comrade A. S. Bright, secretary of the Indian unit of the Revolutionary Marxist Forum. It did not take Shiv Shanker long to discover that these were one member societies and did not suffer from any shortage of funds. Another resident of Constitution House living more luxuriously than Bhavana Sheekant and A.S.Bright was Dr. Louis De Souza, president of the Abraham Lincoln Society of India. Dr. De Souza was sending every week twenty five packets of Marxist, leftist and pro-Soviet literature to individuals and libraries in U.S.A., the import and distribution of which was banned in that country. Dr. De Souza had made arrangement with Indian publishers of books of the same format to provide him with spare jackets and initial pages upto preface or introduction. He would camouflage those books with these jackets and first few pages of innocuous books before posting these to U. S. A. The packets mentioned Abraham Lincoln Society of India as sender.

Miss Bhavana Shreekant of the Society for the Promotion of Democratic Freedom wanted Shiv Shanker to find out an astrologer for her. He should not look like an ordinary Brahmin but should have all trappings of a godly hoary sanyasi, possibly having matted hair and an ash smeared body. He should have a trident, a jug made of hollowed gourd and rosaries with biggish wooden beads. Payment can be more if he is the look-alike of a holy man coming straight from the jungles of Himalayas. The idea was that when foreign journalists, cine cameramen, press photographers came to cover and to record his Press conference there should not be the slightest doubt that he was a very divine person, a soothsayer and an oracle. Miss Shreekant wanted that astrologer to predict in that Press briefing that the next World War will commence in May 1949 with attack by Soviet Union on Berlin and will end in January 1950 with the defeat of the Soviet Union and the end of communism. About India's Prime Minister Pandit Nehru, he should at least be willing to say that his days were numbered.

C.M.Chopra came to know that Miss Bhavana Shreekant was a married woman with two daughters. After second daughter, her in-laws got her horoscope made which indicated that she would have five more daughters and no son. Her husband deserted her and his parents married him again. Later when his new wife also had a daughter, it became known that horoscope was faked and his parents wanted to marry the son again for dowry.

Shiv Shanker assured Bhavana Shreekant that he would be able to arrange an astrologer as per her requirement, he will be dressed as she wanted and predict as she suggested but she would have to pay him a proper remuneration for this. He asked her to check up with Professor Sanyal that whenever he promised a job he did it perfectly well. She was not invited to the reception held in his honour but knew about it and also that he was a member of the delegation to the Soviet Union. Soon after that Comrade A.S.Bright of the Revolutionary Marxist Forum took him into confidence and wantd him to do for him an interesting but dangerous job. He seems to be aware of his standing and was always deferential to him whenever he met him in the Constitution House,· where he loitered all the day. One day after lunch time was over, he took him inside the. restaurant and they sat in a comer of that empty hall. He said that one Mr. Mickiewitz Miloz was a senior Counselor of the Czech Embassy in India· He was a well-known poet of that country. He was freely movig about in India and meeting people to collect material for a book on Indian culture. Some among them who were close to some western Embassies tried to persuade him to defect to West. He was given very tempting offers but he firmly and angrily rejected them. Now Comrade Bright wanted the Czech Counselor to be thrown down from a high building or otherwise made to appear to have committed suicide. While doing so a note by him was to be pushed into his pocket. The note stated that he was committing suicide on his own free will because he did not want to return to the communist prison again. Shiv Shanker saw the supposed suicide note. They -came out. Standing in the sun he examined it carefully in broad day light. There was a possibility that it could, without much difficulty, be proved to be a cleverly done forgery. Shiv Shanker put off Bright by saying that he would see him after he had thought out how this could be planned.

Shiv Shanker had begun to visit Constitution House regularly and to stay there longer. While relaxing in the lounge or moving about in the corridor, he often met people with little. education and ability harbouring great ambitions. He also came across persons, not even half as clever as he, who had achieved their lofty goals. His brain became a beehive of go-getting plans and he felt a successful political career within his reach more than ever before. He became determined to contest elections to India's first Parliament in 1951. There were persons here who had won elections and those who lost. He tried to learn from them tricks of the trade. Some had bought votes, enrolled bogus voters or got names of those likely to oppose him deleted from the rolls. Others had influenced, by various inducements, the electoral or administrative set up. He learnt how to obtain Congress ticket for the election and how to manage those who could not counter the feeling in the electoral staff that it was their patriotic duty to make the Congress Party win. He also learnt how to buy the votes of the poor and the lower castes and if necessary how to prevent them from voting. He was in no doubt that an election had to be planned as meticulously as a robbery, calculating every step, carefully working out every detail, methodically making every move and anticipating and off-setting possible impediments.

Pandit Ram Lochan lived in the room opposite that of Chopra. He used to be an independent member of the Central Legislative Assembly and got elected by defeating six candidates, four belonging to different political parties. He had set up candidates with exactly the same name as the four belonging to political parties, so that the voters who came to vote for them got confused. He had also set up against the Congress candidate a man of the same caste so that votes of that caste could be divided. In the 1946 elections he was defeated by a Congress candidate by a narrow margin. Knowing that the Congress candidate was a notorious gangster and law breaker, he had set up a terminally sick man as a candidate so that if he appeared to be losing, the sick candidate's demise could help in rescheduling elections in that constituency. The Returning Officer was influenced by the rival candidate to rule that death of the candidate took place too late and elections need not be countermanded. What that gangster candidate had done was to offer two hundred rupees per vote to a community of four thousand low caste voters who had agreed to vote for him at the rate of one hundred rupees per vote. On the polling day that candidate brought busses to take these voters to the polling booth but instead took them to a temple town twenty miles away where they were forced to stay till evening and not paid anything. Pandit Ram Lochan's regret was that he lost election with a number of votes less than that.

Shiv Shanker also learnt from Ram Lochan how easy it was to make money once one had made one's name in politics. He knew the Governor of United Provinces during War years. He offered to bring out a Hindi daily in support of the War effort. A quota of subsidized newsprint for fifty thousand copies was sanctioned and advertisements were arranged for him for the same print order. He actually printed four thousand copies only to supply to the advertisers, distribution list of libraries received from the government and for display at Wheelers book stalls at railway stations. He sold the balance of the newsprint in the black market. He had thus garnered several hundred thousand rupees during War years.

Pandit Ram Lochan was always complaining that people had lost faith in God and human values and that mutual trust was fast disappearing. Shiv Shanker first thought this could be due to his dissatisfaction with the Constitution House catering. He had often publicly expressed his displeasure with the catering contractor. He belonged to that subsect of Bhojpuri Brahmins of eastern United Provinces who ate mutton but believed in totemic taboo for chicken, egg or fish. As the Constitution House mess had common pots and utensils for all non-vegetarian dishes, Ram Lochan did not have mutton dishes from there. Later on Shiv Shanker guessed that reason for his complaining that people had lost faith in God was altogether different. There was a girls' hostel just across the road. Some working girls from his district were living in that hostel. Ram Lochan had been giving them lavish gifts and inviting them to his room. They would accept the gifts but avoided the Constitution House.

Pandit Ram Lochan was the only person in the Constitution House who did not want to keep the journalists and newspapermen in good humour and who never curried their favour. He blamed the Press for the partition of the country and for all the problems of India. He would pontificate: "If the Indian Press had not encouraged Gandhi to create himself as a god on earth and juxtaposed Nehru to him as Laxman was to god Rama, they would have exhibited more down to earth attitude. Jinnah was an eminent nationalist leader before Gandhi and Nehru appeared on the scene. In order to establish their hegemony and to capture leadership they left no stone unturned to sideline and to belittle Jinnah. The Press helped to knock down Jinnah from his acknowledged position as a national leader and to ensure that Gandhi was unrivalled. The Indian Press is a wild elepant and journalists are small men who sitting on the elephant think that they are taller than the elephant. "

Pandit Ram Lochan's expletives against journalists made Chopra look inwards sometimes. He himself was astonished by the success of his recent journalistic cuisine. The news of land slide near Badri Nath in northern Himalayas was received at a time when a Chinese delegation was in Delhi.

The story he gave had the full page banner: 'China to claim Badri Nath area as Tibetan territory' the news story written from this angle was lapped up by the Western Press. Again, it was reported that some rusted guns of 1857 Mutiny period have been found below some rocks at the Delhi ridge not far from the Victory Tower commemorating the Mutiny. Chopra turned it into a front page news item saying that communists had dug a tunnel and were storing weapons there. A Home Ministry top official complimented his paper for this news report because the government was then adopting a hard line against the Communist Party. "Is truth so fleeting, facts so ephemeral and actuality so transient?" Chopra would think again and again. He would ponder: "Have not the world's problems arisen because the newspapers have helped the political leaders to be cock sure of their faultlessness and presented their pronouncements as gospel truth" More Chopra thought about these, more he was filled with remorse. He asked himself: "Must the truth have the ringing tone of a gold coin? Like the face of a woman, has truth to be dressed up, embellished and made attractive with every variety of cosmetic? Is truth a harlot who comes to every patron as a virgin? Has truth a different colour for different people, white, red, gray, black? Must truth be dressed up with layers of clothes so that one does not feel aghast at seeing it naked?" Ruminating on this Chopra thought how easily truth could be proved false and falsehood established as gospel. How easily a man could be made to have faith in one truth in place of another. The people who were unquestioning adulators of Mahatma Gandhi only a short while ago, were now crying hoarse that he should die. Those who were till recently shouting at the top of their voice slogan like 'Long Live Pandit Nehru' now wanted him to lick dust. Chanan Mal Chopra looked back at life in his village, in Lahore, in Amritsar and later in Delhi. He recollected how the nature and complexion of truth hss been changing for him. As he attempted to fathom his mind, he was gnawed by the feeling that it was not truth that was changing but he himself was metamorphosing.

He sometimes talked these things over with Shiv Shanker. Both of them had seldom been in doubt that what they had been doing was not good and correct. This was unlike Ram Lochan or Acharya Ram Krishan, who far from harbouring a feeling of wrong doing, were convinced of their righteousness. However wrongly he and Shiv Shanker might have acted to achieve their pursuits, they always had a nagging conscience. It appeared incredible to them that others while falsifying truth or perpetrating a blatant wrong could convince themselves that they were upright and truthful. They were self righteous enough to believe that the armchair of their moral life could stand on one or two legs or even hang in the air.

CHAPTER THIRTY EIGHT

Shiv Shanker had made up his mind to contest elections in 1951 to first Parliament of free India. Acharya Ram Krishan and daily Desh Bhagat had acquired much influence among the refugees. Chopra had told him that if he fought election on the ' ticket of the Congress Party, Acharya will oppose him tooth and nail. Mela Ram, editor of Desh Bhagat, had confirmed that he should not expect any support from Achrya ji if he is going to be a Congress candidate. He had been paying fixed amount to Mela Ram every month, but he was receiving publicity in the dak edition of the paper only. This publicity was of little use to him as he was proposing to contest elections from Delhi on Congress Pary ticket if possible and without that if necessary. Shiv Shanker had been trying to make out how Acharya Ram Krishan's opposition could be lessened if not neutralized.

The underlying policy of Acharya Ram Krishan ever since he launched daily Desh Bhagat in Lahore was dissemination of hatred. Some criticism of British rule was necessary so that he could pose that his newspaper was nationalist. The first target of his hate psychosis was the Muslim community, which gained in virulence as the demand for Pakistan acquired momentum. Next were the Sikhs, though editorial comments against them were subtle, the news display had a pronounced slant against them. This was followed by Sanatanist Hindus who had distanced themselves from his Arya Samaj because of its opposition to idol worship. There were two groups in Arya Samaj. One Gurukul Section stood for ancient hermitage type of education and the other College Section which advocated modern system of education. Acharya Ram Krishan belonged to the latter and he missed no opportunity to belittle and to attack the Gurukul Section Arya Samajists. He also attached relentlessly any group in the College Section which in any manner challenged his leadership of College Section of Arya Samaj.

In Lahore the paper subsisted mainly on black mail and scandals. Except near Partition, when Hindu-Muslim tension reached its peak, the sale of the paper never exceeded two thousand copies. He had large ancestral property in Chauk Khatrian, a boulevard in the heart of the old city. The rental value of unoccupied portion was not much. He, however, had good income from discourses at religious gatherings. His son and daughter-in-law made full use of the free passes supplied by cinema houses in lieu of a few lines in 'Cinema Today' column about the picture on show. Both of them were spendthrift, with the result that Acharyaji had to be very thrifty. He had two daughters, both died before they were a few months old. There was much gossiping about it.

After shifting to Delhi the sale of the paper picked up soon. There were more than half a million refugees from Pakistan in this city and a few hundred thousand in the neighbouring districts of the Punjab and United Provinces all anxious to know about their fate. By fueling hatred against the Muslims and the Congress Party and by sensationalizing news reporting, the paper reached a circulation of thirty thousand copies in its third month in Delhi. This gave him a net income of over rupees thirty thousand per month. That was ten times the salary of the Prime Minister of India. His editorials, pedantic and hauteur as ever, now had the tone of an oracle ten times wiser than the Prime Minister of India. His house in Aurangzeb Road was bigger than Pandit Nehru's York Road residence. He had always measured a man's wisdom by these criteria and now applied these to himself.

It did not mean that he was happier than he was at Lahore. Rather he was very miserable. His daughter-in-law Sushila had second' miscarriage soon after arrival in Delhi, which within a week turned her hair gray, though she was yet in early twenties. This came as a shock to everyone in the family. Her husband Naresh particularly felt stunned and humiliated. The other problem arose because Acharyaji had put the names of his son and daughter-in-law on the staff of the paper, both on a salary of rupees two thousand per month, which he pocketed after they had signed the salary register. To Acharyaji's consternation, both of them started claiming the full amount while signing the receipt. This was a shock for Acharyaji greater than losing the hope of having a grand son. All his life Acharyaji had been sermonizing against smoking and drinking and that a woman should strictly follow the ideals of mythological Sita and Savitri. Naresh now smoked and drank openly and Sushila got her hair bobbed and dyed. He felt as if his nose had been cut off. His fair complexion had acquired murkiness as a result of constant unhappiness and worry. However, his big saturnine eyes, with pouches and well Proportioned nose and chin continued to create the impression that he was both a wise and a worldly wise man;

Developments in the newspaper office made him still more miserable. After he had fixed the salary of his son and daughter-in-law more than ten times the highest paid to any member of the staff, there was demand from them for higher pay. All along he had raised the salaries by a few rupees at a time. Now he had to double and in some cases triple their wages. Soon after Chanan Mal Chopra left the paper, its oldest employee Mohammed Ali, whom he had specially brought with himself from Lahore, also resigned. This greatly added to his headache.

Acharya Ram Krishan was at heart a God-fearing man. The present luxurious life and unexpected prosperity had not changed his simple habits, nor the rigid discipline of his life. He had seldom departed from it during last forty years of his active life. He would get up at 4.30 a.m. without the need of an alarm clock. The morning necessities, half-an hour'sfoot-slog within the house, pranayam, breath control regimen, etc. would be over by 6 a.m.Then there will be quick bath and Vedic puja concluded with recitation of mantras which took an hour. All the morning English, Hindi and Urdu newspapers would be placed on the center table of his room on a stack of other papers and periodicals. He would leisurely drink a liter of milk, hot or:old according to the season, while scanning these papers and working up ideas for his editorials for Desh Bhagat. At 8 a.m. sharp Mohammed Ali would arrive. Acharyaji strolled in the room and muttered his thoughts in a mixture of Urdu and Panjabi with an occasional Hindi or Englsh word. Mohammed Ali moving behind him would go on taking notes. He would later on arrange these ideas in a proper order, adding the missing links and put the material in readable Urdu.

The Iiielligence Bureau had been making use of Mohammed Ali as a stool pigeon to know about the activities of some suspicious Muslims in the Jama Mosque area. He had been appointed as Inspector (Intelligence} on a whole time basis for the same purpose. Mohammed Ali' s departure made him more heart broken than other recent. mishaps. It greatly added to the load of his work.

The office of Desh Bhagat was in a large flat in the outer circle of Connaught Place and Acharyaji came to office after lunch at 2.30 p.m. Knowing how lonely and unhappy he was, Shiv Shanker began to see him in his office at reasonable intervals, Acharyaji was very fond of gossip and

Shiv Shanker had enough of that from Constitution House. Shiv Shanker informed Acharyaji of the son of an important national leader who had recently come to Constitution House as guest of a member of the Central Legislature. He had floated a 'People's Provident Fund' and wanted some Central Minister to lend his name as a patron so that those, from whom he sought deposit, gave money less diffidently. Acharyaji said that he could go to any Minister with a gift of five thousand ruees and he would readily agree. Shiv Shanker informed him hat he did go to an important Minister with a gift of five thousand rupees. The Minister concerned kept the money but refused to lend his name unless he was paid ten per cent of the collection. He could have paid one per cent but paying ten per cent would force him to turn the scheme into a racket. Shiv Shanker told Acharyaji about Miss Bhavana Shreekant who wanted him to arrange an astrologer to make the prediction which she would suggest. Acharyaji told him of monthly astrtological magazine 'Bhrigu Sanhita Patrika', editor of which might himself like to do the job provided the payment was attractive. He could also suggest someone else. When Shiv Shanker briefed Acharyaji about A.S.Bright's scheme about the Czech Counselor, he had a hearty laugh and revealed: "His real name is Amar Singh Chanana. He has translated Punjabi word for light into Bright as his name. It might be he has links with Indian Inelligence and is· being used to spot persons who undertake such work."

In a reminiscent mood Acharyaji talked somewhat lightheartedly and added:
    "In Lahore he wore a turban and properly tied his beard but now he has a flowing beard and hair hanging down his back so as to be a look-alike of Karl Marx."

His elder brother who is a very competent versifier is giving me much headache. In order to divide Hindus and Sikhs before the forthcoming general elections, the Punjab Congress government has given him money to start two newspapers from Jullundur, one espousing Sikh cause and the other appealing to hindu sentiments. He has, however, begun publishing the two papers from Delhi because this city has the largest concentration of refugees from Pakistan. The pro-Sikh and anti Hindu paper is called 'Sher-e-Khalsa' and pro-Hindu and anti-Sikh paper is called 'Bajrang Bali', names which have religious connotation. Both carry every day poems against the other community which have both humour and malice. This is helping the two papers to pick up sales at the expense of Desh Bhagat. Victims of Partition in both the communities in East Punjab harbour a feeling of bitterness against the Congress. The two communities are being divided so that fear of the Sikhs would enable the Congress to garner bulk of votes of the Hindus in he next general elections. Nehru does not realize that in the new situation anything that fans communalism among Sikhs would in the long run do the country more harm than good." Acharya gasped after his long discourse.

To change the subject Shiv Shanker put in some good words. about his son and daughter-in-law. Like fathers in general he did not seem to be flattered or humoured by this. Thinking that having good relations wih Naresh and Sushila could be useful at the time of elections to Parliament, he had been trying to establish good relation with both of them whIle trying to further their estrangement. He found Naresh bohemian and Sushila whimsical. He introduced Naresh to Miss Bhavana Shreekant but she kept him at a distance. There was an English girl whom Shiv Shanker saw many times in the Constitution House and Chopra had nodding acquaintance with her. Shiv Shanker discussed this with Chopra who said that it should not be difficult to make Naresh and the English girl know each other. He invited both of them for dinner in a Connaught Place restaurant. The English girl had once enquired from Chopra about Agra and what would be the most convenient mode of visiting that place. At dinner Naresh readily agreed to Chopra's suggestion that he took her to Agra next day. Despite much persuasion by Naresh she refused to spend the night there and they returned the same day though quite late. This was enough to make Naresh fall in love with her. They began to have lunch or dinner together often in the same restaurant. She however insisted that he should become a Christian before she could talk to him on anything other than occasional get together. This sunk him deeper in infatuation for her. After a few weeks she returned to England leaving her address with Naresh. Both Chopra and Shiv Shanker saw her off. Shiv Shanker gave her a gift and assured her that if she kept insisting in her letters on his becoming a Christian and migrating to England, she was bound to succeed. When Shiv Shanker talked this over with Acharyaji, the latter told him clearly that even if the English girl became a Hindu she would not be acceptable in his house. Naresh was already married under Arya Samaj rites which mandated monogamy and these marriages are indissoluble. Acharyaji threatened to disown and disinherit him.

Shiv Shanker's plan was to woo Sushila after she became sole beneficiary of Acharyaji's properties and of the newspaper. He had invited her for dinner in a restaurant and quietly pushed into her vanity bag an expensive set of earrings which he had picked up from one of the houses of Muslims. To his surprise she looked for him next day and returned the earrings, with the remonstrance: "Don't do such stupid thing again".

Shiv Shanker went to see Pandit Kirpa Saran Vidyankar, editor of Bhrigu Sanhita Patrika, which Acharya Ram Krishan had mentioned dealt with astrology. Pandit Vidyankar refused to divulge the address of the President of the Vedic Astrological Society who made horoscopes for the journal. He first wanted to know the purpose for which he required the information. Later on Shiv Shanker picked up a clerk of the Bhrigu Sanhita Patrika when he was leaving after office hours and took him to his Mon Gate residence. After entertaining him with sumptuous tea, he gifted him a shirt and pantaloons of his size out of his large stock. The clerk told Shiv Shanker that Vedic Astrological Sociey or its President did exist except in the advertisements. The Patrika has been publishing since 1935. During this long period it had accumulated several hundred horoscopes of various types and sizes catering to all sorts of requirements. According to the advertisement in Bhrigu Sanhita Patrika, fee for full horoscope was rupees fifty and rupees five for providing answer to a single question. There were different types of predictions and forecasts for rupees thirty, twenty and ten. A senior clerk in the office cooked replies in accordance with information supplied and specification of questions asked on the basis of horoscopes in the stock catering to 'similar requirements. These would be written in florid Devanagari script in ocher ink on light orange hand made paper specially made for this purpose with auspicious gyatri mantra embossed on the top. This clerk was familiar with astrological terminology but did not have a suitable personality. He also did not want to risk his job. He could not suggest how and where Shiv Shanker could find an astrologer of the type he was looking for. When he narrated this to Acharyaji, he replied that he had suspected this all along but was not quite sure about it.
Shiv Shanker asked Acharyaji: "Do you have horoscope of Naresh? It should be able to reveal to you whether he will have one marriage or more and also whether he will be a source of happiness or a cause for worry for his parents. It should also be able to indicate whether Naresh is destined to have overseas voyage or not. If the horoscope does not forecast two marriages, then you need not worry."

Achryaji remarked sneeringly: "When one accepts Arya Samaj faith, one throws away some of the backwardness of Hindu mind. I donot believe in horoscopes and did not get one made for Naresh. My father got one made for me. It forecast that I will die before I was forty and that I will have five sons and one daughter. Normally when a horoscope turns to be wrong, one explains it by saying that particulars about the time, date and place of birth were not correct. In the case of my horoscope my father was quite sure that there was no mistake about it."

"Why do not you have a young beautiful girl on your staff" Shiv Shanker suggested: "If Naresh takes fancy to her your problem will be solved. I do not think Arya Samaj marriage rituals prohibit short-term extramarital relationships". Acharyaji replied:

> "Life is not as simple as that. Matters of love are complex and complicated. Love is an insurgence against one's self. It is an inverted ego and a misconstruction of emotions. If a man is charmed by an ugly woman, even the most beautiful woman would be unable to break her spell Love is an incurable debility of the mind. Ved Vyasa recounted in Mahabharata how as a result of love a man gets imprisoned in sentimentalism and willingly undergoes every tribulation."

Shiv Shanker interjected: "Naresh said that one of your uncles fell in love with a Muslim girl, became a Muslim to marry her and shifted to Muslim quarters of the town. Thereafter the entire family broke away from him, even not recognizing him after conversion. Naresh is afraid that the same will happen to him if he becomes a Christian to marry the English girl. My own impression is that he does feel much attachment to the family."
Acharya Ram Krishan replied: "It is true that when my uncle became a Muslim, there was total break off, complete cessation of relationship. He began to live in a different part of the town and we turned our face whenever anyone of us came across him. With a Christian it is slightly different. For example even orthodox Hindu homes have Christian girl as a maid but not a Muslim girl. Dr. Rajendra Prasad and some other Congress Ministers have quietly weeded out Muslim government employees from their personal staff but not Christians."

"Acharyaji I have often thought about it" Shiv Shanker commented, "I have lived among Muslims as one of them. I have known and met Muslims of every type and class. I have never noticed any difference between the quality, manner and nature of life amongst the two communities. I have always felt that the proportion of honest, upright, intelligent and cleanly persons is more or less the same among Hindus and Muslims."
Acharya Ram Krishan concurred: "What you say is correct. That is my experience also and that of most other unprejudiced Hindus. But inborn

prejuidices can make one blind to factual position. A Hindu child imbibes it with mother's milk that Muslims are unclean, etc. Similarly a Muslim also acquires as a child mistaken prejudices against the Hindus. Gandhi by putting all the blame for Hindu-Muslim schism on the British rulers made us blind to the underlying cause of the Hindu- Muslim polarity which has been the bane of our social life. Many of the Hindu prejudices against Muslims are so absurd that the British could not have created these. Take for example the prejudice that Muslims are not cleanly. Compare a Hindu temple with a Muslim mosque and then decide who have a better sense of cleanliness."

After a brief pause Acharyaji continued: "Our prejudices and superstitions go back to the time when a child's mind awakens. Many of these, including religious prejudices, are part of our inheritance. Societal suggestions and imbuing over the long period of adolescent life play their part in engraving, fostering and directing these prejudices. Since man is a suggestible animal, he is very much influenced by the social pattern of his early life and Hindu-Muslim separateness has been part of that. Centuries ago when prejudices against Muslim invaders took birth in the mind of the Brahmins and other high castes, these were defensive in nature. They had passively accepted Muslim rule. What kept human the jumble of Hindu castes and sub-castes was this prejudice, their exclusiveness, their sense of loftiness and that of a peerless past. In a completely heterogeneous community sundered by castes, cults and totems, this was what stitched them together. When the British rulers came on the scene, first reaction among the Bengali high castes was outburst of these anti-Muslim prejudices. The same happened in other areas also, though it differed in degree but not in kind. This communal feeling gradually declined as the sentiments of nationalism and patriotism sprouted among the people with the consolidation of British rule and spread of modem education. That was the time when new societal atmosphere for Hindu Muslim amity and mutual goodwill could be created and the education of the child and family in new values taken up in right earnest. What actually happened was the opposite of it."

Butting in Shiv Shanker remarked: "All this is beyond my understanding. I think these communal prejudices are the result of our downfall. What I see all around is moral anarchy more than political freedom. More unscrupulous and self-serving one is, more quickly one climbs the social ladder in independent India."

Acharyaji closed his eyes, bent his back and kept sitting motionless for

sometime. Shiv Shanker was waiting him to open eyes so that he could take leave. Acharyaji got up with back bent and went to the attached bath room, keeping the door open. Standng near the wash basin, he splashed water on his eyes with hollowed hand. Without wiping his face he came back and sat back on the chair. This time he sat erect with hands clenched above the belly. His saturnine eyes were almost unblinking. He seemed to be feeling the burden of an unbearable weight of ideas. The entrance door of the room was at the back of Shiv Shanker He saw the shadow of a man standing at the door but not moving in. He turned back and saw Naresh standing there. "Come in Naresh", he suggested and pointed to the chairs.
Naresh moved in apd took his seat in a chair on the right side of his father's table. Acharyaji grumbled: "Last night you came so drunk that you had to be helped to find your room."

Naresh replied apologetically: "Pitaji I avoid drinking now but last night I could not help. As advised by you, I had gone to Gandhiji's prayer meeting. What he said there, created such a stonn in me that I had to drink and drink hard."

Acharyaji had not wiped his face after splashing it with water. A few drops still nestled on his eye bags. His face looked more somber and slightly shrunk. His long thin lips which were mildly quivering when he returned from the bath room were now closed tight.

Shiv Shanker looked at Acharyaji and then more keenly at Naresh. Except their height and a well proportioned nose there was nothing common in the features of father and son. Naresh's medium height was more noticeable because of his better built body and robust shoulders. His bountiful black hair looked like a skull cap and lent oddity to his personality. His face was light brown and cheeks wore a hectic flush. There was something coldly smug about him. His glance was sometimes furtive, at others darting or brazen.

Shiv Shanker recollected Naresh's wife Sushila. Even though physically attractive, she lacked a feminine personalty. She had in her features many elements which lent comeliness to a woman, yet it was not a stare at me face, nor did she arouse sentiments commonly associated with a woman. She treated everyone casually as if she would not take the trouble of liking or disliking a person.

Shiv Shanker ruminated over the societal structure which made persons with altogether different traits to live together: He was also wondering how a son so lovingly brought up could have a diametrically different personality from his father. Suddenly Acharyaji shouted: "I advised to go to Gandhi's prayer meetings in the evenings so that you keep away from drinks and not for having more of it. What did Gandhi say that created a storm which could only be subsided by whiskey?

Naresh muttered: "What Gandhiji said is his long, winding discourse after prayers purported that he wanted an innocent harijan girl of great purity to be President of India."

Acharyaji fumed: "This is usual Gandhian flim-flam which he has used for thirty years now to ensure that his. title Mahatma becomes bigger and bigger. Why this created a storm in you?

Naresh submitted: "Pitaji, I began to think that if Gandhiji sincerely wanted a Harijan to be President or Prime Minister of India why should he not have preferred Ambedkar to Nehru? On all counts Ambedkar would have been a better choice. Gandhiji often avers that one should think of the poorest of poor whenever taking a decision. If he had really thought of the poor he would have preferred Ambedkar to Nehru. Nehru is a dandy born with silver spoon in his mouth. As against that Ambedkar has risen to equal heights from poverty by the dint of hard work."

Shiv Shanker responded: "Achryaji you have been giving the impression that Naresh is an utter bohemian. This is not so. He might be right or wrong but he does concern himself with vital moral and political issues as much as you do."

Acharya Ram Krishn bowed his head, closed eyes and was lost in thought for some minutes. Everyone remained silent. He straightened his back and ruminated: "I have been wondering why of all persons Gandhi chose Nehru to be Congress President in 1946 so that he was invited to become Prime Minister. Most of the Provincial Congress Committees and all the Chief Minisers belonging to the Congress Party were against him and preferred Sardar Patel. Gandhi knew that Nehru did not believe in simple living or a clean life. Gandhi was aware that Nehru's flirtation, in Allahabad, with young female volunteers, during the freedom movement, was possibly the cause of his wife's illness. He also knew that Nehru was not for decentralization nor did he have any faith in self-the reception held in his honour. He invited him for dinner and entertained him lavishly. In the course of their rambling conversation he mentioned that the Communist Party was trying to plant its moles in government departments and as an example casually mentioned the case of Nigam in Governor General's Secretariat. Within two weeks Nigam's services were terminated and Allauddin was appointed in his place.

After joining service in Governor General's Secretariat, Allauddin faced another problem. Whatever translations from Hindi and Urdu newspapers he did, whatever clippings from newspapers in English he sorted out, Under Secretary Shastri kept it on his table and did not send these onwards. In fact not a single paper or file was moving out of his room. Not only his table but shelves on his right and left were getting more and more cluttered with piles of office papers. He was not showing any inclination to dispose off these files. He had come on deputation from the pre-Independence Department of Education, Health and Lands. After Independence it was split into three Departments - Department of Education, Department of Health and Department of Agriculture, each having its own Secretary, with appropriate number of Deputy Secretaries, Under Secretaries, etc. The result was that many persons junior-to him had become Deputy Secreetary. That could be a reason for Mr. Shastri not attending to his work but not for Mr. Allauddin's labour coming to naught. Some of the Press comments he had translated were very· important. He was afraid that if the Governor General became aware of these from some other source he would be in difficulty. Mr. Shastri was trying to have his post here upgraded to that of Deputy Secretary but the Department of Finance did not agree to it. Allauddin went to that Section of the Department of Finance which had rejected the proposal. After some negotiations the Section Officer agreed to upgrade Shastri's post of Under Secreary to that of Deputy Secretary on an under the table payment of rupees four thousand .. That Section Officer asked Allauddin how many words are there in a newspaper, last time ten newspapers only were mentioned which did not justify the proposal. Allauddin told him that about a hundred thousand words are there in a newspaper in English and half that number in Urdu and Hindi newspapers. That Section Officer advised him: "In our new note mention that five hundred thousand word· in English and three hundred thousand words in Urdu and Hindi are to be examined every day, double that number on Mondays. Also ask for the post of Superintendent (Information] and five more posts of Assistants [Information], three clerks and two daftris, so that the post of a Deputy Secretary can be justified."

Shastri agreed to pay rupees two thousand and desired Allauddin to shell out the other two thousand because he too would get promotion, becoming Superintendent [Information] on double the salary. When Allauddin asked Shiv Shanker for a loan he was so elated to know about this, that he gave him a gift of rupees two thousand. He told him that this had given him an idea that would help him solve his problem. Immediately after Partition, Muslims living in the villages around Delhi had been attacked and killed by Hindu jats from neighbouring Gurgaon district to settle some old scores. The land in these villages was being disposed off at throwaway price. Shiv Shanker thought a tract of land quite near Delhi very suitable but that village had been completely laid waste and there was no trace of any owner or previous resident. Shiv Shanker thought that if things could be thus managed in government offices, it should be possible for him to own this land without paying anything for it.

CHAPTER THIRTY NINE

On hearing of Gandhiji's assassination, Lord Mountbatten had rushed to Birla House. His Private Secretary and other members of his Staff were waiting for his return. The evening dusk had deepened and stars had begun to-twinkle dimly in the January-end sky. There had been an early warming of weather after a heavy downpour three days ago. The fresh breeze coming from the Mughal Garden carried the aroma of newly sprouting buds and offshoots. Shortly before evening they had seen hundreds of thousands of ants moving out of their winter-time hibernation towards the garden in a long black ribbon. Dicey an Assistant Private Secretary was standing near the window, looking at remnant of the swarm of ants moving towards a tree trunk in the garde.n. He thought to himself that. India had perhaps the largest population of ants in the world. He visualized long dense lines of human beings moving towards the place where Mr. Gandhi's last remains would be cremated. He might have been sidelined by the Congress leadership and his passing away was unlikely to have any tangible impact on their policies, but people firmly held the belief that he lived for them and now died for them.

Another Assistant Private Secretary Lockhart entered he room. Both sat down on easy chairs near the wall. Dicey initiated thc conversation: "His Excellency must be encouraging the persons present there to discover problems so that he can suggest solutions. He has a knack of creating the impression that the problem is knotty and that he alone has the solution."

Lockhart added: "One great quality of Lord Mountbatten is that he can look at a problem calmly and objectively. He does not shy away from a solution if it is unpalatable. If he is behaving like a bull in a china shop, it is not his fault. He has been pushed into a china shop which is so much cluttered with chinaware that there is absolutely no standing room."

Dicey opined: "There is no doubt that Lord Mountbatten will have the longest face of all and his eyes also would occasionally shed a tear or two. It is likely that he will take some time to return. He is in the habit of listening to everyone before he decides what should be done."

They saw Moti Chand of the Hindustan Times coming. As a local reporter of the paper he had been a frequent visitor. "Come in Moti Chand, What news?" Dicey beckoned him. Moti Chand was medium statured with thinning grey hair. His eyes had few lashes and there were no eyebrows. His well fed distended cheeks looked clean shaven so smoothly that -it gave "the 'impression of his not having normal growth of hair on his face. He was wearing a full sleeve woolen shirt over a pant of the same shade. While the skin of his hands appeared normal, that of his face was patchy and pimply. Soon after that, Mr. Chopra of National Times walked in and both Moti Chand and Chopra sat down on office chairs facing Dicey and Lockhart. They knew the decision about Gandhiji's last journey would be taken by Lord Mountbatten and would first become known here

On coming to know that Chopra was coming straight from Birla House, they wanted to know from him about the activities there. Chopra explained: "In a room next to the one in which Gandhiji's remains are lying, Lord Mountbatten is engaged in discussions with Congress leaders. The desire of the Gujarat lobby that Gandhiji's mortal remains should be taken to his Sabharmati Ashram for cremation was rejected outright They want the last rite to be in Delhi, making it an extraordinary occasion with incomparable memorability. They want full political mileage out it."

Moti Chand joined the issue: "Gandhi has to be cremated in the most glorious and spectacular manner possible with utmost deification, so that people do not think of the cavalier manner in which the entire corpus of his teachings has been discarded by these leaders.

Mr Lockhart intervened: "When we received the news about Mr. Gandhi's assassination, we began discussing whether Gandhi's philosophy was devalued by Gandhi himself or his followers are now cremating it along with his body. This is something about which there will always be two opinions. Let us first hear from Mr Chopra about Birla House. First it was thought that Gandhi should be cremated near the river bank at a point nearest to India Gate. Then it became known that the whole river bank upto Delhi Gate side of Red Fort gets flooded every monsoon season."

Mr. Chopra explained: "Opposite south eastern end of the rampart of the city the level of the ground is quite high. Lord Mountbatten seems to have suggested that out of all the alternatives available, including one near the sacred Nighambodh Ghat, this place is best for cremation. Even the monsoon high tide of the river remains half a mile away. This ruled out the carrying of Gandhiji's arthi - the bier - on shoulders, as is the traditional custom. The question perhaps is whether the cart carrying Gandhiji's last remains should be drawn by national leaders or by bullocks. Lord Mountbatten has been patiently listening to these suggestions and indicating his disagreement with a grimace. He has not uttered a word yet As has been happening in other cases, Lord Mountbatten will take the decision, inform Congress leaders about it, come here and announce it. It is only here that the decision will be known to Press. He should be coming shortly."

Mr. Lockhart observed: "Mr. Dicey has given many reasons for Mr. Gandhi reneging his philosophy, for closing his eyes to whatever he professed earlier. First was his support to military intervention in Kashmir. When World War broke out in 1939, he had declared that in every war both sides were equally wrong and it made no difference who won. He even suggested that there should be no resistance to Hitler so that there was less bloodshed. He advised the Jews to commit collective suicide. The second was his opposition to Cripps and Cabinet Mission proposals which ensured unity and integrity of India which he vehemently declared to be his desire. 1 he third was his upholding Congress leaders in their fulsome support to the Partition of India after he had declared that Pakistan would be formed on his dead body. Mr. Jinnah had proposed peaceful transfer of population after Bihar riots. If Gandhi had accepted this all the present bloodshed could have been avoided. The fourth was his selection1Mr. Nehru as India's Prime Minister. Gandhi fully knows that Nehru does not believe at all in devolution of power to villages but wants concentration of power in his hands at the center."

Dicey interrupted Lockhart and remarked: "What is noteworthy is the special treatment the British Government accorded to Mr. Gandhi. That he was treated with extreme gentleness can be understood. He was useful in preventing violence which could be much more troublesome than his non-violence. If need be he could be an effective counterweight against socialists and communists. So far it was all right. By singling him out for an excessively privileged position, the Government unwittingly promoted in him an attitude of unbending self-righteousness which brought all negotiations to a dead end. The British Government is, therefore, equally responsible for the failure of any settlement between Hindus and Muslims." Lockhart added: "If events jumped into saddle and trampled on the flower bed, Mr. Gandhi is not free from blame. At every moment when clarity of thinking was needed most, he refused to see beyond his nose. In 1940, he wrote to Viceroy: "This man . slaughter must be stopped. You are losing. If you persist it will result in greater bloodshed. Hitler is not a bad man. If you call it off today he will follow suit." In connection with transfer of power also he took a rigid stand and wanted compromise and settlement only on his terms. There was unwillingness to understand the other's point of view. There was complete absence of a spirit of give and take so necessary for a solution. His opposition to both Cripps and Cabinet Mission poroRosals was a surpise to everyone who desired India to remain united. He wrote to Cripps that his proposals were worse than Pakistan. He wrote to Hindu Chief Miniser of Assam to oppose Cabinet Mission Plan."

Moti Chand remarked: "One man alone could not have vitiated the prePartition atmosphere. The entire Press and all the leaders did their best to paralyze the ability of the people to think clearly."

Mr. Dicey changing the subject observed: "Last week Sir Shivalingaswami came to see the Governor General. As he was not there he waited for him in his Private Secretary's room. They began discussing whether Partition could be avoided. Sir Shivalingaswami was of the view that when Gandhi came to India he erased the line between political and religious behaviour, thereby paving the way for Pakistan. He talked about Ram Rajya and sanctity of the cow side by side with demand for home rule. By using religious themes and symbolism for political ends he unintentionally set into motion a process which was to lead to the Partition of India. When Gandhi came to India after the start of First World War, he was an eccentric specimen of an England returned young Indian. Mr. Jinnah at that time was an eminent secular nationalist leader. Jinnah and scores of other Muslim public men had joined hands with Hindus to build a strong secular nationalist movement. That was the time when Dr. Moonje and Mr. Savarkar were propagating that Hindus and Muslims were two nations. Gandhi turned turtle all that. He tried to usurp all the national space and tried to undermine the position of anyone he could not lead by the nose. The more he made himself a deity and a mahatma, the more he was isolated from the Muslims. His fast against separate electorate for scheduled castes convinced Muslims that he was more a Hindu leader than a national figure and that his vision of free India did not envisage aD equal positio,n for Muslims."

There was a brief pause. Moti Chand. broke the ice: "Nehru. was . loved by Gandhi because he permitted himself to be ruled by him. Nehru and Gandhi made a combination about which future historians would speculate much. Gandhi looked to the distant past and Nehru to distant future. Yesterday, today and tomorrow did not exist for them. If in British India some were more slave than others, in free India the position is likely to remain similar.

There was a message that Lord Mountbatten had arrived and had desired that the Commander-in-Chief and the Area Commander should be sent for immediately. It seemed the Army was to be in-charge of Gandhiji's last journey. The newspaper men rung up their offices about this decision of the Governor General. They informed their office that while waiting for Commander-in-Chief and other Military Officers, the Governor General was helping his Secretaries to work out details. They were calculating how many Army units would be needed to fully line up the seven kilometer route so that there was no stampede. One journalist suggested that in order to mollify Congressmen a spinning wheel could be put on the gun carriage carrying Gandhiji's last remains. Another journalist said that Gandhiji wanted his writings to be cremated with his dead body, because what he had done would endure and" not what he had written. Certainly his genius lay in action. Disagreeing with him another journalist remarked: "This was just a paradoxical statement. He often delighted in paradoxes imbibed from Hindu metaphysics, such as: 'God is truth but He is also untruth; He is motionless yet always moving; God is atheism of the atheist'. True he was a man of action but he seldom let his action reach a culmination. The best example is the 1922 movement, the only time since Mutiny when there was Hindu-Muslim united action. He called off the civil disobedience movement just when it was gathering momentum."

Another journalist expressed the opinion: "Gandhiji said that God is both a person and an idea. Gandhi himself was both a person and an idea. Now that the person is dead, the idea can be killed best by raising Gandhiji's writings to the level of scriptures, which in India are venerated and not followed.

On enquiry by some journalists, the Military Secretary came out and informed the waiting Pressmen that a Press Communiqué was being cyclostyled and would be made available soon.

267

The journalists again got busy in chitchatting. One of them said that Lord Mountbatten gave the impression that everything was amenable and every problem could be solved in a trice. Another commented that what was remarkable was his meticulous and methodical nature. He was one of those men who measured the cloth three times and cut it once, unlike Indian leaders who did the opposite. Another journalist felt that if Lord Mountbatten could teach the Indian leaders to measure the cloth carefully before they cut it, it would stand them in good stead in free India. Another retorted: "It would be safest if they do not take the risk of cutting the cloth and use it as such, like the Indian sari. A single uncut cloth wraps the whole body. I wish they had similarly treated the Indian landmass."

While distributing the Press Communiqué to the journalists the Military Secretary asked them" "How much crowd do you expect when Mr. Gandhi's last journey takes place?"

Pat came a journalists reply: "That depends on to what high pitch the All Indian Radio and Indian Press work up the patriotic fervor."

CHAPTER FORTY

Shiv Shanker had been amassing funds to finance several schemes intended to build him as a successful politician. He had been borrowing from banks and investing in property and elsewhere. He had been soliciting grants and donations mainly from abroad for his English medium public school and other educational institutions which he organized as lucrative businesses. He got literary works ghost written in his name and managed to win prestigious honours and awards He seldom paid back the principal or interest on the loans from banks. When it became absolutely necessary to repay the loan, he borrowed from that bank a larger amount, returned the loan and kept the balance. He never bothered that several crores of rupees he had borrowed from commercial banks kept on multiplying. He knew that umpteen politicians and businessmen were doing the same. He was in no doubt that these pending debts would, sooner or later, be written off, scaled down or have a long moratorium.

With this money Shiv Shanker had been organizing toughs, hoodlums, desperadoes, racketeers, mobsters and unemployed youth in various areas as his support base, making many of them take up positions of leadership in local committee of the Congress Party. He believed that in the prevailing situation in India, the politicians and the lawless elements must inevitably coalesce, just in some earlier centuries sea merchants and pirates worked hand in hand. These gangs were told about several ways of making money for him as well as for themselves. They made sure that tender for government and other works were accepted only from a party which had paid him his dues. They made sure that only a contractor who had gratified him got the contract. They cooperated with local policemen to allow the shops to be illegally kept open after closing hour. They collected the charges for this and shared these with policemen. Everyday they found new avenues for making money. A landlord would like his tenant to be evicted. At another place a tenant would want his landlord to be chastised. An industrialist desired a rival trade Union to be set up or a strike by workers in the factory of his rival. Another factory owner wanted his labour unrest or his raw material problem to be solved. He kept the police and the administrative set up happy. He made regular payments to those who acceptd these and provided occasionally expensive gifts to others who wanted to keep a clear conscience.

He had also become close to some Ministers both in the Central Government and the States. Whenever their guest needed a car for moving about in Delhi, he provided it. When their sons or kith and kin had lavish parties in an expensive restaurant he paid the bill. When a senior Minister and a veteran Congress leader came to know that Prime Minister's Private Secretary was maintaining a file about his wrong-doings, he decided to keep a file for Pandit Nehru and sought Shiv Shanker's help. Shiv Shanker picked up a Teen Murti house security guard from his residence. Took him to that Minister's house and helped them to settle terms for information he would supply about the goings on at Pandit Nehru's residence

Study of the English language was now more in demand than under the British rule. Knowledge of English was the stepping stone for any job in government or in a business enterprise. It had also become necessary criterion for a status in life. There was therefore a craze for English medium schools. It was a situation where one would not be considered an intellectual unless one knew English nor could one make headway in any industry or business without the knowledge of English. Even those who had not learnt English language did not want their children to be left behind. This made the proliferation of English medium school inevitable. Some of these schools turned out to be lucrative businesses, which gave further stimulus to their growth. An elitist public school of this type could also be a good way of enlarging one's sphere of influence, because' admitting someone's child to such a school became an act of favour. For these reasons Shiv Shanker wanted to set up the most elitist English medium public school in Delhi, but was finding it difficult to find suitable vacant land for the purpose.

There was an eleven acre vacant plot of land attached to the temple of goddess Jagdhari. It had been in public use for so long that claim that it was the private property of the Brahmin custodian of the temple was not acceptable to the general public. Every time the hereditary priest of the temple built a boundary wall large gaps were breached in it and it's public use continued unhindered. The Municipal councilman elected from this area got track laid in it for morning walkers and swings, parallel bars etc fixed for boys who came to play there. Finding that he was gradually losing his right over this land, the priest thought it prudent to agree to Shiv Shanker's suggestion that the land be leased to him for a public school. As he asked for a nominal lease money only to establish his right over the land, Shiv Shanker agreed to make his second wife, who had a doctorate in Hindi, to be trustee of the school.

Shiv Shanker decided to make it the most expensive and the most elitist public school in northern India. As a popular elitist public school was called Doon School, he decided to name his school Royal Doon International School. The teaching blocks were Roosevelt Hall and Kennedy Hall, and the hostels, King George House for boys and Queen Victoria House for girls. All the buildings, including hostel buildings, were air conditioned so also were the buses which brought day scholars to the school.He was able to get some grants and donations and with loans from commercial banks the school was running full steam in two years. He had put a large board at the entrance of the school, which announced: "Speaking in any language other than English is strictly prohibited. Hindi is taught in this School through the medium of English." Parents of day scholars   were   advised to speak to their ward in English when they returned home.

What surprised Shiv Shanker was that all this made his school the most sought after school in the city though its fee structure was at least four times more than the next expensive school. That even girls in the school had to wear necktie and that English medium was compulsory even for learning Hindi greatly added to the importance of the school. Shiv Shanker many times discussed this with Chopra. The pe-Independence generation of educated Indians had an excellent command over English language but they were equally well up in the mother tongue. Gandhiji wrote in Gujarati with as much facility as in English Poet Tagore had mastery both over Bengali and English languages. Pandit Nehru might never have written much in Hindi but he could make a speech in Hindi for more than an hour without using a word of the English language. The pride which a journalist in Hindi or a man of letters in Hindi used to feel peviously is now missing altogether. Writers in Hindi languages are made to feel smaller and smaller as the English language is acquiring ever greater supremacy in this country. The pun that in expiring, the British Raj was perpetuating iself in its successors was coming true with a vengeance.

One could understand that there was some lowering of moral tone, when Indians were left to themselves. That this downward slide would get accelerated was beyond comprehension. The cinema, television and daily Press was creating a hunger for luxurious living, not only persuading the people to buy more than they needed but even to buy articles they did not need. Resultingly, a majority of the people had become Un-mindful of scruples. They hankered after all the good things in life by hook or by crook. What was difficult to understand was the down-grading of all intellectual endeavors, rather their atrophy. It was not merely the supremacy of brawn over brain, but the glorification of the glittery, the sporty and the risque. Before Independence English language helped to broaden the mind and to enrich the intellect. It produced a galaxy of some brilliant and scholarly men and women of great intellectual eminence, who towered not only in legal and educational fields but also in other professions. After Independence that intellectual vigour and richness of mind had abated. Journalism and other writings in Indian languages had lost both influence and excellence. English language has shown them the door. Journalism and other writings in the English language were day by day augmenting its gloss of frivolousness and trumpery. More and more news columns were occupied by sports and the antics of sportsmen, by film stars and their sleazy world of adultery, drinking brawls and endless cycle of marriages and divorces. Where the neo-rich ate, what they ate and the circuit of their carnivalesque parties stood out prominently in today's newspapers. If it was held that cinema and over-doze of songs and music on All India Radio could only produce slaves, it could be said, with equal veracity, that the newspapers' highlighting of the bizaree, vulgar and the trite was intended to create moral and intellectual morons.

This made Shiv Shanker heart-sick. He felt that a crook like him did less harm to India than these morons and philanderers which the media was creating these days. Chopra agreed with him but there was no other way he could keep his job. There was race for more circulation in newspapers and in order not to be left behind he had begun to front-page stories of rape and sex crimes. He had twice a week special features on the luxurious and boisterous life of film stars and sportsmen. He had introduced a weekly special supplement featuring the lives of film actors and actresses and the back-stage sluttishness of film making. He made these more punky and sleazy than the wildest rumours in the film world. Finding that this gave them charisma and glamour, the world of actors and actresses began to mould itself to the level of these erogenous stories. He had a separate page for cricket. Reuter's news report based on a scientific journal stated that professional footballers had gradual depletion of yellow matter in their brain. He had guessed that the same was the case with professional cricketers. He however suppressed the news because he was, as a sales promotion gimmick, floating the idea that cricketers are our gods and cricket is our religion. There was now additional coverage for yoga and naturopathy and the daily feature 'What Stars Foretell' now covered half a page instead of a column. The newspaper was going to persist with these whether he was there or not, Chopra consoled himself with this thought.

In this featherbrained world of frivolity and slush, a man like Shiv Shanker could hope to have a great future. Somehow he was gnawed by the feeling that he had reached a dead-end. Despite all the money he had amassed and the gang of hoodlums he had at his command, he felt pessimistic and despondent. He knew that he had little chance of being elected to Parliament from Delhi or Punjab, regardless of the money he spent on his election campaign. He was told that long time Director, Intelligence Bureau, was very close to the Prime Minister and had often much say in his political decisions. Shiv Shanker made every effort to cultivate him. The Director would accept his gifts but went on increasing the distance he kept from him.' He knew his Deputy S. Dayal who did not accept any gifts and put him off with a joke or a cutting remark. When he explained his problem to him he advised him to forget not only Punjab and Delhi but also United Provinces. He told Shiv Shanker that Bihar is a State, where Intelligence Bureau had not been able to corner anti-Nehru groups.

Shiv Shanker had befriended Pandit Ram Lochan who lived in the Constitution House in the early years of Independence. He was member from Bihar of Central Legislative Assembly of the British days. Shiv Shanker had given him a flat and in return he had transferred to him the ownership of a house and some land in Kusumpur in his constituency, half way between Hazipur and Patna. When Shiv Shanker discussed his problem with Pandit Ram Lochan, he advised him against contesting for lower House of Parliament from Bihar and told him that with much less money he should be able to buy enough members of the Bihar Legislative Assembly to get elected to the Upper House of Parliament. Pandit Ram Lochan himself was a sad and dejected man. Thakur Man Singh who had defeated him in the election. to the Central Legislative Assembly shortly before Independence had now become a very powerful person with more land 'and influence than he had before Independence. He was very close to.all the successive Chief Ministers of Bihar, was a heavy weight of Bihar Congress Comittee and was with Prime Minister Nehru whenever he visited Bihar. He had a regular formation of armed thakur toughs and kept a stockpile of weapons for their use. He had built up such an awesome presence in this area that none could dare to fight election against him. He got elected to the House of People unopposed in 1952 and 1957.

Shiv Shanker explained: "All these strong-arm methods will not have been helpful to Thakur Man Singh if our form of representative democracy had been free from serious defects. I will just mention one. For a static population of forty million direct election to British Parliament of five hundred members was a practical proposition. India's population has already reached six hundred million and in a decade of so it will cross one thousand million. This will make each constituency bigger than three-fourth of the countries in the world. Only men with muscle and money can contest election from such big constituencies. "

Responding to Shiv Shanker, Rarn Lochan observed: "It is not merely the enormous size of the constituencies which precludes free elections. There is much else which negates democracy. When B.N.Rao Constitutional Adviser placed the draft constution before the Constituent Assembly speaker after speaker denounced it as a fraud on the Indian people. Dr. Rajendra Prasad its Presidednt was as vehement in its denunciation as others. Finding that it was a mere rehash of Government of India Act 1935, some members described it as a grafted monstrosity. A committee was appointed which did not function. When Nehru saw that the draft provided a highly centralized government with States at the mercy of he Centre, he used his influence to have the same passed by the Assembly with the addition of some high sounding flamboyant clauses."

Shiv Shanker interrupted Ram Lochan and said: "Let us first tackle the problem we are facing. Your Thakur has to be destroyed not only politically but also socially so that both of us can have any political future in Bihar. Pandit Ram Lochan ji, if you act like sage Chanakaya, we can make mincemeat of your Thakur in no time. First you have to find 'a suitable astrologer and glue him to your Thakur. He will put into his head that he was a supreme mighty chakravarty emperor in all his previous births and is destined to be so in this also."

Noticing that Ram Lochan was sceptical about what he had proposed, Shiv Shanker explained: "Seth Ram Krishan Dalmia held that Mahatma Gandhi's selection of Pandit Nehru as India first Prime Minister was a misfortune for the country and his paper Times of India sought every pretext to virulently attack him. In view of Dalmia's. blind faith in astrology and the supernatural, it was quite easy to plant an astrologer in his household." Shiv

Shanker explainbed to him in detail how that astrologer helped in silencing Seth Dalmia and added: "It took two years for Seth Dalmia to be destroyed. We cannot wait so long. We have to reduce your Thakur to dust in less than a year."

Pandit Ram Lochan now felt quite enthused about the proposal. Slowly he muttered: "I know a few astrologers and will probe them toe find out who will suit us best. I will also think out which earlier incarnation will elate Thakur Man Singh so much that he will make an immeclate dash at least for the post of Chief Miniser of Bihar. It is unlikely that the present Chief Minister will ever forgive him for this."

Shiv Shanker added: "You will also have to think of a king who had several wives so that the astrologer has to put it in mind to marry at least once again. This will create problem for him with his family. After this episode is over I will send a journalist from Delhi who will stay in Kusumpur, collect details of his atrocities and irregularities, embellish them and report these in a series of articles in his paper. We will subsidize Patna and Gazipur papers to carry out a campaign against him. Once his reputation is mauled it will be easy to destroy his political career, particularly with the help of the present Chief Minister. After he marries again his half a dozen children can be pitted against him and we will have a drama worth watching."

Ram Lochan was lost in thought and was silent for sometime. Speaking thoughtfully, he said: "If Man Singh is not there another person will be selected as a Congress candidate, may be his eldest son. A congress candidate has many advantages. I will mention only three. Firstly a mental makeup ha:; been nurtured for over a decade that makes a government employee believe it as his patriotic duty to make Nehru and . Congress win in the election. Secondly votes of Muslims have been ensued. Riots between Hindus and Muslims are engineered either by giving a long rope to Hindu fanatics or through Inelligence agents planted among them. Thus an impression is created that Nehru and the Congress Party are savior of Muslims. Thirdly there is monopoly of the votes of the poor and the depressed classes. Either they vote for Congress or are not allowed to vote at all. Despite all talk of land reform, the social relations in the villages have remained unchanged. The position of the landlord has rather got strengthened. It is wrong to think that only dictators want to remain in power all their life. A democratic ruler can be equally determined to do so."

Before Shiv Shanker could comment on this, Ram Lochan continued:

"Intelligence Bureau is as much involved in these elections as the Congress Party. Central intelligence men are there in all the districts. In Hazipur there are two men who work inconspicuously in the room behind a ration shop. in Patna, there are few more, having a room behind a hosiery factory in the main bazaar. These have been taken on rent under a fictitious name."

Cutting short Ram Lochan, Shiv Shanker affirmed: "Let us deal with Thakur Man Singh first. Other moves can be planned later. Elections in India are no doubt cloak and dagger affair. I think we will have to find out issues on which agitation can be worked up, resulting in arrests, lathi charge, firing and more. That will create ill will against the Congress and may be against Nehru."

Ram Lochan muffled his laughter and remarked: "Lathi charge, arrests, firing, etc., have become so frequent and routine that these have ceased to make news and over ninety per cent of these go unreported in the Press. These do not in any way influence the electoral chances of the Congress Party. Before" Independence, British Officers were afraid' of opening fire especially after Jalianlwala Bagh firing, afraid not only of India public reaction, but also of their own Parliament arid 'the Press in Britain. An officer could never be sure whether the government will standby him or drop him like a hot potato when he found it necessary to take strong action. They will be afraid of an adverse remark in their personal file such as: 'Cannot be depended upon to keep a cool head in a hot spot'. Now the administration and the police have a free hand."

There was silence for sometime. Shiv Shanker smiled and remarked: "An attitude of unconcern towards meaningful social and moral issues is being deliberately cultivated among the people. It is being made overwhelming by feeding the people with drivel and flim flam through the media. This tends to make the very idea of scrutiny, hope and change irrelevant. If we plan properly we can exploit to our advantage this attitude of amorality and flippancy among a large section of the people. Only after Thakur Man Singh hs been dealt with, the position will become clear enough to think of the next move."

Disagreeing with him, Ram Lochan opined; "I think after the astrologer starts his work, you should befriend the Thakur. Feed him on friendship more luscious than the most delicious sweetmeat. Convince him that you are his best friend and a real bosom friend. Make the fire of friendship blaze so much. that you can roast him."

CHAPTER FORTY ONE

Panditji had disurbed sleep many times, but that night it was nightmarish broken by one ugly dream after another. He dreamt that he was a centipede as big as he himself. For years the centipede had not moved at all, as it was unable to make out which of its hundred feet should move forward first. The second dream was that he was walking on water, sometimes leisurely, at others at a brisk pace. Suddenly he disappeared in water, only his Gandhi cap remained wafting on water. The Gandhi cap became bigger and bigger till it acquired the size and shape of a battleship. He just had a few winks of sleep when there was another dream. He was addressing a large gathering of admirers. All the entrances to the hall were blocked by persons anxious to hear him but unable to find space inside. As he started speaking, th$_y$_ audience began to dwindle. In no time the hall was empty, except for an old man, wr;llkled and dwarfish like Gandhiji. He also removed from his ear the plug of hearing aid but kept sitting there. Panditji had therefore to continue with his speech.

Next dream was that he was hiding behind a large montage in the exhibition hall of Anand Bhawan, Allahabad, which contained panels desdping his life from birth till he became Primr Minister ofIndia . A boy fifteen years old, looking just as he did at fifteen, walks in holding a small mirror in his left hand. There was a full size picture of his when he was fifteen. The boy went straight to that panel. He looked at himself again and again in the mirror to compare the picture of fifteen years old Jawaharlal with his own reflection in the mirror he held. Suddenly he dashed the mirror down and further splintered the broken pieces on the floor by striking these with his footwear.

It was half past one. Dreading lack of sleep for the rest of night, Panditji swallowed a sleeping pill with a sip of water. Shortly he was fast asleep. He was shaken out of sleep by the rocking of his shoulder. He opened his eyes and saw Gandhiji by his side. Blessing him by placing his hand on his head,

Gandhiji said: "I made you my heir in the hvpe that you would serve the poorest of the poor in this land. You have been ruling over India for one and half decade. Why donot you have a guise and go about incognito to find out how much the common man has gained from this." Gandhiji had wings and after saying this he flew away.

He sat up in the bed, thinking of the disguise he should assume and the places he should visit. In his distressed mood he recalled the advice of Shardha a young woman yogi who had spent a few nights with him in 1948. She had advised him on two issues.

She informed him that Zamorin ruler of Cochin in South India used to go to a temple in the center of his capital on completing twelfth year of his rule. He announced the new ruler there, cut his throat and ended his life. She had said that he was not a king but head of a democracy. He had just to relinquish office after holding it for twelve years otherwise there would be ignominy for him and calamity for his family. The second point she told him was about the golden Buddha of Saigon. When a clay statue of Buddha was being removed from a temple.to another, it started raining. The clay was washed off and they discovered that it was a golden statue of Buddha. In order to prevent its' plunder by marauders from Burma and South China, this statue of Buddha had been given a plastering of clay. Shradha had told him that there has been a thick deposit of dust and clay on him. He should remove it and let the gold shine again. He had not acted on any of her suggestion. All at once he became alive to an event in November 1949.

A convent in Kamataka had sent a decent looking person to Delhi with a bundle of letters to be delivered to him personally. He said a young woman from north India arrived in the convent a few monhs ago and gave birth to a baby boy. She refused to divulge her name or to give any particulars about herself. She left the convent as soon as she could move out but left the child behind. She forgot to take with her a small cloth bundle in which, among other things, were found several letters in Hindi. Mother Superior, who was a foreigner, got the letters examined and came to know that these were from the Prime Minister. The person who brought the letters surrendered them but he declined to give his name or the name of the Mother Superior or address of the Convent.

Panditji could comprehend the rationale of his dreams last night. He could understand why he dreamt about the centipede. A white embroidered skull cap lying in his wardrobe came to his notice yesterday. It was left by one of Muslim divines who had come to see him in 1950 and 1951 to demand the removal of Hindu idols from the Babri Mosque in Ayodhia. In December 1949 these idols had been surreptitiously placed in that mosque with the help of D.P. Armed Constabulary. He had then written to U. P. Chief Minister to have these idols removed immediately, otherwise the country would be heading to some kind of disaster. When nothing was done, delegations of Muslim divines came to see him again to demand the removal of idols from the mosque. The embroidered white skull cap left behind by one of them reminded him of his long inaction in the matter, the gravity of which had not lessened in all these years.

This was the first time Gandhiji came to him in his dream. He began to think seriously how he should disguise himself to move about incognito in the country. The skull cap with him, bifocal glasses with thick frame, a short beard like Maulana Azad and a long coat and pajamas like him should make a good guise. In a few days Panditji was ready to adopt the guise of an upper class Muslim. He hopefully looked forward to his encounter with people who were his first lov):. His short pointed beard was thicker than that of Maulana Azad and covered the cheeks and chin fully. The rest of the face was properly covered by thick crimson frame of eyeglasses. These were bifocal and needed to be put on all the time. The embroidered white skull cap completed the camouflage. He decided to call himself lohar Khan.

He decided to move out of Luttyen's Delhi and first visit one of the new colonies which had sprung up all around. He looked at the sky. The clouds tom into small shreds were scurrying towards the northern horizon. The sun peeped often out of these silvery fragments. This filled lohar Khan with hope and enthusiasm. He reached lawahar Bazar on the right side of which stood out busy Nehru Market. He was bewildered by what he soon noticed. The way Hindus looked at him as a Muslim was not the same as they beheld another Hindu. It was neither the presence nor the lack of fellow-feeling, but something different, reflecting otherness, if not aloofness. He failed to figure out all this.

There was a policeman standing near the crossing. He was a corpulent baldish tall man. He had a broad ridge of a nose. His balck eyes were so big that these appeared nearer to ears than is normally the case. lohar Khan asked him whether there was any house agent nearby, who could help him in renting accommodation. The policeman glanced at him from head to foot and asked him wherefrom he had come.

Johar Khan replied: "I come from Pilibhit where I have an estate. One of my sons is sick and requires long treatment in Delhi."

The policeman advised him: "I donot know about Pilibhit but here in Delhi, Hindus and Muslims live in different areas. You should go to a Muslim colony to look for a house." After a minute's pause he said: "I may be able to help you with a house in this area but first you will have to spare fifteen minues to come with me. Let us first help a beggar woman."

Finding that lohar Khan had reacted favourably to what he had proposed, the policeman pointed finger towards a beggar woman siting by road-side near a bus stand about forty yards away. He explained: "The woman is nearing her full term.Unless something is done for her immediately she will deliver on the roadside and she and the newborn might not survive. Some youngmen in the area found out from a neighbouring nursing home that delivery there would cost her, as a special case, rupees three thousands. They collected from neighbouring houses a little over four thousand rupees. They decided to celebrate their philanthroic act by spending the extra amount on a get together. Once inside the pub they drank away the whole amount. The poor woman has been left in the lurch as before. I have thought out a plan for her. I will get her arrested for pickpocketing and she will have free delivery in jail. She begs near a bus stop. She and both of us will get into a bus. After the bus has moved a few hundred yards you cry that this woman has picked your pocket. I will recover from her your purse. Take out much of the money from that purse and give it to me. We will go to nearby police sation. I have already talked the matter with the policemen there. It will take a few minutes to file the First Information Report - FIR as it is called. There your address will be recorded as "House No 14, New Station Road, Aligarh", which does no exist. After delivery in jail when the woman is brought to the court for prosecution, she will be released on the first hearing, because the plaintiff will not be traceable."

They walked back briskly from the police station to that crossing. On the way Johar Khan asked the policeman: "Why the passers by do not miss having a glance at me? Is this area generally not visited by Muslims?"
The policeman smiled and replied: "You have all the appearances of a well bred person, of a gentleman, an exception to what Hindus associate with Muslims in general. You donot appear to be one of the riff-raff, an uncouth, which a majority of the Hindus believe a Muslim looks like."
The policeman again looked at Johar Khan from head to foot and said: "I

told you no Hindu in this area will let out his house to a Muslim. However, there is a landlord here, who may be able to help you. I will take you to him."

The policeman was unusually good natured. It was a pleasant surprise for Johar Khan to find anyone particularly a policeman so humane. He had a full look at him. He not only had a large heart but also a robust physique. The small balding patch on his head was surrounded by a thick crop of black hair. His large eyes peered through equally thick projection of black eyebrows. There was an impression of alertness and readiness in his manners. Johar Khan noticed that when he dropped his hands, they almost touched his knees. He appeared long past Afs youth. Johar Khan asked: "How many children do you have? Do they go to school or college?

In a pensive voice he replied: "I have two sons both go to a government high school. Half the teachers' posts in that school are lying unfilled, because only those who can give hefty bribe can get the job. The teachers come to school at their sweet will and teach half-heartedly Most of them give free tuition to children of officials and thus have all the freedom. There is a carom board in teachers' common room but not black boards in all the class rooms. Only about five per cent of the students appearing from this school for high school examination are able to qualify. My sons are still hanging in the tenth class. Most of the policemen send their childen to a public school where the monthly fee is as much as their monthly salary. I cannot employ the usual methods of a policeman for making extra money." Johar Khan commented: "You seem to have been quite long in the police department"

The policeman replied without a tinge of regret: "I joined as a policeman seventeen years ago and will retire as a policeman. Firstly, I do not extract bribes and therefore cannot pass on any money to the higher ups. Secondly I cannot rough up people and make a brute of myself. There is a saving grace in my position. Even if you are one step above the post of a policeman they will not tolerate you if you are honest and will find some way of getting rid of you."

They had by this time left behind the crossing and reached the beginning of a street with a large road sign. "Shiv Street". The very first building in that street was a palatial mansion. The name plate outside the gate read: "Shiv Shanker Ex. M.P. President All India Farmers Welfare Association". The policeman took him in and asked the doorman to inform Shiv Shanker sahib that there were visitors. The policeman asked lohar Khan to have his seat in the gallery and remained standing waiting for Mr. Shiv Shanker. When Shiv Shanker arrived, he saluted him and said: "Sir, you wanted me to bring a respectable Muslim in need of some accommodastion. That is why I have brought this Khan Sahib here." Shiv Shanker patted the policeman before he left. He asked the doorman to have the visitor seated in his office.

Johar Khan had to wait for Shiv Shanker for about five minutes. He stepped in with long steps, fully dressed as a leader. His Gandhi cap and Nehru jacket were perperly ironed and what was not usual properly starched. That made him look spick and span. Shiv Shanker enquired from him his name and other particulars. He replied: "My name is lohar Khan. I am a Muslim Rajput. I have a jagir in Pilibit. I have to live in Delhi for the medcal treatment of my son. I want to rent a place for at least six months.
Shiv Shanker glanced at him thoughtfully. He was not able to hide the fact that he was of two minds about him. lohar Khan could not decide how to react to it.

CHAPTER FORTY TWO

When lohar Khan saw Shiv Shanker, he immediately recognized him. He was a member of First Parliament and was then President of Refugees Welfare Associaion. Elected in 1951 from a constituency in Delhi, he was youngest member of the Parliament, twentysix years of age. None of the Congressmen could explain how he got Congress Party's ticket, but he defeated a popular stalwart who had been in public life of Delhi for decades. There were charges of puchase of votes, of bogus voting and forcibly preventing many from voting. An election petition was filed against him. Much after he completed his five year term, his election was declared void. He was popular among some Ministers, but members of Parliament generally disliked him. He was regarded as an example of crookedness restricted by no principle or rule. He used his proximity to some Ministers to spread the impression that he could have any work done. Many people approached him for favours and he took money from all. The Minisers in the Central and Punjab Governments were unhappy with him not because he took money on their behalf but because he did not give them proper share. In the 1956 Parliamentary elections, the Punjab Chief Minister gladly agreed to give him a Congress Party ticket from the Punjab. He, however, made sure that he was defeated. There was even a suspicion that he had a hand in the murder of former Punjab Chief Minister Pratap Singh Kairon.

Shiv Shanker had no more his boyish looks. He still looked less than his age of about forty years but had an overfed body which he planted majestically in that ornate chair with a high back and velvety red uphostry. Soon after Shiv Shanker entered the room his private secretary also came in.

Shiv Shanker asked his private secretary: "You were in Pilibhit. This Khan Sahib is a jagirdar from there. Do you know him?" The private secretary replied: "I was a student at the medical college and seldom went to the city."

Shiv Shanker explained to Johar Khan: "My private secretary Lal Chand is from Allahabad and belongs to the Chamar low caste. The family is too poor to do any tanning or shoe-making business normally associated with Chamars. His father and three uncles earned a living by plying hand diven rickshaw. As Lal Chand was well up in studies, the family pooled together reasources to educate him. In the pre-medical test for admis~sion to medical colleges conducted by the government he got tenth position out of several thousand candidates and was first among those from Allahabd. He did not need the benefit of reservation for schedules castes but was, against rules, put in that quota to keep down the number of schedules castes selected for admission to medical colleges. Despite having first position among Allahabad candidates, he was not allotted to medical college, Allahabad, where he lived, but was sent to medical college Pilibhit. There were officially four scheduled caste students in his class, three Brahmins who had a bogus certificate obtained on payment from the office of the District Magistrate. Lal Chand was made to fail four times in the first year and after he was kept down two times in the second year, he left the medical college. He started plying Rickshaw in Delhi as his father did in Allahabad. In a chance meeting he told me his story and I decided to have him as my private secretary.

"How can a Brahmin get a certificate that he belongs to a scheduled lower caste" Johar Khan voiced his surprise.

"Thanks to this government it is very simple" Shiv Shanker replied "Before you turn for Shiv Street, there is on the right side on the main road a three storey building. Outside second floor hangs a sign board 'Diamond Careers Institute'. The proprietor of the Institute sells forged birth certificates, school leaving ceriticates, univeristy degrees of all types, ration cards, driving licences, import or export permits, passports, visas and much else, including scheduled caste certificates. Once he came to me for a favour. I asked him how he manages to give to a member of the upper caste a certificate that he belongs to a scheduled caste enabling him to get wrongly benefit of reservation. He said that these forged certicates are being issued everywhere through various devices, but he does it in a matter of fact way. The forms for these certificates have serial numbers and are bound into books of hundred forms each. He buys one such book from the government office concerned for rupees one hundred thousands. In many cases these are duplicates obtained through an underhand arrangement with press which prints these forms."

Johar Khan now asked Lal Chand: "You should have written to Prime Minister or seen lagjit Ram and other low caste leaders"

Before Lal Chand could say anything, Shiv Shanker elucidated: "All the hundreds of letter received in the Prime Minister's office are summarily passed on to the Minstries or Departments concerned where these remain struck in red tape. As regards Jagjit Ram, I personally took to him five low caste students, who had met with most outrageous treatment at the hands of high caste authorities of their college. They were six low caste students in that class. These were addressed not by their name as were the other students but were called cobbler, tanner, barber, weaver, sweeper, according to his low caste. Once they insulted these students so hurtfully that there was a fight between six low caste students in the college and several dozen upper caste students. The low caste students got severely thrashed. One of them died. The other five were expelled from college. The policeman who brought you here guided these five studerfs to this house. They all had bandages on more than one part of their body. One of them had both arms plastered and in slings. I took these five low caste studens to Jagjit Ram. Two of them belonged to his own low caste. Jagjit Ram promised much but nothing happened. The upper castes assert that everything should be purely on merit but at the same time ensure that the low castes are unable to acquire any merit or show any sense of dignity."

Shiv Shanker directed Lal Chand to spell out to lohar Khan what was required of him. Lal Chand explained: "You will have free furnished house in a Hindu locality. As you know a Muslim is not let out a house in an area inhabited by Hindus, and the living of a Muslim in his neighbourhood is distasteful to an ordinary Hindu. When Shiv Shankerji buys a house in a Hindu locality and makes a Muslim live there, the value of property in the neighbourhood goes down. After Shiv Shankerji has bought property there at its depreciated value, he makes that Muslim gentleman shift to anoher Hindu residential area where he has purchased a house. After that Muslim leaves the place, the value of the property appreciates and he makes some profit. All the purchses and sales are duly registered and all transactions are by crossed cheques. The various taxes are paid in full. The previous Muslim gentleman who helped in this has gone back to his native place. The three youngsters who threatened him have been arrested and there will be no problem again."

Johar Khan made a request for a glass of water. Lal Chand called the servant and asked him to bring a tumbler of water. The servant came near Lal Chand and whispered:

"The tumbler kept for Muslims has got broken. Can I use the other one. Shiv Shanker removed the lid of glass filled with water lying on the able and offered it to lohar Khan. Addressing lohar Khan, Shiv Shanker said: " I have lived and eaten with Muslims, do I become less of a Hindu? Pandit Madan Mohan Malaviya and Lala Lajpat Rai complained to Gandhiji that Pandit Moti Lal Nehru has his meals with Muslims. Are Motilal and lawaharlal less of Hindu, because of that? They say I play fraud on Hindus in the way I earn a million or two every year. Do I tell a Hindu to feel outraged if a Muslim happens to have a house nearby?"

Johar Khan had a few long sips and placed the glass tumbler on the shelf near him. He had a look around the room. The walls were bare, except for the head of a twelve-horned antelope mounted on a brass sheet. The table was of right size for the room which had eight chairs for visitors. On the right side of he table was an expensive penstand with a golden pen on each side and a four inch square time piece in the center. On the left side of the table was a telephone with telephone book under it and a desk diary nem$t, the crimson cover of which showed signs of frequent use.

Johar Khan had a full look at Shiv Shanker. He was a different person from the days he came to Parliament in 1952, and yet he was the same. He no more had the agility and fervency of those days. His body had become more muscular but not fat. His face had the same, if not more, over-confidence and his eyes were as assertive as before. Unlike that time, he had one or two millimeter of stubble on his upper lip like a worn out took brush. His face was filled. His hair line had receded a little giving a commanding presence to his personality. lohar Khan remembered that there was a case against him of having grabbed land worth a few hundred crores illegally. The file was put up to him many times but he was not sure whether much could be done about it. He asked Shiv Shanker "Are you a refugee from Pakistan."

Shiv Shanker replied: "No, I am not a refugee. I was born in a district now in Pakistan.All my kith and kin, my parents, brothers, sisters, uncles, aunts, cousins and other relatives were in Pakistan at the time of Partition. Most likely all of them got killed, because I was unable to trace anyone of them. The saving grace was that I came to Delhi some years before Partition."

Johar Khan consoled him: "Yes, that saved your life. At least one member of the family has survived."

Shiv Shanker responded: "It was a blessing in disguise for a different reason.

If I had been unable to prove that I was in Delhi before Partition, the government would have hanged me. They were after my blood when I denied to some Ministers free plots in this land."

Shiv Shanker lowered his head and became pensive. There was complete stillness in the room, even the fly which was buzzing occasionally had disappeared. In this ambience of quietude, lohar Khan unrolled in his mind all that had come to his knowledge about Shiv Shanker during the last decade and a half.

He was than living at one end of York Road. Despite the outcries of policemen and guards on duty, someone had pushed inside his horse cart from the gate on the Man Singh Road side. Saying that Indiraji wanted to have some pickles, he unloaded five large twenty kilo glazed jars of pickles. On seeing much commotion, he had come out. Though he momentarily felt amused, it was something to be angry about. Seeing the Prime Minister knitting his brows, the boy who had unloaded the pickle jars, jumped into the horse cart and made the driver rush out as speedily as he had barged in. Later, on Indira's birth day, someone came with half a dozen silk saris wanting her to select one as a gift. As she hesitated to accept the gift or was otherwise undecided, he disappeared quietly leaving all the six saris there. From the description given by Indira he seemed to be the same boy who had brought jars of pickles. When lohar Khan saw him in Parliament he had no doubt that he was the same person.

During five years in Parliament he did not even. once rise to speak or to ask a question. However, he was one of the talked about members and among a section very popular. He claimed to be the right hand man of the President of the Punjab Congress Committee and was with him most of the time he was in Delhi. Punjab Congress chief later turned against him. When he was given a Congress Party ticket from the Punjab in 1956 parliamentary elections, both arch enemies in Punjab Congress, the Punjab Chief Minister and the President, State Congress Party combined to make sure that he was not declared elected even if he managed to poll more votes than others with the power of his money.

On a few occasions Shiv Shanker came to Tin Murti house with someone but never alone. He always avoided meeting him. After he ceased to be a member of Parliament, something or the other kept cropping up about him from time to time.The latest was his grabbing government land worth a few hundred crores. lohar Khan was now siting on this very land. Ruminating over this, he asked Shiv Shankr: "I donot follow you, Why should the government be after your blood? You appear to be a very respectable person."

Shiv Shanker had by now got over his introspective mood. He replied: "Khan Sahib I am contemplating to give you a very big role and not just provide you with a free house. This will catapult you from the small position of a jagirdar to an all India figure with more importance and money. Let me first answer your question why government was after my blood. What I am going to tell is known to everybody. It is better that you hear it from horse's mouth. At the time of Partition this village of Muslim jats was completely ravaged by Hindujats from Gugaon to settle some old scores. No one was left here. I found out from the land record the name of the Muslim jagirdar to whom almost half of this village land belonged. I got a legal document prepared of his selling this land to me one year before Partition. It was duly entered in patwari's records and registered with the revenue department, showing a date week after that of the sale deed. On the basis of this I claimed the possession of land but the government contested this claim on the plea that I was a refugee. The court decreed in my favour when I produced register of the New Delhi Municipal Committee accepting rent from me for a room in the Gol Market years before Partition. I also produced the register of Lady Harding Sarai of having lived there from time to time before that. As I refused to give free plots of land to Ministers and senior officials, the matter was again taken to the court, where again I won. For years efforts were made to trace the original owner. No one knew whether he was killed here or on way to Pakistan and ifhe was alive, where in Pakisan he was."

Shiv Shanker's voice had become husky. He asked for a glass of water. He had a few large mouthful of water and placed the tumbler on the table near his pen stand. In a tone of self-justification, he continued: "There is a market nearby. Out of twelve shops there at least ten have a daily turn over exceeding fifty thousand rupees. None of them pays any income tax. Over ninety per cent of the merchandise is sold in India without paying sales tax, excise duty and other government and municipal dues. Almost all commercial, industrial and government dealings have become devices for generating black money. None calls them a cheat as some call me at my back. There is a parable many times repeated at Hindu religious discourses. I believe Gandhiji also used to narrate a similar parable. There was a beautiful wq~an making a luxurious living by the oldest profession in the world. In the morning anctbed time she would recite for half an hour the sacred word 'Rama'. She had a parrot whi6h uttered the word 'Rama' all the time it was awake. When ttJ! prostitute died the devil came to take her to hell as she had lived a life of sin. Soon, god Vishnu was there to take her to heaven. She had recited the word "Rama" in the morning and at bed time all her life, which absolved her of sins and made her achieve salvation."

Shiv Shanker stared at the blank face of lohar Khan and continued: "If this is somewhat trite there are other methods of achieving salvation and atllne fOL sinB, which are less simple. There are religious rites and variety of offerings to Brahmins. Then there are pilgrimages and baths in sacred tanks and rivers. About one of these, it is believed that a crow having a dip in it, will come out as white as a swan. No wonder our Ministers, government officials and businessmen feel no compunction when they do wrong or commit a sin. Khan Sahib you do not know how easy it is for a Hindu to have a spotless conscience whatever sin he may commit. For him praying at a temple is more beneficial than wasting time in being good."

Johar Khan did not want to comment on Hindus or Hindu religion. He coolly remarked: "Muslim shopkeepers dodge income tax and all other taxes in the same manner as do the Hindus. This is human nature which, I believe, even communism has not been able to curb."

There was silence again. For lohar Khan it was somewhat eerie, because Shiv Shanker was thinking of something with eyes closed fast. He was undecided whether to , stay on or take leave. Lal Chand had gone out. As he entered the room and as Shiv Shanker caught the sound of the feet he opened his eyes. After a glance at lohar Khan, he asked his private secretary to ring Sharma to find out the position of the house they were to purchase. He went to his room, came back shortly and said that registration of the house had been fixed for Thursday next week. Addressing Johar Khan, Shiv Shanker explained: "We have finalized the purchase of a house in a Hindu locality. All formalities are complete and we will take possession of the house soon after registration of the deed in Registrar's office. Furnishing the house will take a week or so. You can plan to bring your family here in about three weeks. In the meanwhile, I will try to arrange for your temporary stay. Professor Saraswat lives in this very street a few houses away. He is among the few Hindus I know who donot have usual prejudices against Muslims. He has two rooms vacant on the back side of his flat. He asked Lal Chand to find out whether Professor Saraswat was in. Looking at the time piece on the table, he said that he should be back from college.

Lal Chand replied that he saw him returning home just a while ago.

Addressing Johar Khan, Shiv Shanker informed him: "We will be going to see Professor Saraswat. He is very liberal, absolutely secular and non-communal in attitude His wife also is a very broad-minded lady. This is the only house in this area which has Muslim visitors from time to time and where they do not have separate crockery and utensils for a Muslim. A young lady used to live in the two rooms on the back side of their flat. It is vacant now. I will persuade him to let it out to you for a month.

When Shiv Shanker reached the residence of Professor Saraswat, they were welcomed most warmly. Putting on the electric kettle Professor Saraswar said: "I returned from college a short while ago and have not had tea yet. I hope you will kindly have a cup wih me. Turning to Shiv Shanker, he said: "You know I donot have separate cups and saucers for Muslims and hope you will not mind having tea in these cups. I can serve you tea in a glass tumbler which has not been used before. I bought this set last week."

Shiv Shanker laughed and remarked: "When I came to Delhi before Parition, I used to live and have my meals with Muslims from a restaurant run by a Kashmiri Muslim." Addressing Johar Khan he said: "Unfortunately the wife of Professor Saraswat had to leave because 0 f d i sda 1 n of neighbours. Because they did not have separate plates, cups and tumblers for Muslim visitors and used one common set for all, none of her friends in the neighbourhood had tea or even a glass of water in this house. He is Saraswat and wife is from a Bharadwaj family. Both are Brahmins of high gotra, while their neighbours are all Rajputs, Aroras, Khatris and other middle castes. The neighbouring ladies virtually ostracized her. This created tension and some psychiatric problem in her. She has gone to her parental home for sometime. Distance between Hindus and Muslims is increasing and not decreasing after Independence."

Professor Saraswat butted in: "Shiv Shanker sahib, I have now decided to maintain separate utensils for Muslim guests. Firstly, I want that when my wife comes back she has normal atmosphere around and neighbours feel less estranged. Secondly, and more importantly, I am not likely to have visits by my Muslim friends for sometimes. "

"Why? What has happened?" Shiv Shanker could not contain his surprise.

Professor Saraswat replied: "Absolutely nothing on my part. The whole thing is incredible. Palestinian leader Yasir Arrafat was in Delhi and we laughed at the way he hugged and kissed everyone he met. We began discussing Israel-Palestine relations Everyone held that the killing of innocent Palestinians by Israel army was a heinous crime. I expressed the opinion that Palestinian gunmen and rocket launchers also should, as far as possible, avoid killing innocent Israeli children. Quite innocently I added that there should be peace between them. To make that possible the Jews should restrict themselves to the area given to them under United Nations mandate and that Palestinians should give up threatening to throw them into the sea. I told them that eversince Spanish Inquisition, when both Muslims and Jews were driven out of Spain relations between the two communities have been cordial. The Sultan of Turkey had sent ships to Spain to rescue Jews from there and gave them asylum. After that, it did not take long for the rumour to spead that I am anti-Muslim and for my Muslim friends to shirk my company."

There was a brief silence. Professor Saraswat added: "My wife is coming back with a new set of kitchenware and crockery. The old ones we will keep for Muslim friends when they start visiting us again. Both of us hope for the day when all this will not be necessary and there will be real feeling of brotherhood between the two communities. "

Shiv Shanker felt very sad about it and opined: "Professor Sahib, it will take very long."
The silence that followed was sad, somber and full of unshed ears. One could feel how heart broken Professor Saraswat was for surrendering to prevailing prejudices and for diluting moral and social values with which he had sought to fortify himself all these years.

The lines of an over clever guy, if not crook, which had formed on the face of Shiv Shanker subsided for sometime. He was full of compassion and fellow feelings. Cups of tea and a plate of biscuits had been placed on the center table which no one touched.

In his long life Johar Khan had had several occasions of profound sadness sadness that drowned him, as if he had fallen in a deep sea of sorrow and sadness that was so bitter that every drop of his blood became acerbic with grief. The sadness which Johar Khan now felt was of a different type. Even the feeling of lying on a bed of nails did not fully convey the pain of it.

Professor Saraswat broke the silence: "Shiv Shankerji do you know how last weeks riots in Hapur started. The Press has given a garbled version of it. A Muslim student of Government College there took, a fellow Hindu girl student and daughter of a colleague of his father, on the back seat of his scooter to her home on way to his house. Some Hindu stdents of that College followed them on their scooters and after he had dropped the grrl at her home, took hold of him. They all started giving him blows and kicks shouting all the time, how he dared to give lift to a Hindu girl. They thrashed him till he fell down. He was taken to a hospital and died after a week, which provided fuel to these riots. Shiv Shankerji the situation is being pushed to a direction where it will be worse than 1946 and 1947."

Shiv Shanker felt a deep heartache, the like of which he had seldom felt before. Johar Khan also showed signs of anguish. He had lowered his head and beads of cold sweat glistened below his skull cap.

Shiv Shanker said, as if asking himself: "Whom would they blame now for the communal tension in India? The Britishers left long long ago."

Professor Saraswat muttered: "They will now put all the blame on Muslims and invent many reasons for this." Johar Khan was dumbfounded. There was now a silence which had the sting of a thousand hornets.

After sometimes Shiv Shanker explained: "I might be a rotter, a swindler, but I have a conscience which pricks. Often my heart bleeds for the country. Gandhiji had many failings, Pandit Nehru has more. I have been feeling unless something is done forthwith, Indian people are going to rue in the next century. I have been seriously thinking of a plan. Now Johar Khan can playa very important role in it. If he play it well, it will be a turning point in Indian history" Facing Professor Saraswat, he continued: "I have come here to request you give your two vacant room to Johar Khan for a month In. the meanwhile I will prepare blueprit of my plan."

There was silence. Finding Professor Saraswat dumb to his suggestion, Shiv Shanker added: "I could have accommodated Johar Khan in my house but that will not be wise. When I let you know my plan you will agree that I should remain in the background. "

Professor Saraswat replied: "I told you my wife is coming back. If a Muslim is living in this house, reconciliation with neighbours will become impossible. The poison of communalism was there before Independence. The atmosphere is now very dense with it. Gandhiji evolved his own criterian for communalism. Blaming the British for division between Hindus and Muslims, he became blind to the communal feelings which the social mores nurtured in the minds of the people since childhood. Our leaders encouraged vainglorious adulation of our past. If we have some things in our past to be proud of, we also have equal if not more legacies to be ashamed of. Gandhiji and other leaders made us blind to this, otherwise communalism would not have acquired the dimension it has today. Not having learnt the lesson of our history, we are repeating all the mistakes. I donot know how you are planning to save the counry?"

There was silence again. Shiv Shanker was about to say something, when he noticed Professor Saraswat continuing after the pause: "For Gandhi truth was something sublime. It is a human artifact the utility and veracity of which have to be tested continually as we live with it. It has to be taken out of the recesses of our mind and tested on a touchstone and may be sharpened on a grindstone of every day life. I personally feel that in our hatred against the British we missed to learn from them their spirit of give and take, their probity in public life and their always regading counry above self."

There was silence again, a silence that gave a feeling of loss of face. For a while it painfully pierced everyone of them. This silence was broken by Shiv Shanker who addressing Johar Khan said: "Khan Sahib I mentioned that I have a special role for you and am not merely providing you with free accommodation. It can be an earthshaking role."

Shiv Shanker looked at Johar Khan. He did not show any positive or negative reaction nor any sign of interest or indifference. He only eyed both of them sharply. Shiv Shanker continued: "I want you to contest election to Parliament against Prime Miniser Pandit Nehru, from Dholpur or whichever constituency he choses. I will make sure that you defeat him. A Muslim with your dignified personality can give him a better fight than a Hindu. A Chief Minister used to say that an election campaign should be planned as meticulously as a robbery, working out and calculating the minutest detail. I will in this election engineer precisely every piece of this campaign and assemble these systematically as if I am making an atom bomb. An atom bomb it is going to be."

Johar Khan interrupted: "But he has done so much for his constituency, provided irrigation tanks, tube wells, hospitals, schools, etc. His name has a great pulling force and attracts votes with a greater pull than magnet has for iron filings"

"All this is half truth" Shiv Shanker explained, "Money was sanctioned for the digging of irrigation tanks in Dholpur. On paper these were dug and filled with water as required and money appropriated. Then there were letters and representations on the file that the tanks have become breeding ground of mosquitoes and the whole area was ravaged by the epidemic of malaria. The filling of tanks with earth was sanctioned, completed and money pocketed. These places are as flat as before. About tube wells, schools and dispensaries, the story is he same as elsewhere. It will be easy to expose it. In the case of Dholpur dispensary, the post of one peon had been sanctioned as elsewhere. There were strong recommendations for four persons, all by powerful politicians. Four peons wee appointed, leaving no money for medicines, etc. The doctor now visits the dispensary whenever he wants to have picnic in the village."

After a brief pause Shiv Shanker continued: "All these are secondary and subsidiary parts of the election campaign. I am planning an altogether different thrust and propose to spend from seventy to seventyfive crore rupees on it. The technique of Gandhi and Nehru has been to say the same thing again and again and eventually people start believing it and repeating it. It does not matter that your actions are in variance with your words, or what you say is a lie masquerading as truth. You get hold of an idea and then go noisily beating drum about it. Then you shift to a new idea which lifts you further higher and makes the people adore you more. Adoration is an aphrodisiac and one would need more and more of it."

Shiv Shanker's shirt had become wet with sweat. Drops of sweat glistened on his forehead. He stretched his eyelids and continued: "All this is unprecedented in the history of modem world. Think of Giuseppe Garibaldi, Sun Yet Sen, Mustafa Kamal, De Valera and others who fought for the freedom of their country. None wanted to be paid over and over again for the sacrifice they made for their country or adored and worshiped. I will need only a month or two to demolish what they have built over decades. I will make each and every voter in the constituency tap the colossus and find for himselfthat it is hollow."

Shiv Shanker looked at Professor Saraswat and then at Johar Khan. The face of the latter showed some tension. In a confident voice he added: "I will collect more than hundred boys born after Independence, who have never had milk in their life after their mother's milk, never had even a bellyful. Who never had since birth, new clothes or a footwear. Think of these bony striplings, with their skinny ribs peeping out of tatters, moving from person to person demanding justice for tens of millions like them in the counry. There will be more than fifty men and women with stony eyes, wrinkled faces and misery etched on their person moving from house to house. They will relate how they became victims of lawlessness, corruption, avarice and oppression. Their grim tales will make the hair of listeners stand on edge or make their blood boil in anger. The whole constituency will become a pulsating being seething with anger and crying for justice. There will also be a group of Gandhiji's followers moving from village to village describing to the people how Gandhiji has been betrayed by Nehru. Khan Sahib you will have to do nothing except sit in a chariot and move about in the constituiency with both hands joined together."

Shiv Shanker took a long breath and looked at Khan Sahib carefully examining his face for his reaction to what he had said. Johar Khan showed signs more of restiveness than of eagerness. He bowed and gazed at the floor. He suddenly raised his head and looked roofwards as it was sky he was staring at. His face became both thoughtful and vexed.

Johar Khan raised his back, looked straight at Shiv Shanker and said confidently: "I donot think such gimmickry can help defeat Nehru in the next election. It is not living in a fool's paradise but worse. We will be making a laughing stock of ourselves." Johar Khan kept his gaze fixed at Shiv Shanker's perplexed face and remarked bluntly: "Can you claim to see everything? Can you see your back?

Shiv Shanker felt nonplussed. He put his little finger in his ear and quivered it lightly. Taking the little finger out of the ear, he said: "Why? No one can see one's back."

Johar Khan said in a tone of certitude: "There are people who can see their back and there are others who see their back only. They are the people who quarrel with history as if they are having an altercation with an estranged wife. When they are asked to do something, they would start thinking that the right thing to do would be to do the opposite. They would not lift even the little finger without clearly understanding the advantage of doing so and after debating whether it should be little finger of the right hand or ofleft hand."

Shiv Shanker felt taken aback and was still making up his mind how to clarify his point, Johar Khan continued: "I am not wise like you Shiv ShankeIji but it seems to me that Nehru is always talking about future because he is appalled by the present. He sees in it the blaze of burning coal. For him present is like a child walking in the middle of the road about to be run over by the dray of history. To talk about future one only need to be a visionary. To talk about present seriously requires determination, courage and heroism. For this a war has to be, waged in he minds, hearts and squls of people. One cannot think of the present while letting the sword sleep in the scabbard."

Johar Khan got up. He decided to go back and give up the guise. As he turned to move out Professor Saraswat chuckled, Shiv Shanker squirmed and stared at Johal Khan angrily.

A knock at the door roused Panditji from sleep. As Haria entered the room with tea, he sat up in the bed and shook off drowsiness. Seldom he had slept so late and never before he had such a long running dream.

CHAPTER FORTY THREE

Bradford, correspondent for a chain of American newspapers was again in New Delhi. It was October 14, 1962, and he did not keep under his hat the fact that he had come to Delhi to cover for his newspapers war between India and China. Nobody in India had the slightest inkling at that time that there would be acual fighting between the two countries on the northern borders. When in March 1959, Mr. Bradford had earlier come to Delhi he had said that he had come to cover Dalai Lama's flight from Lhasa and arrival in India. None in government or journalist circle knew at that time that Dalai Lama intended any such thing. Bradford had met Dalai Lama's brother Mr. Gyatso in New York and he could have been, at that time, his source of information about Dalai Lama's :intention to make a dash for freedom. However, in mid-October 1962, none in New Delhi saw, immediate or distant, possibility of war between India and China. Bradford did not mention the source of his information. He merely remarked: "The Indian Prime Minister has given orders to Indian Army to drive out the Chinese from every inch of Indian territory. The Chinese dispute the claim and should, as a matter of course, hit back when Indian Army advances into a territory,which Chinese claim to be theirs. If this is not war, what else is?"

Bradford was told that when Pressmen met the Defence Minister Krishna Memon, he laughed it away and had quickwittedly remarked that the Prime Minister's statement was a political statement. His orders could be given effect to after ten days, hundred days even after a thousand days. Bradford's terse reply was that the Chinese leaders were unlikely to have as much grey matter as Krishna Menon. They would think, as anyone else would, that such explicit orders were meant to be obeyed forthwith.

In the later half of his last visit to Delhi, Mr. Bradford was guest of Shiv Shanker. This time he had been accommodated at the Asian Trade Union Training Institute at the instance of his newspaper syndicate. He had come to see Shiv Shanker where he had invited Chopra to meet him. Shiv Shanker expressed the opinion: "What is implied by war cannot well-nigh happen between India and China, because one lizard cannot eat another lizard. At worst it will be kissing and hugging between two hermaphrodites, who swear by love and hate in the same breath. There will be a few bites and scratches and thereafter both of them will recoil hurtfully to their old state of affronted virginity." Chopra was surprised to hear this from Shiv Shanker. Believing that Pandit Nehru was the main hurdle in his political advancement, he was behind the scene doing everything that would harm him. When referring to Aksai Cheen area in the western sector Nehru said that not a blade of grass grew there, Shiv Shanker had financed groups in the Congress Party and others against his belittling the importance of a vital Indian border area.

Last time, when Bradford came to India in early 1959, to cover for his newspapers the arrival in India of Dalai Lama, Chopra was of great help to him. He had provided not only background material for his dispatches to newspapers but had also helped him to make the main story a world scoop by getting delayed the news reports' of others till these missed the next morning edition. This made his fellow journalists in Delhi very hostile to him. It took him a year to normalize relations with them.

Last time Chopra had accompanied Bradford to Tezpur after it became known that Dalai Lama was not far from MacMahon line and that he was expected to reach Tawang across the border in a few days. The Government of India had arranged a special train to Tezpur for Indian and foreign journalists. Officers of Press Information Bureau were accompanying them to facilitate their meeting with Dalai Lama. Bradford preferred to charter a plane so that he could reach Tezpur much ahead of others. Tezpur air-strip was quite far from the town. They reached the main bazaar of the' Tezpur town in a taxi. Bradford felt cheated, when he came to know that there was no hotel worth the name in the town. Above a row of ten shops there were eight rooms available for short stay. On one comer was the kitchen and on the other end were common bath and other conveniences. A string cot was the only furniture in the room. It was meant for the local travelers to spend the night there and leave in the morning. On enquiry Chopra came to know that there was a Planters' Club about ten miles uphill towards the north, where they could stay comfortably provided the caretaker of the Club allowed this.

Bradford was thrilled to see the Planters' Club. It was a log house in the style of eighteen and nineteen century country houses in Britain. Built by British tea planters in the last century, it was not in regular use after the British tea planters sold their tea plantations and left India. Seeing a European after a long time, the caretaker .saluted him smartly. Chopra pushed a hunded rupee note into his palm and commanded him to arrange meals and to open the best suite there for sahib.The caretaker made them members of the Planters' Club on nominal payment and unlocked for them a commodious suite in the central portion of the club building. The furniture was Victorian and much of it in bad shape. The caretaker selected the best and set it properly in the rooms. The entrance room was quite large and on the right there were almirahs full of thick bound volumes. Bradford was ecstatic to find that these were bound volumes of well known British journals of the nineteenth and early twentieth centuty, such as Illustrateed London News, Tattler, Punch, Spectator, Nation, Woman and Home, etc. He observed that such a rich collection of old journals would be available only in the British Museum and perhaps no where else in Engand. He said that furniture like this made of reddish mahogany was now a rarity even in England.

He had some news stories ready to be filed from there. He made a minor addition to it and gave it to the caretaker to file at the telegraph office before he got busy with arranging meals for them. He had given the story dateline Twang. It stated inter alia that Dalai Lama was camping ten miles north of that place awaiting Government of India's signal to enter India. The story mentioned that Dalai Lama decided to flee from Lhasa only after the oracle Dorje Drakden through the body of young monk Lobang Jigme cried: 'Go, go, go tonight.' To prove that Tibetan resistance would now become headless, Bradford referred to Younghusband's expedition to Lhasa sent by Lord Cuzon in 1904. The Tibetan held bunting in their hand, which they believed had charm and would save them from any harm. Several hundred Tibetan monks thus got killed in cold blood. Younghusband had reported that Tibetan army had only medieval weapons and no leadership or training.

The train carrying journalists from New Delhi arrived in the afternoon of the next day. The District Magistrate had somehow got the rooms in the hotel in the bazaar cleaned and furnished each with a table, a chair and a proper bed. He also got the empty rooms of the Planters' Club unlocked and cleaned. By 4 p.m., the whole place wss buzzing with journalists. A Press Room and two telephone booths had been set up in the open space outside the District Courts. At 5 p.m. it was announced that Dalai Lama had entered India. Some Pressmen drove as high up in the hills as they could to meet him first, others were soliciting Government Press Officer's briefing about the time Dalai Lama would arrive in Tezpur. The announcement that he would speak to Pressmen only after reaching Tezpur, gave them much relief.

Bradford already had a story with him about Dalai Lama's arrival in India and his interview with him. He seemed to have worked it out in New Delhi as he was typing it from his notes. He datelined it Lumpu, less than a day's journey south of Tawang. It stated that Lukhangwa, a Minister of Dalai Lama, avowed that he left Lhasa on the bidding of Oracle and would act in India as commanded by the Oracle. There was detailed description of Khampa and Amdo tribal armed men who had escorted the Tibetan god-head to the Indian frontier. He drew a graphic picture of how they all wept bitterly as they bid adieu to their living god. Even Dalai Lama could not hold back his tears. He gave this story to Chopra for tranmission to New York via New Delhi. He wrote "Most Immediate" on it and asked him to rush to the telephone booth. He asked him to request Delhi to connect him to New York. He gave him a telephone number where what he read out on the telephone would get recorded automatically.

When Chopra returned from the telephone booth, Bradford looked at his watch. He said that if the telephone lines could be snapped for an hour, other journalists would not be able to transmit their story in time for the morning edition of their paper. His news report about Dalai Lama having entered India would thus be a world scoop.The telephones in the booth were a make shift arrangement with telephone wires drawn on the hills on three feet high stays. As desired by Bradford, Chopra gave the caretaker a few currency notes and asked him to go up the hill, and tie together witlr a string the two pairs of parallel running telephone wires.

When the newspapermen came to file their stories, they found both the telephones dead. It took more than an hour to set the telephones in working order again. When the Pressmen came to know how the telephones were short circuited, they were in a whirlwind of anger. It made their blood boil. They rushed to the Planters' Club to thrash Chopra who hearing the noise had bolted himself in a store room. Early next morning when there was still more than an hour for the dawn, Bradford arranged for Chopra leaving the place in a taxi for Gauhati, from where he took a flight to Delhi. It took a year's explaining, lying and cajoling on his part to assuage the hurt feelings of his collagues in the profession.

This time also Bradford sought his help in covering the impending war between India and China. Chopra explained his inability politely as he recollected what happened when he assisted him in connection with Dalai Lama's flight to India. He told Bradford that the war was most unlikely. He along with other journalists had met Defense Minister Menon and Intelligence Chief Mallick. Menon had said that there was absolutely no possibility of war between India and China and Mullick was firm in his belief that China would never attack India.

Bradford replied: "I donot know what Menon's motive is in nursing this illusion. I will try to guess it tomorrow when I have breakfast with him. I came to know him well in London. I can only guess Mallick's intentions. The Director General, Asian Trade Union Training Institute, with whom I am staying this time, told me that the Intelligence Chief Mullick was the author and executor of forward policy in Ladakh area. When he tells Nehru that this will never lead to a war, Nehru should have asked him if two plus two do not make four here, what new sysem of calculation he had invented in this case. Just three years ago there was hue and cry in Indian Parliament about allegations against Nehru's long time Private Sectretary M.O . Mathai. It was openly alleged that he was an American mole. He was forced to resign. Who knows Mullick is doing all his at the behest of those who want to make a shortshrift of Nehru's pet policy of non-allignment."

Shiv Shanker interrupted: "Do not go to see Menon empty handed. Whenever I go to see him I take a nice shirt, an elegant walking stick or something else. He has hundreds of these things but loves to have more. On my last visit Menon said that he was tired of driving the Indian political car from the back seat. I suggested to him to persuade Nehru to hand over the reins of office to him. When Indira Gandhi succeeds him, none would in that case point an atusing finger at her father."

CHAPTER FORTY FOUR

On October 20, the Chinese armies attacked with great force Indian positions both in the eastern and western sectors. Having infiltrated behind Indian positions I during the previous day or two, they were easily able to overcome Indian units, in much smaller numbers and with insufficient equipment. Bradford frantically tried to contact Chopra but he avoided him. Chopra received a message through Shiv Shanker that he should positively see Bradford between ten and eleven in the forenoon on October twenty fifth at the place he was staying.

This was the first visit by Chopra to Asian Trade Union Training Institute. He has been watching baggy trousered R. Sanyal, Secretary of the Society for Cultural Freedom, transforming himself to Dr. Rabindranath Sanyal, Director General, Asian Trade Union Training Institute. Sanyal had shifted from a lower middle class suburb in the slums of wesern Delhi to the most expensive posh colony in New Delhi. He chanced to meet him off and on. Without a visit to his Institute, Chopra would not have imagined the prosperity and importance he had managed to acquire during the last few years.

On the top of a three storey bungalow on the main arterial road in Greater Kailash was fixed a twelve feet into two feet red board on which bold black letters announced the premises as: "Asian Trade Union Training Institute". Outside the gate there was a cabin on the left side for the guard and on the right side was inscribed on a shining brass plate: "Dr. Rabindranath Sanyal, Director General". The Gurkha guard was in a suitable uniform. He had information about Chopra's visit and took him to the Secretary. The Secreary, a smart beautiful girl in her early twenties, made him comfortable on a sofa in Dr. Sanyal's office room, served him coca cola and informed him that both Dr. Sanyal and Mr. Badford had gone out together and would be returning soon.

The big hall on the ground floor of the bungalow meant to be a drawing cum dining room, had been transformed to an office room and a lounge for meetings and had enough of elegant and expensive furniture. The office table of Dr. Sanyal was quite big and stylish, so were half a dozen chairs around it. Dr. Sanyal's own chair had a high back, velvety center and ornate golden lining encircling the back and on its arms. More than half the hall towards the front lawn had a rectangle of elegantly upholstered sofas and settees of modern design. About ten foreigners were sitting, reclining or lazing there. Center and side tables had many varieties of drinks and snacks. They were chatting and laughing. From their vivacious mood they appeared to have come for some festivity or celebration.

Chopra got up from the seat and strolled around the passage. The room opposite, third from the entrance, had three tables, near two were sitting young girls probably typists or clerks. The next room towards entrance was of Dr. Sanyal's private secretary. It had many chairs for visitors. Outside the first room from the entrance side he saw a name plate indicating that it was accounts section. Chopra was surprised to see in that room Hari Ram Bhonchal, who was introduced to him two months ago. Bhonchal earthquake - was the pseudonym of Hari Ram as a poet. He was a competent versifier and wrote verses for Urdu and Hindi dailies and weeklies according to their policy and requirement. He also wrote panegyrics for marriages, birthdays, etc. and obituary in verse for death ceremonies.

Chopra had mentioned to Shiv Shanker that meetings held every month by a group of Diplomats in Delhi played a silly joke with Indians. At these parties they had one Indian who claimed to be strict teetotaller. He would refuse to accept any drink other than soft drink when the party commenced at 8 p.m. However, by the time the party ended between 1 and 2 a.m., he could be coaxed to have hard drinks. This made other Indians present there look very small. So far not a single Indian had stood by 'no' till the very end. Shiv Shanker invited Hari Ram Bhonchal to his house. Introducing him to Chopra, he said: "Bhonchal drinks like a fish but he has made a solemn promise that he will not accept any drink at the Diplomats' party. I have told him that if he keeps his word, I will stand him one peg of whiskey every day for three months and if he does not I will make him drink from a gutter." Next Dipolomats' paty was at the residence of a French Diplomat. Bonchal kept eating very greedily but s~id no to repeated offers of dri~.He accepted nothing except water to gulp down all that he was devouring. After midnight when all present began to exhort, coax, urge and coerce him to drink, Bhonchal in order to reinforce his resolve began to continuously shout 'no', 'no', so much so, they had to close early.

On seeing Chopra near the entrance of the room, Bhonchal came out and began strolling with him in the corridor. Bhonchal said that the doctorate degree of Dr. Sanyal was bogus. When he went to U.S.A. last time, he bought it for a few dozen dollars fro'm a nondescript university. Bhonchal said that the top floor was full of boxes and crates which Sanyal said contained study material for the training of trade union workers. Bhonchal, however, believed that these contained anti-Nehru posters and booklets. He said that Sanyal had arrangement with prisons in north India who apprised him of the names and addresses of criminals being released from the jail. He supplied these t6 politicians and others who needed toughs. Bonchal drew Chopra's attention to the editorial which appeared last week in his paper National Times. It had expressed concern over the acquittal of a criminal of central Uttar Pradesh of more than twenty cases of murder, dacoity, extortion and assault because all the witnesses had been bribed to turn hosile. He said this criminal, popularly known as Billa Pehlwan, came yesterday to see Sanyal. He was planning to contest next elections to the Legislative Assembly of his State. He wanted five toughs for five segments of his constituency. Dr. Sanyal charged him rupees twentyfive thousands, as commission, for providing him five criminals released from jails.

Seeing Dr. Sanyal near the gate, Bhonchal went back to his room. Chopra shook hands with Mr. Bradford and Dr. Sanyal. Dr. Sanyal put his arm affably around Chopa's waist and they entered the drawing room toward his office table. As Dr. Sanyal and Chopra sat on a settee, Bradford requested Sanyal to send Chopra to his room when he was free. Seeing them in the hall a drunken voice enquired from the other side: "Has Nehru resigned?"

Bhonchal came there. Sanyal introduced him to Chopra as Comrade Bhonchal and they shook hands as if they did not know each other previously. Bhonchal said that Dr. Sanyal was creating an institution unique in the whole of Asia... His Ph. D. thesis, 'The Problems of Dishwashing in New York State' is indicative of his great love for the working class. After a few more similar sycophantic remarks, Bhonchal left that place.

As always in his conversation, Sanyal began to shoot crisp sentences at Chopra. 'Early European traveler in Africa, Mango Park, was astonished the way Africans ridiculed his white skin. In India today white skin is worshipped more than it was during British rule.', 'In America political decisions are made by majority of dollars and no by majority of men.', 'If past was a golden age we live in an age of gold', 'God is dead everywhere except in India, particularly among those who have nothing to eat'. Many times Dr. Sanyal made some comment which would end up with deriding Nehru but Chopra would manage to shift the gear. When Dr. Sanyal said that India had freedom but not liberty, Chopra laughed this away by the remark that a statue of libety, bigger than the one in New York, should have been erected in New Delhi. Finally he succeeded in firing his volley: "In recent history we had one man dictatorship and earlier many autocracies. What is unique in India today is one man democracy. Immense renown, superiority, peerlessness, adulation and triumphant greatness have been built around Nehru over years. It is not a question of his wishing something and getting it fulfilled. His personality has been made so dominant that the various institutions created by the Constitution and others, anticipate his wishes and act accordingly."

Noticing that Chopra was not enthused by what he had said, Dr Sanyal changed the subject and explained: "Asian Trade Union Institute has become a success even before it has been formally inaugurated. For twentyfour seats for six-month course next year, there are more than hundred applications. A majority of these have been sponsored by political leaders in the northern Indian States for their party cadres." As Chopra rose to take leave, Dr Sanyal came forward to shake hands with him and remarked: "I see success, I hear success, I smell success, I feel success; I have unbreakable patience to remove any obstacle that is placed in the path of my success."

Chopra climbed the stairs. Mr. Bradford's room was at the end of the corridor. The rooms he crossed were as full of hilarious chitchat and mirthfulness as was the gathering of foreigners in the hall below. Noticing Chopra's grin at the festiveness at that place, Bradford commented: "All of them are not journalists. Most of them are members of some international labour, social and cultural organizations from various parts of the world. They are looking forward to a drama after their own heart, as the Chinese armies move down the Himalayas.

After a thoughtful pause, Bradford added: "Chinese had forewarnings for more than a year and had attacked in strength and with full preparations. As Indian leaders were smug about Chinese reaction, they left the Indian Army unequipped and ill-trained for this type of war. But I donot think anyone can muster strength to replace Nehru. Firstly Indians do not have the tradition of debunking false gods. Secondly, a man who has managed to stay at the very top of national leadership for more than thirty years, under varied circumstances and situations, must have mastered the art of staying there as perfectly as does a trapeze walker. As he adjusts his policy under the pressure of changing circumstances, these very people will applaud him more than before."

Bradford informed Chopra that he was flying to Kathmandu that evening or next day. He will try to move via Bhutan and Sikkim behind the Chinese lines and send news messages from there, via Peking, adding another laurel to his career. Bradford himself said that it would not be proper for Chopra to join him in this.

The next ten days were very busy for Chopra. As the Indian Army withdrew from position after position and rolled back to Tezpur in the eastern secror, there was unprecedented upsurge of patriotism and strengthening of national unity, as had never before happened in the history of India. Thousands of persons were volunteering for service in the Indian Army. Even before "Ornaments for Armaments" posters and hoardings were displayed, the people started donating as much cash and gold as they could. Office staff became punctual, trains began running on time, and many government employees began to attend to public work without greasing of palm. Air raid shelters were being dug by people on their own at many places and blackout in the night was observed strictly. Chopra was required to report this accelerating upsurge'of patriotic fervor in Delhi and the neighbouring districts of Punjab, Rajasthan and United Provinces. He did it with as much flourish as would appear credible. After the resignation of Krishna Menon as Defense Miniser, attacks on Nehru became mild and ineffective. Dr.Sanyal, whenever he chanced to meet him, however, could not hide his belief that Pandit Nehru would have to resign by the end of November.

Shiv Shanker had also fully involved himself in War effort. Through his group of toughs he was making collection of ornaments and cash in various areas. His informers among them made sure that none pinched more than a trinket. Even though Shiv Shanker deposited more or less half the gold collection with Reserve Bank of India and cash in the Defense Fund, none could find fault with him as his was the largest single collection. Shiv Shanker organized the digging of trenches and air-raid shelters in many areas. His gangs helped in organizing groups to oversee blackout in the night. As Chinese armies halted at north east Himalayan foothills, digging of trenches and black out by exercizes became less and less. Drive for recruitment for the Indian Army and for funds for its armaments however, continued to gather momentum. Both Shiv Shanker and Chopra actively participated in this as much as any other prominent person and made sure that it came to the notice of public in general.

Bradford after his return from Kathmandu tried to conact Chopra almost daily but he avoided him because he noticed that his dispatches to his American newspapers had an anti-India slant. This was a great surprise for Chopra. On his last visit at the time of Dalai Lama's flight to India, he was all praise for India and every thing Indian. When he went on a sight seeing excursion and saw the various monuments he kept exclaiming:
"Wonderful, wonderful; what a great job Indian people have done in ten years time. This Secretariat, this Rashtrapati Bhawan, this Parliament House, this Red Fort, this Jama Mosque, this Connaught Place, wonderful, what a miracle in just ten years." Even after Bradford was told that some of these building were there when the Briish left, his praise for India did not become less profuse. His news reports now made acrid remarks about India, though these were not pro-Chinese. If at some places digging of trenches had been left incomplete, he generalized and reported that only cats could find shelter in these trenches. When Intelligence Bureau Chief B.N.Mullick informally told some Pressmen that he had prepared a guerrilla force of half a million fighters in north east of India, Bradford went to Assam to report about it. He did not find any evidence about it there and reported this disparagingly. He reported that Nehru was surrounded by persons who bluff and bluster and how easy it was to befool him. Bradford gave details of his meeting various section in Assam and elsewhere in north-east of India and stated that none there whether in police, army or general administration had ever known about this guerrilla force.

On Novembr thirteen, a day before Pandit Nehru's birth day, city walls were plastered with glossy posters demanding his resignation. By the morning of fourteen most of these posters had been tom off by the Police or some Congressmen. On that day the procession demanding that Nehru should resign started with more than a thousand participants from Red Fort and thinned down to a few hundred persons by the time it reached India Gate lawns. As against that the procession in support of Pandit Nehru began with a few thousand persons and kept on swelling as hired buses brought more and more people from the neighbouring districts. More than an expression of support for Nehru it was enthusiasm for the war effort. Bradford emphasized more the hiring of buses to augment the crowd and described it as the last ditch battle by Nehru to save himself.

Bradford invited Chopra and Shiv Shanker for dinner but both of them did not want to be seen with him. Instead, Shiv Shanker invited him to his house. They wanted to find out from him what he really thought was wrong with India. He said that he would be a little late which both of them welcomed. There was much off-the-cuff talk Mr. Bradford was sure that China was not interested in India, nor its military preparations were directed against this country. He was of the firm opinion that China will go on increasing its military might, much more than Russia and possibly more than United States. The Chinese were likely to have their eyes on the uninhabited, minerally rich land of Siberia bordering their north and not on over-populataed poverty-stricken India in the South. He thought that by the end of the twenty first century if not earlier, Siberia will have several million Chinese inhabiting it, as part of China if possible and without it if necessary. This statement was as confounding as the one he made on his last visit about Dalai Lama. He had said then that Dalai Lama was leaving Tibet not because of Communist as is made out but because of his Advisory Council of Lamas which is a semi hereditary body. None of the pevious Lamas had lived beyond the age of thirty five, most of them died before they were twentyfive. This enabled the Lama Council to continue its control over the State of Tibet. This Dalai Lama wisely decided to get out of Tibet before he neared thirtyfive years of age.

Mr.Bradford hesitated to speak about India and after much prompting he opined: "There is exaltation and deification of leaders in India as happens nowhere else in the world. Jesus or Buddha were not worshipped in the lifetime in the manner Gandhi and Nehru are worshipped. An aura of a paragon and of faultless excellence makes Nehru keep under wrap his normal human failings. He is all the time afraid of a finger pointed at him. Other leaders in the Congress Party take advantage of this. As against Nehru's pardonable sins, such as his weakness for splendor and for women, they commit worse sins and indulge in unpardonable vices. Nehru will not put his foot down because he is afraid of someone spilling a black dot on his immaculateness. The sooner the people know truth about their leaders and take them as normal human beings, the better for India. The people degrade hemselves to the same extent as they exalt their leaders to a supra-human position."

Chopra was taken aback by this forthright expression of opinion. Shiv Shanker knew many reasons for the present malaise of corruption and mismanagement. He had always thought that greed and personal ambition of men like him had much to do with it. An Indian's trait of obeisance, his servile hero worship had contributed so much to it had not occurred to him with such clarity. There were some tense moments of silence. Digressing from the subject, Shiv Shanker asked him: "Now that India had almost licked dust, what would be the next course of war?"

Bradford replied: "I am thinking and thinking, but the picture is not clear to me. All I know is that these are not medieval times when a war could drag on for decades, when there could be a thirty years war or even a hundred years war.A modem war, if it cannot be concluded in a few weeks has to end forthwith."

As Bradford was getting up to take leave, Chopra asked him: "How was Krishna Menon? You went to see him before he resigned"

Warmly shaking hands with them and bidding them farewell, Bradford observed: "He was under the influence of some drug. I cannot tell you what he said. I have not included this even in my news reports."

Sometime after Chopra became Senior Accredited Corespondent of his newspaper, he was allotted a government flat in Kaka Nagar. It was on first floor. The ground floor flat was occupied by Dr. Ram Sulakhan Joshi, a Ph. D. in Chemical Engineering and a Director in one of the Defense Services Research Institutes in the city. However, his main interest was astrology. It ws generally known that he was great expert in making and interpretting horoscopes. Often Ministers and senior officers were visiting him for this purpose. After Krishna Menon resigned, Joshi said that he had predicted this. When Chopra remarked that Menon never told anyone the time, date and place of his birth, Joshi affirmed that in Indian astrology there were other indices also for making a horoscope. He was, like many orthodox Hindus, against Prime Minister Nehru. Whenever Chopra asked him about his prediction about Nehru, he would smile wryly and mutter: "Let us see, let us see"

Chopra had been visiting western Uttar Pradesh and East Punjab to report on war effort in these areas and often returned home late at night. While going to office late next day, he would find Joshi basking in the sun outside his verandah with many horoscopes in his hand. With the situation in a flux, many Ministers wanted him to make or interpret their horoscope. Dr. Joshi had taken leave from office to attend to this work. Coming down from his first floor flat Chopra would greet him: "Pandit ji namaskar". Dr. Joshi would smile, sometimes sardonically, at others blandly and utter a curse for the Chinese and a cutting word for Pandit Nehru. The news, about setback at Tembang, at the bottom of the Bailey Trail, was received on seventeenth November. On eighteenth November Walong and later Bomdi La were evacuated. Retreat of the Indian Anny was continuing on nineteenth and twentieth November. Most of the infonnation received during these two days was contradictory and confusing. When Chopra greeted Dr. Joshi on way to office, his curses for the Chinese would be more bitter and his remarks about Pandit Nehru more cutting.

When Chopra came down the stairs on November twentyone, Dr. Joshi was reclining on an easy chair crestfallen, with head bent sideway sOlTowfully. When Chopra looked at him enquiringly, he blurted in a painful voice: "First they gave us a thumping slap, now they have spat on our face." When Chopra could not understand him and looked at him puzzlingly, Dr. Joshi shrieked: "Donot you know the Chinese have announced ceasefire."

There was stunned relief mixed with shame and sorrow in office also. The direction of news reporting had to be changed completely. The purpose was to show it as victory for India. The Chinese felt compelled to announce ceasefire in view of the upsurge of patriotism and massive mobilization that was taking place in India. Shortly before he was to leave office, there was a telephone from Bradford saying that he was flying to Hongkong that night. He wanted to leave some personal effects with him. He would get these back from him after a week on his way home via New Delhi. He requested Chopra to come as early as possible to collect these.

When Chopa reached Asian Trade Union Training Institute, sometimes after dusk, he was aghast to see everything topsy-turvy there. There was an atmosphere of utter confusion and disorder. The gate was half open, guard's cabin had glass window smashed and not only he but his chair was also missing. He walked over torn posters and booklets to enter the building. He noticed the entire front lawn clutterd with broken flower pots and heaps of torn, shreded and burnt papers, booklets and posters. Even the flower vases had been hurled down the first floor and the;. broken pieces and crumpled flowers were lying scattered hither and thither. It seemed that the place had been vandalized in a fit of disgust and anger. The drawing room was in a state of greater desolation.The sofas and settees were lying in a disorderly manner. The side tables were scattered hither and yon. Both the center tables had their glass top smashed and one was lying upside down near the entrance door. The carpet was smudged and was littered with empty wine and beer bottles, soiled plates, cutlery, empty, half empty packets of cigarettes and, burnt cigarette halves. Torn and shredded papers and booklets were lying in a heap in the center of the hall. There was an amosphere of debacle everywhere. Though the building was standing, everything else seemed to have crashed down.

Chopra climbed up and went to Bradford's room. There was no sign of life, much less of previous mirth, in the rooms he passed by. Bradford gave Chopra a locked handbag with his name embossed on it. He had his luggage ready and both of them stepped down the stairs hand in hand. He said that the turn war had taken was quite contrary to the expectations which had brought these people here, but he did not expect everything to turn topsy-turvy in this manner. Bradford had gone to Dr. Sanyal's room to say good bye but he was not there. They found him sitting dazed on the floor near his office chair in the drawing room. His long droopy face had swollen eyes. Chopra had never before seen such a heart-rending spectacle of gloom and despair. On seeing them standing near him, Dr. Sanyal's lips moved but there was no sound. Chopra poured water in a tumbler from a bottle on his table. Bradford lifted him, seated him in the chair and made him sip half a glass of water. He slightly regained his self. Bradford held his lifeless hand and thanked him. Suddenly, he held Bradford's hand fast and without shaking it bewailed: "Could not these pigs have waited for ten or twelve days before they showed us their back."

Chopra was thinking whether to pity Sanyal, have contempt or him or just to treat him as a guttersnipe. Bradford lifting his suitcase meaningfully looked at Sanyal and remarked: "Pigs, yes pigs. A man's brain is not yet an organ of thought, but is like a pig's snout an instrument for foraging. If a man's brain could be used for thinking and not merely for snouting for satisfying one's ambitions, there would not have been any wars, not even the smaller one we have experienced just now."

They came out of the building with devastated mind. As they sat in the car, Bradford put his hand on Chopra's shoulder and remarked distressfully: "I donot know whether anyone here has learnt any lesson from this melodrama, but it has shaken me. It appears incredible to me that a democratic leader should be as determined to stay all his life in seat of power as does a dictator. When necessary he can be as ruthless as a dictator. He uses all the media to promote his worship as a super-hero capable of achieving spectacu1l:ir triumph."

There was a pause and before Bradford could say more, Chopra observed: "It is said that truth is the first casualty of war. These days it is in peace time that truth is put under the hatchet"

After a month lights were on. One could see bright shops and homes. Passing vehicles were flashing beams. It appeared to be brighter than it previously did. There was silence again. Bradford kneeled on Chopra's shoulder and said in a thoughtful voice:

"Darkness all around in the city was appalling, so also the murkiness in the minds of men. Let us hope that thoughts of the people in the two countries and elsewhere in the world will be lighted by wisdom."

END

ABOUT THE AUTHOR

Mr. Shamsher Singh Narula. Or Uncle Ji as I call him is one of the Grand Old Men of Indian Literary World. He is been writing novels, erudite books, historical fiction and other forms of literary works since before I have known him.

He has written novels in Punjabi, Works in Hindi, Urdu, and English. He is a consummate master of each of these languages and one reading of any work embeds that belief in the reader.

He words are sure, speech and meaning subtle to plain when he writes. The emotions, the descriptions, the period, all come alive.

I leave the readers to make their own judgment. But his books portray language as it should be written and only a learned person with a life time of knowledge, as he has, can pen such books. God Bless him and Grant him Good Health and Happiness.

Narula, S. S. (Shamsher Singh) (1915-)

1. Social roots of Indian linguistics / S.S. Narula
   [Book : 1979]
2. Hindi language : a scientific history / S.S. Narula
   [Book : 1976]
3. Bharatiya bhashavijnana ka samajika dharatala / Shamsher Singh Narula
   [Book : 1977]
4. Scientific history of the Hindi language
   [Book : 1955]
5. The man who stole rainbow / Shamsher Singh Narula
   [Book : 2004]
6. Woman who sold tears / Shamsher Singh Narula
   [Book : 2006]
7. Jale : giyarah afsanon ka majmuah / Shamsher Singh Narula
   [Book, Microform : 1900]
8. Society and languages in Northern India / Shamsher Singh Narula
   [Book : 2009]